What readers are saying about The Black S

"The author's own experiences of living in a. ....
*book are coupled with her extensive knowledge of Egyptology, Greek and
Latin. The reader is not only drawn in by the steamy, fast-paced story, but
by the historically accurate backdrops and customs." - Michael, Chicago*

*"The Black Scroll takes the themes of ancient history and modern political
intrigue, mythology and magic, romance and reincarnation, and somehow
wraps them up into an erotic yet strangely plausible thriller. I couldn't put
any of the books in the "Isis" trilogy down!" - Eugenia, Oregon*

*"In the Isis Trilogy we witness the transformation of a shallow Las Vegas
socialite into a powerful, spiritually aware heroine as she experiences the
lives of three priestesses from three ancient historical periods. Some say
that the same tribe of souls is reincarnated in each generation in order to
guide and protect each other. This Circle of Protectors guides our heroine
throughout her dangerous, mysterious, and frankly, very erotic, transformation. Highly recommended!" - Deborah, New York*

*"The same roller coaster ride, ever more twisting, through history. Gore has
an amazing talent for description. I felt like I was there." - Peter, Dallas*

*"Great characters take the stage again. In her own special way, Gore blends
eroticism, adventure, history, and a modern day thriller all under one
cover." - Sunny, London*

*"Past or present, the story intrigues, grips and captures. The Black Scroll
doesn't disappoint lovers of The Red Mirror and The Emerald Tablet. Gore
keeps the action going with plenty of suprises." - Nasr, Washington DC*

*"In the most amazing way, The Black Scroll ties up all the ends of The Isis
Trilogy yet leaves the reader wanting more." - Odile, Paris*

*"I love Gore's unique take on the death of Antinous, Hadrian's fabled lover."
- Gustavo, Miami Beach*

*"Growing up in the Nafusa, the Mediterranean Sea breeze (bahri) is a
treat especially in the dry hot summer nights and days. Reading about the
'Northern Wind' and Leptis Magna brought back awesome memories of
Libya. Gore makes it so real." – Khalifa, Canada*

*"With the Isis Trilogy, Gore provides so much rich detail about all aspects
of the ancient and modern worlds that it is easy to suspend disbelief and
be completely caught up in the fast-moving and gripping story." – David,
California*

ISIS TRILOGY

BOOK THREE

THE
BLACK
SCROLL

ONE LIFE IS NOT ENOUGH

S. L. GORE

2018.06.03 Edition

ISBN 978-1-940304-03-8

Published by Tajine Publishing, Las Vegas NV
This book is available in eVersion

Author website: www.SLGore.com

AUTHOR'S NOTE
This book is a work of fiction. Names, characters, places and incidents are the product of the author's imagination or are used fictitiously, and any resemblance to actual persons, living or dead, or events is entirely coincidental.

Gratitude always and forever to my Muse Jesper
for believing in my magic and me.

Special appreciation to beloved Ann,
gone to her eternal journey on the Nile.

And sincere thanks to Horace of Rome
for his words of wisdom 2000 years ago.
"If you want to be a writer, write."

TABLE OF CONTENTS

Roman Empire 130 AD
MARE NOSTRA

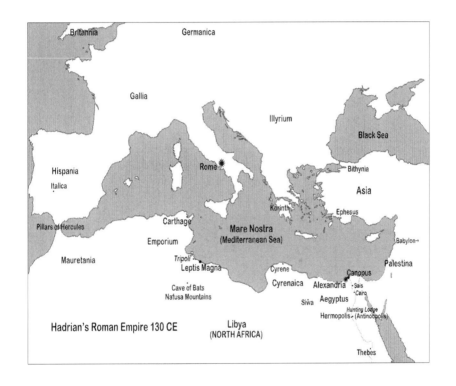

PROLOGUE
ISIS AND THE RED MIRROR

"You traverse the world in search of happiness, which is within the reach of every man. A contented mind confers it on all." – Horace

It began again with a dream. The vague evanescence coalesced into a film noir scene of black shadows and high-contrast bright white. Save for a blue promise of sky at the top of the abyss, the only color was the woman's shining red hair. Her long waves, the coppery auburn of an Irish Setter, swirled as she swam through the air.

First we were two. Then we were one. In that crazy way of dreams, when you see yourself from the outside, I watched her struggle as they say a soul watches its body at the moment of death.

Down and down through the shadow, glowing hands on four pairs of long rubbery arms stretched closer and closer.

Turning desperate, glittery emerald eyes on me, the woman begged, "Come back. Come back and save me."

I reached to snatch her from forty grasping fingers. Before I could take firm hold of her pale shoulders, fiery Medusa tendrils snaking all about, the dream dissolved into golden fog, and I opened my eyes to the Red Mirror.

In the bright morning sun, fragile Chinese chrysanthemums popped bright blue and snow white against the red-lacquered frame. Once dusty and coated with grime, the glass now sparkled. The wood gleamed. But not the metal starburst in each corner—or the parallel struts bracing each side. Those were still tarnished, except for a single pair of struts, one over the other.

For it is in the polishing of the silver that the magic happens. The magic that took me back. Back to Isis and Athena.

Today nothing about the Red Mirror suggested its power. Only a purring Aisha, with black fur gleaming against a yellow silk bed, reflected in the glass. But I knew the Spirit was there; we had become old friends.

And thinking of old friends, I sighed and began to plot how I would convince Barb yet again to help me. But even then, I think I knew this trip would be unlike the others.

"You're selfish," Barb snapped. "It's always about you. What about *me*? I don't want to do this anymore."

We sat each at an end of my teal leather sofa with the splendor of the Strip framed in the terrace sliding doors. Neither of us was looking.

Barb wore new frames, hot pink and a little crooked on the sharp ridge of her nose. Right above the nose, the crease between her eyebrows was a canyon deep. I had this sudden vision of her always-neat platinum helmet hair spiking out in all directions. From frustration. From anger. Maybe even desperation.

"You're asking me to play Russian roulette. I hate it. You know that I hate it." Then she grabbed my hand, squeezing my fingers. "I'm so afraid you won't come back."

"I don't really *go* anywhere, Barb. You see me here all the time."

"But what about your *mind*? Where does *it* go? I don't know how this works. *You* don't know how it works."

She was as close to tears as she'd ever let me see—she who prided herself on being from 'good stock.' That's Scottish-Canadian code for emotions held in check and spine held straight with feet firmly planted on the ground.

When I didn't answer, she let go of my hand and demanded, "Why would you take such a risk when you finally have everything?"

"If I thought I had everything, I wouldn't go, would I?"

She glared at me, and then fuming, took a sip of wine.

"Remember the old me, Barb? You said yourself I was wasting my life. Now you say that I have everything. But I didn't get here on my own."

"Yes, but you *are* here. *Be* here for a change. You always want to be somewhere else."

"I'm needed." I said it quietly but firmly. I meant it. I believed it.

"*Needed?* Listen to yourself. Those women are dead. Long dead. The past is over. *Over.*"

"It's not true."

"What's not true?"

"That I don't make a difference."

Her breath caught for an instant. If ever I were to describe someone as looking flabbergasted, it would be Barb in that moment.

"So now you think you can *change* the past. Do you realize how delusional that is? You really *are* scaring me. You do know that?"

"When the dreams start, Barb, I have to pay attention. If I don't, they won't stop."

Her answer was a look that said, Good stock people don't live their lives according to dreams.

Now it was my turn to reach out and take *her* hand. Her skin was cold to the touch. She had such elegant, aristocratic fingers. Such long arms and legs. Regal, angular and, when angry like tonight, spiny.

"*Please*, Barb. This last time."

She started to say something but instead closed her lips into one of her thin puckers of disapproval laced with vexation. I waited. Another word—the wrong word—might tip the scale. Her eyes were fiery blue in the hot pink frames before they dulled. And then I heard the sigh of resignation and saw the slump in the shoulders that told me I'd won.

So our dance ended as always—Barb unhappy but acquiescing, fearing I wouldn't wake up without her, and me relieved, yet remorseful. Mildly.

The sun disappeared in a coral blaze behind the purple mountains that separate Las Vegas from Bonnie Springs. In silence, we sipped our chocolaty Merlot and watched the horizon mellow to tangerine and the pastel lights of high-rises and casinos brighten.

I had Barb to thank for the view. She'd come to me with the penthouse of wide terraces and floor-to-ceiling windows when one of her clients went bust.

"He's in a bind, Isis, and needs to unload fast," she'd urged over martinis at the Stirling Club. "He can't wait for an appraisal. Come with a cash offer, and he'll take it."

What I didn't have in my brokerage account I got from the General at favorable interest. Strictly business. No strings attached. Despite Barb's warnings, I'd managed to keep him just where I wanted—orbiting my world, coming only as close as I allowed.

But my universe of orbiting men hadn't behaved quite as I planned. Elaine had been right—she was always right, all the way back to college. I didn't have to choose between my four men. It turned out some choices were made for me.

I hadn't heard from Hector since he stroked Aisha one last time and walked out the door of my old condo, closing it firmly with a solid click.

If ever I had a champion, it was Hector. He'd come through the Red Mirror once to save me. Into a world he didn't believe in.

From time to time, I run into his mother Isabel—*my* mother in another life. She's always polite, never friendly, and waits for me to approach her. Once, at a Paris auction, she accepted, albeit reluctantly, my invitation to lunch at a tiny, mirror-walled bistro in *Saint-Germain-des-Pres*.

When I asked about Hector, the slightest dilation of her pupils told me that I'd touched a nerve.

"Hector is in Argentina managing family affairs."

Only someone who knew her well would sense the faint whiff of accusation in her tone.

"You hurt him, Isis. But sometimes good comes from evil, and at last, Hector is taking charge. I have more time now to travel."

After *salade niçoise* and a chilled bottle of *Côtes de Provence*, she relaxed a little over espresso served in tiny white cups. I'd never seen her use sugar or order dessert. She was just thin enough to be elegant without the bony look older women often have. Her black and silver hair, pulled back into a *chignon*, gleamed. Antique emerald studs pierced her regal earlobes.

As always, she wore the dazzling Asscher-cut family diamond on her slender finger with long, scarlet-painted nail. The ring would have been mine, if I had accepted Hector on his terms.

"We should do business together." Her offer took me quite by surprise. "Hector was right about you in some ways. I've come to respect your… abilities."

I heard a reluctant note of admiration in her tone. She'd never expected that I could evolve into a woman worthy of her respect.

Isabel seldom referred to our past lives together. Her loyalty in this lifetime—she made very clear—was to her son. To Hector. But her soul and mine were bound by the eternal connection of mother and child. I felt it, and as much as she wished to distance herself, she felt it too.

I'd seen her black eyes soften with affectionate approval when I vanquished a particularly aggressive bidder. Isabel admired strength and had no stomach for weakness. How was it that she'd raised diffident Hector, who surrendered me without a fight?

Every few months, I go to Princeton for a long weekend in Tony's storybook house with a broad wooden porch on an elm-lined street. Azalea bushes bloom pink and red in the spring. Last Christmas, Thomas Kinkade snowmen waved from tidy front yards.

Curled up in front of the fireplace of porous gray stones, hickory logs smoking and crackling, we sipped icy Plymouth martinis garnished with plump green olives. The rainbow hooked rug had seen better days. I don't think there was anything in the room that was new—not antique, but comfortable and worn, like a favorite pair of slippers.

"How do you know when you're going to win?" Tony asked about my auctions.

"I don't. You're never sure how high the competition will bid until they stop."

"And you? How far do you go?"

"As far as I have to."

"Gr-r-r-r," he roared, locking me in one of his wrestlers holds. "I love it when Isis talks tough."

Happy to have me for however long I could stay, Tony never pressures. Like the Greek Antinous he doesn't remember, his mind is occupied with cosmic concerns—far distant galaxies and mathematical models of events that happened light years ago.

But it is Jenny who comes first in his life. A remarkably well-adjusted girl for a thirteen-year-old who lost her mother, she reads a lot and demands little. She keeps an elaborate shrine in her room with pieces of jewelry, old birthday cards, a bottle of flowery perfume, and a collection of family photos in silver frames. Her pretty young mom, unaware of the cancer growing in her body, smiles back at me from the Jersey Shore.

In the beginning, I was loath to tread on such fragile ground and quite nervous to be the first woman Tony brought to her mother's bed. Against all reason, it turned out that Jenny didn't resent my intrusion into their quiet, private life. The first time I arrived at Princeton station—

to my surprise and great relief—she hugged me and squeezed my hand.

"My dad's been smiling all day," she whispered in my ear. "And I'm Jen, not Jenny."

I believe her soul, Jason's soul, recognized and welcomed me.

I see Rasheed as often as he'll see me. He shows up for a day or two when I have business in Europe; he hasn't been to Vegas since the night he gave me the Hathor Ring in my old condo. Always with Marcos and Gamel, he appears with little notice and gives no hint of where he's been, where he's going, or when I'll see him again.

Once we spent a whole week at Sharm el-Sheikh in the Sinai. We rarely left the marble-floored room with lush king bed overlooking the Red Sea. Always taking his time, never hurrying, Rasheed lingered over those secret places he's caressed through lifetimes.

No one has a touch like Rasheed. Like Black Falcon. Like River God.

I don't ask if he still works his deals with the General. Questions are off limits with Rasheed.

I have my secrets, too. I make certain Rasheed knows nothing about the General and me. Not the present. Not the past.

Just as he'd promised the night of the ring, Rasheed tries to let me be free. But his jealousy lies always just beneath the surface, smoldering in his long silences after the heat of making love.

Without warning, I feel him retreat into his dark world of suspicion and jealousy, and I cease to exist. My magic has never worked on him.

"I'm going to be out of town for a few days, General, but I'll be in Paris as arranged." My tone was all business. This was a courtesy call from one associate to another.

His response was a chuckle. "I take it, Ishtar, you're not asking my permission."

As always, he called me Ishtar. It was his way of reminding me of what happened in his Persian tent.

I steer clear of talking about our past, whether in this life or others, and he's gracious enough to let me play that game. But even as our mouths form safer words, our thoughts carry on silent, dangerous conversations.

He didn't ask where I was going, but I was certain he knew. I don't believe though, that he had the whole picture; he's never mentioned the Red Mirror.

I was about to ring off when he said, "This may not turn out as you expect."

I thought about challenging him, asking *what* may not turn out, but in the end said nothing.

"Ishtar?"

"Yes, General. What is it?" I managed to sound confident and even a little impatient.

"You are going to need help."

"Then I will count on you."

He laughed then and said in a good-humored tone, "I shall look forward to that."

I poured myself a couple fingers of Dalwhinnie single malt and wandered into the bedroom. Aisha curling between my crossed legs, I settled on the silvery-gray carpet.

With all the reverence due a magical icon, the Mirror hung in the altar-alcove where the previous owner had showcased an erotic 19th-century oil painting of a buxom blonde.

Barb had a key, I told myself. She'd take Aisha home. After two days, Barb would wake me up, and all would be well. Even better.

Still, the General—and Barb—had unnerved me more than I liked.

On impulse, I dialed Eben. Strange, sweet Eben with his Kabbalah chants—trapped in his awkward body, most likely autistic—cursed perhaps by some evil deed in the distant past.

Not long ago, he had sat across a table at a penthouse party to tell my fortune.

"Go back, Isis," he'd begged, body shaking, hands so cold they burned my skin. "Go back and save yourself."

The landline rang and rang. No voicemail for other-worldly Eben. No answering machine for a psychic. After the tenth trill, I gave up. I was on my own.

I caught the faint, telltale glint of one of the dull struts and, letting the Spirit guide my hand, began to polish it with the oiled cloth. Breathing slowly and deep, I focused on the reddish glow behind my eyelids.

The room grew hot, as it always did, and after a few brief moments, the redhead from my dream stared back from the Mirror.

I wouldn't have recognized her if not for the fiery hair; she looked a far cry from needing help. On the contrary, she appeared very much in control. No Medusan snaking tendrils. Her coppery waves were piled high on her head in an elaborate array of twists and curls.

"Come," she whispered. "Taste of the goddess."

She was a force, this woman. This woman I once was. I felt her power, and I coveted it.

With a final stroke on Aisha's thick gleaming coat, I flowed weightless through the Red Mirror.

PART ONE
LIBYA

CHAPTER 1   LEPTIS MAGNA

"Woe to the conquered." – Livy

Even before I opened my eyes, I knew this time was different. Terrifyingly different. Fierce heat slammed me. And the overwhelming stench of sweat, urine and feces. My tongue filled my cotton mouth. Every cell in my body screamed for water.

There were about twenty of us crammed into an iron cage with a rough plank bottom. Straw had been strewn once; what remained was foul with excrement and alive with vermin. When I held out my hand to push myself to a more erect seat, my palm slid in the rot. I gagged and brought up sour bile.

Wedged next to a dark giant, I couldn't move. His massive arms stretched out; yellow pus oozed from sores where iron shackles chafed his wrists.

In horror, I looked at my own unbound wrists; the skin on my forearms was a shocking white tinged with blue. My long slender fingers ended in jagged, blackened nails. Vivid red hair, tangled and filthy, hung in my face.

This was nothing like exotic Isis lolling on sweet grass beside the Nile. This was nothing like golden Athena greeted by an Aegean breeze.

Barb, wake me up! Bring me back! But Barb wouldn't wake me for two days—forty-eight long hours in Las Vegas that could be a lifetime on this side of the Red Mirror.

A mass of woolen robes blocked my view, but from the clamor of voices and wailing of pipes over the braying of donkeys, I guessed that the cage stood on the edge of a marketplace.

What I saw of the sky was bleached to white. Judging by the short shadows, the day had just gone noon. Already, heat shimmered off the paving stones. Over our heads, a strip of tattered canvas gave some shade. That small comfort was the sole human charity afforded us.

There wasn't the breath of a breeze. Dust from hundreds of scuffling feet choked the air.

A brute of a soldier, with a face as flaming as his cape, rattled at the lock on the cage while a second banged on the iron bars with his sword. Sunlight flashed on their helmets and polished eagle breastplates.

"Out!" he bellowed. "Out, you rats!"

Latin. Crude. Not a native speaker.

The gate clanked open; the brute reached into the cage, yanking on chains, hauling us onto the burning stones. Those who were too weak to stand, he dragged by the hair. I think we were all half-dead, most nearer to death than to life.

I made it to my feet by gripping the arm of the giant next to me. He jerked away without a glance; I lost my footing and slammed into the bars. Every joint screamed. My muscles cramped. Hammers pounded in my head. I would have given anything for one drop of water.

The giant moved ahead of me, the cage so low he bent double at the waist to squeeze through the narrow opening. I followed close behind, slipping and sliding in my bare feet, warm sludge oozing between my toes. Though he hadn't looked once in my direction, I was desperate to stay by his side.

Once in the relentless sun, a thousand needles stabbed my tortured flesh. Still it felt like heaven to be, at last, out of the stinking, cramped cage. I stretched my spine and drank deep of the air.

We weren't far from the sea; I could smell and taste the salt. Seagulls circled above, their cries as loud as the vendors.

"*Fly! Fly!*" I willed myself. But no wings sprouted.

"*Wake up! Wake up!*" But I remained firmly here in this nightmare.

A third soldier, this one wiry with the narrow face of a rat, shoved the men to the left and the six females to the right.

No sooner were we separated from the men than a foul-smelling mob grabbed at our breasts and between our legs.

More soldiers rushed to beat them back with swords and shields and threats. "Don't touch the merchandise, worms!"

The rat-faced one tightly bound my wrists in front with a leather thong. Then twisting a long length of coarse rope around each of our necks, he tied the six of us into a chain.

The other females wore rough wool sack tunics ending mid-calf and belted at the waist with rope. My long gown was of grass green wool intricately embroidered at the hem and bodice in crimson silk. Underneath, I wore a yellow linen tunic that ended at my elbows. Dark splotches stained the front of the green gown and the right tunic sleeve. I was certain it was dried blood but didn't think mine. At any rate, I didn't feel any wounds other than my aching muscles.

Immediately beside me trembled a lissome black female about eighteen with a face marked by ritual scars. Tiny raised dots circled lush lips bright pink against glossy ebony skin. She had raven hair, shorn close to a petite head slightly pointed at the crown and a little flat in the back. I was struck by her tiny seashell ears.

A long white beach framed by swaying coconut palms flashed through my mind; like me, she was far from home. Her wide obsidian eyes mirrored the terror we all felt.

The three girls behind her were olive-skinned and looked to be in their mid-teens. They kept their faces hidden behind long matted hair of various shades of brown. They never looked up—not around them, not at each other.

The girl in front of me couldn't have been more than twelve. Short dark blonde curls framed a tanned face dominated by large, clear hazel eyes. Swamped by her tunic, of slight build with only a hint of budding breasts, she could easily have been mistaken for a boy.

She met my look only briefly. Of course, I saw fear in her eyes, but I also saw defiance. She had not given up.

Rat Face jerked on the rope, and the elfin girl followed, the rest of us stumbling along in single file.

"Make way!" he shouted, brandishing his sword, shoving with his shield.

The men who were slow to move felt the broadside of his blade.

I refused to look other than in front of me, but from what I could see, the crowd was all men, most dressed in dark woolen robes or knee-length suede tunics. They had a savage look about them—hardened and wind-weathered. I caught sight of an occasional white toga and a great many soldiers in crimson capes and bronze helmets. Here and there, the close-sheared heads of more sub-Saharan Africans stuck up from the crowd. Giant Nubians like the man in the cage.

We were somewhere along the coast of North Africa, of that I was certain, but not Egypt. There was a harshness here born of an unforgiving desert never softened by the Nile.

As we made our way toward the stalls hawking bright vegetables, mounds of spices, and fly-swarmed haunches of sheep, all haggling ceased. An uneasy lull fell, out of which a hum turned into a buzz that became a low rumble.

It wasn't until the girl turned to me with a wide-eyed questioning look that I realized every eye trained on me. Or more precisely, I sensed, on my impossibly red hair flaming in the sun.

"*Lamia*," a deep voice hissed. Vampire.

The man stood just next to me, his lizard eyes cold in a sun-ravaged face. I glared back, summoning a force I knew not from where it came or what it was. It gathered in me. I felt it leave my body to break upon his. He stumbled backward; I thought he might fall. Those closest moved quickly to avoid touching him, and then he melted away into the wall of dark wool.

In the silence, only the seagulls squawked.

The circle around me widened. With a hiss, an old man in a black-hooded cloak made the sign of a cross in the air.

"Get moving, cows!" Rat Face screamed. "Or you'll feel my gladius on your backs."

On and on, he dragged us. The heat pressed in. My head throbbed. I sucked on my swollen tongue hoping for moisture.

Then the chaos gave way to some semblance of order with utterly wretched stoop-shouldered men, women and children herded into bunches, strung together with ropes around their necks, their heads hanging down. I couldn't begin to guess how many they were. In the roar of the marketplace, they stood silent.

We halted beside the steps of the auction block and not far from a corral holding twenty or so well-fed man slaves. Crude placards on their chests identified trades, origins, ages and character traits. *Parthian scribe, Greek marble worker, Persian accountant. 24 years. 40 years. 35 years. Clumsy. Irritable. Good with numbers.* Like other prized slaves, they would be auctioned individually.

Not so the group of emaciated and defeated men next herded up the steps. At a fast clip, the dozen went to one bidder for 4000 *denarii*. Destined for the mines. All dead in a month.

Two women were then hauled up and stripped naked. One had great pendulous breasts; the second a gaping overbite. The mob crowed.

"Look at those cow tits! I'd pay to suck those."

"Keep those horse teeth away from *my* cock."

"Put a bag over her head, and I might fuck her up the arse!"

The women were dragged away. A delicate boy of about eight, with the face and golden curls of Cupid, appeared on the podium. He stood all alone, sobbing for his mother.

No sooner had the bidding started than two scrawny old men went at each other with fists and fingernails. The crowd went wild, whistling and cheering, shouting out wagers. Centurions forced their way through and towed the two away, arms still flailing, in a cloud of dust.

The mob booed. Hunks of bread flew through the air. Then small stones. A dozen soldiers banged on their shields with swords until the rock throwing slowed to a few pebbles and then ceased altogether.

In the end, the child was sold to an invisible buyer behind the curtains of a litter. A blue-skinned blond giant flung the boy over his shoulder, and a head slave shouted, "Make way! Make way for a Roman citizen!"

Like the parting of the sea, a path opened for the Roman in his litter and the Gaul with the howling boy hanging upside down. No sooner had the entourage passed than the mass closed ranks again.

"The redhead. The redhead," they began to chant.

Save me. Save me, I begged the Universe.

"You'll get the redhead," the auctioneer promised. "But first another prize."

At his signal, the Nubian from the cage was pulled up. Two slaves in loincloths dumped buckets of seawater on his massive front and back, and for a few fleeting moments, his long powerful muscles, more navy than black, glistened in the sun. A fine white layer of salt coated his chest and arms.

"Look at these shoulders and the power of those legs!"

Using an ebony camel crop with brass tips on both ends, the auctioneer slapped the giant's biceps and thighs while turning him in a full circle by the rope around his neck. He then forced the Nubian's lips open to expose strong, straight ivory teeth set in blue-black gums.

"This beast was born for the Arena. Do not insult me with anything less than five thousand denarii."

The bidding ended with eight thousand denarii, and the Nubian was led down from the block. He passed so close by me that I could see tiny beads of sweat pooling in the hollow at the base of his throat. Just at that spot—so green against his ebony skin—hung a glassy medallion etched with a seven-pointed star. A septagram.

I grabbed his arm, and for the first time this day, we looked straight at each other. He blinked and then blinked again. I could see every tiny red capillary in the white of those wide, surprised eyes.

Goliath recognized me, but by the baffled look on his face, I saw he didn't know from where.

"Help me," I pleaded, although I had no idea how one slave could help another.

A soldier wrenched my hand away, but Goliath's eyes and mine stayed locked until a forceful tug on my arm pulled me in the direction of the block.

I had no reason for hope, but I no longer felt alone. The Universe had a plan. Goliath was here.

I was back in the Circle of the Protectors.

CHAPTER 2   SLAVE AUCTION

"To some extent, I liken slavery to death." – Cicero

Viewed from the top of the block, the mob was impossibly more vicious. It was from that vantage point I saw how many they were and how utterly vile their faces.

A voice cried out, "*Praecantrix!*" And then another and another. "Witch." "Witch." "Witch."

O blessed Hathor! Did they burn witches in Rome? My skin already felt on fire.

The sun was a white orb in a white sky. When I raised my bound hands to shield my eyes, the auctioneer knocked them down with his brass-tipped baton.

"Strip the witch!"

"Strip her! Strip her!" They kept at it, baying louder and louder, more like packs of rabid dogs than men. "Strip! Strip!"

This is not happening. This isn't real. But, of course, it was real enough.

A northerly breeze sprang up, bringing cooler air from the sea. I took a deep breath—drawing strength from its freshness—and braced myself.

But the auctioneer didn't tear off my gown. Instead, he stood back and grinned a broad, gummy smile with missing front teeth. Sweat pasted strands of strawy hair to his cheeks and forehead. At the back of his neck hung a greasy ponytail tied with a leather thong.

In a grand theatrical gesture, he raised both hands for silence. Legionaries beat in unison on their shields with the flat side of their sword blades until the mob calmed.

He moved up close to me, making a great show of stroking my hair with his stained fingers and rubbing back and forth across my breasts with his crop. The mob cheered and screamed again for him to strip me.

"You say *praecantrix*," he shouted. "I say *enchantress*. Who will hold this red mane between his thighs tonight? Whose cock will she suck?"

"No bids 'til we see 'er naked!"

I looked straight ahead, fixing on a mammoth bronze statue of a Roman emperor with his arm outstretched in an orator's pose, his finger pointing right at me. Behind the statue towered an incongruously magnificent theater with elegant stone colonnades and graceful arches.

Wake me up, Barb. Wake me up.

"I regret, my good citizens, but only he who pays has the privilege to see. It is rare we have such a prize as this in Leptis Magna."

"Is she a virgin?"

"If your taste is for virgins," he yelled out, "I'll throw in this sweet young thing."

The hazel-eyed girl was dragged to my side. He took her face in his hands and licked across her lips. She spat at him. The crowd roared. She tried to pull away; he held her jaw fast in his grip and licked again. They roared louder.

"Not so sweet maybe, but she can be tamed. Now this goddess," he said, tracing the baton over my breasts, the curve of my belly and down the length of a thigh, "knows how to please a man."

He lifted a lock of my hair, ran it under his nose, dramatically inhaling the scent and, with a flourish, sucked on the tip, making smacking sounds. "I'm told she craves the thrust of a cock, no matter where."

The mob surged. I was terrified they'd storm the block, but a handful of soldiers repulsed them with spears and shields. Fistfights broke out among those jockeying for the front rows. Soldiers dragged men away. The mass shoved forward again. More soldiers arrived, locking shields to form a wall at the foot of the platform.

"Five thousand denarii!" The opening bid.

There was a flurry of back and forth on all sides in a pace of frenetic bidding that didn't stop until a voice to the right called out, "Twelve thousand."

I had resolved to stare straight ahead but found myself unable to resist assessing him. A Roman officer. Not a General. Likely a Legate.

He held himself erect with the arrogance of a man accustomed to having what he wants. A nasty scar ran the length of his left cheek. He stood with two other Lieutenants a little outside the crowd, as if they'd been passing by and stopped on a whim.

"I see we have a connoisseur today," cried the auctioneer. "A man of discerning taste. Do I hear—"

"Fourteen thousand." This bidder didn't shout out; he didn't need to. He was that close.

Striking in a savage way, he was all lean muscle a few shades darker than the golden-tan of his suede tunic. Dried reddish mud matted his beard; feathers stuck out from his braids. His yellow-green eyes stared into mine with the non-blinking gaze of one who spends his life in vast spaces. A desert man.

"I have fourteen thousand," shouted the auctioneer. "Do I hear fifteen?"

The Legate nodded. One of his companions said something, and the three laughed.

I cast a side glance to Desert Man, holding my breath, dreading his counter. I had to stay in the city. There were places to hide in the city. In a city, I could find help until Barb brought me back. Once he took me to the desert, I would have nowhere to escape. And escape was all I thought of.

But the next bid, "Twenty thousand," came from a little round Roman in a red-trimmed toga. His bony slave, all knobby knees and elbows, shielded him from the sun with a green parasol trimmed in gold fringe.

I liked this new bidder. He looked overly pleased with himself when the crowd cheered him on. A man who craved approval. A man who could be manipulated.

"I have twenty thousand denarii!" crowed the auctioneer. "Who will say twenty-two?"

The mood had shifted; the tone was relaxed, as at a sporting event. Clearly enjoying themselves, men laughed and joked, shouting out bets, wagering whom of the three bidders would go highest.

From below, Desert Man stared up at me. I felt him probing my mind and refused to meet his yellow eyes. I pushed him out of my head. He pushed back in. I put up a wall. He took down a brick. Of anyone here, I feared him most.

"Twenty-two," he bid.

"Twenty-three," countered the Legate at once.

I turned my gaze on the fat Roman. Across the space between us, my smoldering eyes promised him everything.

"Twenty-five!" he called out bravely.

The auctioneer turned to the Legate. There was a bit of a hush while the Legate weighed if the pleasure he would gain from me was worth the investment.

"Thirty-five thousand." The stunning bid didn't come from the Legate but from the back, near a pair of octagon pavilions.

"I have thirty-five thousand denarii!" boomed the auctioneer. He was beside himself, his eyes agleam, a toothless grin cracking his face.

I'm certain he'd never dreamed of such a commission.

He yelled out, "May we see the bidder?"

A relative quiet fell while the crowd thinned around a very tall man with thick chestnut waves—handsome, athletic, with an easy posture that said he was born to privilege.

Even from this distance, there was no mistaking him. Hector.

I didn't know if he'd come through the Red Mirror, or if he was from this life. It didn't matter. He was here. Hector was here.

"Thank you, Universe," I sobbed. "Thank you."

"Do I hear higher?" challenged the auctioneer.

There was to be no counterbid from the Legate; he was already walking away with his companions.

For a moment, it seemed that the fat Roman would counter. Men shouted out, "Bid! Bid!"

He beamed with as much eagerness as a child at holiday, until his slave whispered in his ear and the glow faded from his face. When the auctioneer made a plea for a final bid, he shook his head, his eyes cast down, ashamed to face me. He was a pathetic excuse for a man, much less a Roman.

"And you," the auctioneer put to Desert Man. "Do I hear thirty-six?"

Silence. Over and over I chanted, *Don't bid. Don't bid. Don't bid.*

"Going once," the auctioneer cautioned. "Going twice."

I held my breath, avoiding Desert Man's eyes, fearful that if I looked at him, encouraged him in any way, he would counter.

An eternity passed before I heard the auctioneer shout, "Sold! Both females to the tall stranger for thirty-five thousand denarii!"

It was over. The nightmare was over.

A soldier bound the girl and me together with a rope around the neck and hurried us down the stairs. Elated, buoyant even, I didn't feel the wood slats beneath my feet.

No sooner was I off the steps than Desert Man stood so close, he pressed into me. I glanced quickly into his face, expecting to see disappointment, but instead, he looked amused, as if he knew something I didn't know but soon would.

He lifted his hand, and a small green object flashed in the sun. Like a hypnotist's charm, a faience circle etched with a seven-pointed star swung back and forth from his middle finger. A second septagram.

I reached out for the medallion, but Desert Man was gone as quickly as he'd appeared.

Here on the ground, in the crush of the mob, not a breath of air came off the sea. The marketplace began to spin. I couldn't seem to put one foot in front of the other. I tripped; the girl caught me before I fell. Iron hammers in my head pounded and pounded.

Water. I had to have water. *Hector will give me water.*

But that wasn't what the bare-chested Egyptian with shaved head and gold slave collar was saying to the sales agent.

"Have the two females delivered to the villa of Marcus Quintillus."

"No-o-o!" Without a thought to consequence, I grabbed his forearm. "Your master," I demanded. "Where is your master?"

He had the most dumfounded expression, poised between shock and panic. He tried to pull away; I hung on, digging my fingertips into the cobra tattoo coiling up his arm.

Then I felt a blow to the side of my head, and all around me went white. There was silence until, in a sudden rush, the sounds of the market hied down a long corridor to explode in my ears. Edges hardened, and the world snapped back into focus.

Not ten feet away stood Hector.

He stared at me for a long moment then turned away to leave, but not before I saw the triumph in his eyes.

"Hector!" I screamed after him. "*Hector!*"

He kept going and never looked back.

CHAPTER 3   VILLA BY THE SEA

"Fortune favors the bold." – Sallust

Surely if my mind were strong enough and I willed hard enough, I could wake myself in Las Vegas. But either it wasn't possible or my mind was too weak, because I stayed firmly in hell.

A cretin of a soldier with a Neanderthal face snarled, *"Move it!* We've got far to go."

"I need water," I told him, "You shall end up having to carry me."

His answer was to slap me across the face. "Shut your trap, or I'll drag you the whole way by the hair."

He jerked hard on the rope around our necks, and the girl lost her footing and fell before I could catch her.

"Get up, cow!" he screamed, kicking her in the side with his thick-soled monster sandal.

While I helped her to her feet, he fumed and spouted abuse.

In spite of his threats, I plowed on. "Do you not fear the displeasure of Marcus Quintillus when he receives damaged goods?"

I braced myself for a second blow, and when it didn't come, I said, "I need protection from the sun."

Uneducated lowlife that he was, it confused him to hear me speak patrician Latin. He clenched his fist but didn't strike me. I clearly unnerved him. I was not the kind of slave to which he was accustomed.

He gnawed a little on his lower lip, glancing a bit furtively at the crowd gathering around us.

"She's right about Marcus Quintillus," someone offered. "Look at that skin. Whiter than the belly of a toad. Better wrap the witch up before she fries."

He chewed more on his lip. I saw his little mind struggle with one simple decision before he loosened his red cape from the bronze clip at the shoulder and tossed it over my shoulders.

As best as I could with my hands tied, I dragged the cape over my head to shield my face.

"Hey, Legionary! Hire a litter for her!" The laughter sent him into a towering rage.

Crimson-faced, snorting like a bull, he yanked on the rope to haul us along the scorching pavement in our bare feet. While the girl seemed oblivious to the burning stone, each step was searing pain for me.

Marble-faced three-story buildings pressed right up to the roadway, leaving only a narrow curb. Not a single tree or flowering bush relieved the crushing hardness of stone.

The soldier, no doubt wanting to escape the brutal sun himself, elbowed his way to the shady side. Everywhere street vendors hawked foodstuffs from small carts on two wheels. I didn't remember when I last ate, but I didn't feel hunger—only a relentless, tortuous craving for water.

My head was a balloon expanding, shrinking and expanding again. My tongue filled my mouth. There was no saliva to wet my lips.

"Please!" I begged when I stumbled against a water vendor with a red-tasseled goatskin bag hanging across his chest.

He flashed a wide grin of yellow teeth set in black gums and waved a copper cup in my face. Clear sparkling water splashed on stone.

Blurry vision was the first warning. The second was a dampening of distinct sounds to a muffled roar. Then the world went black.

When I came to, we were by the sea. Not on the beach itself, but so close as to hear the tumbling waves. Scores of seagulls squawked overhead.

The light was vividly bright, as it is at the shore, with a fine salt mist softening the cruel sun.

I lay on the side of a gravel road, next to double wood gates set in a whitewashed wall. A gold laurel crest with the red letters 'MQ' was painted on dark green. The villa of Marcus Quintillus.

The soldier was banging on the gate with his sword hilt. The girl stood close to me, but we were no longer bound together. When I met her eyes, she stared stoically back, guarding her fears to herself.

The right-hand gate opened, and a wall-eyed round face with an astonished look peered out at us.

"Dominus has said nothing about the delivery of slaves." He disappeared, closing the gate with a clang of the iron latch.

The soldier glared at me as if it were my fault we were kept waiting in the sun.

He must have given me water; my tongue was not as thick. I didn't feel any more bruised or scraped, so he'd carried and not dragged me by the hair as threatened.

"*Grātias*," I told him.

He grunted and spat on the ground.

The villa appeared to be quite on its own. A stand of olive trees separated us from the nearest house across the road. The cerulean sky, unrelieved by a single cloud, stretched forever. By the western sun, I judged it early afternoon and decided that we weren't far from the city, certainly less than an hour's walk.

The gate opened again, and out stepped a tall coffee-colored Syrian with an oiled, shaved head gleaming in the sun. A heavy gold slave collar glinted at his throat. Impeccably dressed in a knee-length, blinding white tunic and solid, quality sandals, he had the telltale smugness about the mouth of a man who wielded great power. The major domo. Head slave of the household.

"On your feet," he snapped.

When I didn't move right away, the soldier stepped over, grabbed a fistful of my hair and hauled me up.

He took his time, this Major Domo, undressing me with his nasty hawk eyes, before saying, "Dominus can suck her teats when she's cleaned up. And that hair is worth something."

Then he glanced quickly at the girl. "We'll take the boy, too. He's the age the cook likes."

The gates opened into a blessedly cool hall with bright-colored columns and ochre walls painted with hunting murals. An immense earth-tone square mosaic with the head of Jupiter, encircled by gods and goddesses, covered the floor.

Directly across from the entrance, the hall opened to a vast peristyle courtyard with a lavish rose garden blooming around a rectangular reflecting pool. I heard the tinkle of fountains and the incongruous sweet medley of birdsong.

On the left was a smaller hall with a staircase leading to the second floor where slaves would be quartered and household goods stored. To the right were closed, richly painted double doors.

Major Domo opened the door on the right, and we entered a long black-and-white tiled corridor with a paneled ceiling painted with birds. Pastoral scenes decorated brick red walls. Above, a clerestory of green glass windows let in light. Standing brass lanterns evenly spaced along the hallway waited to be lighted at dusk.

We stopped midway down the corridor at an atrium. Directly under a square opening in the red-tiled roof, deep green lotus leaves floated on still water.

The atrium was quiet in a most unpeaceful way; a vague undercurrent of malice hung in the air. I became aware of the girl's light, too-rapid breathing and reached out for her hand. Startled, she pulled away, mistrust in her eyes.

Leaving us in the corridor, Major Domo made for a divan where two female Nubians massaged a reclining man.

"Can you not see I am occupied?" The voice, in every way commanding, was yet uncommonly high, as if arrested somewhere between puberty and manhood.

"Yes, Dominus. Please forgive the interruption. Two slaves have just arrived. A female and a boy. I understand they are sent by one Rufus Hektor Ptolemais."

"I know no one by that name."

"I believe Rufus Hektor is from Alexandria, Dominus. A Romanized Greek. Dominus may recall that he has requested an audience on a number of occasions."

"These are gifts from Egypt then? Let us have a look."

"My understanding, Dominus, is that the slaves have come directly from the slave market."

"The market! Great Jupiter! Get them cleaned up before they infect the whole house with vermin!"

The slave bath was reached from a kitchen garden ringed by tall white walls topped with broken glass. Clay *garum* pots with fermenting sardines and herbs lined the villa wall. Three female slaves with short-cropped hair bent over neat rows of rosemary, onions and lettuce.

A young boy was drawing water with a leather bucket from a well. Behind him, in the back wall, was a single red door. I wondered if it gave directly onto the beach. The splash and rumble of surf sounded not far away.

Major Domo turned us over to a round, honey-skinned woman with broad hips and navy blue diagonal lines tattooed on her forehead and chin. Her hair, more gray than black, was shorn close to the head. On her neck below the left ear was a thumbnail-sized brand. 'MQ.'

"Bathe them," he ordered. "Shave their heads. Send the boy to the cook."

"T'wud be a pity to shear that red mane." Her rough Latin had the guttural harshness I'd heard everywhere today.

"We need water," I told the woman. "I do not know how long it has been since we drank."

It was suddenly still. At the well, the boy with the bucket stopped and stared.

"Did you not understand me?" I repeated impatiently. "Water. The girl and I need water."

At my mention of 'the girl,' I heard a few snickers and saw those nearest exchange glances. My first mistake. Humiliating Major Domo in front of the others. I don't know which was more deadly, the way he looked at those snickering or the way he looked at me.

"Well, I'll say," jeered the woman. "Ain't you the fine one? Where did you learn to speak Latin like that?"

"I am Roman," I told her coldly.

"Roman!" Major Domo knocked me to the ground with the back of his hand. "I've got news for you, missy. You're a slave now."

Our eyes locked. If my stare had cowed men in the marketplace, it had no effect on him. Not long ago, I would have slapped that the smirk off his slave face. I would have had him whipped.

Instead, I allowed my disdain to show. In that moment, he declared war.

No murals adorned the brick walls of the slave bath. Sunlight streamed through round cutouts in a plain ceiling to fall in long, dust-filled shafts onto the concrete floor.

I washed my hair and sponged my aching body in a concrete pool filled with clear, tepid water. A thin nut-brown girl with a sparkly green headscarf filed my broken nails, pumiced away my pubic hair stubble and shaved my leg hair with a copper razor. With a look of pity in her eyes, she gently massaged warm olive oil into my screaming sunburned skin.

My flesh was on fire, but it was wonderful to be clean again. I felt almost alive.

The girl sat on the bath floor, watching everything and saying nothing. Only her head had been shaved; she was too young for body hair. Bubbling blood dried in tiny beads on her white scalp.

My hair hung thick and wet down my back.

"Give me the cutters," ordered the woman with the tattooed face.

My hair! My beautiful hair! Even that was to be taken away. I clenched my teeth and stared stonily ahead.

The shears turned out to be a huge affair with long clumsy bronze blades that didn't look sharp enough to trim a rosebush.

She grabbed a handful and lifted the hair up and out, pulling so hard that I felt the tug on each follicle. Metal scratched against metal close to my ear, and then I heard the sound of the blades meeting resistance. I closed my eyes and waited for the shears to chew through.

"I should not do that, if I were you."

The shears stopped. The hair dropped. We all turned in the direction of the voice.

The youth was about thirteen years old with a sullen face marked by a high cunning brow over vulpine eyes. He was dressed in a schoolboy's knee-length white tunic with a wide crimson border on the hem and sleeves. His brown wavy hair was trimmed short and combed forward from the crown. A heavy gold *bulla*, the protective amulet worn from birth until manhood, hung on a leather cord around his neck.

"Major Domo ordered it, Master," murmured the woman.

"It shall not be he who feels the rod when my mother discovers what you have done."

The two women stepped quickly away from me, crying out, "Forgive us, Master! We did not know Domina had interest in this woman."

"She herself does not yet know." His eyes took in every curve of my naked body. "But she *will* be interested when she sees her. You may be quite certain of that."

CHAPTER 4   DOMINA

"There's no such thing, you know, as picking out the best woman; it's only a question of comparative badness." – Titus Maccius Plautus

After our bath, the girl and I were taken to the kitchen and given a wedge of chewy black bread and a bowl of paste-like wheat porridge boiled with goat milk.

Using all my discipline, I ate as slowly as I could bear.

The cook, a swarthy Greek with a sloppy belly, watched me spoon each mouthful. He'd once been a thief but forgiven. 'F' for *fure* scarred his forehead. The household 'MQ' had since been branded on top.

"We'll see how uppity you are," he mumbled in a peasant's Greek, "with some cock up your arse."

I put the spoon down in the bowl, looked directly at him and said in flawless Greek, "Yes, I suppose a Thracian *would* prefer the dirty hole."

He looked confused, no doubt trying to decide if I were Greek myself. But whatever my origin, my accent was not that of a slave.

"Just wait, bitch. I'll come for you in the night, and you'll eat those words along with my dick."

It was impossible to know how many of the kitchen slaves spoke Greek, but they definitely picked up on our tone. They slowed their work, glancing in our direction. To be absolutely certain that I got my message across, I switched to a precise Latin that all could understand.

"I should be very cautious about that. The last man who forced himself on me choked on his 'dick' down his throat."

An abrupt, piercing clap of hands shattered the quiet that followed my words. At the same time, a female voice snapped, "Enough chatter!"

Every man, woman and child went to their knees with foreheads to the floor. I alone sat on my haunches.

In the latest Empire fashion from Rome, the woman wore a six-inch high wig of tight strawberry curls parted in the middle and decorated with an elaborate pearl-studded part barrette. In her hand she carried an ebony baton very like the auctioneer's. Hers was tipped in gold.

Domina. Mistress of the house with absolute power of life and death and every misery in between. I knew at once by the curl of her lip and the way she held her head what kind of mistress she was.

She'd been a great beauty once; she still had fine bones. Today any vestige of good looks were spoiled by unfortunate stark white lead makeup and cruel black-red lips. Even more than in the eyes, her evil showed in that mouth.

"You do not bow?" She had a treacherous voice, vibrating with menace.

In a sudden movement, her ebony rod slammed the crown of my head, and I put my forehead to the stone floor.

"There," she said, pressing her sandal with all her weight on the back of my neck. "That was not so difficult, was it?"

The kitchen was breathlessly silent. A bird sang in the garden. Beyond the wall, waves tumbled to a beach.

"Bring her to me," she ordered. "Just the way she is."

Her bedchamber was smoky with a cloying cloud of myrrh. I could see daylight as a faint glow around thick shutters. Tall bronze lanterns cut with stars and crescent moons cast dancing patterns on a black and white mosaic floor and blood red walls.

"Closer!" Domina commanded from across the shadows.

Major Domo pushed me forward into a hazy halo of amber light. "Leave us."

She reclined on a sofa with a raised gilded armrest. At her feet lounged a leopard with a golden collar. The leopard was chained, but I saw at a glance that the silver chain was long enough for the cat to reach me.

"Turn around."

I did as she commanded, pivoting slowly.

"Closer."

I stepped up next to her couch, so close the leopard lay only inches from my feet. It hissed, curling its lips to show me sharp teeth the color of ivory. Forcing myself to breathe evenly, I blocked visions of those teeth tearing at my throat.

"Untie your right shoulder."

Slowly, so as not to provoke the cat, I loosened the cord, and half of my tunic top slipped to my waist. Domina's eyes widened; her breath came faster.

In the dim light, her lips were blacker than black against her stark white face. The light falling on her hollow eyes and cheeks cast dark shadows that gave her the look of a corpse. But she was very much alive. Her mouth hung a little slack; the pointed pink tip of her tongue appeared between crooked teeth.

"Your skin is like milk," she breathed out.

If my heart raced, so did hers; her breasts rose and fell quickly.

"Untie the other shoulder," she whispered.

Just as cautiously as before, I loosened the second tie and the rest of the tunic tumbled to my waist.

For a long moment, Domina was silent, taking in my white glowing breasts with hungry eyes, moistening her lips with that reptile tongue.

Try as I might to control my breath and heartbeat, blood pounded in my temples. My palms were wet with sweat. It wasn't her lust that frightened me; I'd seen lust before. It was the not knowing what it would take to satisfy her appetite that unnerved me. And the leopard. I'd seen that too. It was an ugly end.

"Æsa!" Domina hissed.

An Amazon with thick blond braids to her waist appeared from nowhere.

"Yes, Domina."

"The black one—and the Gaul."

Silence. The leopard shifted position and began to lick its paw in an idle, languid way. Long, curving claws unfurled. For the moment, it seemed to have lost interest in me. My eyes kept going to the pink tongue and the razor claws.

"Look at me," Domina snapped. "Where are you from?"

"Hispania."

When her eyes narrowed, I hurried to add, "Domina."

"Say something else. I want to hear you speak."

"What does Domina desire me to say?"

She studied me, no longer mesmerized by my breasts but looking me hard in the face.

"They tell me you were born Roman?"

"Yes, Domina."

"I heard you tell the cook that you murdered a man."

"Yes, Domina."

"Well," she demanded impatiently. "Who?"

I hesitated. There were a dozen stories I could invent but none with the shock factor of the truth. I wouldn't tell her all, though. All would be too much.

"My father," I said evenly.

She jerked back, recoiling with such force that I might have put a deadly asp to her face. The leopard tensed, lifting its ears. A low growl rumbled in the stillness.

I thought I might use her shock to my advantage, but I hadn't counted on the men. They came out of the black into the ring of light. Two beasts in horrid pewter masks with huge round eyeholes and thick bulbous lips.

When they saw me, naked to the waist, their already monstrous penises swelled.

One was a black giant. Oiled muscle moved toward me on silent bare feet. Even before he came close, I saw the eyes of a sadist glittering from behind the mask.

The Gaul had skin so blue, he glowed. His wild straw hair was braided into long ropes twisted with colored glass beads that caught the flicker of the lamps.

His broad, bare feet were soundless, too, on the mosaic floor.

With the arrival of the men, Domina morphed once more.

"You. Black One. Take her from behind." Her voice, husky and terrifyingly breathless, told me she was one of those who finds her pleasure in watching. "You. Gaul! Down her throat."

I knew that if I looked at her, she would be aroused, flushed under her white makeup, nipples rock hard in her silk gown. But I didn't look at her; I couldn't tear my eyes away from the blue Gaul.

"Make her squeal," Domina whispered.

The black giant grabbed me by the hair, forcing my head down, bending me at the waist, hauling up my tunic, ripping away my loincloth.

"All the way in," she screamed. "I want you all the way in."

I felt the searing thrust in my anus at the same time the Gaul rammed the back of my throat.

My mind shouted, *This isn't real! The real me is on the other side of the Mirror.*

But the pain was real. I couldn't breathe; a log tore me.

"STOP! Stop at once!"

The command was shouted in the too-high, vaguely adolescent voice of the man from the atrium. Dominus. Master of all, even Domina.

The black giant and the blue Gaul dropped me and went to their knees. I collapsed between them, sucking in great gulps of air.

"Fool!" Domina shouted. "She is a murderess. She could be an assassin! You know nothing of this Alexandrian who sent her. He is Greek! Who can trust a Greek?"

"A Roman citizen nonetheless. And well-connected. I want this woman in one piece until I discover why he sent her."

He snapped his fingers. Major Domo dragged me on my knees to Dominus and then hauled me to my feet.

I stood before him, careful to keep my eyes cast down as was proper for a slave.

"Look up," he commanded.

And when I did, I saw the Crown Prince Psamtik. I saw Ptolemy IV. Now Dominus. I held my breath for a moment, waiting for him to recognize me. Dreading him to fathom that he controlled, at last, what he long had desired—the time and means of my death.

This incarnation was not much taller than me, with thick lips in a doughy face pitted from the pox. He had cunning, nakedly ambitious eyes with no more soul than a shark. Eyes that didn't know me. Not yet.

I kept my own expression blank, showing him nothing. If I were to survive, I needed his protection. To gain his protection, I had to prove my worth. Behind my mask, I searched for clues as to what his needs might be—in the rate of his breath, the pulse in his temple, the blinking of his eyelids. Of one thing I was certain, he was not the weak Ptolemy I'd once manipulated.

Whatever he saw piqued his interest. I could only hope he wasn't beginning to see our past.

"Get her cleaned up," he ordered Major Domo. "And keep her away from knives. If you value your life. If we all value our lives."

CHAPTER 5   DOMINUS

"Great fear is concealed under daring." – Lucan

The same nut brown slave with the sparkling green headscarf cleaned away dried blood and applied a soothing ointment in my torn anus that stung hot before it chilled. And when the salve cooled, the pain was a distant throb.

"What are you called?" I asked her.

"Shinuba," she answered and then added in broken Latin, "I from South."

The hairdressing slave piled my hair on my head in an elaborate maze of plaits and curls. Using a curved needle threaded with silvery twine, she sewed the braided coils as one might a hooked rug.

While she worked, the two talked together quietly in a language with a cadence reminiscent of the Egyptian I once spoke in another life.

"What are you speaking?"

"*Tamazight.*" When she saw my blank look, she added, "Berber."

"Shake head," commanded the hairdresser.

I obliged, and not a hair shifted.

Satisfied, Shinuba helped me into a soft leather bra and underpants, then a long *tunica* of sunny linen. She covered the yellow undergown with a *stola* of green Milesian wool soft as cashmere. Silver twine gathered the wool at the shoulders; more silver rope crisscrossed from my shoulders around and under my breasts, and then crossed again in back.

Over the *stola* and *tunica*, she draped a sapphire blue *palla*, also of fine wool. As soft as it was, the fabric chaffed my sunburned arms.

"Drink. Help pain." She urged a small vial of bitter liquid to my lips.

"ANA A A NANA A A NANA," she murmured in the throaty vibrating drone of bees.

When I'd emptied the vial, she breathed, "ABLAMGOUNOTHO ABRASAX."

Glancing around to make certain no one was near, she unfurled her fingers just enough for me to glimpse in her palm a green faience talisman carved with a septagram.

"Where did you get this?" I whispered.

Her answer was to lower her eyes and shake her head.

"Eat nothing," she hissed in my ear. "Only me give you."

I wanted to ask about the hazel-eyed girl, but my tongue grew numb and thick, too thick to form words. My ears hummed as if listening to the roar of the sea in a conch.

A cosmetics slave had outlined my eyes with *kohl,* spread carmine on my lips and begun to dust my sunburned face with white lead when Major Domo appeared.

"You are to accompany Dominus to the baths." It must have pained him unbearably to speak those words; he made no attempt to conceal his hatred for me.

"I cannot go more in the sun." My nose and lips were numb, but my tongue worked again. "Dominus would not desire my skin further spoiled."

He raised his hand to strike me but thought better of it and dropped his clenched fist to his side. In a disconcerting flash, I saw his thoughts snaking through his mind, inventing foul ways of making me suffer.

"I would skin you alive if given the chance," he snarled.

"You should speak to Dominus about a litter," I told him. "Impress him with your foresight."

He turned abruptly on his heels and stormed out, scattering the beautician slaves in his path. Shinuba clicked her tongue against the back of her teeth and began to chant under her breath. "ANA A A NANA A A NANA."

When I arrived in the front hall of the villa, the reception area I'd entered only hours before, a flurry of slaves buzzed around Dominus, settling him onto a litter. Major Domo glowered beside a second one with a matching green-striped awning.

Dominus watched me with frank curiosity as I climbed on with an ease and grace that made clear I was born to this.

He didn't owe a slave any explanation, yet he said, "If I do not take you with me, you shall not be alive when I return."

Resting on my elbow, I stretched my legs and settled on my right side. A stack of pillows in a rainbow of colors supported my shoulder and arm; filmy curtains hung down from the awning.

Four broad-shouldered slaves of identical height took the ends of polished cypress poles and lifted the litter into the air. The double doors with the crest of Marcus Quintillus opened into blinding white light, and with Major Domo leading the way on foot, we entered the road. Each step of the bearers fell in practiced unison.

The sound of the lazy sea was a quiet lullaby broken only by the cries of seagulls. The litter swayed with the rhythm of a light boat in a gentle swell. My head was still light from the drug; I didn't feel quite connected to my body.

Through voile drapes I saw sparkling turquoise water kissing white sand. When I closed my eyes, I saw the green septagram circle glowing on Shinuba's hennaed palm.

We turned sharply inland and entered a rough paved road framed on both sides by neat rows of silver-leafed olive trees whispering with the wind.

The ghastly stench fouled the air long before we reached the killing field.

Just outside the gates of the city stood a grove of wooden crosses hung with wretched bodies in various stages of decay. Birds had been at them. Around one corpse's neck hung a wooden sign with crude block letters. FUGITIVA. *Runaway female slave.*

I turned my face away, pulling the blue wool palla to my nose, determined not to let her wretched end influence what I knew I must do.

Once through the gates, we joined the river of foot traffic and litters on the Cardo running north and south through the center of the city. For as far as I could see, Corinthian columns painted in scarlet, emerald and cobalt lined both sides of the avenue. Midday was sliding into late afternoon; the pillars cast long indigo shadows.

After the calm of the shore, the street rang shrill with clanking wheels, piercing shouts and protests of donkeys and camels. Urban odors replaced the reek of the rotting crucified—garbage, animal waste, burning incense and wood fires roasting meat. Silhouetted against the cloudless sky rose the magnificent towering *scaenae frons* of the theatre I'd seen today from the auction block.

We passed by the slave market with its twin octagon pavilions, then through a massive square limestone structure of four triumphal arches. Deep-carved Latin block letters expressed gratitude to Emperor Trajan for granting Leptis Magna full status as a Roman *colonia* with all free-born males made Roman citizens. After the Latin came what I took to be a Neo-Punic translation in that alien alphabet of the ancient Phoenicians who once ruled here.

"Make way! Make way for the Procurator!" cried Major Domo.

Great marble monuments blocked any sea breeze. Heat radiated off baking stone. I waved a feather fan and dabbed the sweat from my lead powdered brow with a corner of the palla.

Shortly, we turned off the Cardo onto a narrow street that ended abruptly at a mighty bathing complex on the edge of a river. A half-acre of orange-red ceramic tiles covered an intricate array of sloping and domed roofs. Inside would be the *caldarium,* hot room, the *tepidarium,* warm bath, the *frigidarium,* cold pool, and the *laconicum,* sauna.

Green spiky tops of cypress and date palms poked up above the high wall of an athletic field. In the cool of the morning, Roman young men would wrestle there, throw javelins, and swim laps in the open-air pool. My brothers had spent their days in just such a *palaestra* in Spain.

I felt no guilt when I thought of them—or shame for the price I made them pay for their abuse. When I went to that place where my heart should be, I felt nothing.

We made a dramatic entry through wide doors under a carved inscription declaring the baths built by the Procurator Marcus Quintillus in honor of Emperor Hadrian.

Fountains splashed under a high vaulted ceiling pierced with scores of compact blue glass domes. Green marble floor tiles gleamed. Painted on the walls of the foyer, life-sized muscular tanned men embraced voluptuous ivory women with nude backs.

Our arrival caused quite a stir. I had the impression Dominus didn't come here daily as was customary for the elite. While greeters fussed over him, their eyes kept going to me. *Who is this redhead with Marcus Quintillus?* Roman ladies bathe in the mornings.

There was nothing about me that said slave. My hair was not shorn; I wore a stola and palla.

"*Striga*," a hushed voice hissed. Witch.

I thought I would stay with the litter, but instead Dominus signaled for me to follow with Major Domo. We passed through the dressing chamber, ignoring the statue-like slaves waiting to disrobe bathers, and entered the frigidarium with triple-height ceiling. Hunting murals with lions and giraffes covered the cinnamon red walls.

It was wonderfully cool after the heat of the street. So quiet. The air was fresh.

A dozen Romans in long loincloths reclined on divans near a circular plunging pool. Here, too, they showed surprise to see Dominus. And the same stealth curiosity about me.

"*Salve*, Marcus Quintillus!"

A pair of male anointing slaves rushed to unwind his toga, trotting in a circle around him as he walked. By the time he reached a fur-covered couch, the toga was gone. A third *unctor* removed his tunic, revealing a pasty, puffy body utterly lacking definition.

Two sinewy black female slaves went to their knees, each massaging a foot; a third kneaded his neck and shoulders. A boy slave appeared with a chalice of wine.

"I have come about a silphium shipment," Dominus announced.

His words, simple enough but delivered in that menacing half boy-half man voice, created another stir. A thin, balding man of about forty sat straight up in alarm.

"Silphium, Most Excellent? Which shipment? There are many."

"I trust, Sextus Julius, there is only one with a fraudulent bill of lading."

"Fraudulent, Most Excellent? Might I inquire of what nature?" He had the dense look in his wide eyes that told me straightaway he wasn't cunning enough to be guilty.

"Of the nature that evades export duty."

No one spoke. Dominus had quite electrified them. By his off-hand sipping on a goblet and nibbling on a hunk of cheese, I saw he thoroughly enjoyed their unease.

We all knew the punishment for cheating a Procurator's treasury—confiscation of property, exile or death. Dominus, final judge of all crimes, would render judgment. If he chose to be merciful, suicide might save the family.

I studied each man in turn and focused on two. One had a withered left leg, the other a great fleshy stomach that hung in a sack to his side. They exchanged looks, then the Pig spoke in a voice too oily for an honest man.

"Most Excellent, I know of no citizen in this company who would prove so disloyal as to betray the Procurator's trust. Certainly not with silphium, of all goods."

My mother had taken great pride in her exotic dishes flavored with the Libyan herb and paid its weight in gold to get it. When she lived, that is.

"I accuse no one, Hostus Flavius," answered Dominus. "I have come to you, my trusted friends, to seek your counsel."

"If there is a discrepancy in weight, Your Excellence, might I suggest slave error." He was a shrewd one all right, this Hostus Flavius the Pig.

The others leapt at once to his laying of blame on slaves.

"Yes! Slaves are a deceitful and incompetent lot."

"Tricksters!"

"We shall uncover those slaves responsible," growled the man with the withered leg, "and they shall be punished!"

Dominus took his time, allowing the fervor to run its course. He focused on a pear, sucking the juicy flesh, making little slurping sounds. From across the room, I made out a tiny erection under his loincloth.

The group stilled, watching Dominus as if never having seen anyone eat fruit. The chamber was very still. I hadn't noticed until now how loudly the water played in the fountain.

"The fault *could* lie with the slaves." Dominus paused to finish off the pear and toss the core to the tiles. "Yes. We should all take measures to monitor them more closely."

"Especially the Christians," the slow-witted one called Sextus Julius shouted. "Heretics! Thieves all!"

Looking positively delivered, the men relaxed back onto their divans; wine slaves hurried to refill goblets. The Pig and Withered Leg glanced a little too long at each other. I had been forgotten; they were quite unaware of my eyes on them.

When Dominus waved away the masseuses and stood, an unctor rushed over with his tunic. Two dressing slaves came running with his lengthwise-folded toga.

An assistant held the bulk of the cloth while the master dresser draped, back to front over Dominus' raised left arm, a length long enough to reach the ankles. He then took the remainder of the wool and unfurled it across Dominus' back, under his right armpit, across his chest and then over the left shoulder. The last bit hung halfway down the back.

There were no pins; the sheer weight of the wool held the toga in place.

The dresser fussed with the folds on the chest until Dominus brushed him aside, and we left with as little ceremony as our arrival.

We were about to exit the adjacent dressing room when Dominus pivoted without warning to face me.

For one dreadful instant, I thought he'd recalled our past lives, but instead he asked, "And what did my witch see?"

Slaves stood a few feet away, shallow-breathing statues with eyes staring straight ahead. The notes of a lyre drifted in from the frigidarium. From the main hall came the bustle of bathers arriving and departing.

I didn't insult him by pretending not to understand his question. Nor did I show pleasure that he sought my opinion. He could have me blinded me for the slightest hint of triumph in my eyes.

My first impulse was to invent an answer that wouldn't accuse a Roman. For that offense, Dominus could have me beaten, face disfigured, or slowly crushed to death. Perhaps all three.

But only truth would prove my value, and my value was all that would keep me alive.

"I saw that it is Hostus Flavius and the man with the withered leg who deceives Dominus."

I looked down, steeling myself, repeating in my head Shinuba's nonsensical sounds. *"ANA A A NANA A A NANA."*

But instead of ordering my torture, he remarked in an idle way, "I am told you are from Hispania."

"Yes, Dominus. The provincial capital, Italica."

"Italica? Birthplace of Hadrian? Look at me, woman!"

I met his eyes in the proper way of a good slave, carefully subservient, shielding all my thoughts, hiding my feelings. A slave's survival depends on never revealing anything.

"Are you acquainted with the Emperor?" he demanded. "Do you know that Greek sodomite he has taken to? Antinous of Bithynia?"

"I was a child, Dominus, when last I saw Caesar."

"And now you are a slave. And a gift from a Greek. I find it most curious. I find *you* most curious."

I thanked every god in the Universe that he remained yet unaware of why I so intrigued him. At the same time, I anguished that some memory deep in his subconscious could, at any moment, awaken him.

"Locate this Rufus Hektor Ptolemais of Alexandria," he said to Major Domo. "I desire his company at my *convivium* this evening."

Major Domo shot me a murderous look before hurrying off. I focused on the mosaic dolphins swimming in glassy waves at my feet.

What was Dominus up to? He knew which men were guilty before he entered the baths. Slaves had already talked. They would have been made to.

"You are correct in your judgment," he confided.

I sensed he expected me to look at him. And when I did, he truly astonished me by asking, "What course of action would you counsel?"

If I failed this test, would he toss me to Domina?

"The fraud shall cease now. Dominus has wisely seen to that." I spoke slowly and very cautiously, alert for any sign that I went too far. "If Dominus believes Hostus Flavius has value in other matters, then I counsel using him to full advantage. Retribution can come later. When he has no more use."

He almost smiled. At least, that's the way I took the twisting of his mouth.

"It is clear that you are no ordinary woman—much less no ordinary slave."

With that, he turned his back on me and went through to the grand foyer. Our bearers jumped to ready the litters.

In the flurry of departure, fingers pressed a cool, hard object into my palm. The hand was quickly gone, but not before I glimpsed a cobra tattoo on the arm. I looked up into the face of the Egyptian slave from the slave market. He held my eyes, shaking his head slowly back and forth, warning me.

"From Hektor Ptolemais," he whispered.

In my palm glinted a gold-horned ring. The plump lapis lazuli stone, marbled with golden veins, was the deepest of blues.

O praise be to all Gods! The Hathor Ring!

Hektor would surely come for me tonight.

CHAPTER 6   CONVIVIUM

"The greatest pleasures are only narrowly separated from disgust." – Cicero

By the time we returned to the villa, only a golden glow on the horizon remained of the brutal sun. A tiny sliver of the moon hovered in a tangerine sky. The sea was shimmering mauve satin.

Peals of laughter and shouts of gambling carried across the peristyle gardens and echoed through the halls. The guests were ensconced in the library, no doubt dicing or playing *latrunculi*, a form of checkers that had become wildly popular. Some must sit at backgammon boards, sipping *mulsum*, a favored sweet aperitif made of fermented honey.

"Tell my guests I shall join them after I bathe," Dominus instructed Major Domo, who had caught up with us only minutes before.

I wasn't able to hear if he'd located Hektor Ptolemais of Alexandria but was certain he had. The ring in my hand would bring Hektor here.

"And you," Dominus said directly to me. "Come."

I felt Major Domo's eyes stabbing into my back as I went down the corridor, the Hathor Ring heavy as a rock in my clenched hand. How long before it would be discovered and taken from me?

The villa had its own baths with a series of rooms *en suite*—the hot room, followed by the warm pool and finally the cold plunging pool. Outside, torches lighted a fifty-meter lap pool set in yet another peristyle garden, this one with a view of the beach. An array of marble statues stood poised around the pool and among gazelle topiaries.

The floor of the tepidarium, the warm bath, was tiled with black and white marble squares set on the diagonal. Bright murals of dancing *maenads* and satyrs covered blood-red glossy walls. In the daytime, the dozens of opaque glass bubbles in the domed ceiling would have let in natural light. Now, in the twilight, oil lamps glowed.

A slave brought a silver tray of pigeon eggs on a bed of rock salt, chunks of white cheese, black and green olives with marinated peppers, a small silver bowl with olive oil, and a round loaf of dark bread. I was suddenly ravenous. I couldn't help but stare at the food.

"Eat," Dominus said.

Eat, drink nothing.

When he saw my hesitation, he gave me an approving look. "It is meant for me. It has been tasted. But you are right to be cautious. Domina has her fingers everywhere."

He turned his attention from me to bathing; a half-dozen slaves hovered around him. The ring would soon be discovered if I didn't hide it. Easing closer to the wall, I spotted a crack where the tiled lower section met the painted base of the mural.

When certain that no one was looking, I slipped the ring into the space. But the crack was deeper than I anticipated, and the ring disappeared. I almost gasped out loud.

Where I had felt hope, I now felt despair. The ring was my omen of good fortune. With it, I was saved. Now that it was gone, I was doomed.

"Well, what are you waiting for?" Dominus snapped impatiently. "Eat."

I put a tiny peeled egg in my mouth and washed it down with watered wine; the nourishment exploded into all my cells at once. I chewed another egg and then a piece of cheese, dipping a chunk of bread into olive oil. My eyes kept going back to the crack in the wall.

The slaves busied themselves scraping Dominus with a bronze *strigil,* then massaging scented almond oil into his doughy flesh. His body was an enigma. His breasts were as soft and well formed as a young girl, his tiny penis limp as a fat worm.

What aroused him, besides intimidation? He wasn't in the least excited by me. Perhaps he needed props. Some lashes on the buttocks, a leash around his neck?

"Is it true that you murdered your father?" he asked abruptly.

"Yes, Dominus."

"Why?"

"He abused me beyond bearing, Dominus."

He looked surprised. Abuse is not a Roman concept. *Potestas* gives fathers absolute power over their children. Like slaves, they belong to him.

"How?" he asked.

"How did he abuse me, Dominus, or how did I kill him?"

"You *are* a clever one." He paused, then revealed what was truly on his mind. "Well, are you a witch, then? The slaves fear you are."

"What makes one a witch, Dominus?"

"Perhaps the red hair is enough to convince them. Or the green eyes. But I think it is more the light in your eyes—a light of Seeing."

He pushed the strigil away impatiently and turned to look directly at me. "*Do* you see?"

"I see what I see, Dominus."

"But you must know that you see what others cannot. Is that why Hektor Ptolemais believed you to be useful to me? Because you can see into the hearts of men?"

"I know nothing, Dominus, except that I am a slave."

"*My* slave."

I didn't say, of course, what I thought. *Not for long, Dominus. Not for long.*

No sooner had we arrived in the library than the *vocator,* a sinewy slave with the hawk nose of a Syrian, announced the meal. The guests in their silky gowns and glittery jewels rose from the divans and wandered into the *triclinium* with its sweeping vista of the sea.

The dining area was built in the shape of a truncated cross, with three alcoves facing a central courtyard opening onto white sand. A chariot race mosaic of earth-tone ceramic and glass tiles covered the courtyard floor. Water danced in a gold lion fountain; the inky Mediterranean, *Mare Nostrum,* Our Sea, lapped at the nearby shore.

The walls of the three dining alcoves displayed a series of remarkable banquet murals executed in rich fresco finished with layers of marble powder to give a mirror gloss. Strewn about the mural's triclinium floor were lifelike fish and fowl bones, oyster shells, lobster claws, nuts, cherries and bits of vegetables. Half-nude revelers in couples, trios and foursomes sprawled on the frescoes' couches. In every possible combination and position, women copulated with men, men with men and women with women.

The sky had gone violet; the first stars twinkled. Lush velvet air pressed on my skin. Somewhere, out of sight, musicians played softly on pipes and lyres.

I assured myself that the loss of the ring meant nothing. Soon, very soon, Hektor would come.

In the central alcove, directly facing the sea, waited three broad divans of carved imported oak; gold-embroidered imperial eagles, heads in profile, dotted the crimson cushions. A semi-circle low table stood inside the U.

Dominus, his odd little body in a sea-green lounging gown trimmed with silver braid, took the head *lectus.* He lay on his left side against a cushioned armrest. In his right hand he held a silver chalice.

Straight away, two slaves arranged on the lounge to his left a bloated man in the shiny *toga candida* of a politician running for office. The couch to Dominus' right was vacant until Domina, hennaed hair tightly curled and piled a foot high, made her dramatic entrance. She shimmered in yellow silk and was hung with so many emeralds and pearls, I wondered that she could stand.

Her eyes surveyed the dining area until they fell on me. I felt her icy hateful look but didn't meet it. There is no gain in provoking a cobra.

The Syrian vocator scurried about, directing guests to their couches in the facing pair of alcoves to each side. Most guests dutifully took their assigned places. Relaxing on left sides in pairs or threes, they settled on royal blue cushions with broad yellow stripes.

There was a bit of a scuffle when a thin-armed man in a wine-stained blue caftan shoved away a teenage slave attempting to lead him to his couch.

Like the other men here tonight, he'd adopted the distinctly non-Roman, flamboyant Eastern habit of draping himself in gold and jewels—every finger held a ring, gold chains hung on his chest, elaborate armbands encircled his wrists.

"I am Septimus Julius Severus!" he bellowed. "I demand to be seated with Marcus Quintillus!"

The vocator snapped his fingers. A bull-necked slave propelled the stumbling Julius Severus to his place next to a plump woman bursting from her green silk gown. She flashed a mouthful of horse teeth and slid obligingly aside to make room.

Food appeared in aromatic clouds of spices and herbs. So many slaves hurried about that I doubted Dominus knew any of their names. Wine slaves filled silver chalices embossed with flying cranes. Serving slaves passed *gustus* to tempt the appetite—fresh goat cheese, small peppery pork sausages, dormice simmered in honey.

As was the custom in a prestigious home, the servers were young males with barbered curls. They had been shaved of all body hair, then oiled and perfumed. Their short white *chitons* exposed taut thighs and bronzed biceps. I thought them most likely Greek, but as they didn't speak—a serving slave must never speak in the dining room—I couldn't be certain.

While the guests ate, drank, and fondled under slaves' chitons, strolling musicians strummed lyres and sang psalms.

I believe Hektor was meant to dine beside the politician on the third couch at Dominus' table. When the first course of the *cena* was announced and Hektor hadn't arrived, the vocator moved a stunning young blonde in a turquoise caftan from another alcove.

Dread swept me; I was awash with black warning that not Hektor, but something unspeakably evil, was coming.

Turbot from the house fish pool—served with garum, the ever-present salty sauce of fermented sardines and herbs—came out in silver dishes. After the turbot, slaves passed platters of mussels and a seafood fricassee smothered in black pepper.

I was too agitated to feel hunger.

The convivium cheered and threw mussel shells when roast boar, complete with glassy eyes and razor tusks, arrived in a fanfare of trumpets.

Boy slaves holding eagle feathers and silver vomit bowls kept their eyes on the guests, ready to move instantly to their sides. As a reminder of what might happen if a slave moved too slowly, a dark-haired boy of about thirteen, with arms ending in black stumps, stood to attention by the entry. His desiccated hands hung on a rope around his neck.

With the *seconda mensa* of cheesecake, pear soufflé and dates stuffed with ground pine nuts, the dinner show began.

Against the night sky, six slaves in red chitons blew trumpets hung with crimson banners. Acrobats burst upon the lion fountain courtyard in a frenzy of somersaults and leaps.

A squat man with the chest of a bull swallowed the blunt end of a long spear. In a crude tableau of Asclepius and his snake-entwined staff, a thin naked boy slithered up the protruding shaft. Guests applauded politely. A few tossed copper coins.

"If you can swallow that spear," someone shouted, "maybe you can swallow my cock!"

Three tattooed men lighted oil-soaked cloth heads in the braziers, lifted the torches dramatically into the air, and then smothered the fire in their mouths. When they pulled out the torches, the heads burst into flames again.

It was an old trick and brought no applause. Some guests threw food.

"Let us see your lips suck some pussy."

Next up was a brute with long blond braids and Hercules arms holding a pole twice as tall as himself. Attached to one end was a rope ladder. While he walked in a circle around the fountain, balancing the pole on his forehead, his arms stretched out, the same nude boy climbed the ladder to the top and down again.

"Stick that pole up your ass, and then we'll watch the boy climb!"

The guests had grown bored with the entertainment. The air in the room, in spite of fresh breezes from the sea, reeked of vomit and stale wine. Just as in the murals, *sputa*, tiny bits of real half-chewed food, littered the floors.

Domina ate little and drank less. She didn't engage in conversation. She was tense, on edge. A slave moved to refill her chalice, and she slapped him.

Clearly, Dominus had drunk more than his share; slaves often refilled his cup. His eyes glazed over; his high-pitched voice was higher still.

With one last frenzy of somersaults and leaps from poles and shoulders, the circus was gone, leaving the courtyard empty. I could hear again the musical fall of water in the lion fountain.

"No elephants, Marcus Quintillus?" a guest jeered.

Domina snapped her fingers, and slaves began to douse lamps. As the lights went out, everyone stilled. In the end I heard not a whisper. A sinister pall marked the electric air. Perspiration beaded under my lead face powder.

Three ladies rose from their divans and, attended by their personal slaves, exited the triclinium.

"Flee! Flee!" my brain screamed.

"Where?" I screamed back.

The triclinium was dark. The sea was black. One by one, a brazier glowed until the gold lion fountain in the center of the flickering orange circle turned fiery.

I heard the pulsing rhythm of a drum and the undulating wail of a single flute before I saw the musicians. Coalescing from the night with skin so black, only their scarlet turbans were visible at first. They sat in hook position, drums clamped between their thighs.

Unseen hands cast powder on coals; the room filled with perfumed vermilion smoke. The dense cloud lingered for a few moments, then cleared.

The woman was a vision of greased ebony flesh—tall as any man, all toned muscle, not a hint of fat on her long limbs, narrow hips and flat belly. Gold bangles encircled her slender ankles and wrists; gold hoops pierced her ears. Close-cropped jet hair glistened like an obsidian helmet.

Specter that she was, it was the python that stopped my breath. The undulating thick cord of one continuous muscle coiled up her never-ending leg, around her long midriff and between her high, tight breasts with hard nipples. In her right hand, she held the great snake just below the head. Its mouth yawned in a bright flash of pink showing no fangs, but two rows of razor-sharp teeth curved backward.

A flutist trilled high hypnotic notes on a slender wooden pipe. The sway of the dancer and the rippling of the serpent were one with the music. There wasn't a murmur in the dining room; even the retching had ceased.

Wearing the horrid pewter masks, the blue Gaul monster and the black giant moved into the circle of orange light. The black giant held her shoulders from behind; his erection was that of a stallion. The Gaul took the snake's head from the woman's hands.

I couldn't say whether it was the music or the effects of a drug, but she was in a trance. Her eyes rolled back in her head. Only the whites showed. A fine sheen of sweat glistened over her polished onyx flesh. Her nipples were copper points.

The blue Gaul put the serpent's mouth to her breast, and the python latched on. Writhing and shuddering, the woman moaned and sobbed.

Bright crimson began to trickle down her black torso.

It was the sight of the blood that inflamed the guests. They sat up, straining forward. Even Domina showed interest. She was too much in shadow for me to see her face clearly, but I could imagine her ravenous eyes.

The black giant slowly penetrated the woman, sliding his monster penis into her anus in time with the music, always swaying, keeping pace with the rhythmic, rippling contractions of the snake. He lifted her, impaled on his erection, by the back of her thighs and spread her long legs into the air.

With great force, the Gaul dragged the snake's jaws from the woman's raw breast and placed the head between her legs. She screamed when it bit down, setting its jaws. And when she screamed, the dining room went mad. Two men close by ejaculated into slaves' palms.

The snake kept convulsing in a vain attempt to swallow her. The woman kept shrieking and shrieking. The drums pounded faster and faster. The wail of the flute soared.

I covered my ears with my hands but couldn't stifle the slave's cries or the applause of the guests. Oh, if I could have, I would have merged with the wall. I would have put myself right out of existence.

"Death!" "Death!" they chanted over and over, until Domina herself rose from the divan and made her way to the fountain courtyard.

What a fool I was to think she meant to stop the show. What a fool I was to think her human.

It was only when she came into the orange circle of light that I saw she wore the dull metal mask with round terrible eyes and cruel mouth. In her hand, the burnished steel of a dagger flashed like a tongue of fire.

Swiftly, without any hesitation, she slashed right down the woman's belly to the groin. Wet, coiled pink intestines tumbled to the floor. Before I could squeeze shut my eyes, she drew the blade across the soft underside of the woman's jaw open in mid-scream.

I so wish I truly had a witch's sight to have known what Domina would do. Then I could have spared myself the image that I shall never erase from my mind.

I couldn't watch the woman die, but I heard the guests roar. Like her crimson blood coming in a sudden rush, I shall never forget their cheers.

When I dared open my eyes, the son stood next to me. His formal *toga praetexta* had the purple stripe of a boy not yet a man; the gold *bulla* of childhood around his neck glowed red in the orangey light.

With the vilest imaginable smirk on his face, he took my hand and put it on his hard erection standing up in the white wool.

Then and there, I vowed that, no matter what, I'd never again pass through the Red Mirror.

CHAPTER 7   WITCH

"Men are always ready and willing to believe what they wish." – Julius Caesar

W here is the witch?"

Too much wine slurred Dominus' words, but there was no mistaking the menace in his tone.

"They're coming for me now!" shrieked my brain.

"Here, *Pater*," called out the son. "She is with me."

That a child so young spoke with so sinister a voice. But what other than a monster could a pair like Dominus and Domina spawn?

Everything in me wanted to run, but there was nowhere to escape. I was vaguely aware of my feet moving mechanically across the mosaic tiles as the son pulled me forward to Dominus.

A euphoric, giddy Domina had returned to her divan. Her gown dark with blood clung to her breasts and belly. A slave boy tried to rinse her hands, but she kept taking nervous sips of wine, giggling like a girl.

Dominus had the vapid grin on his face of a drunkard. I had thought him clever, but clearly he was a weak man who let alcohol dull his wit.

I suspected he had a hard time focusing on me. I wouldn't have been surprised if he suddenly vomited; he had that look about his mouth.

"Your Greek of Egypt did not come tonight," he challenged me. "Do you not find that impolite?"

When I didn't answer, he screamed, "Speak!"

"I know nothing of the man, Dominus. I know nothing of his habits."

"Insolence!" hissed Domina.

"But do you not see into the hearts of men?" Dominus asked slyly. "Is that not your special talent?"

"My talents are those which Dominus tells me they are."

"Hear no more abuse from a slave!" Domina commanded.

I balanced on the thinnest of edges. One tiny slip, and I was doomed. I no longer had the Hathor Ring, but I had the chants of Shinuba.

"ANA A A NANA A A NANA." The sounds came from deep in my chest; I felt each syllable vibrating, first in my throat, then in my ears and finally all over my body.

The more I chanted, the more distant I was from the room. High, excited voices came from afar. The drone in my ears grew louder. I felt the room turn and opened my eyes to a swirling kaleidoscope. Each flame of every lamp split into a shining prism.

Then I heard my voice, so penetrating I barely recognized it, bellow like a clap of thunder. "ABLAMGOUNOTHO ABRASAX!"

With razor-sharp clarity, a stunned Dominus came into focus.

"*Periculum!*" I breathed out in a hush.

"Danger?" His boy-man voice was hoarse for him; his eyes, wide with alarm, popped from a face bleached of all color. "What danger?"

"Do not force me to say, Dominus," I pleaded. "Words might make real that which is only a vision."

"Is it *me* that you see?" he whispered.

"It need not come to pass," I whispered back. "It has not yet been written."

"Tell me everything!" He leaned far forward, as if he would reach out and grab my arm. "Everything you see."

I let a full minute pass, fluttering my eyelids dramatically, willing my body to shudder.

Finally, I exhaled a long, deep breath that came out as a heavy sigh of regret.

"The vision has faded," I murmured. "The energy in this chamber interferes with the Sight."

Even Domina was rattled; she'd drawn back as far as she could into the divan. The son no longer stood beside me but had joined his mother on her lectus, his arm tight around her waist.

Slaves melted away. The convivium guests, only a short time ago frenzied with the bloodlust of death, were now hushed. They sank deeper into the plush pillows of their couches. I think they all would have risen in unison and fled, if not for fear of the consequences of deserting Dominus.

"Shut the house," ordered Domina. "Lock out the night!"

The grating of heavy wood on metal rails rumbled as slaves rolled giant gilt and painted doors to close off the beach.

The air grew hot and close; the pungent stink of slaughter mixed with the cloying perfume of incense. The black woman lay perfectly still in a black pool of blood. The python was nowhere in sight.

"I am exhausted," I whispered. "I must rest."

Dominus waved for the vocator who, although immediately at my side, was too terrified to touch me.

"Take her," Dominus commanded. His voice was near cracking point. "Take her to…to the slave quarters."

Then he changed his mind.

"No, not there. Not with the others." He turned to Domina. "What do you think? Where shall we put her?"

"Well away from me."

"Yes…Yes…" he stammered. "Of course. But *where?*"

There was absolute silence while the room awaited his command. But he came up with no solution, and I saw that his equivocation caused yet more fear. I wondered if anyone had ever seen him in such a state.

"I need the girl," I demanded in a tone that said I expected to have her. I don't know why I asked for her. I had no plan that I was aware of. My challenge was to steer the next critical moments to my advantage.

Instead of calling for me to be flogged for speaking without permission or my tongue ripped out for making a demand of a master, Dominus turned in bewilderment to Major Domo.

"Girl?" he demanded. "Of what girl does she speak?"

"Also a gift from Hektor Ptolemais, if Dominus recalls," Major Domo soothed. His voice was wholly devoid of the fear infecting everyone else and very smooth in glossing over his earlier error. "She was delivered with the redhead this morning."

"For Hades, fetch her!" Dominus shouted, clearly having forgotten that Major Domo had identified her as a boy. Male, female. What was one more slave to him?

Two slaves immediately rushed to find the girl.

It was far too easy. I expected someone to cry out, *"The woman is a fraud. She has done no magic. She has no special power."*

I didn't need to look at Major Domo to know he saw through my ruse. A non-believer. He turned out to be the cleverest of all.

With that one exception, all present seemed overly eager to accept that I could see what they could not. All that was required was a roll of my eyes and the mumbling of a few chants for them to believe me a sorceress.

A single demand for proof, and I would have been doomed.

But no one asked. They believed. It took nothing more to convince them of my power than red hair, green eyes and much nerve.

And I intended to make full use of those blessings.

CHAPTER 8   MAJOR DOMO

"Don't think. Just do." – Horace

I stumbled through the dining room, pretending to be in a trance while casting around desperately for something—anything—I could use. A glint of silver caught my eye. A fat Roman stinking of vomit sprawled passed out at my feet. Next to him lay a serving fork, two-pronged, a bit longer than my hand.

Under normal circumstances, a slave would have long since dragged the comatose drunk back to his divan, but this was not a normal night.

I allowed myself to trip over his thick ankle and fall, dragging my stola over the fork.

"Pick her up!" wailed Dominus.

The vocator hesitated, then took my elbow with as much enthusiasm as one might take hold of a leper.

"Great Jupiter, man!" Dominus bellowed. "Get her up!"

His grip tightened only slightly. Then I felt a rough jerk by another hand and was hauled to my feet. I didn't need to look up to know it was Major Domo.

I clutched the fork in the blue folds of my gown.

"She will be secure enough in the wine storeroom, Dominus."

"Yes! Lock her up there. With the girl."

Cooking fires in the kitchen still smoldered; a score of slaves washed golden plates and polished silver chalices. The air was stifling hot. A single door stood ajar to the garden with its glass shard-topped white walls and red door opening to the beach.

Rows of clay *amphorae* lined the outside wall of the storeroom. At the roofline were two openings for air and light so narrow that not even a child could crawl through them.

"Perhaps the witch can make herself disappear?" Major Domo sneered.

Shortly, the girl stood in the doorway, her hazel eyes wide with fright and confusion. It occurred to me that she didn't speak Latin—how petrifying for her to be in this nightmare and understand nothing of what was said. On her neck flamed a fresh brand. 'MQ.'

Major Domo shoved her inside and tugged the door closed. I heard the key in the lock and then muffled arguing. The door opened again for Shinuba, who came in with a clay cup.

"Drink slow," she cautioned, then murmured, "EĒ IE IE ĒI IŌ... IAŌIĒ IYE IA IAŌ Ē...OUŌ."

The door shut behind her, leaving us in total darkness. Easing back until I felt the wall on my spine, I sank slowly to the stone floor.

The girl didn't speak. I wouldn't have known she was there except for her rapid breathing.

My mouth was dry, my tongue thick. I took a sip of bitter herb tea and waited. My head stayed clear; I took another cautious sip. When I was certain that the tea wouldn't drug me, I gave in to my thirst and swallowed deep.

Immediately I gagged on a thin leather thong. Lifting the cord, I pulled a weight from the cup. The light was just enough that I could see the shiny faience; my fingers felt the inscribed septagram. With a wave of relief, I pulled the cord over my head.

Hotter than my skin, the septagram warmed the base of my throat.

"EĒ IE IE ĒI IŌ...IAŌIĒ IYE IA IAŌ Ē...OUŌ," I whispered.

My heart calmed. My mind ceased racing.

I repeated the chant and felt calmer still.

My eyelids grew heavy. For a brief moment, the image of the screaming black slave floated across the stage of my mind. Then the curtain fell, and I slept.

The sound of a key in the lock woke me. I sat up. The light from the kitchen, dim as it was, blinded me for a moment before my eyes made out Major Domo's devil shape with the fiery-red aura of the cookfire glowing around him.

Before the door closed, I saw Domina's rod silhouetted in his hand. The gold tips flashed.

He must have remarkable eyesight. Or he'd memorized the room while he still had the light, because Major Domo was on me at once, shoving my head against the wall with his hand at my throat.

I groped with my fingers for his eyes, and he choked me harder. I would have scratched, but my once long nails were dull stubs. My legs thrashed; my heels scraped on the rough floor. Twisting my hips, I tried to dig my feet into his genitals, all the while beating at him with my fists.

"Where is your magic now, striga?"

It was too dark to see his face clearly, but I heard the wicked smirk in his voice.

With his other hand, the one that held the rod, he pulled up my gown and jerked down my leather underpants. I tried to press my thighs together, but he had his knee in my groin.

"I'll not give you the privilege of my cock in your cunt. I shall let you taste my little friend."

I felt the cold metal on my hot skin and opened my mouth to scream, but no sound could pass my choked throat.

We struggled, him with one hand crushing the back of my neck into the wall and the other looking to open me, to shove the stick up. I fought back as best as I could, trying to gouge his eye with frantic fingers while my left hand clutched at the wrist in my groin in a vain effort to keep the rod at bay.

His face was only inches from mine; his open mouth panted hot, sour breath.

The fork! Where was the fork? I gave up on his eyes and felt along the base of the wall until I touched the tip of the tines, and then the handle.

At the very moment he found my canal with the rod, I plunged the sharp prongs into the side of his neck. He went rigid. His eyes went huge, so huge that even in the gloom, I saw the shock.

He let go of my throat to put his hand to his neck. I must have hit his carotid artery, because blood spewed in a dark fountain, streaming down his neck and flooding me.

In his effort to pull out the fork, he released pressure on the rod. I pulled on his wrist with all my might. But even with blood pumping from his artery, he overcame me. I felt the rod again.

"Die!" I hissed. "Die, you bastard!"

Whack!

His body collapsed across my lap.

Standing next to us, holding in her hands an amphora big as herself, was the girl. I don't know how she carried such a weight, much less lifted it into the air to bring down on his head.

And then, as if the effort had drained all her strength, she dropped the jar. The clay would have shattered on the stone floor and caused a terrible racket if it hadn't landed on Major Domo's still legs.

The amphora teetered for a few seconds before sliding without a sound to the floor and rolling. The girl stopped it with her foot.

I shoved his dead weight aside and jumped to my feet, wiping his blood from my hands on his tunic.

"*Adios*, asshole."

His face was forever imprinted with an astonished look asking, "How could this happen?"

"His keys," I whispered, forgetting the girl didn't speak Latin.

Perhaps language isn't necessary in such a state of tension. Our fears speak to each other in a universal tongue of survival.

She bent, rustled about at Major Domo's belt and stood again with a ring of iron keys in her hand. Ever so silently, I opened the door a crack. A fire glowed; a snoring slave stretched out beside it. A second slave lay curled in a corner. He rolled over and farted, and I held my breath for fear that even the whisper of an exhale might waken him.

Motioning for the girl to come out, I eased the door shut after her. There were so many keys on the ring, but the Universe guided my hand and the third key turned the lock. I had bought some time before the body was discovered. Now to get to the sea.

Somehow we would have to scale the garden wall—or find the key to the red gate on the ring. It had to be there; a head slave would carry a key to every lock.

Tiptoeing across the kitchen, we squeezed through the slightly ajar door into the night. Sunrise was still some time away; the sky had yet to lighten. Even the cocks slept.

The damp air was pungent with the scent of rosemary, savory and mint. Overhead the stars blazed in a canopy of wonder. On the nearby beach, slow hypnotic waves tumbled in the magnetic seductive rhythm that is the Mediterranean. A sea breeze rose as we stood, taking our bearings, deciding the next step.

In the starlight, jagged rows of glass shards on the high wall sparkled. I might have lifted the girl onto my shoulders for her to climb over, but I could never scale the top on my own.

I looked around for a table, a stool, a ladder, but there was nothing in the garden besides the well at its very center and pots of fermenting *garum* along the side of the kitchen. The scattered pomegranate and apricot trees grew too far from the wall for me to climb up and over.

A lone bird called out and was answered. My heart pounded. Blood rushed in my head. Every nerve screamed.

I had tried the first dozen keys when the girl touched my arm to tell me we weren't alone.

Just outside the kitchen door stood Shinuba in her green scarf. Beside her was the son. At first, I thought he must be an apparition born of my fear. An evil *djinn* come to test me. But he was real. Too real.

He wore a white linen sleeping gown; his dark wavy hair stuck out in a way that said he'd come directly from bed—had come with Shinuba. *Why? After all she had done, why betray me now?*

I thought he would sound an alarm in that odious voice of his, but instead he walked directly up to me and held out his hand. I avoided his vulpine eyes, dreading the malice I would see there.

"Give me the keys," he whispered. His hushed tone confused me; he sounded not at all the same.

"The keys," he repeated impatiently.

Then Shinuba reached out her hand and whispered, "Give me."

I hesitated, but not long. Soon, very soon, someone would discover Major Domo missing, and then us. And when Dominus woke, he would realize I'd made a fool of him. One thing he was not when sober was a fool.

Against all reason, I handed the ring over to Shinuba, who promptly passed the keys to the son. I thought all hope gone until he stepped to the red gate, selected a key and turned it in the lock.

The hinges creaked with a deafening roar, and the gate swung open toward us. Framed in the doorway were iridescent white dunes with waves crashing behind them. The tide was coming in. I imagined I felt salt spray on my hot skin.

Now was the moment of no return. If captured, there could be only one outcome for me, no longer Roman, but a runaway slave. Crucifixion. FUGITIVA. I pushed aside the image of the bits of rotten corpse hanging from the cross.

Out there I had a chance. Here, I had none. I saw Death waiting for me in Domina's chamber. Before she finished, I would welcome Him.

In truth, I don't know which I feared more, death by crucifixion or death by Domina.

The girl took my hand, pulling me through the open gate. "Come!" her wide eyes begged. "Hurry!"

She, too, knew her fate in this house.

The son grabbed my arm to stop me; I was certain he meant to keep me from going. Instead, he held out Shinuba's emerald green scarf.

"Cover your hair. You are too easily seen."

Metal at his wrist flashed in the starlight. Embedded in a thick gold armband gleamed a green glassy circle. A fourth septagram! Not on the arm of a Protector, but a devil.

For the first time since he came into the garden, I looked fully into his face. There was the same high intelligent brow, but instead of that sullen curl to his lips, I saw a resolute set to his mouth. He appeared weary, as if his eyes had seen more than he cared to bear.

"We are not all monsters here," he told me in a solemn voice. "I am not my brother."

It wasn't until that moment that I grasped he was a twin, identical in all ways to the monster—except his soul. The soul of Jason.

I wanted more than anything to take him in my arms, to cradle and comfort him. The boy I had once rocked to sleep in a long ago life, the boy I'd risked all to save. Now he risked all to save me.

"Go!" he urged. "Now! When the sun rises, they will know you are gone."

I kissed him lightly on the lips and once on each eye.

"May the Gods protect you in this evil house," I whispered.

He stood outside the red door in the white wall when I looked back the first time. But when I turned at the crest of the last dune before the dip to the beach, he was gone. The red gate was shut. The villa was dark with no light shining around closed shutters.

Only the brightest stars shone in a sky softened to lavender. It would not be long before the glow of a rising sun lit the horizon.

At the bottom of a shallow rocky rise, the beach was broad and white. The girl and I took each other's hands and headed into the waves, running in step through the foaming surf. The straps broke on my sandals. I flung them far into the water.

Our bare feet sank in the wet sand, leaving deep prints. A wave rolled in, tugging at our ankles, washing away our tracks. We turned to the west, away from the sun, away from the city, away from the villa of horrors.

CHAPTER 9   HORSEMEN

"Gentleness is the antidote for cruelty." – Phaedrus

Even the force of the sea didn't mute the earth thundering behind us. I looked over my shoulder to see three galloping horses in a halo of ocean spray, sand flying from their hooves.

I plunged into the sea, clutching the girl's hand. My long wool stola dragged at my body, making each forward step as if through quicksand. The girl weighed nothing; she was a sea nymph, floating at the end of my arm.

The sand sucked at my feet; the waves did their best to push me back to shore.

Did I have time to drown? Would one great inhalation of salty sea fill my lungs and stop my last breath before they captured me? A few desperate moments of thrashing in the water, my body struggling to live while my mind willed surrender. A few moments compared to days of agony on the cross.

"Barb," I screamed into the roaring surf. "Barb, wake me up!"

I dread death as do all who live. But my fear was more than the end of this life—it ended centuries ago. I feared what experiencing my death on this side of the Mirror might mean in Las Vegas.

A horse was at my side; an iron arm plucked me from the water, hauling me up in front of him. I tried to hang onto the girl's hand but lost my grip, and she slipped away.

I fought back, but the horseman held me fast. At breakneck speed, he rode out of the surf, along the beach. I beat at him with my fists, twisting wildly to break free from his arms, but his grip was steel. The harder I struggled, the tighter he held me, until I couldn't breathe.

"ABLAMGOUNOTHO ABRASAX," he hissed in my ear.

I froze, turned my head and looked into the face of Desert Man.

"Shinuba?" I asked in wonder.

He grunted and whipped the horse to a faster gallop.

Once I stopped struggling, he maneuvered me into more secure seating. I looked back to see the girl mounted with a second horseman. The third horse thundered beside them.

After a few hundred yards on the beach, we turned landward, the horses clamoring up a shallow stony knoll and sprinting across a narrow field into a grove of olive trees.

Just above the far horizon glittered the morning star bright white in a plum sky fading to lilac at the edge of the eastern hills.

The horses slid down the steep embankment of a dry *wadi* in a cascade of stones. We galloped on hard rocky sand past stands of pink oleander bushes and clumps of date palms. With each pounding hoof beat, the sky grew lighter. Venus grew dimmer. We were in a race against the sun.

The wadi divided. Desert Man veered to the right toward a low range of purple-tinged mountains far in the distance.

We rode hard, hooves pounding, sweat welling on the horse's hide, white foam at its mouth. Only when we reached the first ridge rising sharply up from the plain did Desert Man slow.

The sun had risen on our left, casting long shadows on the hard ground, bathing the purple ridge in gold.

They would have discovered the body of Major Domo by now. Before the end of this day, all Leptis Magna will hear of the murder and my escape. Dominus would surely hire slave hunters. Such humiliation required my capture—and a punishment to strike fear in the hearts of all his slaves.

We stopped and dismounted at a grouping of giant boulders. The third horseman, younger than the other two, passed a goatskin of slightly salty water and then filled a leather pouch for the horses.

I knew the breed from Spain as Libyan or *Mauretanian*. At least fourteen hands and sparsely-fleshed, they were valued as high-spirited, exceedingly swift, and slow to tire.

The ground was dry and stony, yet I sank to it gratefully, resting with my back against the canyon wall. The girl collapsed beside me and fell asleep at once.

The sun, not long risen, was already hot. I closed my eyes.

It was his presence that woke me. The third horseman. Startled, I sat up straight, tense, ready to defend myself.

He lowered himself to his haunches, pointing first to the sun and then to my sunburned arm. As he would handle a skittish colt, his gestures were solicitous and unthreatening; his honey-colored eyes assured me that he meant no harm.

With slow deliberate movements, he removed his wool cape and gently wrapped the rough cloth around my shoulders, pulling it carefully into place to cover me. He had the most delicate touch; his fingers barely grazed my skin.

He stroked once my bruised neck where Major Domo had tried to strangle me and frowned.

"Grātias tibi ago," I thanked him, not knowing if he spoke Latin.

His eyes held mine for a long moment before he stood and went back to grooming the horses.

He had caramel-colored, lean muscular calves and biceps. Rows of geometric bracelet tattoos encircled his wrists and ankles. Broad shoulders narrowed to slim hips with no surplus anywhere. He wore his rich honey hair, a few shades darker than his eyes, in feathered braids like the other two. But unlike them, his braids weren't matted with red mud.

I watched his hands with long, graceful fingers curry the mare, stroking her steaming black coat while he whispered soothing words into her ear. I couldn't remember anyone who'd ever treated me with the tenderness he showed his horse.

"Quo imos?" I asked Desert Man. Where are we going?

"Nafusa."

When I frowned, he said, *"Montes."* Mountains.

Only yesterday, what I most feared was him taking me to the desert. Today, I would follow him anywhere as long as it led away from the villa by the sea.

When we were ready to ride again, the honey-eyed Horse Tamer gestured that I was to ride with him.

Assuring me again with his eyes, he expertly twisted Shinuba's emerald sparkly scarf into a turban, covering my forehead. After wrapping the final swath across the lower part of my face and over my nose, he tucked the end into a fold above my temple. Only my eyes showed.

He then lifted me astride the black mare and mounted behind me. I took a handful of the thick mane to steady myself. He slid his left hand around my waist, taking the reins in his right.

There was nothing more natural than leaning into him, his arm tight around me. I relaxed into his chest and belly. I felt him grow hard. He dug in his heels, and we set off, the girl behind us with the same horseman and Desert Man in the lead. Someone, maybe the Horse Tamer, had tied a dingy brownish cloth around the girl's shaved white scalp.

We rode southwest through the day, stopping only twice to water and rest the horses. Each time we stopped, he dismounted and held up his arms to help me from the horse and set me carefully on my feet. Each time we remounted, he lifted me astride and then climbed on behind me, pulling me back into him.

Soon after the sun slipped below the horizon and the air cooled, the crescent moon, higher and fatter than it had been the night before, brightened in a coral sky. Then the moon, too, disappeared below the plain.

After a meal of coarse bread and dried goat meat, I lay down with the girl on a rough blanket spread on sandy ground and covered us both with the wool cape. She was out as soon as she relaxed beside me.

The Milky Way arched in a broad hazy river across a blazing field of stars dotted with the familiar constellations I'd known all my lives. Orion, the Big Dipper, Berenice's Comb. Seeing them gave me a strange kind of comfort in this savage world. As I watched, the orange ember of Mars rose above the silhouetted mountains.

Desert Man snored. The second horseman, the grim one, rolled to his side with his back toward me. With steady, quiet movements, I tugged away the heavy cape and wrapped the girl with the blanket.

My bare feet made no sound on the sandy ground. A shadow might have made more noise. I barely breathed. My heart drummed in my chest; in the still of the night, I thought surely he must hear it beat.

He was awake as I knew he would be. Hands crossed under his head, lying on his back, he, like me, gazed at the wonder of the desert night sky.

I slipped the emerald scarf from my head and pulled the pins and threads from my hair; lush waves fell around my shoulders.

My body was one pain, but still I lowered myself onto him, draping the cloak over us. That's how starved I was for tenderness in this nightmare world. How desperate I was not to be alone.

His calloused hands might have been gloved in velvet, his touch on my bruised flesh was that soft.

Cradling me in his arms, he gently eased me beside him. I moaned softly, and he breathed, "Sh-h-h." But he never stopped stroking me.

Those velvet hands calmed me as he'd calmed the mare. His magic fingers sensed where they gave pleasure or pain. And there was a lot of pain after Major Domo.

In my ear, he whispered soft sounds that didn't form words. I felt safe. Safe in the hands of a wizard.

I wanted to take him inside me, to envelop him, for him to drown in my warmth. I needed for him never to want to leave me. But when I tried to guide him into me, he stopped my hand. His lips brushed my bruised throat and then my breast.

The desert night was still, the camp silent in sleep. I didn't feel the hard ground; my body no longer ached.

In the way of a wizard, his fingers knew where, and where not, to go.

A wave began to rise, and then rise higher. There was no time or space; I no longer breathed. With the crest, I tumbled into a satin sea.

He kissed my tears away, and I kissed him on his chin, down his throat, all over his chest and across his flat belly. With the tips of my fingers and the heat of my hand, I fondled him, taking my time, setting the pace of my caress to the rhythm of his breath, until he convulsed in a shuddering release I felt my own.

In the dark under the cloak, he traced with his fingertips the deep ridges of the carved septagram at my throat. Two miracles had happened since I'd hung Shinuba's amulet around my neck. Jason and Horse Tamer. The septagram was a sign. A sign of a new beginning.

If this was not magic, I don't know what is.

I woke. The sky was light; the metallic horizon said the sun was soon to rise. Rocky, sage-colored mountains, dotted with crooked olive trees, surrounded our camp. I sat up. The black mare was gone. *He* was gone.

The girl was folding the blanket. Desert Man busied himself boiling water for tea. The grim one readied the horses.

"Where is he?" I demanded and immediately regretted it.

Desert Man turned, saw my face, surely full of panic, and glanced at the emerald scarf on the ground next me. It seemed to say everything, that castaway silk lying in the dirt.

I felt naked before him and wrapped the cloak more tightly around me.

In that brief moment, his eyes appraised me and found me wanting. He saw my need. He saw me as weak. I felt weak.

Then he grunted and went back to his fire.

I picked up the scarf and went to sit next to the girl. The wound on her neck from the brand had begun to fester.

"What is your name?" I asked her in Latin.

She didn't answer.

I tried in Greek. Still no answer.

"I cannot keep calling you '*the girl.*' I shall name you. Dido, perhaps. Queen of Carthage."

She looked at me with those clear hazel eyes and said nothing. She could have answered me in her own tongue. Said something. But whatever language she spoke, she wasn't forthcoming. Neither was Desert Man nor the grim one. I might have been with a band of mutes.

He had never spoken to me except to croon nonsensical syllables in my ear. I didn't know what language he spoke. I didn't know his name.

I didn't know if I'd ever see him again, much less feel his horseman's taming touch.

CHAPTER 10 SORCERESS

"The only problem with seeing too much is that it makes you insane."
– Phaedrus

When the sun was at its zenith, we arrived through a maze of labyrinthine canyons at the cave. The gaping black mouth, deep in shadow, was a third of the way up the face of a sharp treacherous rise.

Desert Man halted the horses, and we dismounted to begin the slippery climb. My bare feet felt each stone edge like a knife blade. Dido moved easily on the loose rock, effortlessly finding a smooth place for each step.

We had reached the narrow shelf outside the cave when Desert Man faced me.

Just as in the slave market, the septagram on a leather thong dangled from his finger. By the jerk of his wrist, I took him to mean I should take it. He edged past me then to start his descent.

Incredulous, I asked, "Are you not staying with us?"

When he didn't answer, I demanded, "Where are we? Why did you bring us here?"

Still he kept moving away. I took two quick steps to grab his arm. A shower of small stones tumbled down the craggy cliff face.

"Speak!" I commanded him.

Faster than I could prepare myself, he had hold of my jaw, fingertips digging into my cheeks, and dragged my face to within inches of his.

"Do not press your luck," he spat. "I would sooner cut the throat of a Roman—mistress or slave—than breathe the same air."

I watched them scramble, the grim one and Desert Man, nimbly down to the horses, mount and ride off in a cloud of dust.

Behind us, the mouth yawned black and forbidding. It was a roomy entrance, high enough to walk upright and wide enough for three men abreast.

I gave myself courage by reasoning that the septagram was a sign; surely a Protector waited here. Hermes Trismegistus perhaps. He always buries himself in dark, mystic places.

Motioning to Dido to wait on the ledge, I stepped inside the cave. A foul, burning stench seared my nose and throat.

Something flew by my ear, followed immediately by another swoosh, then another. I yelled out an involuntary "Oh-h-h-h-h!" In pure reflex, I ducked my head and covered my face with my hands.

A strange kind of whirring echoed about. Slowly, I lifted my head, looking all around me, peering into the shadows. Even more cautiously, I raised my eyes to the ceiling. Ten feet over my head, a black mass breathed.

Bats! The dome of the cavern was alive with bats.

And at that moment I felt the squish of guano between my toes. My feet! Covered in open cuts! I flew out of the cave back onto the ledge. Leaning against the rock face, I frantically wiped at the bat shit with the hem of my cloak.

Then the girl Dido was pressing on my shoulder to say I should sit. Together we cleaned my feet as best we could without water. And together, I decided, we would stay here on the ledge. Whoever waited in the cave would have to come to us.

I clenched Desert Man's septagram so tightly in my fist that a seven-pointed star would surely be imprinted forever on my palm.

The sun was directly overhead. I'd been forty-eight long hours in this world. Two days. That's what Barb and I had agreed. But forty-eight hours for Barb might be weeks on this side. If I went back right now, would it be to discover that only an hour had passed in Las Vegas?

Barb! Barb! Wake me!

The girl stared so hard at me that I must have cried out loud. I gave her a small smile of reassurance, as much for me as for her.

"Someone wants us alive, Dido, or we would not be here. Whoever they are, they mean us no harm."

I saw nothing in her expression to indicate she understood a word I said. But the sound of my own voice, surprisingly calm, soothed my nerves. The heart is like a pressure cooker. Words let off steam.

So we sat with our backs to the rock wall while I prattled on for a few minutes, asking where she was born, if she had always been a slave. My questions and comments all went unanswered. Soon we both waited in silence for someone to come.

And come they did—but not at all who I expected.

He moved as silently as a shadow and was standing over us before I knew he was there.

Horse Tamer.

He reached out his hand and pulled me in one long smooth motion to my feet. My joy and relief must have shone too bright, because he frowned, warning me with his eyes.

Behind him loomed two tall men with his same spare, lean-muscle build. And they wore the knee-length tunics of worn suede painted with geometric designs in bright colors. One had braids streaked with gray; the other's were nut-brown. No red mud. These weren't Desert Man's men.

They had a cautious air about them, with resolute faces and steady eyes revealing nothing.

"I cannot walk into the cave," I told them, pointing to my bare feet. When I got no reaction, I lifted one foot, showing the lacerations.

I pointed to Dido's bare feet. "*She* cannot walk."

Horse Tamer said something in the Berber of Shinuba. The younger of the two men picked Dido up and tossed her over his shoulder like a bag of grain. Horse Tamer carried me with my feet hanging over one forearm, his other supporting my waist, and my arm around the back of his neck. I might have weighed nothing.

We moved from the hot sun into the cool dark, quickly through the antechamber under the canopy of bats into a second chamber with two passages, one to our left and one directly ahead. A small brazier glowed beside a throbbing orange wall.

The gray-haired man lit a torch in the brazier and led the way into the narrow man-made tunnel facing us.

Horse Tamer's arms held me firmly but not tightly. It was like the long day on horseback, with bodies close, the air rife with tension.

I looped over his head the leather thong of the septagram clenched in my palm, letting my fingers linger at the base of his throat.

His arms tightened in alarm, and he leaned to my ear, whispering in Latin, "*Periculum.*" Danger.

I dropped my hand.

We traveled deep into the mountain along a shadowy corridor running perfectly straight. I would have thought it more prudent, if one didn't want to be found, to make a crooked passage with a few dead ends and booby traps.

The tunnel ended abruptly at double wooden doors with a luminous white septagram the size of a man's hand scored into each. The doors swung open to a thick cloud of incense. Horse Tamer carried me in and stood me on my feet; the younger one dropped Dido roughly to hers.

Outside on the ledge, the sun blazed down. Here all was shadow. Bronze oil lanterns with heads of gargoyles spluttered at the end of long chains. The sides of the chamber curved upwards to a point high overhead, as I would imagine the interior of an immense beehive.

Against the black walls pulsed a bewildering splash of glowing Punic and Greek letters scattered among Egyptian hieroglyphs and alien symbols I didn't recognize. The glyph for the moon, a lustrous white crescent, throbbed beside an ochre ankh.

Amorphous shapes coalesced from the void, dancing in the flickering light for a heartbeat before vanishing into the shadows. More birds than I could count squawked from straw cages.

Just inside the door perched a raven on a lifeless, leafless branch. Alert, missing nothing, he stared at me, his glassy eyes glittering.

I had no sense of direction or place and was seized by a terrible premonition that I'd never leave. That I'd be entombed here for all time.

I can't breathe! I need air. I must see the sky!

A smoky voice, deep for a woman, gave a vibrating command in Berber. Horse Tamer and the other men left, closing the double doors behind them with the sucking sound of an airlock.

Do not leave me! Do not lock me in!

Close by, a voice sweet as a lullaby purred, "Do not be afraid."

A vision stepped from shadow to light. Glossy black braids, thick as sailor's rope, framed the face of an angel. The long ivory wool tunic draped the lush curves of a goddess.

When her hand took mine, her skin was warm and dry, her touch as velvet and soothing as Horse Tamer's.

"Lemta desires to welcome you," she crooned in a Latin with only a whisper of accent.

She'd lived long in a Roman household. Had she too escaped a villa of horrors? Under her gentle grace and silver tone, I sensed the steel of a Viking shieldmaiden.

With a soft squeeze of my hand, the Maiden led me forward to a low dais bathed in the yellow halo of whispering oil lamps.

She reclined on rich carpets and plush cushions, this Lemta with the vibrating voice. A wild mane of curly hair, black as black can be, gave her a savage jungle look. More handsome than beautiful, she had a broad intelligent brow, dark overripe lips, and the too-large, high-bridged nose of a natural leader. Her pearlescent skin glowed white as the glyphs dancing above her head; her black eyes gleamed with the uncanny light of all-seeing.

I couldn't determine her age. She was neither young nor old.

I kept my gaze level without a trace of boldness; this woman was too potent to challenge. But when I spoke, I did so not as a slave, but as a Roman.

"*Grātias ago vos.*"

Lemta said nothing. No one spoke. Except the birds. *Caw. Caw.*

"I lack sufficient words to express my full gratitude for your beneficence."

Still silence.

"May I inquire as to why I am here?" I was most careful to modulate my tone as to be formal and courteous, but firm.

She waved me closer with an impatient flick of shiny, talon nails. I took her to mean that I was to join her on the dais. My mind went through a dozen possibilities as to what Lemta might want of me, none of them reassuring.

"I am not clean," I told her.

Those crimson lips of hers curved into an amused little smile. She nodded to the Maiden, who rang on a bronze bowl. Immediately, a red door opened in the black wall and a dusky beauty, sleek as a cat, glided into the Hive. She, too, was dressed in an ankle-length, unbleached wool tunic. A few words in Berber were exchanged in a hush.

"While we wait," sang the Maiden in her lyrical way of making every phrase a melody, "you must take some nourishment."

Conscious of Lemta's eyes never leaving me, I forced myself not to show my hunger but nibbled on small chunks of coarse bread dipped in olive oil. Slowly I sipped honey-sweetened herb tea. Dido gulped hers in one long swallow, dribbling a bit at the corners of her mouth. A whole loaf of bread disappeared with an odd sideways chewing.

At last, the red door opened again. The cat beauty brought a stack of neatly-folded ivory wool; three other young women in the requisite long tunics carried earthen jugs and steaming brass bowls. Thick braids of caramel-colored hair tumbled over their breasts.

They undressed me, taking away without reaction my stola and tunica stained with Major Domo's blood. Their touch was gentle; their auras serene. I sensed none of the fear living always in a slave. They were acolytes, I decided—in the cult of Lemta. What kind of cult that was, I could not guess.

The salve they dabbed on my bruised and cut feet brought instant relief, faster even than Shinuba's ointment. First tingling, followed by numbness, and then the pain was gone. Entirely. Soft suede boots caressed my skin.

I held out my hand for the ointment jar, took salve on my fingertips and reached to soothe my anus. Again that tingle with a slight chill before going blessedly numb. At a word from the Maiden, a slip of a girl with the eyes of a doe massaged a mixture of the salve thinned with almond oil into my flaming arms.

Once bathed, oiled and dressed, I joined Lemta on the cushions. The downy folds of the ivory tunic clung to my breasts and loins. Lemta's eyes, bottomless black pools, traveled without shame from my hair to my toes. So, she was like the many others I'd known.

To satisfy her shouldn't be difficult; I didn't sense a sadist like Domina. But if she wanted me willingly, I had my price.

"You have not told me why I am here."

Giving me that curved, lush-lipped smile rife with secrets, she said, "You are brazen. I like that. It is a good thing to have courage." Her Latin had Shinuba's coarse, throaty note.

She leaned back, relaxing into the scented pillows, radiating an electrifying sexuality impossible to ignore. Great sensuous waves rolled off her. I felt myself pulled into her tide, helplessly lured by the inexorable ebb and flow that she, and she alone, controlled.

Unbearable moments of silence ticked away; a slight hum in my ears buzzed louder and louder. My vision blurred, my lips numbed. My tongue grew thick. I felt inferno hot, then glacier cold.

They'd drugged me! Alarmed, I tried to focus my eyes to find Dido.

"My ladies will take good care of her," Lemta oozed in her low, hypnotic, undulant voice that sucked me nearer and nearer.

Her perfume, a heady scent of sweet gardenia infused with an alien bewitching spice, rose off the satiny pillows. My head whirled.

"How is your skin now?" she asked, reaching out to trace her long, curved, hennaed nail down my arm. "Do you still feel the sun?"

Unnerved, I jerked away, not because she was a woman—women had found diversion in my body for as long as I could remember. My mother had seen to that.

It was fear of *her* touch, falling under *her* spell that terrified me—the surrendering of my soul.

She laughed, but not cruelly, and the intensity between us relaxed a fraction.

"You are very beautiful, just as I saw." She wet a lock of my hair with her tongue and ripe lips. "Such glorious hair. Like living fire."

Just as she saw? I wanted to ask where or how, but my tongue was too thick to form words.

And then nausea consumed me, and I no longer cared. I succumbed to an irresistible need to lay my head down—to lay my whole body down.

"Do not struggle," I heard her say from far, far away.

I closed my eyes. The room swirled in an eddy. As hard as I tried, my lids were too heavy to open.

Her hand on my cheek was hot, hotter than my burning skin, too hot to bear. I struggled to move my head, but her fingers held me still.

Her moist lips, close to my ear, breathed, "BERBELŌCH CHTHTÖTHŌMI."

I lost all strength. Or rather I lost all will to resist.

I was no longer in my body but floating beside it, studying the fluttering of my eyelids, wondering at my long red hair on the pillows snaking out like Medusa.

There was a profound silence broken only by the squawks of the birds. If I opened my mouth to speak, I, too, would squawk.

Then the low vibration of Lemta's voice drew me back into my body.

"You have had carnal knowledge of one of the men," she accused.

"Is it a crime to know a man?" I slurred.

"*This* man, it is."

"Why?"

"Because he is *my* man."

Her husky rich voice went gravelly, and I opened my eyes.

Gone was her glowing milky skin. Gone was the wild mane of raven curls. Dull gray frizz hung in thin strands on razor cheekbones and a skeletal jaw. Creased lips sunken in a ravaged face mouthed her words.

I'm sure I stared at her in horror. Horror was what I felt.

She laughed a toothless cackle and stretched out a black-veined hand with twisted fingers, laying her pointed yellow index talon on my forehead, right between my eyes. Blinding white light flooded the Hive.

I was back in the bleak abyss of my dream, struggling to rise to the top toward the promise of blue sky. My fiery hair flowed around me. My skin was pale as death.

Hands on rubber arms grasping down through the shadows belonged first to Horse Tamer, then to the General. In that strange way of dreams, I knew it was him without actually seeing him, without knowing from which lifetime he came. He took my wrist, and I swam upward, weighing nothing.

I thought the General would pull me from the inky well, but just as I came within reach of the vast expanse of cerulean freedom, he showed me his face that wasn't his, but that of Dominus. I screamed, and my scream was the screech of a bird.

I tumbled further and further until there was no longer any trace of blue, but only a coal-black void. Void, that is, until I crashed through the Red Mirror, shattering the glass into a thousand shards.

When I woke on the cushions in the Hive, Lemta was gone. It was impossible to know how long I'd slept. There was no change in the light in the room. The same lamps burned. The air still choked with incense.

A small clay jug stood near my head. Cautiously, I sniffed the water. The scent was fresh and sweet as a cool mountain spring. I was painfully thirsty, but did I dare drink?

"It is pure," I heard the Maiden say. "You need not fear."

She poured water into a clay cup, drank deep, filled the cup again and handed it to me.

"You are soon one of us," she said in a tone I'm sure she meant to reassure.

I had a sudden, startling, terrifying image of her as wrinkled and coarse with absolutely white hair. I didn't want to be one of them. I wanted to leave.

"You will take the voyage again," she continued in her voice like a melody in the breeze. "But you will do it at your own will."

"Is that why I am here? To become an initiate?"

"You know why you are here."

"Do I?"

"You know if you let yourself see."

"See what?"

Her answer was a maddening smile like Lemta's that held too many secrets.

"See what?" I demanded.

"Many things. Perhaps all things."

"The future?" Oh yes. I wanted to see the future. I wanted to see Barb. Then I remembered the dream. O Gods! I wanted to see the Red Mirror.

"Possibly," she said with a shrug.

"How do you know that to be possible?"

"Because you are the Chosen One."

With that, the Maiden slipped silently from the Hive, closing the red door behind her.

I was alone with the crowing birds.

CHAPTER 11   ESCAPE

"When defeat is inevitable, it is wisest to yield." – Marcus Favius Quintilian

I found a brass chamber pot and urinated. My feet didn't hurt to walk. When I took off a suede boot, my sole was perfectly smooth, without a scratch or bruise. The skin on my arm was smooth and white, with no trace of blistering.

I opened one of the double doors to the corridor. The long passage was empty, dark and silent.

It wrenched me to leave without Dido, but I had to seize this chance to escape. If I thought about it a moment too long, it would be too late.

Grabbing the jug of water and a ceramic oil lamp, I stepped out, closed the door silently behind me and started down the passageway.

I didn't ask myself where I would run—or how far I could go before they found me. My only thought was to get away.

Horse Tamer stepped out of the rock wall—or as it appeared—so unexpectedly that I ran right into him. Oil from the burning lamp splattered on his tunic and braids. The feathers caught fire.

If it had been anyone but him, I would have run past, leaving him to burn. But I didn't. I couldn't.

I splashed water from the jug, and the flames died. The acrid stink of burnt leather and hair filled my nostrils.

His thanks were to take me by the arm and turn back down the corridor to the Hive.

"No!" I begged. "Please not *there!*"

He pulled me along, not rough, but with the gentle firmness he would use with an unruly mare. I sat down, refusing to walk.

Sitting on his haunches as he had done when he wrapped me in his cape in the desert, he took me by the shoulders and forced me to look at him.

You cannot escape, his eyes said. *It is as it must be.*

"I cannot go back in there," I pleaded. "I must breathe fresh air. I *must* see the sky."

Over and over, I kept seeing the Red Mirror break into a thousand shards of glass, each shard a shattered hope for returning home. And with the thought of never leaving the black Hive, I lost all pretense of pride. Shaking, weeping, begging, I clung to him.

"*Please!*" I sobbed. "Take me to see the sky for one moment. Then I will come with you. I will not resist."

In my mind, I was scheming that if only I could get outside, something would happen—I didn't bother to imagine what. I even entertained for a moment the idea of throwing myself from the ledge.

He looked so incredibly desolate when he kissed my tears that I thought surely he would weaken.

"*Help me,*" I whispered, touching his lips with my fingertips.

He rose to his feet, lifting me with him, cradling me in his arms as he had yesterday—or was it today? I had no sense of time. For one bright moment, I believed that he would take me away. Instead he turned back toward the Hive.

"What kind of man are you?" I hissed.

But he walked on in silence, eyes straight ahead.

The Maiden waited outside the open double doors. The raven glared at me with his glittery eyes. Lemta had appeared and now sat cross-legged on the Hive floor in front of a steaming pot on an open clay stove. She was that indefinable age again. Her black lion's mane hair bushed out around her head.

Dido sat beside her, seeming perfectly at ease. The festering brand on her neck was a faint white circle. She looked up only briefly before turning her focus back to something she was doing with her hands.

One of the acolytes who had bathed us was feeding the birds.

No one showed any particular surprise when Horse Tamer carried me in and set me down in the middle of the chamber. I straightened myself fully erect.

"I want to leave," I declared in an imperious tone. "I do not wish to be here."

How absurd I must have been to them, standing there, chin stuck out in defiance, wet eyes blazing. It was plain to everyone that I'd been crying. They'd probably heard me wailing and pleading in the passageway.

"You are not ready," Lemta said. She was utterly calm, her tone matter-of-fact.

"When will I be?" I demanded.

"When you are ready, you will know."

"I am ready *now*," I insisted.

"Stop this foolishness," she snapped. "We have work to do."

It wasn't until Lemta dismissed Horse Tamer with a wave of her hand that I noticed she wore the faience septagram around her neck, the one I'd given him. I glared at her with hatred.

Without looking up from her steaming pot of mystery potion, she said, "The amulet belongs to me. It has always belonged to me."

That she could read my thoughts was unbearable, but that her tone was so smug, infuriated me. That Horse Tamer did her bidding maddened me more.

I wanted to scream after him, *Why did you tell her about us?*

Instead, I called out in a defiant mocking tone, "Tell me your name! You who call yourself a man."

He turned and faced me with a pathetic look of helplessness, but still, he stopped. I saw he asked me to forgive him, which I would never do.

Lemta's eyes flashed black fire before she veiled her displeasure. She growled something in Berber, and he went out the door.

I glared at her, livid at both of them, despising them for making me a fool.

"Is it a crime, as well, to know his name?" I asked acidly.

"He is *Nemo* to you," she answered an equally caustic tone. No man.

"You will pay for what you are doing to me," I warned her. "Others have paid."

She chuckled and gave an order in Berber to an acolyte. The woman left through the red door.

"You must wonder how your cuts healed so rapidly," she remarked in an exasperating affable tone.

I fumed, refusing to answer. All around me, women went about their tasks. Lemta helped Dido sort stems from dried flowers.

The acolyte returned with a small packet of herbs, which Lemta added to the pot. A rich, savory scent steamed up, stronger even than the incense smoking from the burners.

"The balm that restored you was made from silphium," she explained as she stirred. "Quite miraculous, would you not admit?"

I had to begrudge her that. Dido's ugly sore from the branding was virtually gone. My cut feet and sunburned skin had healed without a mark. There was no discomfort at all in my anus. The rape might never have happened.

"The salve is only one secret—a very minor one—of the many I intend to share with you." She paused and added, "When you are ready."

She looked up at me with a teasing little smirk on that enigmatic face that might or might not be hers. Was that one of her secrets? Eternal youth—or the illusion of it?

"Ready for what?" I asked cautiously.

"Your destiny, of course. What else?"

I glanced at Dido absorbed in her dried herbs. Had they drugged her as well? What could she tell me about the other side of the red door? Most likely not much. She'd never spoken to me. How *did* they communicate with her?

I found myself jealous that she'd been allowed to leave the Hive and not me. She appeared to be at home here; I was the isolated one. *I* who had saved her from the villa. But she'd saved me from Major Domo. She'd killed for me.

Stop it, I told myself. Stop these thoughts that lead nowhere and gain nothing. All my focus must be on one thing and one only—getting out of here. If cooperating was the path, then it was the one I must take.

In that way she has of reading my thoughts, Lemta stopped her stirring, lifted her black eyes to fix on mine, and asked. "Are you ready to start?"

I plunked down on the floor opposite the cooking fire, crossing my legs in the same way as she.

Never had I seen skin such as hers, whiter than faces dusted with lead powder. I felt no sexual energy from her at all. She was beyond gender, beyond corporal, beyond time.

"I am ready." And I meant it. Ready to learn how to get home.

"*Bene.* Then let us begin."

CHAPTER 12   INITIATION

"Whatever you do, do with all your might." – Cicero

Hours merged into days without the movement of the sun or phases of the moon to mark time. Only by the fuzz on Dido's shaved head growing steadily into short curls did I have a sense of the passing weeks. My bleeding came. Then again.

I slept only when exhausted. Each time I woke, I went through the same crushing disappointment that I was still in the cave and hadn't awakened in Las Vegas. Each time, I vowed to redouble my efforts, working ever more feverishly. I gave up the idea of escape.

And when I convinced Lemta of my resolve, she allowed me through the red door.

What I found was eerily domestic. A kitchen had large vents on the outside wall that let in fresh air and natural light. Along the inside wall were storerooms with upside-down bunches of dried herbs hanging like laundry on a clothesline. Hundreds of clay urns of all sizes crammed wall niches. Labels written in the indecipherable alphabet of the Phoenicians identified the jars' contents and the phase of the moon when collected or distilled.

The last storeroom held cages of snakes whose venom we milked for potions. There, too, were kept the monkeys, white doves and black rats whose organs we harvested for spells. Spiders wove their webs freely, entrapping insects fed to them by acolytes. Scarabs in wooden boxes tirelessly moved balls of dung with their hind legs.

Past the kitchen was a small steamy Turkish bath where we sat on a crude tile floor and washed each other with hot water from copper basins. An inward passage next to the bath led to a row of sleeping cubicles. Beyond the bath, acolytes wove cloth, molded clay pots and prepared powders for potions.

The final workshop, furnished with rough-hewn tables and ceramic urns tall as me, had two closed doors—one of wood and another of stone imbedded in the exterior wall. The heavy slab had been crudely beveled to fit flush into the rock. Dust filled the cracks.

I imagined the sun shining bright on the other side. So close.

"Where does the wooden door lead?" I asked the Maiden.

"A corridor to the cave entrance. We may not go there. It is forbidden."

"Is that where the men live?" *Is that where Nemo is?*

I hadn't seen him since the day I resigned myself to what Lemta called my destiny. A destiny without his Horse Tamer touch.

Lemta proved a hard taskmaster, driving me as I drove her. I grew more and more in awe of her, especially of her remarkable ability to recall hundreds of spells and potions without effort.

"I have been doing this for many years," she told me.

"How many?"

She only laughed.

Just as the Maiden promised, Lemta hadn't spiked my tea since that first time, at least, not that I could tell. It was always with my permission that she gave me the drug that enhances memory.

I would close my eyes and listen to her incantations of nonsensical phrases whose origin no one knew. *ABRACADABRA. ARBOTH ARBATHIAO.*

"Where does the magic come from?" I asked.

"From the South. From beyond the desert."

Step by step, session by session, drugs and mantras reprogrammed my psyche. Deep in a restful trance, I repeated each alien word, chanting in the exact rhythm as her vibrating voice. When I came to, I could recite the mantras as perfectly and effortlessly as Lemta.

"We are the guardians of the Sacred Arts," she told me. "I pass that knowledge to you. The magic must not be lost."

And lost it would not be with me, for I had begun to appreciate Lemta's curse tablets and the immense power of her leading and binding spells.

I thirsted for that magic. I hungered for that power.

"Are you ready for another voyage?"

"Quite ready," I assured her.

It was a solemn ceremony. Lemta, the Maiden and a dozen acolytes held hands in a circle around me, droning over and over in a slow mesmerizing hum the chant of Shinuba.

"ANA A A NANA A A NANA."

They had loosened their hair from the thick braids. Heads rotating far back and far forward in wide circles, in time with the droning, they swung their long waves round and round. Their voices grew louder, the rhythm faster, the arcs wilder.

I lost myself in the chanting. Muted colors exploded in neon. Floating glyphs throbbed.

Lemta held a silver chalice to my lips; embossed septagrams rimmed the edge. I closed my eyes and swallowed a full mouthful, holding the potion only an instant on my tongue. The taste was slightly bitter but not unpleasant. Warmth spread through my chest, filled my belly and caressed my thighs. My toes tingled; my fingers vibrated. Every cell ignited. My ears hummed.

Then out of black nothingness, thousands and thousands of angry bees swarmed round my head. The roar of their wings deafened me. I felt one sting, then another, and then another. In panic, with arms flailing, I tried to protect my face.

At the center of the attacking black swarm, the Queen Bee—Lemta with giant wings—seized my wrists with her sharp-barbed forelegs.

My eyes flew open, and she was there, gripping my arms, pulling me close to her face.

"Do not choose this journey! Choose *only* the reality you control."

She placed her index finger on my forehead, intoning, "BERBELŌCH CHTHTÖTHŌMI."

White light flooded my brain.

I was on the Nile, gliding through green satin waters on a gilded barge festooned with red and gold banners woven with silver septagrams. All around me were riches and sweet flowers.

The air was tepid and moist, the sky a remarkable cobalt above a mercury fog. Nothing could touch me in that shimmering velvet mist. I was protected.

In my hands I held a black scroll. If I did not hold tight, it would fly away. I thought at first the papyrus was black, but then I saw that the scroll, rolled around golden rods dressed with silver tassels, was encased in an ebony tube.

In the teal dusk, the quicksilver mist snaked in long fingers over the gunwale, morphing into rubbery arms with grasping hands.

But I wasn't afraid. I had nothing to fear, for I had the Black Scroll.

"ANA A A NANA A A NANA."

I heard in the distance the faint chant of acolytes singing to a molasses, undulant beat.

A searing touch tapped my brow, and I opened my eyes.

The Nile was gone, replaced by the vivid glyphs and bright symbols floating in the Hive. I reached out to touch a golden ankh, and my finger went right through it.

"What did you see?" I heard Lemta ask from as far away as the stars.

"The future."

"Ah-h-h, it is as was foretold. You have the Sight."

It was the Maiden who settled me on the pillows and removed my gown. Her angel touch bathed me in the scent of jasmine. She spread my long fiery waves in a corona around my head and shoulders.

Against the bare skin of my hips and loins, the pillows were satin soft. I sank deeper and deeper, becoming one with the silk.

I let her do with me as she willed, transfixed by her arranging my limbs, my arms over my head, the back of my hands on my flowing hair.

Her lush mantle of crinkly black tresses, luminous under the light as a raven's wing, tumbled over her shoulders and onto my white flesh.

When the Maiden breathed, I breathed with her. We were two. Then we were one.

My breasts were glowing mounds with rosy tips. I felt her wet tongue. A shock wave rolled through me.

Another angel coalesced from the swirling Hive; her long, musk-scented waves mingled with those of the Maiden's. Her soft lips and tongue caressed my other breast.

In the ecstasy of their tenderness, I moaned "O-o-o-o-o-o-o."

When I tried to caress in return, warm fingers held my wrists gently in place, above my head. I was permitted only to receive.

Soft fingertips lovingly spread my thighs and opened me, massaging, stroking, exploring. Hot breath, then warm lips and a knowing tongue teased my womanhood. Tongues on my breasts. On my belly. Tongues dipping in my ears. Lips sucking my tongue. All with the same rhythm.

We were one, the women and I. One in the Feminine. One with the Mother. One with the Earth. One with Eternity.

I convulsed in a roll of waves cascading through my soul.

When I opened my eyes, it was into the upside-down face of Lemta leaning over me. Her lion mane hair hung in my face; I breathed in the fragrant, exotic, seductive herb that was her unique scent.

"You are blessed, our Sister," she whispered, stroking my lips with her long talon nails. "The world is yours. You must seize it. It is your destiny."

I must have dozed off. The women were gone. Lemta was gone. The room was silent. Even the birds were silent. So silent I heard the whispering of lamps burning oil.

Lemta had been right. *When you are ready, you will know.*

I was ready. Ready for Egypt.

CHAPTER 13   NEMO

"First say to yourself what you would be; and then do what you have to do."
– Epictetus

Keep well away from Roman settlements."
Lemta unrolled a parchment map of Libya and Egypt showing the sea to the north of a vast empty space. "The journey is long. Through the desert."

"How long?"

"Weeks."

I'm not sure what I expected, but it wasn't that.

"You must go south to join the east-west caravan route. You may start with horses but will need camels. The *Imazighen*—the Berbers—will help you along the way."

With her hennaed nail, she traced a line east on the map. "Here you head north for Cyrenaenica. From the port of Cyrene you will find a ship to Alexandria."

The birds squawked, but I'd become accustomed to their constant chattering. I even allowed for the possibility that I might miss them, that the world would be too silent without them.

"You shall manifest everything," she assured me. "You are a Mistress of the Sacred Arts. Few have the strength to resist your spells. Even I feel your power."

"Nemo resisted well enough."

She laughed. "Poor Nemo. A man caught between sorceresses."

"Why did he tell you about the night in the desert?"

She threw back her head and laughed even harder. "Nemo tells me nothing. He does not have to. You see, dear Sister, while you have the power to see into men's hearts, I have the power to read their minds."

Then before I could make my demand, she announced, "Dido will not be going with you."

In truth, the news came as no surprise; I couldn't fail to notice how content Dido had become. I'd even seen her smile.

"Are you certain this is what she wants? Does she speak to you?"

"Speak?" She seemed genuinely surprised by my question. "Dido cannot speak. She has no tongue. It was cut out by her Domina when she was five."

I thought of Dido dribbling when she drank, and how she chewed her food in that odd, sideways grinding. For all my powers of seeing, I saw nothing.

The women readied goatskin water bags, bundles of dates, joints of dried goat and sacks of flour for baking bread in the sand under the campfire.

Lemta presented me with a tooled red leather satchel filled with dried herbs, vials of potions and oils, and packets of powdered animal blood and feces.

"You should use your menstrual blood when possible," she told me. "It is more powerful."

"Who taught *you*, Lemta?"

She smiled. "Another old hag, older even than me."

Then she grasped my hand in a gesture of affection I wouldn't have believed possible a short time ago.

"It was my destiny to bring you here, just as your destiny is Egypt."

"How did you know to send the men to Leptis Magna?"

"I saw you in a vision with your red hair flaming in the hot sun. I saw your power."

"Did you see a black giant? A Nubian with a septagram?"

"The circle of Protectors surrounds you."

"How will I find him? How will I find the others?"

"All things come when they are needed."

I kissed her on both cheeks. "I shall try to keep the faith."

But she wasn't finished with her surprises.

"You *will* go home again. Trust in your destiny."

"Home?"

She smiled and kissed me on the mouth with her hot palms pressing on my cheeks.

"Do you think you have secrets from me? We have all lived many lives."

For the first time in months, I saw the sky. The pale light of dawn blinded me when I came out of the Cave of Bats. I blinked, holding the back of my hand up to my eyes.

Three silhouettes stood on the ledge, all with long braids entwined with feathers. I recognized the wiry one by his thin legs. I no longer saw the man in the middle because I couldn't tear my eyes away from the tall figure on the right.

I would have burst into tears if Lemta hadn't taught me always to be strong and never show what was in my heart.

Nemo.

Lemta had given me Nemo.

Around his neck he wore the septagram Lemta had taken away.

Silently, he wrapped the green emerald scarf in a turban around my hair, leaving loose cloth to cover my mouth and nose. He lifted me up and into his arms, cradling me, my feet dangling over his forearm. His honey-colored eyes didn't close until his lips pressed on mine.

I think we both closed our eyes at the same moment. I know that we breathed the same breath.

No longer did I dread the long voyage on the desert. I saw the sweet passing of each night. I saw the canopy of stars.

I saw the future, and I liked very much what I saw.

CHAPTER 14   RE-ENTRY

"A word once uttered can never be recalled." – Horace

The Red Mirror hadn't shattered, after all. I saw it hanging in its altar by my bed, just behind Barb's silvery head. She was slapping my cheeks. Aisha lay on my feet, purring.

"Wake up, Isis. Come back!"

I sat straight up. "I'm here."

Barb, perched on the edge of the bed, leaned back, her face awash with relief.

"Jeeze! I hate this, Isis. I really do. I'm so bleeping terrified you'll be stuck on the other side. That I won't be able to wake you."

"Oh Barb! I thought I *was* stuck. I had a dream. A dreadful vision of the Red Mirror breaking. I'm not sure how or why, but it splintered into thousands of pieces."

"Well, it's not broken, but it could. Anything could happen. That's what I keep trying to tell you."

"It was *horrible* there, Barb. So unbelievably brutal. I saw Hector, but he was cruel. Not anything like himself."

"I warned you it was only a matter of time before something went wrong. Russian roulette, remember?"

"I'm done with the Mirror. I'm *never* doing this again."

"Humph," she snorted. "That's what you say now."

"I did meet someone new, though. Sweet and gentle."

I could see her thinking, *Will this guy show up here, too?*

Then she said, "That awful Corsican, Cesari—the *General*—has been trying to reach you. I saw his call on your cell."

"That *awful Corsican* helped me buy this place," I reminded her. "Got you a nice commission."

She made her little snorting sound and went into the kitchen to sort out some tea. I headed for the toilet.

After we agreed to meet for lunch at Olives and Barb went off to see a client, I called the General.

He answered on the first ring. "You're back."

As usual, he didn't ask where I'd been. He never questioned my disappearances. I didn't sense it was lack of curiosity or a respect for my privacy, but rather that he knew. That he knew everything about me. Well, almost.

He never mentioned the Red Mirror. The Mirror was perhaps the only secret I had from him.

But then neither did we talk about the Emerald Tablet. It was a taboo subject, like Rasheed. Of course, he still wanted it; he wasn't a man who gave up. I had the impression he waited for the right moment, like a crocodile patiently waits hours in the mud for its prey to come near.

"There's a silver sword coming up for auction in Paris, Ishtar." As always, he used his special name for me, the name that elicited memories I wanted to forget. Ishtar, Goddess of Love, the Evening Star.

"Very old," he continued. "Greek. I'd like you to get it for me."

"I'd like to meet. Are you in town?"

If he'd sat across from me, I would have seen his eyebrows lift in surprise. I'd refused to see him in person since Tahoe. I'd refused to take the risk.

"I can be."

"Petrossian Bar?"

"Eight o'clock," he said without hesitation.

I looked at my watch. He had twelve hours to get here. He could be anywhere, maybe even Paris.

The text from Tony asked me to come to Princeton to see Jen in a junior high play.

Tony: *come if you can. the 15th. promise fresh sheets.*

Me: *might be in Paris. know soon. kisses to Jen. more than kisses to you.*

Rasheed had called three times. With each message, his voice was more irritated. No matter how elusive *he* was, I was expected to be here for him.

I did a quick calculation in time zones. I supposed he was in Dubai. If not there, then someplace else in the Middle East, or possibly Europe. Of course, I could never be sure with Rasheed. He never told me where he was. He might be in the lobby of my building.

"It's me," I said to voicemail. "Call me. I'll answer."

My shower didn't take long, just enough time for me to scrub private parts and wash my hair. I checked my phone as soon as I got out and saw the missed call.

He didn't leave a message. I sighed. Rasheed.

I was just about to hit redial when an incoming call flashed on my cell.

"Has Cesari asked you to go to the Paris auction?" The Argentine accent was more apparent on the phone than in person.

"Hello, Isabel," I said drily.

Undeterred, she demanded. "Well, has he?"

"Who else wants the sword?" I could be as rude and direct as she.

"You didn't answer my question."

"I haven't decided yet if I'm going."

She was quiet. I'm sure she was trying to decide if I'd reconsidered my business arrangement with the General and what that would mean for her.

"How is Hector?" I asked politely.

She took a sharp intake of air.

"Hector is happy. Leave my son alone."

I'm not really sure why, but I found myself in the car and then at a CVS drugstore in the hair products section.

When I finished blow-drying and using a flatiron to make it straight and sleek, my hair blazed like an Irish setter. It was getting long, past my shoulders. I wondered if I should let the bangs grow out.

I just had time to put on eyeliner, mascara, a little blush and some lip gloss. My white jeans hugged my hips and thighs. A lemon yellow, deep-V-neck cotton sweater made my hair even redder. I'd be using valet parking so indulged myself with knee-high, spike-heeled python boots.

The sky was China blue. There was no wind. I wrapped an emerald green scarf around my fiery hair, dug white Dolce & Gabbana sunglasses out of my tote and put the top down on my white M3.

Construction on Flamingo blocked the rear entrance to the Bellagio where I could dump my car at the back valet. From there, a few quick steps through the glass-roofed shopping arcade, past Tiffany and Chanel, and I would have been at the restaurant Olives facing the fountains. But not today. Today I had to confront the madhouse of the main entrance.

Seven cars spilled out passengers and suitcases before the valet took my keys and I headed for the mammoth lead glass doors. Tourists streamed out. A long queue waited for taxis.

Late for my lunch date with Barb, distracted and in a hurry, I walked straight into Hector.

I don't know how long we stood there, staring at each other. I hadn't seen him since he walked out of my old condo, closing the door with that final click. That is, if you didn't count Leptis Magna where he left me to the horrors of the villa by the sea.

What happened next was a blur. I found myself inside the lobby, still with Hector. But he was introducing me to a drop-dead gorgeous blonde.

"Ingrid, this is Isis."

The way he said my name telegraphed that Ingrid knew everything about Hector and me.

She flashed a warm smile of perfect white teeth and held out her right hand to shake mine. Northern European.

Her left hand was wrapped around Hector's biceps. On her ring finger flashed Isabel's five-karat, Asscher-cut family diamond.

A 1000 pound demolition ball slammed my belly. I actually thought I might throw up. Tears were just this side of breaking through.

With an intimate, supportive squeeze on Hector's arm, Ingrid suggested, "Why don't you two catch up? I have to make some calls."

She was unbearably gracious with that musical voice and delightful accent. Scandinavian. Not harsh like German.

Oh, Ingrid was a cool one. Serene, close to ethereal, she stepped away and outside, utterly confident to leave Hector alone with me.

I hated her at first sight.

Hector and I both watched her walk away, tall and lithe, elegant in beige linen slacks, classy tasseled loafers and a pricey white cable-knit sweater. Her hair was a miracle of spun gold, caught up with a tortoise shell barrette into a glorious, effortless fall.

"She's beautiful," I said, hoping the jealousy in my voice wasn't too obvious.

"Sí." Hector was beaming with pride; he positively glowed. "She is." I almost sobbed out loud.

"This is where I first met your mother," I said when we took a table at the Petrossian Bar on the edge of the Bellagio lobby.

I did my best to make small talk while I pulled myself together. "Isabel and I sat right over there, in the second balustrade."

Idiot. Hector wasn't the least interested in what table I shared with his mother. Thank the gods, I stopped before I told him what we drank.

"You've changed your hair," he commented once he ordered a Heineken and two *kir royales.*

He didn't say he liked it. I felt cheap and painfully self-conscious of the python boots. Totally inappropriate for lunch. Ingrid would never make such a *faux pas.*

"I don't need to ask how *you* are," I said a little too coyly, trying my best to keep my tone light.

But Hector wasn't having any of it. His warm brown eyes flecked with red gold were kind enough, but firm. Unwavering. He'd moved on. I saw no guilt. Apparently he had no memories of Leptis Magna.

"Did you think you could string me along forever, Isis?"

"It wasn't forever," I insisted. "I just needed more time. I needed to sort some things out."

"You never give up, do you? *Increíble.*" He shook his head in wonder, yet there was the slightest whiff of the old devotion before he shut it down.

I might have seized that moment, but even then, I couldn't say what he needed—that he was enough.

I couldn't let him go, though; I couldn't stand the thought of someone one else having him. I couldn't stand Ingrid wearing Isabel's heirloom engagement ring. It was supposed to be mine.

"I miss you in my life, Hector."

He gave that little snort of disgust, so like Barb's.

"Think of me as the one who got away, Isis. It happens to everyone."

The server arrived with drinks. My hand trembled, but at least I didn't cry. At the grand piano, a pianist's fingers wove an intricate full keyboard arrangement of "That Old Black Magic."

"We met in Buenos Aires," Hector offered without my asking. "Ingrid's father is the Swedish Ambassador."

Of course. Another step toward perfection. I'd been perfect once, too.

When I was Athena. Hektor had adored me then. I'd given him a son.

"You always did prefer me as a blonde," I said with too much resentment. In truth, *I* preferred golden Athena. I had been Light itself; my vibrations had moved at a higher rate.

"It's not about you, Isis," he said quietly.

I remembered how he'd been the great hunter of women when we met. South American playboy complete with champion polo ponies. His bravado was gone now, replaced by the sobriety brought on by a broken heart.

The buzz of my phone stopped me just as I was about to protest, *But you promised, Hector, that nothing I ever did could stop you loving me!*

It was Barb saving me from devastating humiliation.

"Where are you? I've only got an hour."

"I-I'll be right there," I stammered. "I ran into…someone in the lobby."

I didn't want to tell her over the phone about Hector. She was going to need some special handling on this one. *I* needed some special handling.

Ingrid appeared and said something to Hector in a Spanish too fluent for me to follow. He laughed and squeezed her hand.

"ABLAMGOUNOTHO ABRASAX," I intoned.

"It was a pleasure to meet you, Ingrid," I said with as much dignity as I could muster. "Please excuse me, but I'm late for a lunch date."

It seemed in bad form to say the usual things to Hector, like "Let's do lunch" or "Give me a call"—or even, "Keep in touch."

So I just said, "Goodbye, Hector. It was lovely seeing you again." A total lie. In my mind, I repeated the spell over and over.

Always the Argentine gentleman, he stood up from the table when I rose. I thought he might at least kiss me on the cheeks, in the Latin way, but he didn't make a move to touch me.

Now that I thought about it, we hadn't touched since bumping into each other at the entrance.

Painfully aware that my jeans were too tight and my hair too red, I left them there, wondering if they watched me walk away.

But I knew they didn't. They only had eyes for each other.

I got through lunch with the help of a Plymouth martini. Barb was so furious, she forgot her glass of chardonnay.

"I told you. I told you! You're an idiot. An idiot!"

Her blue eyes blazed under the platinum bangs. She had no lips;

they were pursed that tight.

"I feel miserable enough, thank you very much," I shot back. "I don't need you to beat up on me."

"You screwed up the best thing you'll ever have."

"Hector. Always Hector," I snapped. "You've been pushing him on me since the beginning. It's only because you want him so badly yourself."

As soon as the words came out, I regretted them. I wanted to bite off my tongue. I wished that my tongue had been ripped out like Dido's.

Barb's eyes went wide. She stood up from the table. Her chair scraped on the marble floor.

I reached out for her arm. "I'm sorry, Barb. I didn't mean it."

But of course I meant it. She knew it, and I knew it.

Without saying a word more to me, she apologized to the man behind her for bumping his chair and walked away, her back straight as a spear, her aura prickly as cactus.

Oh great. Maybe I should have stayed on the other side of the Mirror.

CHAPTER 15   ABRASAX

"Do not ask for what you will wish you had not got." – Seneca

Resplendent under the Chihuly glass ceiling, the Bellagio lobby was packed. A big group had just arrived. I pushed through the crowd, forced to walk past the Petrossian Bar.

Hector and Ingrid were gone, but I still saw them there, Hector's thick chestnut waves gleaming under the light.

"ABLAMGOUNOTHO ABRASAX!" I muttered, and Ingrid disappeared from the vision.

"Hey, man! Over here!"

Startled, I turned in the direction of the Barry White voice I never expected to hear in this lifetime. He was not fifteen feet away, his head towering above everyone.

Goliath. Fully dressed, a sports cap with a logo jammed on his head. A gorgeous black chick hung on each arm.

The crowd parted for another giant to join him, and they slapped each other on the back, both of them laughing.

A young kid of about twelve elbowed his way in and held up a pen and magazine. Goliath grinned, took the pen and scribbled.

"Who's that?" I asked a thirty-something guy next to me.

"Him? That's Gareth Greene."

When he saw the name meant nothing to me, he prompted, "Forward for the Chicago Bulls?"

Still not getting the expected reaction, he tried, "The highest-paid player in the NBA?"

I dug in my bag for a pen. "Have you got any paper?"

He handed me the sports section of USA Today, and I squeezed through to stand in front of Goliath, once a slave, once *my* slave.

I beamed up at him and held out the pen and paper. His complexion was smooth, flawless chocolate, certainly without any tribal scars.

"May I have your autograph?" My look was pretty intense; I was willing with all my might that he recognize me.

A small furrow appeared between his eyes. "Do I know you?"

"Maybe," I teased. "Can you dedicate it to Isis?"

"Isis?"

I could see he struggled, trying to remember where he'd met the redhead with green eyes—or maybe where he knew the name Isis.

When he handed me the signed sports section, I gave him my business card.

"Call me," I said brazenly.

He grinned. "You can count on it."

Hector might not have watched me walk away, but Goliath did. I felt his eyes on those tight white jeans every step to the entrance doors.

I tried Rasheed again while I waited for the valet to bring my car. Still no answer. But it was the middle of the night for him. I left a quick message after the tone.

"So now it's my turn to leave messages. Are you punishing me? I thought you didn't like games."

Barb's phone rang twice, and then she sent my call to voicemail.

"I'm sorry, Barb," I apologized to a recording. "I was horrible. You have every right to be pissed."

My tone was utterly sincere; I meant every word. I'd never before said anything to her so bitchy. I had a sinking feeling that the damage done was beyond repair.

The afternoon shift valet at my building was there to open the car door the moment I pulled up.

When I handed him the keys, he asked, "Have you been ill, Miss? You haven't been out in a few days."

I suppose I should have been comforted that he noticed, but today he made me feel watched. When I bought the penthouse, the glamorous lobby and uniformed staff impressed me. Since the Cave of Bats, I felt trapped on a cruise ship with one way in and out. 24/7 concierges, security guards and valets mentally recorded each time I left and when I came home. Each brown bag of groceries or pink-striped sack from Neiman Marcus went through that lobby. Every visitor. They even knew what I had dry cleaned and how often.

"I like your hair," commented the security guard standing in the kiosk next to the elevator.

I ignored him and pushed the up button, staring steadfastly ahead. The rich rosewood doors finally opened, and an old lady with hair a brassier red than mine wheeled out a baby stroller. When I peeked inside, a ratty gray cat glared back at me.

'Ablamgounotho.'

I typed the letters into Google. No match.

I tried 'abrasax.'

The first link was 'Abraxas - Wikipedia'—"a word of mystic meaning in the system of…"

Then, further down the page: "*abraxas or abrasax*—n. an ancient charm composed of Greek letters: originally believed to have magical powers and inscribed on amulets."

I keep going until I found a link taking me to something called the Greek Magical Papyri.

> "Papyri Graecae Magicae in Latin—referrred to as PGM—is the name given by scholars to a body of papyri from Graeco-Roman Egypt which contains a number of magical spells, formulae, hymns and rituals."

A quick search brought up a scholarly English translation of the PGM on Scribd.com. I scanned until I saw ABLAMGOUNOTHO ABRASAX written in capital letters, as were all the nonsensical, untranslatable chants I'd so diligently memorized in the Hive. The stream of vowels and consonants assembled into jumbled syllables had been transliterated into upper-case to indicate no scholar had determined their source language—or their meaning.

I didn't know the meaning of the chants either, but that wasn't important. The magic lay in the rhythm and sounds of the intonation. The vibrating, hypnotic repetition cast a spell on speaker and listener alike. A spell meant to summon the spirits of the Underworld to do your bidding.

The main body of the text, translated from Latin to English, was a cookbook of potions and charms with detailed descriptions of rituals to accompany the spoken spells.

The article went on to explain that the PGM—*Papyri Graecae Magicae* in Latin—had originally been compiled in Greek in the second century AD from Egyptian sources. No one could guess how long the rituals had been practiced.

I knew they went back to the beginning of time.

Hot water steamed in my marble bathroom. Bubbles foamed. Aisha perched on the edge of the soaking tub, settling to purr after she had licked up so many soapsuds I was afraid she'd be sick.

I didn't intend to go so far as to collect dog feces or menstrual blood to concoct potions, but it couldn't hurt to hum the chants, could it?

If I used a binding spell, Barb might get over her anger.

If I chanted a leading spell, Hector might want me again.

I slipped into velvet, jasmine-scented water.

"ANOK THAZI N EPIBATHA CHEOUCH CHA ANOK ANOK CHARIEMOUTH LAILAM."

Aisha's green eyes grew wide. She made small growling sounds. Her thick black tail twitched.

Nemo appeared.

He was so real that I reached out to touch his face, but there was nothing there.

I felt him, though. His lips on my breasts. His hardness between my thighs. I felt the taut skin of his muscled back erupt into a thousand goosebumps, and I climaxed in a wave of contractions and sighs.

The General was waiting for me at a quiet table tucked away in the back of the Petrossian, on the other side of the lounge from where I had been with Hector that afternoon.

He sat alone, although I knew his Corsican bodyguards were not far away. There was more silver in his thick hair than when I last saw him. He still wore it styled a little long on the neck in the European fashion.

With dramatic flourishes of her wrists, a neatly-coiffed pianist in a starched white blouse was at the grand piano playing a flowery rendition of "This Guy's in Love with You."

In front of the General on the round table, two squat, cut crystal glasses with a couple of inches of amber liquid waited. Macallan, 25 year, his preferred single malt whiskey this time of day. Later on, he'd sip Lagavulin.

He stood up when he saw me, his black eyes shining with appreciation. With Old World polish, he moved to pull out my chair.

"You make a stunning redhead, *ma bella*. But then you make a stunning anything."

He unabashedly delighted in the deep cleavage of my black sleeveless sheath. This was an integral part of our game—my tempting and never delivering.

"I have a small gift for you," he said as soon as we settled.

The black velvet box opened to a necklace of plump Tahitian pearls joined at a seven-pointed platinum star set with a huge ruby. A septagram.

I looked up at him. His thick lips turned up at the corners.

"It's beautiful," I said in a hushed voice. I was afraid to touch it.

"May I assist you to put it on?"

I lifted my hair from the nape of my neck. He took the necklace in his thick fingers and leaned across the small table. Our faces were very close. I smelled whiskey on his breath and a hint of mint. His eyes held mine for a moment before he focused on opening the clasp.

When his fingertips brushed my skin, goosebumps rose. He traced the pearls from the back of my neck to the front with his thick middle finger, then sat back with a satisfied look.

The pearls warmed quickly. The platinum septagram touched just below the hollow of my throat, in the exact spot the faience medallion had hung.

"It was made for you." Then he chuckled. "*I* had it made for you."

His eyes went to the lapis lazuli Hathor Ring on my right ring finger.

I saw instantly that he noted I didn't wear it on the left hand as I did when Rasheed first gave it to me. The General never misses anything. But he didn't mention Rasheed. He didn't need to.

"You've changed," he said.

"I want to talk to you about our business arrangement," I said flatly and a little coldly. Colder than I felt.

His left eyebrow arched; his eyes stayed fixed, unblinking, on me.

"You wanted once to be partners, General. I want to explore that possibility."

"But you *are* my partner, Ishtar. Are you asking for a bigger commission?"

"I don't want a commission. I want a share."

He sat back, studying me. The half-smile was gone. His wrist turned slowly, swirling the crystal tumbler of amber scotch.

"A share of what?"

"Of everything. Isn't that what you offered at Tahoe?"

His lids lowered. He had that lazy look belied by a glint in his eye. A crocodile awaiting the approach of its prey.

"You *have* changed."

"I'm talking about business, General," I said sharply. "Nothing else. We're not going to do that. It's not an option."

He laughed out loud, tossing his head just a bit. "You had me on edge there for a minute, Ishtar. Balanced breathlessly on the edge."

Then he signaled the white-jacketed waiter for two more scotches.

"And the Emerald Tablet?" he asked slyly.

"No. Definitely not."

"Why should I make you a partner, when *you're* not willing to share?"

"It's non-negotiable, General. The Tablet is not part of any deal, just as I'm not."

He smiled and leaned further back in his chair. He was totally at ease. His massive bull shoulders barely bulged in the Savile Row gray worsted suit. A repeating yellow crest pattern dotted a maroon silk tie. His starched white cuffs held gold crocodile cufflinks with ruby eyes.

The server set two more crystal tumblers with amber liquid between us and took away the empties.

The General sipped languidly on the scotch, watching me.

I held his gaze, all the while silently repeating *ANA A A NANA A A NANA* to steady my nerves.

I traveled back to his tent. I was his sex slave then; my survival had depended on pleasing him yet never showing weakness. I think he went there, too. Or maybe he returned to another lifetime when he took Athena over the razor thin line between ecstasy and pain.

"Do you think you're ready, Ishtar?"

"More than ready."

"*Bene,*" he said, raising his glass in a toast. "To us."

"*BERBELŌCH CHTHTÖTHŌMI,*" I chanted in my mind.

CHAPTER 16   GOLIATH

"An alliance with a powerful person is never safe." – Phaedrus

M y heels clicked on the paved path leading down to the waiting area for the rear valet—the valet I couldn't use that afternoon because of construction. It was typically quiet for this time of evening. Tourists rarely came here.

A couple waited on the bench under the trees. In spite of the mild evening, two coarse-looking, broad-shouldered men in business suits stood inside the air conditioned waiting room.

The couple's sedan arrived. A fit, thirty-something ponytailed valet in Bermuda shorts opened the door for the woman, took her tip from the man, closed the driver's side and jogged back up the drive-through lane.

The night sky was a colorless void; I never saw the Milky Way in Vegas. Traffic hummed in a constant flow down Flamingo and along the I-15. In the distance I heard sirens.

The men in the waiting room had gone, although I never saw their car. I was alone. I touched the platinum septagram at the base of my throat and felt the General's fingertips brush my skin.

It happened so fast that at first I thought I imagined it. Hands grabbed me from behind. A cloth went over my mouth and nose. A harsh, acrid scent burned my throat. Roaring in from Flamingo, a black van squealed to a stop a few yards away.

I struggled, twisting and elbowing, but the brute from the waiting room had the arms of a gorilla. The side door of the van slid open, and Major Domo stepped out. O gods save me, he had the same murderous eyes!

I fought like a crazed animal, but the ape in the suit kept propelling me forward.

I held my breath for as long as I could; my head began to spin.

This is your last chance.

I stomped with everything I had on the gorilla's foot with my spike heel. I felt the point go in deep. He yowled and loosened his grip. Jerking my arm away, I drove my right fist, the one with the Hathor Ring, up and into the soft flesh of his under jaw.

His hand went to his face, and I twisted away, screaming "Help!"

Major Domo was on me at once, grabbing my hair as I started to run, jerking me backward.

I had nails in this lifetime, and I used them. Blood streamed from his cheek. Just as in the kitchen in Leptis Magna, he slapped me hard across the face with the back of his hand.

Dropping to the ground, I refused to stand; they'd have to drag me into that van. His fistful of my hair hauled me to my feet.

"Hey! What the hell! Let go of her!"

Turning his head in the direction of the shouts, Major Domo hesitated for the split second that I needed. I twisted my hips around, his hand still gripping my hair, and dug my spike heel into his groin.

I think he would have killed me right then and there, if not for the men running toward us.

In a sudden, swift movement, he jumped into the back of the van after the gorilla, and the van sped away, tires squealing as it careened around the corner and out into Flamingo traffic.

I was sitting on the pavement, my dress hiked up to mid-thigh, hugging myself with both arms, when Goliath—or rather Gareth Greene—crouched beside me.

"Are you okay, Miss?"

Of course, I wasn't. But I was here and not in the van.

"You were in the lobby today," Gareth said with surprise. "Isis. Your name is Isis."

I was aware of rocking back and forth in the kind of mesmerized swaying of Jews at the Wailing Wall, like Eben in a Kabbalah trance.

Gareth put his big arms around me and held me close until I stopped shaking.

"Did you know any of those men?"

I shook my head. *Major Domo! Who was he working for?*

"That's some bad ass stuff, man," the giant with Gareth was saying. "We need to call the cops."

But no sooner had he spoken than we were surrounded by armed Bellagio security.

The manager appeared, and then Metro Police with sirens blaring and lights flashing.

"I don't know why anyone would try to take me," I kept repeating.

An ambulance arrived; the medics looked me over. No concussion, no broken bones, only scratches and bruises. The manager was insistent that I stay the night as his guest.

"I want to go home."

"Of course. Whatever you wish. My driver will take you."

As soon as I was back in my condo, I called the General.

"Just say it, so I can believe that it wasn't you."

"It wasn't me."

It was the simplicity of his answer that convinced me. I was expecting another of his riddles.

"I knew one of them," I told him. "He's…he's from the past."

"I'm sending you protection, Ishtar. I want you to use it."

"Do you think someone is trying to get to you through me?"

"There is always that possibility." His tone said it wasn't the only one.

"What else? Tell me!"

"Rasheed."

Copenhagen. *Where is Bayoumi?* The first time I heard Rasheed's last name. It was in the backseat of the Russian's Mercedes that I fully realized why Rasheed was so secretive.

"I thought you took care of the Russian, General."

"Rasheed has more than his share of enemies."

"Are you one of them?"

Instead of answering, he said quietly, "There is a third possibility you need to consider, Ishtar."

I waited, dreading what he would say.

"They could simply be after you."

I called Rasheed—again. How many messages had I left?

His cell went immediately to voicemail.

"Call me, Rasheed. *Please.* I'm scared."

It was really late in Princeton, but I phoned Tony anyway. All I could think of was Tahoe and Jen's terrified eyes on Skype. A young girl kidnapped to extort me.

A groggy Tony picked up on the fifth ring.

"It's me, Tony. I'm sorry. I know it's late."

"What is it, Isis?" He was instantly awake. "What's happened?"

"I don't know if Jen is in danger, but I had to warn you."

"Jesus, Isis. I thought you weren't mixed up with those people anymore."

"I'm not. I mean, I thought I wasn't. I'm not sure that I am. I…I'm not sure, really, that it's me."

"What do you mean, that it's *you?*"

"That it's me they're after."

I wasn't making much sense, but Tony didn't press for details.

"Do you need me to come?"

"No, Tony. No. Stay home. I can take care of myself. What I need is for you to make sure Jen is safe. Don't let her—"

I wanted to say, don't let her out of your sight, but instead said, "Be extra cautious, Tony. At least, right now, for a while, until I figure out what's going on."

CHAPTER 17   CAMINO MALO

"It takes more than just a good looking body. You've got to have the heart and soul to go with it." – Epictetus

Major Domo in a red turban was driving a Metro police car with neon flashing lights when the chirp of my cellphone woke me.

The clock said 7:04.

"Rasheed!" I gushed.

"No," said Barb icily. "It's me."

I was instantly filled with dread. Barb would never call me this early. Not unless something bad happened.

"I thought you should know."

I braced myself.

"Remember Jack, the ER doctor I've been seeing?"

I didn't answer, waiting for the bombshell.

"Hector's been in an accident."

I was mute. Barb soldiered on, knowing full well she'd stunned me into silence.

"Jack called because he met Hector and you once with me. It's totally unethical. But he knows we're friends."

"Is Hector all right?" I whispered.

"It seems he's fine—well, he's banged up a bit—but Ingrid might not make it."

"Which hospital?" I whispered.

"Sunrise." Then, "You're not thinking of *going*, are you? I mean, wouldn't that be kind of…well, inappropriate?"

"Thanks for calling, Barb. I really mean it."

"I think it's a mistake to go there."

"I can't NOT go. Surely you can see that."

By the time we got off the phone, we were arguing like sisters.

I pulled on jeans and a black top lying on the bathroom floor.

It's not my fault, I told myself. There is no such thing as magic. Spells only work if people believe.

"You have a package, ma'am," the guard said when I came out of the elevator. "Special delivery. It just arrived."

He tilted his head in the direction of the lobby. "And those two gentlemen say they're waiting for you."

Standing by the valet kiosk were two tough-looking men in dark suits. Both were stocky, black-haired and heavily muscled with that olive complexion authors call swarthy. One had longish hair and the other a military-style crew cut cropped close to the head. I recognized them. The General's men.

I'm sending you protection. Make sure you use it.

The package at reception was the size of a shoebox and marked "Urgent - Open Immediately."

It was a greyish black handgun, matte and slightly textured. A gun so small it would fit in an evening bag. So small, I might have thought it was a toy. With it was a box of ammo.

Glock 26Gen4 AUSTRIA 9x19 was engraved on the side of the barrel. A baby Glock.

I hadn't fired a pistol since I dated a cop who took me to shooting ranges on Saturday night. He only liked the big guns though. Powerful, with lots of kick.

You're a natural, he'd told me with a teacher's pride. But I'd learned to shoot on my grandmother's farm hunting with my cousins. Fleet-footed squirrels. Bounding rabbits. Tiny, elusive quail. Hold the weapon steady, take careful aim and squeeze—never jerk—the trigger.

The General's goon with longish hair filled the clip, inserted it with a snap and slipped the Glock into my Michael Kors tote.

"Don't I need a permit?" I asked dryly.

He didn't bother to answer but opened the back door of a black

Mercedes sedan parked near the entrance of the building.

I crawled in. He took the wheel, and the one with the military cut rode shotgun.

"Do you want to tell me your names, or shall I call you Curly and Moe?"

"Curly and Moe will do fine," the driver answered. "Where are we going?"

I sat back and fastened my seat belt with a loud snap.

"Sunrise Hospital."

Hector had some bad bruising on his face, and his right arm was in a sling. He was alone, slumped over in an orange plastic chair, long legs with those horseman thighs stretched out. The right knee of his jeans was ripped. He wore cowboy boots as he so often did, and his usual polo shirt, this one blood-stained sky blue. Not his blood that I could see.

I moved aside the familiar worn bomber jacket on the seat next to him and touched his good arm. When he looked up, I took his big, beautiful hand with exquisite fingers in mine.

It took him a moment to focus on me. He had a dazed, shell-shocked look to his eyes.

"The car came out of nowhere, Isis. He was drunk. No license. *Mexicano,* the police said. He ran a red light, *Dios mio!*" He choked back tears.

I mumbled something about it not being his fault and squeezed his hand.

"Ingrid…" he breathed out. "Ingrid took the full force on the passenger side. The Range Rover's totaled."

He rattled on in the way one does to relieve tension. I let him talk, holding his hand, crooning nonsense niceties. Everything was *not* going to be okay.

"She's in surgery. The doctors won't tell me anything."

"Have you called Isabel?" I asked.

"*Sí,* she was in LA. She might even be landing now. I–I don't remember how long ago I called her."

And then, as if by merely mentioning her name, we had summoned her presence, Isabel was there. Elegant even in crisis.

She wore black tailored slacks with a black turtleneck and low-heeled boots. Her silver-streaked raven hair was pulled back into her usual *prima donna* chignon. Emerald stud earrings glittered. Her only other jewelry was a gold Piaget watch. The Asscher-cut diamond engagement ring wasn't on her finger, of course. It now belonged to Ingrid. Like Hector.

Isabel froze when she realized that I sat next to her son. The red hair had confused her at first, but not for long. Her black eyes flashed with anger. One didn't need to be an empath to read her mind.

"Hector," I said gently. "Your mother is here."

She glared at me until I stood up and gave her my seat on Hector's good side.

To ease the tension, I said, "I think I'll get us some coffee."

I was at the elevator doors when Isabel hissed my name, "Isis!"

Her eyes blazed; she gripped my arm with her talon fingers tipped with long, perfectly manicured crimson nails.

"*What* did you do?" she demanded.

"Do?" I answered, stunned. "What do you mean? I didn't do anything."

"Don't try that with me. I *know* you. You couldn't stand it, could you? You couldn't stand that Hector found happiness without you."

"That's not true," I objected, but we both knew it was.

"How did you do it? Did you use the Tablet?"

"The Emerald Tablet?" I couldn't believe what she was saying. "Do you honestly think I'd use magic to cause a *car accident*? To hurt Hector?"

"Yes, Isis. I do."

I stared at her. She was my mother in another life. She'd loved me once.

"What kind of person do you think I am?"

"I do not think, Isis. I *know*. You've changed. Do you imagine I can't *see*? This is *me* you are talking to."

She pressed quite close; her face was inches from mine. Her nails dug into the flesh of my upper arms.

"You are on a bad path, Isis—*un camino malo*. You were given gifts. Look how you use them! You will pay one day. We always pay."

ANA A A NANA A A NANA, I chanted in my head.

Curly and Moe walked me into the lobby of my building, and I was just passing alone by the security station on my way to the elevator when the guard stopped me.

"You have a visitor. His name's not on the list."

As far as I knew, no one's name was on my list.

In his navy suit and starched white shirt open at the neck exposing a triangle of tanned flesh, Rasheed sat on one of the plush leather sofas in the lobby. He looked so perfectly groomed, he might have stepped out of an ad in GQ magazine.

My first impulse was to burst into tears of relief. Rasheed had come. He'd answered my call for help. But he didn't get up when he saw me walk in. O Hathor! I ached to have him hold me. But he just sat there, watching me with a dark look on his face that sharpened his cheekbones. His hair shone jet black in the light.

I felt the security guard looking from me to Rasheed and back again. Curly and Moe were poised by the valet kiosk just inside the glass entrance doors.

If Rasheed was here, Gamel and Marcos had to be close by. I found Gamel at the rear of the lobby near the door to the parking garage. Marcos stood not far from Curly and Moe. I must have walked right past him.

When it became painfully obvious that Rasheed wasn't coming to me, I took a deep breath to garner strength—and yes, patience. Conscious of all eyes on me, I put one foot in front of the other as gracefully as I could to cross the distance between us. At least Rasheed had the decency to stand.

"Thank you for coming," I told him in a soft voice. My eyes pleaded, *Don't make a scene.*

I couldn't believe we were standing like this. We who moved each other's souls. Yet he acted the jerk, rigid as a statue, so like River God below deck on his ship. I wanted to slap his face.

"What are *his* men doing here?" Rasheed demanded.

Not "I missed you," or even "You've changed your hair."

Of course, he'd recognized the General's men. Rasheed and the General had done business together once. Maybe they still did. I never asked what. No questions with Rasheed.

"I told you I was scared," I breathed, reaching out my hand, taking his fingers in mine. "They're protecting me."

Then I dropped my voice a register and murmured, "Come upstairs with me, Rasheed."

He melted a little; he wasn't quite so rigid. *His mouth softened.*

When I saw he was wavering, I urged, "Can you ask Marcos and Gamel to wait in the lobby?"

He locked eyes with me for a moment and then looked away. The tic was there, the one that comes when he's struggling for control.

"It's not like my old place, Rasheed. They can't hang around in the hallway. We have so many rules. The neighbors will complain."

I leaned into him ever so slightly while I spoke, my tone full of reason but my body language promising everything else.

After coming all this way, from who knows where, would he walk out of the lobby, leaving me to stand here alone?

"Rasheed, everyone's watching. Do you know how ridiculous we look?"

Maybe it was his pride that moved him in the end, but finally he gave a nod to Gamel, and then Marcos.

They frowned, exchanging looks that said, *This woman is always trouble.*

Score one for me, I thought but allowed no triumph to show.

Like practiced dancers who move as one, Rasheed and I glided to the elevator, his Italian loafers squeaking slightly on the travertine tile. His palm on the small of my back burned fiery hot. My whole body was aflame.

No one moved in the lobby. In the silence I heard Curly mumbling on his cell, no doubt reporting this new development to the General. From behind the front desk, the concierge watched with her mouth embarrassingly agape. A handful of residents waited without shame to see what happened next. The valet alone had the decency to pretend to be busy with some papers.

The gleaming rosewood elevator doors slid open, and Rasheed and I stepped in to go upstairs to do what everyone knew we were going to do.

CHAPTER 18   RASHEED

"The wounds of love can only be healed by the one who made them."
– Publius Syrus

A neighbor was waiting for the elevator when the doors opened. She smiled cheerfully. "Beautiful day, isn't it?" I didn't tell her what I really thought.

I turned the key in the left mahogany door and stepped into my foyer with mirror walls, mirror ceiling and polished gray marble tiles. Rasheed in all his glory was reflected around me.

I heard the door latch and waited to feel his arms encircle me from behind, pulling me into him like he'd done our first night, the night of the Wynn.

But nothing. No touch. No embrace. Crestfallen, I turned to face him. The angles in his face had hardened again.

"Don't be like this, Rasheed. Aren't you glad to see me?"

"Are you going to tell me why you were with Cesari's men?"

I lifted my fingers to stroke his clenched jaw; his left eyelid spasmed. He wouldn't look at me—his way of punishing, of trying to make me not exist.

"Look at me, Rasheed," I whispered.

He looked straight at me and took my fingers in his to pull them away from his face. His eyes were glassy green—hard and brittle.

"You're a child," I said and turned to go down the short hall to the kitchen laid out like the galley of a millionaire's yacht—rich mahogany cabinetry, shiny brass fixtures, black marble counter tops and bottle-green covers on the chairs.

I was standing by the floor-to-ceiling windows when he finally came to me. He stood close but not touching. The glass sliding doors were open to the balcony edged with a waist-high wrought iron railing. At one end of the terrace was my bedroom, at the other end the bar, all with a sweeping view of Las Vegas from the airport to Downtown. Twenty-eight stories below sparkled a blue pool surrounded by date palms and flowering pink oleander.

From the pool and tennis courts stretched the green fairways of the Las Vegas Country Club. The golf course ended at the old Hilton where Elvis used to occupy the entire top floor. Beyond was The Strip against a backdrop of craggy, dun-colored mountains.

Even in his anger and suspicion, Rasheed was impressed. His eyes drank in the vista of Las Vegas Valley and lingered a moment on the bronze glass tower of the Wynn a long stone's throw away. Surely he, too, was reliving that first night.

I wanted him to peel off my clothes and lick my body all over. Like he did that night. Like River God. Like Black Falcon.

Instead, the air was so thick with his rancor that I could scarcely breathe.

"Someone tried to kidnap me, Rasheed. It was really close. Police. Ambulance. Everything."

Almost in panic, he looked me over from head to foot—I suppose to see if I had any broken bones that he hadn't noticed. Had he noticed anything except the General's men? He hadn't mentioned my red hair.

"I'm not hurt," I said flatly. "It scared me though."

I stopped and then corrected myself. "No. It *terrified* me. If two men hadn't happened along, I don't know where I'd be right now."

I wasn't specific about Gareth Greene. The less Rasheed knew about other men, the better. Even if that man were someone who'd been loyal to him in a past life, someone like Goliath.

Rasheed was shaken but not enough to forget the General.

"What has Cesari got to do with it?" he asked gruffly.

"I saw him at the Petrossian Bar. He offered to see me to my car. I said no. But he was at the Bellagio last night. He knew what happened and sent help. This morning, when I went out, his men were waiting."

It was all the truth. It was only in the telling that it became a lie. In the parts I left out. But how many secrets did Rasheed have?

He stared; his eyes probed. He was deciding whether or not to believe me. I looked at him directly, not showing anything I didn't want him to see. Certainly not that the General was the reason I owned this penthouse and view.

"What was I supposed to do, Rasheed? I was grateful for their protection."

What was unsaid was that *he* hadn't protected me.

"Can't you be happy that I'm safe?"

Whatever battle raged within him, my words had the desired effect. Angles softened; the tic in his eye relaxed. His emerald eyes softened to jade. Reaching out, he lifted a strand of my red hair, turning it to catch fire in a sunbeam. I could see he approved.

At last, he kissed me. A long, deep River God kiss that sucked my soul right out of my body. Never in a hurry, his tongue slowly circled mine; he sucked on the tip, drawing me into his mouth slowly, deliberately.

He was the sun around whom I orbited, and like a star swallows the comet, Rasheed consumed me.

Drawing him down the long mirrored hall to the bedroom, I stroked his face, outlined his lips with my fingertips and caressed his throbbing throat.

I wouldn't let him touch while I pulled my top over my head and unzipped my jeans, peeling them past my thighs, all the while swaying my hips in the undulating gyrations of a Persian dancer. Taking his hand, I guided his fingers under my panties and into the wet. His fingers deep inside, rocking on his palm, I licked his lips and loosened his tie.

After each unfastening of the tiny buttons of his starched shirt, I kissed another inch down his bronzed chest. His fingers made love to me, exploring, caressing.

When his shirt was unbuttoned, I took his hand from my wet and traced his fingers across his lips so he might taste me. With my palm pressing on his hard belly, I pushed him gently onto the bed. Taking my time, as he always took his, I eased the zipper one notch at a time, then pulled his trousers and boxers slowly past his bent knees and down to his ankles.

I kissed the length of his bare thighs, first up one and then another. His erection stabbed the air. But I didn't touch him. I made him wait.

His eyes devoured my every move.

Hips grinding, I swayed over him leaning back on the bed, propped on his elbows, feet still in Italian loafers with his trousers around his ankles.

My bra brushed his chest, then came near to his lips. But I didn't touch. I didn't allow him to touch.

Reflected all around in the mirror walls, body weaving and dipping, my fingertips lowered my panties down thighs, past knees, along my calves to the silvery plush velvet carpet.

With a silent snap, I unfastened my bra, and my breasts fell free. Rasheed took a sharp intake of air. His pupils were huge in the shadowy room; his jet hair gleamed. The afternoon sun coming through the plantation shutters fell in charcoal and ivory stripes across the bed.

Teasing his belly, brushing his lips, my hair swung from side to side in the compelling, hypnotic rhythm of the sacred dance of the Hive.

Rasheed was so tense I could have shattered him with one flick of my finger. He reached out, but I grabbed his wrists.

Don't touch! I told him with my eyes.

Pressing him back, holding his wrists to the bed, I hung over him, letting his lips suckle for an instant one breast and then the other. Pulling away, leaving him with an open, yearning mouth, I buried my mane of flaming hair in his loins and took him deep in my throat.

I knew him so well; I knew just how far to go and when to stop. I didn't bring him to the edge; that would have been cruel. I brought him only halfway and then traced my tongue up his flat belly, past his narrow waist, over his erect nipples to his lush lips.

All the while, I held his hands firmly on the bed.

"River God," I whispered in his ear.

I might have intoned my most potent spell. He grabbed my ass, flipped me over and drove, panting and crazed, deep inside me.

"Oh Isis," he moaned as his back arched and his body shuddered.

And when I heard him cry out my name, I came.

We were one. We had always been one. This time the gods would not set us on our separate paths.

I would have my will.

CHAPTER 19   DEAL

"To keep oneself safe does not mean to bury oneself." – Seneca

R asheed looked more than a little pissed off when I jumped out of bed to grab my cell buzzing in the kitchen.
"I have to get this."
Of course, I was expecting it to be news of Ingrid. Honestly, that's the only thing in the world that would have pulled me from Rasheed.
But it wasn't Hector. It was the General.
"It was very foolish of Rasheed to show up like that. He may have confirmed you as a valuable target."
"This is not a good time," I said in a low voice, quiet so Rasheed couldn't hear.
"But you answered your cell," he objected.
"What do you want?"
"I have a proposal. I believe you'll find it—shall we say?—both intriguing and profitable."
"Email me."
"I need your passport."
"My passport? Why?"
"Give it to Orsini."
"Orsini?"
"The one you call Curly."
Was there anything the General didn't know?
"By the way, congratulations, Ishtar. You are about to become a

journalist."

When I went back down the hall to the bedroom, Rasheed had on his trousers and shirt. The bones of his face were sharp again.

Incredulous, I asked, "Are you leaving because I answered my *phone*?"

"I came to get you out of here," he said in a tight voice, ignoring my question. "I left something critical. I have to get back."

"Just like that? You show up, and I drop everything? Maybe I've got something critical going myself."

The 'don't be silly' expression around his mouth communicated that any business of mine couldn't be as important as his. He was pulling on his suit jacket, clearly on course to leave. Aisha lay at the foot of the bed, watching him with leery eyes.

"You have to come with me, Isis. There's no other way. I can't protect you here."

I bit my tongue to keep from retorting that the General was doing a pretty good job in the protection category.

"Don't pack anything," he said while running a comb through his hair. "You can buy whatever you need when we get there."

"I don't think you're hearing me, Rasheed."

Our eyes met in the mirror. When he turned to face me, he had that hard, unyielding look that morphed his face to stone. From tender to this. It hadn't taken long.

"Why did you call, Isis, if you didn't want my help?"

"I called because I was scared, and I needed to hear your voice. Who else should I turn to when in trouble?"

His answer was, "Are you coming with me or not?"

"Jesus, Rasheed."

"I'll be in the next room. I've got some calls to make." He said it in the cold flat voice I hate.

I barely recognized myself in the Red Mirror. My flaming hair frizzed in wild waves; my eyes burned with a fierce fanatical light.

"ABLAMGOUNOTHO ABRASAX," I said to the image. Then I added for good measure, "BERBELŌCH CHTHTÖTHŌMI."

Just as I stepped into the kitchen, Rasheed came in from the balcony. He looked hard at my face. Not seeing what he wanted to see, he walked past me without saying a word. I heard the mahogany front door open and close.

I never had any magic that worked on Rasheed. He always was the one who could resist my power.

I allowed myself some tears. A girl deserves a good cry from time to time. Why couldn't Rasheed hold me and reassure me—like Hector used to do?

And then in one of those mystical moments when it seems the mere thought of a person causes them to appear or call, my cell rang, and I saw Hector's number on the ID.

"Isis!" he shouted into the phone. "Ingrid's out of surgery! The doctor was just here. It looks good. They say her chances are good!"

His voice cracked. "She's going to make it," he sobbed.

"That's wonderful news, Hector." I meant it, I truly did.

"Thank you, Isis," he said quietly. "Thank you for coming this morning. I was…I was in a pretty bad way."

"I love you, Hector," I said without any embarrassment. "I will always love you."

"*Yo sé*," he said. I know.

"I'm leaving town, Hector, but you'll call me if there's any change? Promise?"

There was just a heartbeat of silence before he said, "*Te amo, Isis. Siempre.*"

If Isabel was there, she must be shitting a brick.

The email from the General had a link to a magazine article on ancient Libya with aerial photos of World Heritage sites, including Leptis Magna.

An amazingly well-preserved Roman theater at Sabratha was a twin of the one I'd seen on the edge of the slave market. I looked at each photo long and carefully before I called him.

"What's the deal?" I asked when he picked up on the first ring.

"The *deal* is the acquisition of some surplus equipment."

"What kind of equipment?"

"The kind that makes people feel safer."

"Safer?"

"I provide a service, Ishtar. Or rather, now *we* provide a service. The use people make of our service is out of our purview. Safety is but one possibility."

I had a lot more questions, but his veiled answers signaled that the details were not for a phone conversation.

"Isn't it dangerous in Libya?"

"It's not too safe in Las Vegas these days, is it?"

Major Domo's eyes stared back at me from the van.

"Don't you want to see Leptis again, Ishtar?"

For a second I thought I'd misheard. *Again?*

He waited a moment before saying, "I'm sorry that it didn't work out with Rasheed."

"Don't press your luck, General," I snapped. "Rasheed is off-limits, remember?"

He chuckled. "It's just that I do so dislike seeing you disappointed. The man really is a fool. Like that polo player. The Argentinean. Odd they can't see you're a treasure ample enough to share. Tony sees it. We have that in common. But then Tony is a smart guy, right? Princeton. Ways and whys of the cosmos. Impressive."

I hated it when he talked about Tony. I always sensed a veiled threat. He was astute enough not to mention Jen.

"Are you truly willing to share me, General? Or are you waiting for attrition in the field?"

He laughed out loud. "You don't want to know, Ishtar. You like a surprise too much, and I never want you *not* to be surprised."

"I'm going on a trip, Barb. I just wanted you to know. Sonny's taking Aisha. You don't have to do anything."

"You're not asking for my help? That's a change." Her voice was still a little cold; she hadn't quite forgiven my comment about Hector.

"It's a trip in now time, Barb. No Red Mirror."

"More work for that Corsican?"

I didn't tell her that I was now in business *with* the General rather than working *for* him.

"His money is dirty, Isis, and you know it."

"I don't know anything for sure."

"I wonder how many people have suffered—or died—to pay for your penthouse. Do you ever ask yourself?"

If I'd come back with a remark about her commission, we might never be friends again.

"I love you, Barb," I blurted out, but she'd already hung up.

CHAPTER 20   MILITIA

"Every man now worships gold, all other reverence being done away."
– Sextus Propertius

The General touched my shoulder, and I opened my eyes. With a tilt of his head, he indicated I should look down.

Turquoise water kissed a white sandy shore. Further out, the sea was cobalt.

The pilot flew low over acres of scattered ruins and stone columns. Leptis Magna.

A crumbling *scaenae* was all that remained of the splendid theatre—that and a vast courtyard of standing or fallen pillars and the broken remnants of stone benches once seating thousands. Clumps of weeds grew from every crack. I spotted the twin octagon pavilions of the slave market and pressed my nose to the window looking for Hadrian's Baths where the Egyptian slave had given me Hektor's Hathor Ring.

The river by the baths was a dry gulch. Centuries ago, it had emptied into a natural harbor now fortified with tumbled stone ruins. Near the old port stood the remains of an immense forum. The *Cardo* still transected the town, but instead of passing between monumental palaces, the broken pavestone avenue crossed sand and wild grasses strewn with massive marble blocks and toppled columns.

At the water's edge, now dangerously close to the sea, traces of the *circus* where chariots raced abutted the oval *amphitheātrum*.

Did Goliath die a quick or slow death in that Arena? How many men and wild beasts did he slay before his inevitable end?

When I turned back to the General, his black eyes were warm with satisfaction.

We circled for about ten minutes, waiting I supposed for permission to land. Tripoli looked to be a sprawling city of mostly mid-rise buildings and rooftop terraces dotted with clumps of satellite dishes. A few modern skyscrapers were evidence of the massive oil wealth of Gaddafi days.

Wide sandy beaches stretched along the Mediterranean. *Mare Nostrum*. Our Sea. The Roman Sea. Italy and Rome were beyond the horizon, to the north.

The airport looked modern enough. A Lufthansa passenger jet took off, and we landed. Rather than taxiing up to the terminal, our pilot veered toward a stand of hangers.

It wasn't until we rolled to a stop and the whine of the engines died, that I noticed the small army of pickup trucks with men sitting in the beds. Some had head cloths wrapped Toureg-style, but most wore baseball caps. From what I could see, everyone wore T-shirts, jeans and running shoes.

And they all carried assault rifles, slung over their shoulders or balanced on knees.

"Kalashnikovs mainly," the General pointed out. "AK-104 and AK-47. Some M-16's."

He'd changed from his business suit into khaki slacks and a blue button-down collar, oxford cloth shirt. On his feet, sturdy buff-colored suede boots laced to the ankle. Desert boots, I'd heard them called.

"There are some newer models that fire 5.56mm NATO cartridges," he was saying. "Massive wounds. Nasty. Very effective."

"Are those grenade launchers?"

"M203 40mm."

"And those?"

"Hand-held rocker launchers. RPGs."

The General's weapon of choice was in a holster lying on the seat next to me. He took the pistol out, removed the clip, checked to make sure the chamber was empty and handed it to me.

"Sig Sauer 9mm. Semi-automatic," he said. "Swiss. There is no better side arm in the world."

"Why not a Glock? That's what you gave me."

"Everyone has his preference, Ishtar. I prefer this. P226. Military grade. Hard-chromed barrel with Nitron finish. M193 Picantinny rail. Night sights. But more than the specs, it has the right fit for my hand. Your Glock is right for you. Have you fired it yet?"

"I didn't exactly have time to get to a shooting range, did I?"

"I think you'll find it smooth as butter."

Orsini, Moe and the others wore roomy, lightweight zip jackets that concealed the machine pistols in their armpit holsters.

Twelve men had flown with us from Vegas in the General's jet. They looked so much alike—hard-eyed, swarthy, stocky like bulls—I could scarcely tell them apart. They said almost nothing, but when they did, they spoke Corsu.

If there was a customs inspection at Tripoli airport, we avoided it. An official in a wrinkled uniform came on board to collect our passports.

"As-salamu aleikum," he greeted us.

"Aleikum as-salam," answered the General.

The official shuffled the stack of Bordeaux-red passports in his hand, opened the sole navy blue, looked directly at me, verifying the photo, and then put it on top. The only American.

"Remind me to get another passport," I remarked as soon as he was gone.

"Next time," the General agreed.

We waited. The General smiled reassuringly. *It's all happening according to plan.*

I watched the armed men milling around the tarmac below. Were they on our side?

At last the official returned, gave my passport to me and handed the rest to Orsini. My stamped visa said "journalist."

"Are *they* journalists, too?" I asked the General.

He chuckled and patted my hand.

Hot sun bounced off the tarmac, blinding me. I pulled on my sunglasses and a canvas Aussie hat. Around my neck hung a lanyard with a clear plastic case holding a photo ID that read, "PRESS." The name of the news agency and the issue date of the credential was in French.

The General handed me a big honking digital Nikon with a massive lens. "Well, Ishtar. Are you ready for a walk on the wild side?"

My jeans were faded, well-worn and not particularly tight. On my feet I wore the same buff suede boots as the General. Of course, he had known my size. I went for the lightest cover-up possible with a loose, long-sleeved, pale blue cotton work shirt over a tank top.

I felt every eye on me when I deplaned; there wasn't another woman in sight. Maybe I should have tied my hair under a scarf. Even with the hat, I was conscious of the flaming red ponytail hanging on my shoulders screaming, *Look at me! Look at me!*

It all happened so fast. A quick descent down the short flight of steps from the fuselage of the Gulfstream. A rapid opening and slamming of car doors.

The General and I climbed onto the leather back seat of a black Mercedes S-class sedan. Orsini took the passenger seat. A strand of wooden prayer beads with a multi-colored tassel dangled from the rearview mirror.

A kid of about twenty was at the wheel. He'd wrapped a red-and-white checked *keffiyeh* scarf around his head; his T-shirt said 'University of Miami.' He grinned a white toothy smile of sheer joy when I got in.

I counted four identical black Mercedes. I didn't get time to count the white pickups. Toyota Grand Tigers seemed the preferred model.

Our sedan pulled in behind two Grand Tigers with machine guns mounted on steel frames fixed to the cargo beds. The three other Mercedes followed us, with more pickup trucks rumbling at the rear.

We sped across the tarmac and turned abruptly onto an unpaved, jolting road that traversed a barren patch of land. At a closed barbed-wire gate, we squealed to a stop in a cloud of dust.

A gangly teenager with incongruous carrot hair jumped out of the first truck, pulled open the gate, then jumped back into the cab. Drivers gunned accelerators, and we raced ahead with chunks of gravel flying from the tires.

The General glanced over at me and smiled. Although he didn't show concern, I noticed that he'd fastened his seat belt.

As if in a dead heat to get somewhere before everyone else, our caravan of trucks and cars barreled down the middle of the two-lane highway, blasting horns to clear the road, forcing oncoming vehicles to careen onto the shoulder. It all happened with a great deal of shouting in Arabic and the waving of weapons. No gunfire, though. They'd apparently evolved beyond the firing bullets in the air I saw on the news.

The kids in the truck directly in front of us grinned smiles of blazing white teeth and gave us the V sign. V for Victory. Not for Peace.

"Did you hire a private army?"

"I believe that in Libya," he chuckled, "the correct term is militia."

He seemed to be thoroughly enjoying our adventure together. I caught him watching me with an amused look that was more indulgent than lascivious. To my surprise, he'd been a perfect gentleman on the trip. I'd been on my guard, but he'd made no advances. Still, I stayed well on my side of the back seat, with my bent legs in front of me, thighs together. His raw animal power filled the confined space of the Mercedes.

We headed east, away from Tripoli. The sun baked a cloudless sky. Our tinted windows were up; the air conditioner blasted cold air. Wild Arabic music wailed on the car radio.

"Orsini," the General said.

Curly leaned over and dialed down the volume. The kid driver turned his head and grinned at me.

"Please watch the road," I said politely.

He grinned bigger and told me, "No worries, lady. I am good driver."

To demonstrate, he pounded on the horn, drove straight up to the tailgate in front of us and slammed on the brakes, then fell a few yards behind again.

All the shenanigans of waving and grinning, the weaving in and out among old cars, white mini-buses and horse carts took place at 70 mph. My heart was in my throat. I couldn't look at the road.

To come all this way and die in a car accident.

"ANA A A NANA A A NANA," I chanted over and over with my eyes closed.

My nerves were pretty well shot by the time we hurtled through the open gates of a walled villa and careened to a halt. Choking dust blew from the rear toward the front. For a moment, I couldn't see the Toyota pickup in front of us.

Within seconds, the men piled out and spread about the grounds, heading, it appeared, for shade.

I was so happy to be out of the speeding car, that I gave no thought to whomever we were supposed to meet here.

The two-story whitewashed villa had a bright blue front door and matching blue shutters. A narrow outdoor staircase led up to a rooftop terrace where colorful laundry waved from drooping clothes lines.

Fat date palms and dusty olive trees grew here and there in no discernible attempt at landscaping. Chickens clucked and pecked at bare stones for whatever it is that they find to eat.

A green patch, more weeds than grass, spread around a water well with a rudimentary pulley and bucket. It was only a few feet from the blue front door. The door opened.

Out came a handful of men, older, better dressed but still with an untamed air about them. Their unsmiling faces were all business.

They saw me at once and frowned. When they noticed the press ID, they grew even glummer. Heated Arabic words passed between them.

"No women," the Libyan who looked to be the boss said in English. "No journalists."

"Of course," the General agreed pleasantly. "My associate is here to photograph Leptis Magna."

The Corsicans had gathered around us, forming a loose circle, but they hadn't drawn their machine pistols. I didn't feel any particular hostility from our hosts other than displeasure at seeing me. The vibes felt safe—at least so far. Which was a good thing. We were outmanned and outgunned.

"Ishtar, I'm going to ask you to stay outside."

"Should I wait in the car?"

The General looked at the Libyan. He shrugged. I took it to mean that he didn't care one way or the other, so I elected to wait in the shade.

Orsini and Moe stayed with me while the General went into the house, taking four of the Corsicans. Two others waited by the well. I sensed their eyes traveling constantly behind their dark sunglasses. Their hands were inside their jackets, no doubt on their pistols.

Now that we'd arrived at the villa, our escorts seemed to lose interest in us. Most were busy on their phones, talking or texting. They lit up cigarettes; a number lit hand-rolled joints. Smoke drifted in the air. The sharp scent of black tobacco mingled with sweet hashish.

I toyed with the idea of taking some photographs but decided against it. A kid in a yellow T-shirt silk-screened with a portrait of Bob Marley came up with a tin tray holding three steaming glasses of a muddy liquid.

"Nescafé!" he offered. He positively beamed.

When I burned my fingers, the kid laughed and showed me how to hold the glass with my pinky on the bottom and my thumb on the rim. The hot coffee, syrupy sweet, was oddly refreshing in spite of the oppressing heat.

Two guys in baseball caps, one Royals and one Mets, set up bottles and cans.

The crack of the guns exploded. Squawking chickens flew for cover.

No one came out of the house to investigate. Maybe it was the rhythm of the shooting that raised no alarms. A gun battle must sound very different from this *rat-a-tat, rat-a-tat* interspersed with cheers and catcalls.

"You want to try, Miss?" asked an appealing teenager with gorgeous long-lashed honey eyes. He held out his carbine to me.

"I have my own," I said, producing the black Glock from my backpack.

That caused some excitement. There was a burst of rapid Arabic, and immediately smiling faces and dancing eyes surrounded me.

"*Yallah, yallah!*" they called out, waving encouragement.

Orsini scowled but didn't try to stop me.

I checked the magazine, snapped it back into place and slipped off the safety. When I squeezed the trigger, the Glock barely kicked. Smooth as butter, just as the General promised.

A tin can flew into the air. The yard erupted in cheers.

"*Allu al Akbar!*"

I let go five more rounds, and five more cans flew.

"*Allu al Akbar!*"

"*Allu al Akbar!*"

Orsini looked positively thunderstruck. I couldn't remember ever having seen him drop his mask.

"*Shouf! Shouf hadee!*" I heard all around me.

"What your name?" a kid in a Chicago Bulls T-shirt asked. Pointing to his chest, he said, "*Ismee Mohammed.*"

"*Ismee* Isis," I said.

"Isis!" My name resounded around the circle. "Isis! Isis!"

"We are Zintani," Mohammed boasted. "*Thuwar*—Freedom Fighters. The best. The strongest. We took Tripoli from Gaddafi."

They crowded around, telling me their names. I could see they were infatuated with me. But no more so than I was with them.

The meeting inside the villa lasted about an hour. When the General came out, he found me surrounded by militiamen practicing their English.

"John McCain very good. He got NATO to bomb Gaddafi."

No insults about ugly Americans here. They were big fans of military intervention.

"Why Obama no help Syria?"

"It's complicated," I said. "Russia. China. Iran."

"And Israel," someone shouted.

"Yes, and Israel."

"Isis buy guns? We have the best. Qatar bought them for us. Belgian, not just Russian. FAL rifles. Mines. Anti-aircraft stingers. Everything."

"Everything!" came the chorus.

"We have too many guns. We don't need guns anymore. Now we need money."

All this they said with Kalashnikovs slung over their shoulders. I didn't bother to ask why they carried weapons if they didn't need them.

CHAPTER 21   CIGAR BOAT

"Things we do not expect, happen more frequently than we wish."
– Titus Maccius Plautus

Would you care to go to Leptis now?" asked the General.
"Do we have to drive with all these trucks? I'm more afraid
of a car accident than any bad guys."

He had some quick words with a couple of the Zintanis, and there
were some shouts in Arabic. Instead of remounting the trucks, they
waved their guns and gave us the V sign. Orsini, the General and I
got back into the Mercedes, and the rest of the Corsicans piled into
the other sedans.

We drove out the gate to cries of *"Ma'a as-salaama Isis!"* Go with
peace, Isis.

I rolled down the window and shouted, "Free Libya!"

"Allu al Akbar!"

"Allu al Akbar!"

"It seems you've made some friends, Ishtar."

"Nice people," I replied, feeling happy and a bit pleased with myself.

"If you pay them enough."

"Maybe. Maybe the ones at the top. But those kids? They're pure
lion. All spirit."

"Ah-h-h-h to be an optimist again. You inspire me."

We had a different driver. Older. Seasoned. He didn't smile much. In fact, he didn't smile at all. He didn't turn on the radio but drove with a stern, concentrated expression, often checking the rear view mirror. Behind us were the other Mercedes sedans, but no pickup trucks.

The General and Orsini talked quietly in Corsu. I tried at first to make out words, but although it sounded like Italian, it clearly wasn't. The arid landscape flew past. We still drove too fast, but without the reckless abandon of the testosterone militia.

"Where are the arms going that we bought back there?" I asked.

"Enjoy the landscape, Ishtar." The General slid his eyes toward the driver.

After a few minutes, conversation stopped. The hum of the tires lulled us to quiet. The General dozed off. At least, he appeared to sleep. I had the feeling that, like a predator in the jungle, one small deviation from the humming background noise and he would be instantly alert.

The shadows were long when we arrived at what the young *thuwar* referred to as 'LM,' the most eastern of the three World Heritage sites— Sabratha, Oea and Leptis Magna. Collectively the Romans called them *Regio Tripolitana*, Region of Three Cities. Modern Tripoli stands on the site of the ancient city of Oea.

In today's Libya, the dry river at Leptis is *Wadi Lebda*. According to Wikipedia, the old Tamazight, or Berber, name was *Lpqy*. A couple thousand years ago, where there is now rocky sand, the wide river flowed into the harbor. The Great *Lpqy*. Leptis Magna.

"We have very little time, Ishtar. Choose carefully what you will see."

"I want to go to the seaside," I answered immediately.

The General nodded and told the driver to head for the beach.

I'm sure we drove where we shouldn't; priceless antiquities must be buried under every clump of grass or rise of sand. But there were no guards that I could see. We moved freely across the rough terrain on a makeshift road.

Once at the seaside, I asked that we drive slowly. Then I saw it. There was no doubt. The villa by the sea. The villa of Marcus Quintillus. A couple of four-wheel drive Nissans were parked outside.

"Stop here!"

The driver pulled off the road, and I jumped out of the car.

Large portions of the ground floor of the villa remained. Quite a number of walls still stood—or were clearly marked by neat stacks of rubble. The upper floor where slaves slept and household goods were stored had disappeared.

Once inside, I easily discerned the layout of the house by the mosaic tile floors. A half dozen or so were as intact as the day of the convivium.

A small group of archaeologists speaking Italian were on their knees around the elaborate floor mosaic in Domina's bedchamber.

They looked up in surprise when I suddenly appeared. Leptis Magna is not on the travel circuit. No giant tour buses belch fumes. No hordes of Japanese tourists take endless pictures of themselves in front of pillars. We passed no one on our way here. The vast site appeared deserted except for those of us here at the villa.

"Press," I said in a crisp, official voice, holding up the plastic ID.

The Nikon hung like a badge of authenticity around my neck.

My heart pounded in my chest when I found the family's private bathhouse, and then the tepidarium. Dominus in vivid Technicolor reclined on a fur-covered divan, a half dozen slaves massaging and oiling his pasty body.

I looked for the crack. Much of the tile had crumbled; if the vision in my mind's eye hadn't been so precise, I would never have found it.

I took out the Swiss pocket knife the General had given me at the start of our trip and, in blatant violation of every archaeological canon, started picking away at the wall.

Chunks fell. Priceless mosaics and sections of masterpiece murals crumbled. I kept digging.

And then, just when I was telling myself that it was insane to expect the ring to be here, I saw it. A glint of never-tarnishing gold. The Hathor Ring. Lost in time and memory for centuries upon centuries. Twin to the one I left behind in Vegas.

I slipped it on my finger, the middle finger of the right hand, the finger for which it was crafted. A perfect fit.

I spit on the corner of my cotton shirt and carefully wiped the lapis lazuli stone. Delicate veins of gold marbled the deep blue.

"Are you ready, Ishtar?"

"Yes, General. More than ready."

The archaeologists were packing up to leave after a day of work. They cast us a few curious looks, but no one questioned our presence. Anywhere in the world, a fleet of Mercedes signals authority.

Navy shadows stretched out long, skinny fingers; the sun was nearing the horizon. A hundred yards away, the Mediterranean slurped lazily at the shore.

"Can I have one more minute?"

"A minute. Not more."

When I climbed the slight rise, I was stunned by how the coast had changed. Erosion over the centuries had worn away most of the broad sandy beach where Dido and I ran through the surf the night of our escape. The white waves on crystalline turquoise water now rolled right up to short rocky cliffs.

Colors deepened as the sun set. The sea was violet; a rainbow ribbon streaking the horizon faded to mauve.

"Now, Ishtar," the General urged. "Now."

The car engine idled. Our dour-faced driver was clearly edgy. The Corsicans waited in the black sedans with their Zintani drivers. The urgency in the air was palpable.

No sooner had I climbed in the back with the General after me than we sped off, tires throwing up stones. I glanced back through the rear window to see a short train of black Mercedes enveloped in a fog of golden dust.

No one spoke in the car. The General was tense. Orsini's handgun of choice—a matte black Belgium-made FNP-9—was on his thigh.

"Military issue," he'd growled when I asked on the plane.

My little Glock was a child's toy next to its power. I touched the Hathor Ring on my finger. The General looked at my hand in surprise but didn't comment. Wound tight, he was distracted; gone was his relaxed, always-in-charge aura.

Our driver was talking in Arabic into a cellphone. The agitation in his voice took on a new edge, and then he was shouting into the phone. I looked behind us to see pickup trucks approaching—fast.

I touched the General's arm, and he turned to follow my line of sight out the rear window. He growled something to Orsini in Corsu, and Orsini was on his cell.

We drove faster. We were the head car; our dust blew behind us. The Mercedes flew over potholes. The car, built like a tank, rattled and shook.

More Arabic that I didn't understand. More Corsu that I didn't understand. But I didn't need to ask what was happening.

We were in a race to the airport. How many kilometers was it? A hundred? More? I looked back to see if the pickups were gaining on us but couldn't see anything for the dust.

The last glow of sunset died; dusk settled into nuances of gray. We roared past silhouettes of spindly trees and squat houses.

Orsini, still on the phone, turned toward us and murmured something in Corsu. The General ordered the driver to take the next turn.

"No!" he shouted back in panic.

Orsini put his FNP-9 to the driver's head, and we careened around a sharp corner past a rusty gate to speed toward the sea.

The other Mercedes followed. I wondered if those drivers also had guns to their heads.

The General turned to me; I'd never seen alarm in his eyes. His apprehensive expression made me want to burst into tears. When he saw my panic, he reached out and took my face in his massive hand.

"We are not going to the airport. Our plane has been seized. The pickup trucks, we believe, belong to a rival militia." Wound tight as he was, he still spoke calmly and factually.

"I am going to need you to do exactly what I say. Can I count on you, Ishtar?"

"Thank you for telling me," I said solemnly. "It's worse not knowing."

ANA A A NANA A A NANA. But the mantra didn't calm me.

We made better time on the new road, which looked to have been recently paved.

How did the General know to take this route? Who did Orsini speak to on his cell? What is a rival militia? I had a thousand questions but asked none. No one had time for me.

We arrived at a small port with fishing boats moored near the shore and lashed along a low wooden quay. A light on the inky water blinked, followed by three rapid flashes.

Orsini was out before I realized he'd opened his car door. My door opened, and he grabbed my arm, dragging me from the car.

The General tossed him my backpack.

"Do everything Orsini says, Ishtar. Everything."

"What about you?" I yelled.

He reached over and pulled the car door shut.

Orsini and I dashed along the shore toward the jetty. Gravelly sand crunched, then wood planks echoed under our footsteps. I ran as fast as I could, but Orsini ran still faster. I stumbled. He grabbed my arm and propelled me forward.

At the end of the pier was a streamlined wooden speedboat, about 45 feet long, with a sharp-pointed prow, shallow hull and powerful inboard motor churning water at the stern. A Donzi cigar boat, used by smugglers. I thought they were a legend, the stuff of tall tales enticed to extremes by shots of whiskey in late night pubs, but this one was real enough.

Orsini picked me up and leapt over the gunwale into the open cockpit. The pilot rammed the gear into reverse, spun the prow around and slammed the throttle full forward, kicking in 3000 horsepower. The pointed bow soared into the air. We were airborne for a second or two before we settled and flew across the water, salty spray drenching us to the skin.

Back on shore, the four Mercedes moved fast along the curve of the harbor, then turned away from the sea. I watched as red tail lights faded into the night.

Heartbeats later, a horde of trucks with only their parking lights burning swarmed the port, zooming frantically in all directions at once like an irate colony of African bees driven from their hive.

I turned back around; my hand clutched the grab rail. If I let go, I might fly from the boat. The wooden hull slapped the black water doing maybe 70 knots. Chop. Chop. Chop.

The crude bucket seats were soaking wet. I couldn't see a thing in front of us. The pilot stood braced behind the wheel, goggles on his face. A billion stars blazed overhead. The Milky Way was a white arch across the sky.

"Where are we going?" I yelled to Orsini over the roar of the engines.

"Malta."

"And Cesari?" I screamed into his ear.

He shrugged and turned his face towards the north, his hard eyes staring straight ahead.

Chapter 22   Phœnicia

"No one knows what he can do until he tries." – Publius Syrus

Our arrival on Malta was in the dead of night. Instead of the capital Valletta as I expected, we pulled into a small harbor with a big ferry.

"Where are we?"

"Gozo."

"Where's Gozo?"

"Malta."

I looked around. The marina was quiet. I didn't see any movement on the other boats. On the hills above twinkled the lights of a town.

"Give me your passports," demanded the cigar boat pilot.

When I saw that Orsini handed over his without hesitation, I surrendered mine.

We waited. A few cars were queuing up by a ferry terminal. A taxi arrived; passengers stepped out and made their way to what looked to be a ticket office.

The pilot returned, handed us our passports and pointed the way to the terminal.

"You can just make this ferry. There will be taxis on the other side."

"What other side?"

"Malta."

Orsini paid for tickets with some euros he pulled out of his pocket, and we climbed the ramp toward a sign reading "MGARR-CIRKEWWA."

The ferry was quiet. The digital clock read 23.25. I was surprised that there were any passengers at this hour. We took a place standing in the stern.

The horn blasted, the crew cast us off, great diesel engines churned the sea, and the double-deck car ferry chugged its way through black water.

The lights on the other shore grew brighter and brighter. In no time at all, less than thirty minutes, we docked at another terminal.

"Where are we now?" I asked.

"Malta."

After negotiating with the taxi driver, we squeezed into the tiny back seat for a drive on a highway of sorts through rolling hills and small dark towns. The few cars on the road seemed to come from—or be driving to—the ferry.

Soon the road widened to four lanes, and we sped past a well-populated area marked with overhead highway signs indicating hotel and resort turnoffs. Straight ahead was Valletta.

"Are we going to Valletta?" I asked.

"Yes."

"Where are we going in Valletta?"

"A hotel."

I clenched my jaw; his terse answers were really getting on my nerves.

"Where is Cesari? Will he join us there?"

It hadn't dawned on me yet that the General might not make it out of Libya.

"You ask too many questions," snapped Orsini.

We rode the rest of the way in silence.

The circular Art Deco white marble foyer of the historic Hotel Phœnicia could have been the set of a 1940s spy film. A black baby grand piano was centered on a black marble Islamic-inspired rosette under a multi-tiered crystal chandelier. I half-expected to see Humphrey Bogart in a white dinner jacket at the bar.

"I'm sorry, Monsieur Orsini. We don't seem to have your reservation. But that is no problem, Sir. Do you prefer a king or two queens?"

"Two rooms," Orsini said, not specifying his bed preference. "Next to each other. Adjoining if possible."

Grateful to have him take charge, I thanked him in Corsu, "*Vi ringraziu.*"

He glared at me for an instant and then headed without a word to the elevator.

After a long soak in the deep porcelain tub, I wrapped myself in the hotel's thick white terry cloth robe and dried my hair with the blow dryer.

When I came out of the bathroom, Orsini sat in a beige wool lounge chair. His military crew cut and slightly reddish face had a fresh-showered look; he wore the same dusty clothes minus the zip jacket.

Fried eggs, sausages and grilled tomatoes—the English breakfast I'd soon discover was quintessential Malta—waited on a table covered with a starched white damask cloth. I was starving; I couldn't remember when I last ate. While everyone else had breakfast on the plane, I'd slept.

"What's happened to the General?" I used my name for him without thinking. "Have you heard anything?"

"What happened to the *General*," Orsini said in a nasty tone, "is that he listened to *you*."

I stopped in mid-drink of fresh-squeezed orange juice.

The General dismissed the militia because I asked him. The side trip to Leptis Magna was for me.

"Why didn't he come with us on the boat?"

"Do you think he would leave his men *behind*?" he snarled back.

It was then that I realized just how deeply Orsini resented being here with me in this luxurious five-star hotel when the *men* were back in Libya.

"When was the last time you heard from him?"

Instead of answering, he looked away, out the open French doors to the stone balcony. Low amber clouds filled a luminous night sky.

Close by was the main gate of walled Valletta built by the Knights of St. John. Not far away, ships sailed in and out of the harbor past medieval stone ramparts mounted with cannon. Below the ramparts lay the long deep fjord where sailors had sheltered since the days of the Phoenicians.

Orsini exhaled one long, terrible sigh. I reached over and touched his arm. Startled, he pulled away.

"What can we do?" I asked quietly.

He turned his face toward me; there was so much pain in his eyes that it hurt me to look into them.

"*We* can do nothing. My orders are to take you back to Las Vegas."

"Well, I'm not going back."

He blinked.

"I'm not going anywhere without the General."

His cell buzzed, and we both jumped.

He listened, said a few words in Corsu, and the call ended. Thirty seconds tops.

"Tell me," I begged. "Don't keep anything from me."

"He's been taken," he said in a flat voice remarkably devoid of emotion.

Like an idiot who couldn't grasp perfectly understandable English, I repeated stupidly, "Taken?"

Orsini didn't bother to respond.

"Is he still…alive?" I whispered.

"Yes. As far as they know."

"*They?*"

He looked at me for a moment before answering, "We have brothers everywhere."

I had enough sense to stop short of asking what kind of brotherhood.

"Why did they kidnap him? Do they want money? Is that what this is about?"

He shrugged. He looked exceedingly haggard—and older, much older than I'd realized he was.

Leaning back into the plush armchair, he unfastened another button of his shirt as if to breathe more easily.

In the open triangle, thick black chest hair curled. In the hair glinted a greenish faience medallion hung on a gold chain. Inscribed on the pendant was a septagram.

I stared at it in shock.

"Where did you get that?"

He knew immediately what I meant; his fingers went straight to the medallion and touched it reverently.

"Cesari," he said proudly.

Had the General given Orsini his own, the one he'd used to convince me to go to Tahoe, or was this another?

Lars in Copenhagen wore two as cufflinks. A family heirloom, he'd told me. Passed down for generations.

This could be number four of the seven I commissioned in Amunia twenty two centuries ago. Seven septagrams for seven Protectors.

Orsini didn't say "Goodnight," or "Tomorrow we'll make plans," but heaved his bulk from the lounge chair and lumbered to the door connecting our rooms.

"Orsini."

He stopped but didn't turn.

"Will they…will they torture him, do you think?" I asked.

He turned then, and when I saw the desolation on his face, a great weight slammed me. It was my fault. It was all my fault.

"No matter what they do to him," he growled, "they are dead men now."

He'd opened the door and taken a step into his room when I called out his name again.

"I love him, too," I said softly. "We will get him back, together."

Rasheed's cell went directly to voicemail.

"Call me, Rasheed. I'm in Malta. Something terrible has happened. I have to talk to you."

I rang off and then called him again.

"Don't be a jerk. If you don't call, I won't ever see you again."

I counted on him knowing I meant it when he heard the steel in my voice.

I was coming out of a lobby boutique the next morning wearing new white jeans and a white linen, boat-neck knit top—outrageously expensive—when I ran straight into tall, blond Lars. Was he here last night when I thought of the septagram cufflinks, or had my thoughts manifested him?

"*Gud!*" he exclaimed. "Is that *you*, Isis?"

I don't know whether he was more surprised to find me in Malta or that I had flaming red hair.

"Lars, oh Lars! You have no idea how glad I am to see you!"

He'd been Rasheed's best friend once. He was there when Rasheed and I met. Lars wore the septagram cufflinks the day the Russian grabbed me in Copenhagen.

"We keep running into each other," he said with a laugh. "What a delightful fate!"

He sobered, though, when he saw the tears in my eyes. "What's going on, Isis? What is it?"

He really was the warmest of men, with that Scandinavian manner of taking charge without being paternalistic. As if women are partners who sometimes need extra help.

Today I needed help.

"I'm trying to get hold of Rasheed."

"Again? Are you still at that game?"

"*He's* still at it."

"Rasheed is a fool."

"That may be, but he's a fool who speaks Arabic. And I'm going to Libya."

CHAPTER 23   POSSE

"Audacity augments courage; hesitation, fear." – Publius Syrus

Y
ou're not going. I forbid it."

"It's not your decision, Rasheed."

My cell had buzzed as soon as Lars and I walked into my hotel room.

"What the hell was Cesari thinking to take you there? What the hell were you thinking to go? Libya, Isis. Libya! Don't you read the newspapers?"

"He didn't take me anywhere I didn't want. But that's not the point. He got me out, Rasheed. He saved me. I owe him."

I heard his breath catch, and then there was a long pause.

"You didn't come with me in Vegas because you already had plans to go to Libya with *him*." He said it in the flat voice of someone who's realized they should have known something and now feels stupid.

"It's business, Rasheed."

"What kind of business could you have with Cesari?"

But without giving me a chance to answer, he demanded, "How long has this been going on?"

"That's not important now," I said firmly, but inside I was quaking.

He'd caught me in the Lie.

"You can come with me, Rasheed—or not. Either way, I'm going."

It was the same argument that I use with Barb. I listened for the same sigh of resignation but didn't hear it.

"I *need* you, Rasheed."

"It's always about *your* needs," he accused.

Although I was tempted to snap that his needs determined when, where, how long and how often we met, I didn't take the bait.

Instead I argued, "You know this part of the world, better than anyone I know. You're Egyptian, you speak Arabic."

"*Coptic* Egyptian," he reminded me. "Christian."

"Can they tell? Do you have a cross burned on your forehead?"

"I have a Coptic last name, Isis."

"You live in Dubai. You must know how to handle Muslims."

"It's not about handling. It's about going into a place without law, Isis. Libya is a jungle. You don't realize what you're getting into."

"I think I do. I think I've had a taste. It's a matter of having enough firepower."

"What do *you* know about firepower?"

"Obviously more than you give me credit for."

"Let me talk to Lars."

Before I handed over the phone, I threw the right hook.

"You're the strongest man I know, Rasheed," I lied. The strongest man I knew was being held somewhere in Libya. "Who else can I turn to?"

The last part was the truth.

Lars listened for a couple of minutes before saying, "She's determined, Rasheed. I've tried to dissuade her, but she'll go no matter what."

Then Lars dropped his bombshell on both of us.

"And I'm going with her. I can't let her go alone."

The door connecting our rooms opened, and Orsini walked in without knocking. When he saw Lars, his hand went to the holster in his armpit.

"He's a friend," I rushed to reassure him. "He knows everything. He's going to help us."

Orsini eyed Lars with suspicion, which I understood. Blond, blue-eyed Lars had the shine of Scandinavian naiveté about him. A hard person from a hard world would have a difficult time taking seriously a man from a world populated with the happiest people on earth.

But it turned out that Lars had contacts in Benghazi, something to do with oil and Norwegian extraction technology. I didn't get all of the details.

He made some phone calls and then said, "Now we wait."

"How many men can you get?" I asked Orsini.

"A dozen by tomorrow."

"Good. Rasheed will be here by then."

Orsini looked none too happy when I mentioned Rasheed. There was obviously bad blood between them.

"We need Rasheed," I insisted. "He speaks Arabic. We can't do this with a hired interpreter. I don't trust anyone. Do *you* trust anyone?"

His silence told me no.

"Can you contact the Zintani militia? Tell them no arms deal if we don't have Cesari. I'm assuming we're talking about quite a bit of money."

Nostrils flaring, Orsini glared at me. I could see he was right on the edge of exploding, but I refused to be cowed.

"Negotiate for them to take us wherever he's being held. I'd have Rasheed contact them, but they don't know Rasheed. They know you. You're the only one who can do it."

"Us?" he said.

I wondered if he'd heard anything else after getting stuck on the 'us' part.

"Yes, *us*. I'm going. I told you I'm going."

"I can't let that happen. Cesari gave me orders."

"Well, I'm countermanding them. Didn't he tell you? He and I are partners now. I'm in charge until we get him out."

Orsini didn't seem to know what to say. The news about partners threw him off; he even looked over at Lars as if to confirm it was true.

"He needs you," I told him. "He needs every resource we have."

I could see the wheels turn in his head as he sat there, no doubt weighing the ramifications of disobeying Cesari against the ignominy of leaving his rescue to someone else. Of that rescue failing.

"Can I take your silence as consent?" I asked him in a quiet tone, not wanting to challenge him more but making it clear he needed to decide. Now.

Another minute passed and then he nodded his head, sliding his eyes sideways again to glance at Lars.

"*Bene*," I said and then went on, making chicken scratch lists on hotel stationery as I gave orders.

"We're going to need a couple of satellite phones. Can you do that, Lars? And some food, water—that sort of thing. Plan for twenty men going and thirty coming back."

"Yes, ma'am," he said with a small smile. "I can do that."

"You *are* taking this seriously, aren't you, Lars?"

"Dead serious, Isis," he answered, this time without a smile.

"I'm counting on you for the firepower, Orsini. What can you get in Malta?"

A second or two passed before he grunted, "Anything we need."

"We need a boat. Something big enough to get us in—and big enough to get the General and his men out. Choose carefully. Nothing that draws attention. I don't want to be tagged as a drug trafficker."

I paused.

"Keep it simple. The more boats, the more outsiders, the greater the risk."

I paused again. Orsini looked glum; his face was dark. In the morning sun, dozens of acne scars pitted his cheeks. His dark gray eyes, large and liquid, protruded a little. As I studied him, he glowered back.

"Unless you have a better idea?" I waited for a reply that didn't come. Then I asked, "Do you have the funds?"

"I'll be ready," was his answer in the flat, resigned voice of one who had capitulated.

I checked the clock and did a quick calculation for time zones before calling Barb.

"I'm in Malta. It's too complicated to explain right now. I just wanted to…to ask you to take Aisha—in case…in case something…happens."

"What do you mean," she asked in a small, scared voice, "*in case something happens?*"

Much more dramatic than I intended, I breathed out, "If I don't… come back."

"WHAT??! You're not going through the Mirror, are you?"

"No, actually I'm not. It's way more intense."

Barb was silent, but her rapid breathing was audible.

"Isis, what kind of craziness are you into now?"

"It just may be the most right thing I've ever done."

"So now you're some kind of Sufi?"

I laughed. "God, Barb. I really love you."

She laughed back. A laugh like the good old days. The days before the Red Mirror.

I tossed and twisted, shaping the down pillows into hundreds of configurations that never satisfied.

Each time I closed my eyes, I saw the General. Bound, gagged, humiliated in a dark cave. His eyes refused to ask me for help. But I saw under the stoic mask.

I woke up terrified and sad.

The landline rang and rang in Las Vegas. Still I wouldn't hang up. Finally, Eben answered. "Hello, Isis."

I doubted he had Caller ID. Eben could barely dial a phone. To answer one seemed a supreme challenge. He knew that I was calling, though. He didn't need electronic wonders for that. Eben the fortune-teller, stuck in his tragic rumpled body, knew what others could not.

Once, he'd seen the nightmare that the past was going to become and insisted I go back and save myself. No wonder he retreated; the pain of Seeing must be unbearable.

"Eben, I want you to look into the future. My future."

"But you don't need me, Isis. You can see yourself. Use what you learned in the Cave of Bats."

I didn't bother to question how Eben knew. Like I said, he has the gift—or curse—of Sight.

"The future is in your hands, Isis. Use your magic."

"Do I have that magic today, Eben? The Hive was so long ago."

"You are everything that you allow yourself to be."

"But am I enough?"

"Look for the Protectors. They are all around you."

I waited. He was silent. Realizing he wasn't going to say more, I said, "Thank you, Eben. You have always helped me."

Then just when I was going to say goodbye, he gushed, "Isis!"

"Yes, Eben. I'm still here."

"You must not forget your destiny. The past is still waiting."

"Do you believe, Eben, that we can truly change what has happened?"

"Sometimes. Not always. *This* past is not written until you play your part. You were trained for it. Lemta trained you."

I couldn't think of anything to say, so said nothing.

"Isis?"

"Yes, Eben?"

"Do not forget the Black Scroll."

CHAPTER 24 MARSAXLOKK

"There is always more spirit in attack than defence." – Livy

Voices echoed. Men's voices. Arabic. Excited guttural sounds rife with anger.

I stepped from the bright sunshine of the ledge into shadow so black I couldn't see the walls or sense how large a chamber.

I clapped my hands, and the ceiling came alive. The whir of thousands of bat wings whooshed madly about my head. My hands over my ears did nothing to dampen the torturous pitch of their squeals.

When the black settled once more into pregnant silence, a light shone from down a long, chiseled corridor. Lemta in her flowing ivory tunic, wild black lion's mane electric around her death-white face, beckoned me with a long nail. Then without warning, a stone door so heavy I couldn't budge it swung open to a bright blue sky.

I sat up. A brilliant Maltese Mediterranean morning filled the frame of the French doors to the balcony. Sunlight streamed across my bed.

Lars answered his cell on the first ring.

"I know where he is, Lars. I just don't know if I can find it again."

No sooner had I set down my phone than Tony called from the storybook land of Princeton.

"I hope you're still up, Isis."

"Still up?" I was confused until I realized that he thought I was in Vegas.

"I just had the most horrific dream, Isis. I never dream. You know that." He paused and then went on in a strained voice utterly unlike him. "But this was *so* real. I had to talk to you. If I didn't, it would come true."

An unsettling admission from rational cosmologist Tony. "You were in a wild place. Rough mountains, not high. Not the kind I climb. Not glaciers. Rocky, dry. Snaking with canyons."

Tony's speech came in the short staccato bursts of a text message or Twitter.

"You needed my help. I couldn't find you. None of the equipment worked."

"What kind of equipment?"

"Tracking devices. GPS. I'm not sure. But involving calculations. Mathematics."

"Maybe it's not a sign of what's going to happen but a sign of how you can help."

"What do you mean, *help?*" Then in a flash of inspiration, he asked, "Where are you?"

"I'm in Malta."

"I'm coming."

"No, Tony. You have to think of Jen. She's already lost her mother. You're all she's got."

"Jesus, Isis. Is it that dangerous?"

"I don't want to talk about it. I don't want to lose my nerve."

We were both quiet. Engines cranking and the babble of voices at the bus terminal drifted up through the open balcony doors. Birds sang.

So many birds here, but not as many as on the Nile where Tony once helped me escape on a Phoenician ship. He didn't remember though. He didn't remember anything from our past lives.

"If I described direction traveled, Tony, and gave you numbers—like so many hours on horseback, could you calculate the miles?"

He calculated distances to far galaxies. A map of Libya should be a snap. If he thought my calculus of hours on horseback odd, he didn't say.

"Could you do one of those 'probable arc' things on a map? I need to zero in on the location of a mountain cave."

Orsini came back from wherever he'd been. He'd bought some new clothes identical to the khaki slacks and black zip jacket he'd worn since the plane.

"It's arranged," he said.

"The boat?"

"Everything."

"I want to see it."

He shrugged as a way of saying yes. I didn't sense resentment. Apparently he'd come to terms with our new roles. Tough as he might be, he was a man accustomed to following orders.

I left a message at the front desk for Rasheed, and the three of us—Lars, Orsini and I—grabbed a taxi. Lars and I in back, with Orsini in the front.

"Marsaxlokk," Orsini told the driver.

We passed through dense neighborhoods of mid-rise Baroque buildings decked out in colorful wrought iron balustrades and shutters. Whole buildings were trimmed in red, others in blue or green. Shops with matching awnings occupied the street level with apartments above.

Traffic thinned, and we drove through patchy land dotted with farmhouses surrounded by stone fences and groves of stubby trees.

Marsaxlokk turned out to be a bustling little fishing port with scores of tourists milling about. A wedding-cake church with a rose tile dome and two bell steeples anchored the square. Along the waterfront ran a promenade lined with fish restaurants. The lunch crowd filled a dozen clumps of tables shaded by umbrellas, each eatery with its own color. Purple, blue, yellow, red and green.

Hundreds of small fishing boats painted bright blue and yellow, or green and red, bobbed in sapphire waters. When you looked closely, you could see that each boat was unique. Wide stripes. Narrow stripes. More blue than yellow. More yellow than blue. Some with kelly green or cherry red gunwales.

Orsini pointed out an old fishing trawler whose paint job had long ago bleached in the Mediterranean sun. On the port side a tarp-covered wooden runabout with peeling paint hung suspended from a pair of davit cranes with rusted booms.

He handed me binoculars. I saw nothing unusual. There was a pile of fishing nets on the working deck.

"Amidships," Orsini said. "RIBs."

"RIBs?"

"Rigid-Inflatable Boats," Lars translated. "Zodiacs. Navy Seals use them." He took the glasses from me. "There. See that stack of black rubber dinghies under the fishing nets?"

Then he asked Orsini, "What kind of power?"

"Two 150 FourStroke Mercuries each." Orsini paused. "They'll do 45 knots in any sea."

"What about the trawler?"

"Hollowed out, gutted. She's got full ballast tanks, so she rides low in port. Once at sea, we'll blow the tanks and pick up speed."

"Power?"

"A pair of 2400 horsepower GE four-stroke V16 turbodiesels."

"Boost?"

"With turbocharger—6000 horsepower combined."

They both looked satisfied—Lars with the boats and Orsini with pretty boy Lars.

"When do we get underway?" I asked.

"Tonight."

"I'll wait until dark to load the supplies," said Lars. "What about lunch?"

When he saw I hesitated, he put his arm around my shoulder and steered me toward the nearest restaurant. "Not eating isn't going to change anything. It'll only cause us to miss a great meal."

And so we settled at a round table covered with red oilcloth and shaded by a red and white umbrella with the logo 'Martini & Rossi.'

Lars knew his way around Maltese cuisine. We started with *Gbejna*, a pungent goat cheese, served with spicy green olives and a crusty loaf of sourdough with a plate of extra virgin olive oil and malt vinegar.

"You must try the local white wine," he insisted, pouring from a carafe, trying to soothe my nerves with alcohol. "A *Ghirgentina* varietal."

I tried my best to enjoy the grilled fresh *lampuki*, Malta's favorite fish, but my stomach churned. Orsini ate stoically and without pleasure.

"Eat, Isis," Lars urged me. "What will happen, will happen. It won't be better if you let your nerves get the best of you. If you're too tense, you'll make mistakes."

I took another bite and dutifully chewed the soft flaky white flesh that tasted and felt like cotton on my tongue.

"Tonight we'll have rabbit. You can't come to Malta without eating *fenek*."

"Maybe we'll have some when we get back from Libya," I said dryly.

"Good girl!" Lars cheered. "That's the spirit."

I wished I could bottle his dauntless optimism and take a swig every hour or so.

Rasheed was there when we got back. If Lars had thought *me* tense, he must have wanted to pour a whole carafe of wine down Rasheed's throat.

The tic in Rasheed's eye spasmed; the muscles in his jaw worked in a kind of controlled seizure. He didn't make a move to kiss me hello. But he was here.

It was the first time ever I'd seen him without his GQ tailored suit—if you don't count naked. He was so gorgeous in jeans and an olive V-necked cotton sweater, all lean muscle, his broad shoulders tapering to a narrow waist and tight thighs, I had to bite my lip to keep from sobbing.

In truth, it wouldn't take much for me to sob. I was barely hanging on; a thousand doubts buzzed in my head. To find the General in the vast expanse of Libya loomed improbable at best. To get him safely out beyond possibility.

Like Elektra, I was bluffing my way through this. So far, it was working. Nobody had called me a fraud. Yet.

Gamel and Marcos were with Rasheed, of course. How many times had they mutely stood by, watching us ride our roller coaster of heartbreak and reconciliation? If they thought I was bad news for their boss before, what did they think now?

The room was unbearably tense. No one looked directly at Rasheed or me. Except Lars.

"*For Satans, mand!*" he cursed in Rasheed's ear. "Can't you *hold* the woman? Do you have any idea what she's been through?"

Maybe it's a good thing Rasheed didn't take me in his arms or kiss me. I might have gone to pieces in front of everyone.

That's when Lars' cell buzzed. Was this the call we were waiting for?

He talked quietly for what seemed like an eternity. No one spoke, all of us trying to make sense of the conversation from what we could hear. "I understand." "Who are they?" "Any word on demands?"

When he hung up, he faced us with the expression of a doctor delivering the worst news to a family. I couldn't breathe. But from his last question, I knew the General wasn't dead.

"He's been taken, with some of his men, by a renegade militia."

"Some?" asked Orsini.

"Men died in a firefight. I don't know how many. I don't know how many wounded."

I gave Orsini a minute to process before asking, "What do you mean by renegade?"

"A gang of Libyan Shield gone rogue."

"Rogue?"

"Under no one's control. Gang stuff. Roadblocks to steal money and cars. Kids driving $100,000 Mercedes kidnapping for ransom. Robbing hospitals of CT scanners and MRIs to sell for pennies on the dollar. Ex-freedom fighters—*Thuwar*—turned thugs."

"So they want money," I said. "How much?"

"It's not that simple, Isis." He paused. "Did you know Cesari was negotiating an arms deal to buy weapons from the Zintani militia for the FSA in Syria?"

Rasheed glared at me. If his eyes had been lasers, I would have been fried.

Neither confirming nor denying, I asked, "Why would a rogue militia gang of kids care about an arms deal? It doesn't make sense."

"Because Cesari wasn't acting alone. He's a middleman for the CIA."

"So this might be political?" I asked.

"It looks like it. It certainly makes him a valuable asset."

"So we can't buy our way out?"

"Doubtful. Word in the underground is that they're looking to do a trade."

"A trade? With whom?"

"Somebody they owe. Islamists is the rumor. Maybe *al-Qaeda* operatives. *Ansar al-Shariah* most likely." He paused. "Maybe ISIS." Then he quickly corrected himself for my sake, I suppose. "ISIL. *Daesh.*"

Islamists sounded scary enough. And *Al-Qaeda*. But Islamic State? I pushed away the image of a massive hunting knife sawing at the General's neck. The irony that he could die by the hand of ISIS wasn't lost on me, but I never cut off his head.

"Time is of the essence," Lars continued. "Wherever he is, he could be moved soon. They might be split up."

Then he said what we were all thinking. "They might eliminate everyone but Cesari. The others are…well, I hate to say it…expendable. Except for dramatic effect. For propaganda. If they end up with ISIL."

I turned to Orsini.

"What did the Zintani say?"

"They'll meet us on the beach when we land."

"*Bene.*" I allowed myself to feel a modicum of faith. At least on our end, events were unfolding according to plan.

"And just *where* do we intend to go from the coast?" Rasheed's tone was acidic, but I took solace in his use of 'we.' He was going. He'd accepted I was.

"I have a lead," I answered in a voice more confident than I felt.

"*You* have a lead?" Rasheed made no attempt to conceal his derision of any source I could have.

"He's being held in the Nafusa Mountains. I'm waiting for more specifics."

Of course, I couldn't say that I'd seen the cave in a dream. No one here would buy that. Oddly, it was Tony, the man of pure science, who came closest to believing the unbelievable.

And then, in yet another of those magical moments when speaking or thinking of someone causes them to manifest, my cell rang, and it was Tony with a map.

"I'm sending it now," he said. "You realize it's not precise. There are too many variables."

There, on a small map on my iPhone screen, was a pie-shaped shaded area south of Tripoli, to the east of a dot called Qawasim. Gharyān looked to be the largest town.

"I've got some friends at NSA," Tony said. "We collaborate on… well—to keep it simple—star wars stuff. Maybe they can help out. Tap into some satellite imaging. Look for unusual activity. Some guys over there owe me a favor."

"Do you think I should have told Tony about the CIA connection?" I asked Rasheed when I got off the phone. "It might help with NASA."

"Not if you want to see Cesari again. They'll want to keep this operation very black."

The rest of the day was spent speaking on cellphones. English, Norwegian, Arabic and Corsu.

Rasheed got on with Orsini to talk to the Zintani, and the conversation switched to Arabic. I could see Orsini was unhappy at this change that locked him out, but I felt good knowing that nothing was being lost in translation.

We broke to meet in Marsaxlokk, agreeing who would ride with whom, not all of us going at one time. To avoid suspicion, we wouldn't check out of the hotel. I told myself that we'd be back in only a day or so.

Lars cleared the room to leave Rasheed and me alone.

The sun had set; light hovered between day and dark. A solitary porcelain lamp with ivory shade burned on the bedside table.

Rasheed stood stiffly in the middle of the room. Stony, like a statue. If I placed my palms on his chest, would I even feel a heartbeat?

"Rasheed," I begged him. "*Please.*"

I put my arms around his neck, molding my body to his.

"Thank you for coming," I whispered.

His left lid twitched like it always did when he struggled for control. Now he struggled to resist giving in to what we both wanted.

I rose on my tiptoes and kissed his lush lips chiseled by a master sculptor. They didn't yield. But I felt him harden against my belly.

I kissed him again, and he grew harder.

Emboldened, my pelvis cleaving to his, I breathed *River God* in his ear.

He drove me to the wall. His fingers tore at my waistband. He dragged at the zipper of my new white jeans and, when it opened, he yanked the jeans and my underpants to my knees.

I clawed at his hair, my fingers digging deep through the thick waves, my tongue down his throat.

His jeans were around his thighs when he shoved my bare hips against the wall. He plunged deep, ramming me, tearing at me as if to inflict maximum pain.

Rasheed, the lover who never hurried, who savored me as one does the finest of wines, pounded and pounded with black savagery. The painting on the wall banged and banged.

His mouth was cruel without a trace of tenderness; I tasted the salt of my own blood. Swept up in his fury, I dug my nails into his shoulders, tearing my lips away to bite him in the neck. And when my teeth sunk in, I was suddenly transported to the General's Persian tent.

Without warning, Rasheed's hand was around my throat. I locked eyes with him and saw hunger for revenge wrapped in raw rage. I tried to tear his hand away, but he held me in a vise. I beat at him with my fists.

He morphed into Major Domo, then into the General, and finally back to a Rasheed I didn't know.

He squeezed tighter and tighter until I couldn't take a breath.

My mind shouted, *Strangle me now. You broke my heart. Finish the job.*

Then he shook all over in one massive shudder and collapsed on me in a series of spasms, finally releasing my throat. I gagged and sucked in air.

His forehead pressed on the wall next to my head, his forearm on the other side. We were both spent; his chest heaved.

"Is that what you want, Isis?" he breathed in my ear. "Is that what Cesari taught you?"

He tugged up his jeans; I slid down the wall, shattered. He stood there for a moment, looking down on me. So many emotions in his face. Triumph. Resentment. Disappointment. Disgust.

"Don't hate me, Rasheed. I am nothing without you."

He didn't answer but went out the door, never looking back. Was it me he crushed, or the General?

Night fell. I walked about the room in a trance, pulling on my battle gear—jeans, tank top, long-sleeved man's shirt, photographer's vest with a dozen pockets, windbreaker, cotton head scarf and desert boots.

In my backpack I stuffed the Aussie hat along with my passport, a thick wad of dollars, detailed maps of Libya, Swiss Army knife, sunglasses, toiletries, satellite phone, my cell, flashlight, rope, two liters of water, three bags of trail mix, a bottle of aspirin and some Band-Aids.

My Glock with three boxes of ammo was within easy reach in the exterior pouch. A short time ago, I'd known only how to shoot a gun. Tonight I knew too much about them—size, composite materials, fire power, reliability. Although he'd never admit it, even Orsini was impressed with how fast I'd learned.

I wrapped the Hathor Ring carefully in an emerald green Hermes scarf and put it at the very bottom of an inside zipper compartment.

Touching the ring gave me strength.

I stood for a moment in the open door, looking around the luxurious room with the sweeping view of the harbor, seeing the ghost of Rasheed defile me. My new white jeans and top hung in the closet.

We'll be back, I told myself as I switched off the lights. *We'll all be back.*

We still hadn't tried the rabbit.

CHAPTER 25   NAFUSA

"How often things occur by mere chance which we dared not even hope for."
– Sallust

A white light blinked onshore. One long and three short. Orsini signaled back to the Zintani.

The sea was black, the shore blacker. A few lights twinkled up and down the coast. The glow of Tripoli was to the west, to starboard.

In what seemed like deafening splashes, the Zodiacs hit the water. We climbed over the gunwale and down rope ladders.

The new band of Corsicans, identical in dark jackets over broad, bull chests, climbed into three of the RIBs. Rasheed, Lars, Gamel, Marcos, Orsini and I piled into the fourth. A fifth Zodiac, empty, was lashed to ours.

With a roar that I thought would wake all Libya, eight Mercury outboards cranked in, and we sped toward the beach. Ashore, parking lights flashed—once, twice—and then all was black again.

A few hundred feet from the surf, I made out a rocky cove with a slight rise where a dark gaggle of trucks waited. A narrow strip of sand glowed white in the starlight. There was no moon.

I first saw the red embers of their cigarettes. About forty Zintanis. They were surprisingly disciplined. No waving of guns, no shouts in Arabic, no laughing or V signs. All business tonight.

The Corsicans quickly dragged the Zodiacs ashore and camouflaged them with nets and seaweed. Two of them would stay with the RIBs;

they scouted the area while the rest of us gathered our gear.

My cell buzzed. It was Tony.

"I'm sending some coordinates, Isis. Nothing certain, you understand. But there's been some unusual traffic in a place where there are no real roads."

32.1836111 / 32° 11' 0.999 North

13.0566667 / 13° 3' 24.0006 East

The GPS map displayed a canyon east of Qawasim near Ghāryan.

Orsini and Rasheed showed the location to the Zintani in charge. I couldn't make out his features in the dark except for a hard face and steely eyes. If he had been at the villa with blue shutters, I didn't recognize him.

There was some rapid-fire, back-and-forth Arabic. Rasheed translated for Orsini, who was nodding his head in satisfaction.

I moved closer to hear. The Zintani leader looked at me and growled in Arabic. I thought I heard something like *neesa*. Rasheed answered him. There was some arguing. More men gathered around.

They all had an opinion and voiced it, waving their hands, looking often in my direction. They didn't want me here. A woman.

The Corsicans had assault rifles slung on their shoulders. I didn't recognize what kind. No doubt, machine pistols were strapped under their jackets. The Zintani militia was armed with the same array of Kalashnikovs and RPGs as the day I'd flown into Tripoli with the General.

I stepped forward toward the leader and Rasheed.

"*As salaam aleikum,*" I said.

A few disgruntled *aleikum as-salaam*s answered me.

"*Ismee Isis.*"

"Isis!" a voice called out, and then another and another. There *were* some men here from the afternoon of target practice. Their recognition of me sparked more back-and-forth debate.

"*Yallah,*" I called out to them in an insistent tone. I couldn't come up with anything better. I knew it had something to do with 'Let's go.'

I didn't know how to say in Arabic, 'I'm going, and that's that.'

Rasheed stepped next to me. My vision had adjusted to the starlight enough to see the surprise on his face.

"*Shouf.*" I pointed to my eyes with two fingers and then to my backpack.

Cautiously, I took out my Glock and held it up. The group stirred.

I emptied the chamber with an expert forward and back slide on the barrel and removed the full clip from the grip. In a flash, I produced another loaded magazine, and using the palm of my hand, shoved the new clip into the grip with a dramatic snap of the catch spring.

The charade didn't demonstrate much except that I knew how to handle my weapon, a mere toy compared to their M-16s and AK-47s. But they watched, and were—I gathered by their silence—impressed.

There was more discussion. Rasheed's voice was firm. And then, quite suddenly, the Zintani leader grunted what must have been agreement, because everyone started mounting the pickup trucks.

"*Allu al akbar*," I said not knowing how else to express my relief.

Not a few faces around me broke into smiles.

Orsini and Rasheed reported that the Zintani were familiar with the area on the map and that the hills there were pockmarked with caves and marbled with canyons.

No Mercedes tonight. Only a fleet of Toyota Grand Tigers, all fully equipped with steel frames and mounted machine guns. Orsini insisted on riding with me, and we crammed into the cab of a pickup. Wooden prayer beads, these with a red tassel, dangled from the rearview mirror. Three Corsicans piled into the bed with a handful of militia.

Rasheed went in a four-door cab with the Zintani leader. I heard someone call him Ahmed. Gamel took the jump seat. Lars climbed into a third truck with Marcos, and we pulled away from the beach and down a dirt road, our tires crunching on the gravel. They didn't use their headlights.

The dirt road gave onto a paved highway of sorts, but we quickly turned off. We kept to minor roads, passing through lightly populated areas with dark houses and small open spaces.

Our driver kept his eyes on the road. Orsini followed our route on the GPS. His eyes scanned the roadside, going between the greenish screen and the black world passing by our speeding truck. He kept in constant contact by cell with Rasheed.

The lights of the airport were first to the east and then north of us.

Eventually we joined a well-paved, two-lane highway heading south. The signs were all in Arabic, but I could see from my map that we were on the Ghāyran Road that connected Tripoli to Aziziyah and then to Qawasim.

We made good progress, eons faster that on horseback, and before long we were coming off the flat plain into terraced rocky hills planted with dark shapes that might be olive trees.

I kept expecting the notorious checkpoint where we'd do battle with a rival militia, but we breezed through unhindered. The Zintani lived up to their reputation. No one challenged our descent south to the Nafusa Mountains.

The road began to wind as the elevation increased. We snaked our way higher and higher before cresting a summit and dropping to a plateau with low mountains on each side. The highway ran straight again. We didn't stay on it long but turned toward the east on a gravelly track ending abruptly at a steep hillside.

The trucks slammed to a halt in a cloud of dust, and everyone piled out of the cabs.

I went immediately to Rasheed's side. He was my lifeline; he could speak Arabic.

"Why have we stopped?"

"The road from here is rough."

After what I'd experienced so far, I took seriously that it wouldn't be easy going.

Lars and Rasheed looked at each other and then at me.

"How sure are you about the tip?" Lars asked.

"This is it," I answered, never more certain of anything. "Trust me."

Rasheed stared hard at me. Not in suspicion. Not in anger. Not with any emotion at all. I met his eyes. Both of us were totally in the moment. And in that moment, I saw that he decided to trust me. To believe in me. Maybe for the first time.

We drove too fast on a narrow ledge that barely passed for a road. The sound of crunching and flying gravel must have traveled miles in the night silence of the hills. Even in the shadowy darkness of starlight, clouds of white dust rose in the air.

We're going to alert them, I kept thinking. They're going to know we're coming.

I dug the Hathor Ring out of my backpack and put it on my finger. *ANA A A NANA A A NANA.*

I must have been chanting under my breath because both Orsini and the driver turned to look at me. I kept my eyes straight ahead and concentrated on breathing slowly. Inhale. Exhale. Inhale. Exhale. The palms of my hands were wet with sweat.

We rounded a curve, and I saw the canyon. There was absolutely no doubt in my mind. The scene was as clear as if I'd been here yesterday.

"Stop!" I shouted. "Stop!"

Our driver stepped hard on the brakes, and I braced myself for the slam of a truck into our rear that didn't come. The lead pickup in front of us continued a few yards before stopping.

"It's here," I told Orsini.

I think he started to ask me how I knew, but instead, he opened the truck door and stepped out.

"It's down the canyon, not far. But the cave is high up. If they have sentries, they'll see us coming."

Ahmed, the Zintani leader, listened carefully. Rasheed started to translate, but he held up his palm impatiently to say he understood.

There was the usual rapid back-and-forth in Arabic among the Zintani militia, with a lot of waving of hands and some arguing.

Rasheed interpreted, "These two are from Qawasim. They're sure they know which cave this is and that it can't be approached from below without being seen. We have to come in from above."

I closed my eyes and brought into focus the day I'd arrived with Desert Man. I recalled in every minute detail the mountain face with the cave's gaping mouth.

"The ascent is exposed. Narrow and steep." I heard myself describing the terrain out loud, still with my eyes closed. "But just before, there is another path leading up the side of the face. It disappears out of sight. Maybe around to the back."

I was aware of Rasheed translating rapidly to Arabic.

Frustrated, I opened my eyes. "I don't know where it goes for sure. I can't see beyond the front."

They all stared at me. The Libyans. Rasheed. Lars. Orsini. The two locals were nodding their heads.

"We go on foot from here," I told them. "I'll know the path when I see it."

We hurried along the side of the canyon, a silent stream of sneakers crunching softly on rocks.

The Zintani had switched to another mode. They were hushed and moved with stealth. It was easy to forget when looking at their young faces absorbed by cellphones, that against all odds, they'd won a war in these mountains. In the beginning, they fought with knives and antique hunting rifles. Until they could liberate weapons and tanks from Gaddafi's soldiers.

Thuwar. "Rebels," the West called them. "Freedom Fighters," they called themselves. Tonight, to me, they were saviors.

Then several hundred yards ahead, precisely as I'd seen in my memory, the mouth of the cave yawned halfway up the hillside. In the narrow canyon at the base of the mountain parked three dusty, but new-looking, dark Mercedes sedans and a dozen or more white pickup trucks indistinguishable from ours.

The desert mountains are surprisingly bright by starlight. A moon would have made the white rocks shimmer, yet still it was easy to see the trail hugging the underside of the ridge. Just as in my vision, the path climbed the craggy outcrop and disappeared behind boulders.

Using a pair of night binoculars, Rasheed checked out the vehicles and then the ledge.

"I don't see anyone standing guard. They feel safe. They're not smart."

"You should wait here, Isis," said Lars.

Orsini and Rasheed clearly agreed. I had the sense they'd decided this, maybe even before we left Malta.

"No. I'm going with you." My tone said this was non-negotiable. "The cave is a maze on the inside. There are many rooms. Only I know the layout."

They exchanged glances; no one asked how I knew.

Rasheed said a few words in Arabic. Ahmed pointed in two directions, and a group of *Thuwar* melted into the landscape to wait in ambush for any who tried to escape.

Orsini said something in Corsu, and three of the Corsicans, assault rifles ready, took cover not far from the foot of the path leading up to the ledge.

The rest of us set off single-file, a line of dark silhouettes creeping up the mountainside. We were halfway up, on the same level as the ledge outside the cave's entrance, when I stumbled and fell on my face.

Damn! Now they'll insist I stay behind.

When Orsini reached to haul me to my feet, I pulled away my arm and put my palms down to push myself up.

Just by my right hand, the one with the Hathor Ring, was a stone too rounded and smooth to be natural. There was a figure of some kind on the surface, but I couldn't make out what it was.

I reached into my knapsack and pulled out the flashlight. Covering the head with the green scarf to soften the light, I shone the beam on the stone. Deep grooves filled with sand and dirt formed a septagram.

I showed the carving to Orsini and then Lars. They blinked and looked back to me.

Yes, I nodded. *A septagram. Like your medallion. Like your cufflinks.*

Rasheed knew nothing about the septagrams and didn't get the connection, but he understood that the glyph had to be significant. He took the flashlight from me and shined the eerie green light on the rock face next to where I fell. I could just make out a shallow depression, maybe five feet high and three feet wide.

Rasheed scraped away some dirt along one edge with his fingers, and a crack appeared. Perfectly straight and marred by chisel marks. Definitely man-made.

I touched his hand, and he met my eyes. Silently I motioned for him to take my Swiss Army knife and for me to hold the flashlight. Then his focus was back on the rock wall.

Slowly, quietly, with the controlled touch of Rasheed the lover, he used the blade to dig out more dirt from the cracks. After a few moments, we could clearly see the outline of a door. With the palm of his hand, he brushed away the dust of centuries.

At the bottom of the slab, at the right edge, was a substantial knob large as a cat's head. When Rasheed took hold, rusty bits of metal flaked off in his hand. We all held our breath when he tugged.

The stone door creaked outward an inch. Then an inch more. And then another until the opening was about a foot wide.

Orsini moved past me to go in.

"I'm the smallest," I whispered.

On my hands and knees, I crawled through the narrow gap into the pitch-black stillness of a tomb. Dry brush growing at the threshold caught my cotton head scarf and pulled it down.

The ground was dry and crusty. Small stones dug into my palms. My skin crawled at the memory of the guano-covered cave floor, but I kept going. A spider web brushed my cheek. I imagined I heard the squeal of a rabid bat. The air was musty, stale, centuries old.

When I was all the way in, I sat up on my haunches and shined the flashlight around the room. The workshop where acolytes ground powders to make potions. Broken urns and decayed wooden tables cast haunting shadows on greenish walls.

"You can stand," I whispered, shoving the door further open with my shoulder. "You can easily stand."

Rasheed, Orsini and Lars squeezed through, and then Gamel and Marcos came in with the Zintani leader.

In the lurid green light, our faces were those of ghouls.

"That door," I whispered, pointing with the flashlight, "is to a corridor leading to the entrance. There might be more rooms, but I haven't seen them. We should send some men down there."

No one asked how I knew. I could only imagine what they thought.

Ancient hinges creaked, and then the wood door opened suddenly. Only black on the other side. The Zintani leader then stepped over to the stone door and shoved it wide open, hissing, *"Yallah! Yallah!"*

A dozen *Thuwar* streamed in.

"Bats," I warned as they headed down the passageway.

Following the Libyans came the Corsicans with their musky sweat of hard men pumped on adrenaline.

"Beyond *that* door are more workshops, a bathing chamber and a kitchen with storerooms."

I switched off the flashlight. No light shone around the cracks in the door.

"And after the kitchen is the Sacred Hive," I whispered into the dark.

When I switched on the light again, the spooked faces around me were startled green masks with wide black holes for eyes.

"From the Hive," I explained in a hushed voice, "double doors open into a straight passage ending at the chamber of bats and the mouth of the cave."

"Are you a witch?" whispered Ahmed.

If he believed that, then I'd no longer be just a woman.

"I trained here," I told him in my best vibrating voice.

Then I opened the door to the next round of rooms.

"Yallah!" Let's go.

CHAPTER 26   REVENGE

"There is hardly a case in which the dispute was not caused by a woman."
– Horace

The adjacent chamber was empty. And the next. On our right, the door to the bath chamber hung open at an angle. Orsini stepped in and out again, shaking his head. By now, he had out his own flashlight. Rasheed had mine.

The kitchen looked much as I'd last seen it. No fire burned in the pit; a copper pot rested on the ancient ashes. There was a faint sweetish, herbal scent in the stale air. Hashish, mixed with black tobacco and the acrid stench of urine.

The door at the far end, the one to the Hive, was closed. Tinny Arabic music—not likely a radio, more likely a CD—wailed through the thick wooden panel. Shouts were followed by raucous laughter. A party.

I took the Glock out of my waistband.

The doors of the storage rooms stretched along the right wall. I wondered for a millisecond if the caged spiders, rats and snakes still lived.

Ahmed crowded next to me; I sensed tension in him but no fear. He'd been through his share of battles in tight places—and plenty of ambushes.

Gracefully, silently, Rasheed stepped to a closed storeroom door and nodded to Marcos and then Orsini. As though they had rehearsed a dozen times, they opened the three nearest doors at the same moment and stepped quickly in, weapons drawn.

They came out and shook their heads once. No one there.

We all heard the moan and reacted as one, stiffening, focusing our collective attention on the last two storage rooms. The doors stood open.

I suddenly had to pee. The pressure on my bladder was so intense, I was sure I couldn't hold it.

No! It's nerves. It's all in your head.

"ANA A A NANA A A NANA," I chanted stubbornly. *You are not going to wet your pants.*

Lars took hold of my upper arm. His eyes asked, "Are you OK?"

I nodded. *Yes, I'm fine.*

Orsini went through the first open door. He came out again, holding up five fingers. His face registered cold, controlled rage.

I stepped through the doorway into the dark with Ahmed right behind me. His flashlight shone on four Corsicans blindfolded, bound and gagged. A fifth lay on the stone floor holding his intestines. The cell reeked of blood, urine and feces.

Ahmed took out a knife with a long dangerous blade and cut the blindfolds. The Corsicans' eyes went wide in shock when they saw me.

I felt a tap on my shoulder and turned to Lars, who gestured for me to step out of the cramped cubicle. He went straight to the groaning man, sank to his haunches and examined the wound. In a comforting gesture, he put his hand on the man's forehead and leaned into his face, muttering what I guessed were reassuring words. Maybe, *Hang in there.*

But when Lars looked up at me, he shook his head.

It was then that I noticed the young kid who slumped against the kitchen wall a few steps away. He appeared asleep when I first saw him. At any rate, he didn't move or react until I touched Orsini's arm and tilted my head in his direction.

The boy sat up straight, so close that I could make out the whites of his eyes even in a room lit only by a couple of dimmed flashlights. He had the most terrified look when he saw me and then the men. He opened his mouth to shout a warning, but the sound that came out was a gurgle.

So quickly that my mind hadn't registered, Orsini had moved across the room and slit the boy's throat. A gaping gash from ear to ear spewed bright blood.

I thought it took forever for the boy to die. I found myself counting to keep calm.

"One, two, three, four…" I reached twenty before the teenager was still.

Sorry, kid. Bad choice. Wrong hostage.

Blindfolded and gagged, the General sat propped against the wall of the last storeroom, the one nearest the Hive door. Clay jars stood in cobwebby niches, the dust of centuries masking neat labels with faded Phoenician letters.

The General's hands were bound behind his back; his stretched-out legs were bound tight at the ankles with plastic zip ties.

He was alert, body tense, taking in every sound.

A man slumped beside him, his head hanging lifelessly to his chest, longish hair covering his face. The front of his jacket was wet; black pooled on the ground around his body. Loyal Moe had bled out next to his beloved Cesari.

Orsini whispered in Corsu. The General grunted. I knelt in front of him. He stank of urine. The kids hadn't allowed their hostages the dignity of a toilet.

Without a word, I untied the blindfold while Orsini cut his hands free.

My face was just inches from the General's when the cloth fell away. His head jerked back in shock.

"Hello, General," I whispered. And then breaking my rule of never bringing up our past lives, I teased, "Now we're even—Cave of Bats for the Tomb of the Crocodile."

Instead of the gratitude I expected, I saw a momentary flash of humiliation that exploded into cold fury.

"Give me a gun, Orsini," he growled.

He was on his feet. The two other Corsicans, bound and gagged when we entered, were on their feet. From out of nowhere, they gripped compact submachine guns in their massive paws.

The General glared at something behind me, and I turned my head. Rasheed.

"Get her out of here, Bayoumi," the General snarled.

"And let you take all the glory?" Rasheed took my arm and handed me over to Lars. "Take her outside. Get her back to the vehicles."

"No! I'm not leaving until everyone is out."

Lars pulled me into him and whispered urgently in my ear, "You don't want to see this, Isis. I'm not going to let you see it."

So I stood by as the Corsicans gathered without a sound, checking their weapons with a practiced silence. Magazines slid into place with steely finality.

A couple of the men held what Orsini called MP-40s—lethal hybrids of machine and hand gun he'd acquired in Malta. Orsini himself carried a Tropov with both burst and single-shot firing mode. I recognized it by the cylinder magazine mounted along the bottom of the barrel.

Music still blared on the other side of the door; the unsuspecting kidnappers hadn't heard anything, hadn't the haziest idea that death waited only seconds away.

A handful of the Zintani militia armed with Kalashnikovs crowded into the kitchen to join the fight, but in the secret silent body language of men, the General made it clear they weren't welcome. This was going to be a Corsican job.

Except for Rasheed.

With eyes fixed on the General, he stepped to within a few feet from the closed door. Flashlight beams sharpened his cheekbones; in the dim light, his hair was shiny as a raven's wing. Gamel and Marcos pushed their way through the Corsicans to stand behind him.

I couldn't believe what was happening. Rasheed and the General faced off like two ham actors in a B movie. I felt Rasheed's heat and the General's ice. I read their thoughts, too, both accusing the other, *You brought her here.*

In his right hand Rasheed held a dull black Glock 18 mounted on a frame shoulder stock. The General was armed with one of the Steyr machine pistols from the black market in Malta. The weapons were still lowered, but in a terrible nightmare vision, I saw them both firing.

Are they going to kill *each other* after all this?

"STOP!" I hissed sharply. "Stop now!"

My voice breaking the utter stillness jolted them both back from whatever crazy place they'd gone to.

Rasheed blinked once, then twice; I could make out the slightest loosening in the knotted muscle of his jaw. And when the General saw the shift in Rasheed's expression, his finger on the trigger relaxed.

The tension all around stepped down a notch, but not enough for Marcos and Gamel to take their eyes off the General, or Orsini his eyes off them.

"Do what you have to do," I ordered in a whisper. "Then let's get out of here."

Lars was pulling me away when the General flung open the door to the Hive, and the shooting began.

The sounds of battle are indeed very different from the *ra-ta-tat ra-ta-tat* of target practice.

Bursts of gunfire exploded. Piercing blasts ricocheted off walls to ceilings and floor. My ears rang. Death echoed again and again. It was impossible to pinpoint where the gunshots came from; I heard automatic fire from everywhere at once.

Lars got me outside and propelled me down the path; I didn't resist. We were halfway down the hillside when the gunfire stopped.

The mountain was quiet. The night was quiet. A bird sang; I didn't recognize its call. The first hint of day lightened the horizon.

Then came single shots. Methodical. One after another. The sounds of execution. No survivors. Just as Orsini had promised.

Whatever they do to him, they are dead men now.

I never got to see the Sacred Hive again. I never saw if the glyphs still glowed after twenty centuries. Lars wouldn't allow me to go back up the ascent, through the chamber of bats and down the long straight corridor to the double wooden doors scored with septagrams.

I never stood quietly under the pointed dome to summon the ghosts of Lemta, the Maiden and Dido.

What did their spirits make of the blood and death? Did they feel my presence? Did they know that I'd returned?

While I watched, the Corsicans made their descent down the main trail, the one I'd climbed up in my bare, slashed feet the first day, and the one I descended with Nemo on the last.

They carried two bodies. Moe, whose real name I never knew, and the brother-in-arms who died holding his intestines in place.

The General led the way, followed by Orsini. Their faces were grim; they hadn't enjoyed the slaughter. For that, I felt relief.

I didn't know I'd been holding my breath until Rasheed stepped unscathed out of the cave and onto the ledge with Marcos and Gamel. He looked around until he found me looking up at him.

"Goodbye, Lemta," I whispered. "Forgive the desecration."

Goodbye, Cave of Bats. Hello, Cave of Bones.

CHAPTER 27 ULTIMATUM

"No blessing lasts forever." – Titus Maccius Plautus

It turned out that the keys were in the ignition of most of the vehicles and all three Mercedes. That's how confident the kids had been of their seclusion.

"I think you'll understand if we don't ride together," the General apologized. "I fear I'm in need of a shower."

He opened the car door for me, and I slid onto the back seat.

"Tell me," he asked, leaning down to face me. "What must we do with Orsini? He disobeyed my orders. You should be in Las Vegas right now."

"I think you should give him a medal."

"And that, my dear Ishtar," he said with an amused shine to his eyes, "is the reason you're not ready to be the boss."

But I knew he could never harm Orsini. He'd given him a septagram.

Rasheed opened the door on the other side and climbed in the back with me. Marcos took the front passenger seat, and Gamel the wheel.

The General leaned further down to meet Rasheed's eyes, but only for split second before he put his fingers under my chin and tilted my face up to his.

"You never fail to surprise me. What a delight you are."

Then leaving me with a glowering Rasheed, he shut the car door.

Two seconds later, Lars opened it.

"One of the Mercedes won't start. I refuse to risk my life in another pickup with a kamikaze driver. I'm lucky—we're all lucky—not to be dead on the side of the road."

I scooted to the middle of the seat to make room for Lars. Rasheed's thigh burned against mine. I wanted to scream at him, *Hold my hand for Christ's sake!*

I didn't have the guts to take his. He put his hands behind his head and stretched, closing his eyes, his knees spread wide open. What would he do if I grabbed his cock?

For an instant, Gamel's eyes caught mine in the rearview mirror. He looked away quickly, hiding whatever thoughts he had of me.

Motors started, engines revved, and we set off. The Mercedes carrying the General followed directly behind us. Behind the General came the caravan of newly acquired trucks.

We drove past the Toyotas we'd left when we set out on foot. A few of the *Thuwar* were already there, gesturing with wild animation, no doubt describing a gun battle they hadn't seen. They didn't appear sad—and certainly not angry—that some of their fellow countrymen had died in the cave.

They grinned, honked and gave us the V sign. *"Allu al akbar!"*

After the slaughter in the cave, I couldn't share their euphoria. I felt slightly nauseated. The sounds of killing still ricocheted in my head. All this death, for what?

Lars, not Rasheed, took my hand and smiled at me reassuringly. I closed my eyes and tried to sleep.

We weren't long on the road when Rasheed's cell buzzed.

After a few words in Arabic, he told Gamel, "Airport."

"Airport?" I asked. "What about the trawler?"

"Wouldn't you rather fly out of here?"

The sun came up, and the day turned instantly torrid. Marcos switched on the air conditioner; warm air streamed from the vents. Rasheed's thigh touching mine was a furnace. Wedged between Lars and him, I burned hot as the sun.

Our car was in the lead, so Gamel controlled the pace. Fast, but not the heart-in-your-mouth-every-second kind of fast.

We met a number of trucks and cars on Ghāryan Road. Heads turned as we sped past, but they didn't look particularly alarmed at a caravan of armed militia.

I wasn't aware that I dozed off until the Mercedes stopped and we were back at the hangers in Tripoli International Airport. The General's jet with the ramp in place for us to board stood on the tarmac where we'd left it. The pilot walked around the fuselage, performing his checks.

"Good work on the jet," the General grudgingly admitted to Rasheed at the bottom of the steps.

Ignoring him, Rasheed turned to me and said, "*Yallah.*"

If I hadn't been standing so close, I wouldn't have noticed the shadow pass over the General's face at Rasheed's use of Arabic and the intimacy it implied. As for me, that simple command *Yallah* gave me hope that Rasheed might yet forgive the Lie.

We boarded, Rasheed launching me up the steps with his burning palm on the small of my back. I turned at the top of the ramp to take a last look at Libya.

Waving weapons and grinning, a cluster of kids shouted, "*Ma'a as-salaama*, Isis!"

"*Ma'a as-salaama*," I shouted back. "*Allu al-akbar!*"

They were lions, brave and full of spirit, but the guns were all wrong. Dead wrong.

I slept on the plane and woke as we landed in Paris. The General was talking quietly with Orsini but came over when he saw I stirred. He smelled of soap and a faint hint of aftershave. He'd changed into fresh clothes. His hair was wet. It had never occurred to me that one could shower on a plane.

"I booked you a flight, Ishtar. You'll forgive me for not taking you back to Las Vegas, but we've got some unfinished business, do we not? If you have no objection, I think I'll wrap this contract up on my own."

He had a most pleasant expression on his face. You'd never suspect what he'd been through only hours ago.

I reached out and touched his rough cheek with my fingertips. "I'm happy you're safe."

"You shouldn't have come," he said sternly.

"Nothing could have stopped me."

"Careful, Ishtar." He raised an eyebrow. "I'm easily encouraged."

Rasheed, Lars, Gamel and Marcos deplaned just ahead of me. I hung back to thank Orsini.

Just as I was about to exit to the platform, the General blocked my way. I took a step backward and bumped into the airlock frame. His fingertips grazed the bare skin in the V of my shirt. Then he curled his thick fingers and thumb around the base of my throat, holding me firmly, but not forcibly, in his grip.

My heart raced; my pulse must have been through the roof. I didn't want to look at him but did.

His face was so close. Tiny red capillaries laced the whites of his eyes. He had that knowing look, the one that stripped me of all pretense. *The ride on a comet, Ishtar. Who else can take you there?*

"I have men at your building, Ishtar. Be careful. Don't forget what happened before we left."

He glanced significantly at Rasheed nearly down the steps.

"He can't keep you safe, no matter what he thinks. No matter what you think."

His lips were inches from mine; I was afraid he was going to kiss me and terrified Rasheed would turn and see.

"Did you use the Emerald Tablet?" he whispered. "Is that how you pulled this off?"

"I have my own magic, General," I managed to say levelly. "It works rather well, wouldn't you agree?"

He dropped his hand, but his sly smile told me I could keep nothing from him.

On the tarmac, a white airport van with the Charles de Gaulle logo on the door waited to whisk us away to the terminals. I looked back when we drove off. The General still watched from the top of the ramp.

Lars was going straight to Copenhagen on a SAS flight he could just make.

"I need a cold beer and some herrings."

He gave me a huge hug and a kiss on both cheeks.

"We'll have that rabbit dinner one day. Promise!"

I grabbed a change of clothes in a shop in the transit area and cleaned up in *La Premiere*, Air France's first class lounge. When I came out of the ladies' room, Rasheed lounged in a leather chair, speaking in a low voice on his cell. Gamel and Marcos sat a few yards away. Their eyes followed me while I crossed the room and took the seat on Rasheed's right.

When he finished his call, I reached over and touched his cheek.

"I don't have to take this flight, Rasheed."

"Yes, Isis, you do."

His cell buzzed again. *"Na'am."* Then he started rumbling in Arabic.

I glared hard at Gamel and Marcos who had the decency to go over to the bar.

Rudely and cruelly, Rasheed talked for what seemed forever.

The instant he cut the connection, I demanded, "Why are you so jealous of Cesari? If I wanted *him*, don't you think I'd be with him?"

"I won't share," he said simply.

"We agreed, Rasheed. Remember? No questions."

"Not Cesari."

"It's *business*, Rasheed. I make a lot of money with him. I'm going to make a lot more."

"You lied to me," he accused.

"What about you?" I shot back.

"I have never lied to you," he said with a look of surprise. "I don't tell you everything because I need to protect you—and me. It's not the same."

I could have said that I never lied either. That I always told him the truth, just not all of it. But I didn't because we both knew my intent.

He walked me to the gate, but we didn't talk.

"When will I see you again?" I asked.

He took my face in his hands, studied my eyes, my nose, my mouth, memorizing each feature. He lifted a strand of my hair and held it up to the light. Then he gave me a River God kiss of tender, yearning lips that sucked my soul right into his.

"Get rid of Cesari, Isis. It's up to you. It's all up to you."

I watched him walk away, further and further down the concourse.

An Air France attendant at my elbow said, "First class passengers may board now, Mademoiselle."

When I looked back, Rasheed was gone. I'm certain he never looked back for me.

I was just about to switch off my phone when it buzzed.

"Yes?"

"Isis, this is Eben."

I started to ask how he got my cell number, but it wasn't really important. Maybe he just knew. Like he knew so many things that no one else could see.

"Hello, Eben. How are you?"

"I'm waiting for you."

"I'll be back tomorrow, Eben. We can meet then."

"No, Isis," he whispered in that raspy, hoarse voice of his. "I'm not talking about *here*. *There*."

"What do you mean, *there*?"

"Egypt, Isis. You must go. There is not much time."

"I can't do that, Eben. You don't know what I've been through." I meant Libya as much in the past as now.

"You are afraid, but you need not fear."

I waited for him to say more, to further convince me, but he was silent. I wondered if we still had a connection.

The stewardess walked by and signaled for me to shut off my phone.

"I've got to go, Eben," I said hurriedly.

"Yes, Isis. You've got to go. Everything depends on it."

The stewardess stood impatiently by, glaring just a little. First class passenger or not, the phone had to be off.

"Goodbye, Eben. I'll talk to you when I land."

"No, Isis!" His tone was urgent, almost desperate. "You'll talk to me in Egypt. I'm waiting for you. Without you, all is lost."

A flute of champagne was in my hand. The great double-decker Airbus 380 lumbered down the runway. The nose lifted, the wheels came up, and we were airborne.

Once Eben pleaded, *Go back, Isis. Go back and save yourself!*

I'd gone back, terrified as I was, and saved not only Isis, but also the Emerald Tablet.

Was he now begging me to save him?

I closed my eyes, suddenly so weary I could scarcely hold my head up. *ABLAMGOUNOTHO ABRASAX.*

Bats flew at my face, and when I brushed them away, I brushed away the dark, and the sky was blue, blue, blue all around me.

PART TWO
EGYPT

CHAPTER 28 CANOPUS

"Alas, I think I am becoming a god." – Vespasian

Pipes trilled. A lyre strummed. I opened my eyes to filmy curtains and filtered sunlight sparkling on still green waters. Through the sheer cloth of my white linen gown, I felt the soft fur of the divan. Sweet jasmine and musky *myrrh* hung in the breathless air.

Egypt. There was no mistaking that intoxicating, mesmerizing scent or the languid, sultry press on my skin.

I was on a barge, but not on the Nile. No current rushed past the cedar hull. Lush with trees in full bloom, the nearby bank appeared so close, I thought I could reach out and pluck a flower.

A canal. Canopus. It all came to me in a sudden rush with only a breath of separation between her thoughts and mine. First we were two. Then we were one.

I recognized at once the rich Persian carpets and massive cobalt-glazed urns overflowing with lacy papyrus. I knew the songbirds warbling from silver cages. Even the tall gilded cobra rising at the prow and the four golden cobras holding the yellow and white striped awning were exactly as in my dream. The dream of the Hive.

No rubber arms reached out for me, though. I held no Black Scroll. *Oh, Eben. I came back for you. You better be right that I have nothing to fear.*

A sloppy kiss on my right foot jolted me. Next to my feet, on all fours like a dog, cowered one of those fleshy little Romans whose too rich life shows in their loose jowls and bulbous noses. He had the most extraordinary ears that poked straight out from his head. Limp strands of gray hair clumped on his sweaty forehead.

A leather collar around his pig neck was attached to a silver chain I used to drag him closer.

"You are forbidden to touch me!"

Whack! I smacked him on his bald spot with a gold-tipped ebony rod identical to Domina's. So similar to Major Domo's. Not enough to cause real harm, but enough to cause pain.

He yelped and tried to pull back. Twisting the chain around my wrist, I tugged tighter and tighter until his thick lips opened and closed like a fish out of water gasping for air. When I saw he was truly choking, I slackened my grip.

"Now I shall have to punish you. Show me your ass."

Whimpering and sniveling, he backed his rear toward me.

I snapped my fingers, and a tall Nubian in a white kilt, yellow-striped headdress and green leather sandals handed me a whip of knotted black silk cords. His identical twin, right down to the scars on his cheeks and matching headdress and sandals, lifted the Roman's toga to expose bare, pasty flesh.

I struck with the whip. He mewled like a forlorn kitten. I hit him again with twice the force, and he urinated on the deck.

"Next time you wear a diaper."

With the third lash, delivered without mercy, his tiny engorged penis, scarcely longer than my thumb, sprayed white milk. He let out a high-pitched squeal and sobbed.

"You did not have permission to ejaculate. A fine. You must pay a fine." I dragged him around in his own filth to face me again. "Give me your ring," I demanded, holding out my palm.

He pulled frantically at a ruby ring on his pinky finger but couldn't get it past the folds of fat.

"Hurry up!"

The ring came off, and with eyes cast down, he put it in my hand. I slipped it on my thumb, rotating the blood-red ruby to capture the light.

It was a high quality stone, masterfully cut and expertly polished. At least five carats. The setting was gold, not pure, perhaps mixed with silver. My jeweler slave would tell me.

"Go to your corner!"

He crawled across the deck as far as the leash would allow, curled up and stuck his thumb in his mouth.

I let him grovel and whimper for a few minutes before ordering the slaves to remove his collar and leash.

"Bathe His Excellency," I told one of the twins, "and freshen his toga."

"Signal His Excellency's barge," I ordered the other.

The Nubian waved a bright red banner embroidered with fierce golden eagles. Oars splashed into the water, and shortly I heard the creak of wood as the ponderous barge trailing astern pulled along our starboard side.

"Ship oars!" shouted the pilot. "Lash on!"

The barge's crew tossed thick braided sedge ropes to my waiting slaves.

"Secure lines!"

While the two crews struggled with ropes and oars, slaves mopped our deck and tied back the draperies. By the time his personal guard crossed the gangplank, the cleaned-up Imperial Tax Collector reclined on a plush lounge, sipping sweet Delta wine.

I stood respectfully for his departure. We all stood with heads bowed, except for the galley slaves, of course, who were chained to the planks.

"I trust, Lady Elektra, that I shall see you next week?"

"As always, we are at your pleasure, Most Excellent Publican."

He waddled across the deck and over the wood plank with his guard clomping after him, their red capes flowing.

Gondolas with drawn curtains, bustling water taxis and all other shapes and sizes of brightly-painted canal boats halted in both directions for the lumbering barge to reverse course.

As soon as the vile creature was at last on his way back to Alexandria, the Nubians brought me wine, white cheese and clusters of deep purple grapes. A female slave sponged my body with gardenia-infused water.

"Home," I commanded.

The coxswain beat the drum. *Thump. Thump. Thump.* Back muscles rippled, and biceps strained. With a quiet eddying of still waters, our silver-tipped oars dipped into jade satin and we began to glide east toward the Nile.

Hidden musicians trilled on flutes and strummed on lyres. A heady whiff of myrrh wafted along the shore. One after another, like pearls on a string, pleasure gazebos peeked out from riotous jungles of exuberant vines. Some pavilions were grand with golden domes, others intimate with glazed-tile cupolas—and all just separate enough to afford the illusion of privacy.

At our approach, revelers called out, "Elektra! Elektra! Queen of Canopus!"

Rome's Las Vegas. Everything allowed. Nothing forbidden. There was no sin.

A party of whistling Roman cavalry officers in shiny helmets and cuirasses shouted in Latin, "Dock here, Elektra! We have plenty of cock to go around."

I granted them the favor of a wave of my ostrich feather fan and blew them a kiss.

They cheered all together, "Elektra! Elektra! Elektra!"

In the direction of Alexandria, a golden sun slipped behind the lace canopy of trees. The heat of the day had passed. Birds flocked by the thousands to feast on swarming insects. We made steady progress through glassy waters sprinkled with myrtle blossoms falling like purple snow.

Just as dusk was settling, quite near the junction of the Canal and the Nile, we met a shiny cedar barge flying blue banners with the Greek letters ΒΣ woven in white. *Beta Sigma*. One of those centuries-old drinking clubs closed to all except men of pure lineage—generations after generations of sons born in Egypt to Greek fathers and Greek mothers.

"O Elektra the Goddess!" the teenagers sang in Greek. "O Golden Gift of Zeus! Bless us with Your Beauty! Bestow upon us Your Grace."

My galley slaves rowed on. In the water—catch. Through the water—drive. Out again—recover. All in perfect unison to the beat of the drum.

Rough bronze cuffs chained their ankles to iron loops in the decking. Each neck, below the left ear, bore the coin-sized septagram tattoos branding all of my slaves. Each naked back bore crisscross scars from the whip. Two men had fresh flaming marks; black gnats swarmed at the dried blood.

I watched them idly, waving my feather fan.

I'm not certain that I saw them as human.

I'm not certain I was human myself.

CHAPTER 29   FLAVIA

"Things forbidden have a secret charm." – Sallust

When we arrived at my date palm-silhouetted island in the Nile, a single boat the size of a water taxi moored on the far side of the limestone pier. I didn't recognize the markings.

Slaves were busy lighting torches along the length of the quay, down the trellised paths, and around the temple *stoa* ringed with Egyptian columns. As every night, the pier would soon be lined with musicians in snowy white tunics and slave girls draped in diaphanous gowns spun with silver threads.

The resort city of Canopus lay not far to the north where the river joined the sea. On a still night, I could hear the waves of *Mare Nostrum* breaking on rocks.

Dusk was thick. A few lights already twinkled across the vast river. As the night grew darker, the fires on dozens of islets would beckon, "Welcome! Welcome to pleasure."

Aeneas waited with an air of urgency on the pier. I was struck by how frightfully thin and stooped he looked and decided I must command him to eat more and worry less. His oiled scalp shone a little in the lamplight. At some point long before I purchased him as my major domo, he'd abandoned his Greek curls and adopted the Egyptian fashion of shaving his head.

By far, the most remarkable of his features were rather protruding keen eyes the color of rain. Eyes that missed nothing, especially as regards me.

"Have Brutus weigh the stone," I said, handing him the Publican's ring. "I desire a pendant."

"Domina has a visitor," he announced with significance.

"A visitor? I expect no one. Send him away. After an afternoon with that dreadful Titus Publius, I am quite beyond patience."

"The visitor is a Lady, Domina. Roman. And I would judge of the highest rank."

"What does she want?"

"She would not say, Domina. She waits in your library. Forgive me, but I knew not where else to put her. I took the liberty of serving the rosemary cordial from your private stock."

My red-roofed villa was hidden away behind white walls on the far side of the island at the end of a portico walkway lined with Corinthian columns. No torches led the way there. It was my private domain.

When I saw the visitor was Barb—or rather a Roman version of her—I almost called out her name. Last time we were together, I'd insulted her about Hector. Last time we spoke, I hadn't told her about this trip through the Red Mirror.

Her wheat-colored hair was piled high in one of those impossible arrangements requiring hours of primping, weaving, sewing and curling with hot irons.

She had that same graceful swan's neck that held her head high and proud. A gold medallion, hung on a gold choker and set with a pearl the size of a chickpea, gleamed at her throat. Her dangling earrings were the latest fashion from Rome. Three slender vertical gold rods, each ending with a pearl, dangled from a thicker horizontal gold rod. A gold cloisonné armband encircled her right wrist; gold snakes curled around her slender upper arms. She wore garnet rings on her long index fingers and a cameo ring on her right thumb.

Rather than availing herself of the hundreds of manuscripts on my shelves, she stared into space and switched her feather fan in impatient, nervous flicks of her wrist. A miniature cobalt blue glass goblet stood on the round table next to her divan. My best cordial.

Two of her slaves hovered close by. A centurion, built close to the ground, with powerful thighs and calves, stood at attention by the atrium door. His iron *gladius* hung from a red sword belt.

"I do not permit weapons in my villa," I said in lieu of a greeting.

Startled, Roman Barb sat up abruptly, nearly spilling her glass.

I could tell by her expression that she didn't recognize me. How nice that might have been. We could have sat together, sipping wine and laughing as we did in Las Vegas. But that was not to be.

"You are Elektra?" she asked.

"And you are?"

She chewed a moment on her bottom lip, trying to decide if she should tell me the truth or a lie.

Her makeup had been exquisitely applied—just enough to bring out the fine line of her cheekbones, augment her smallish eyes and give fullness to her narrow lips. The overall effect was one of a fragile beauty, utterly aristocratic with that indefinable air of breeding.

"You might as well tell me the truth," I said in a matter-of-fact tone. "My slaves shall soon know. We have no secrets from them."

Breathing out the slightest of sighs, she took a sip of the cordial as a way of buying time. I stared boldly at her, not attempting to mask my impatience. Barb or not, she had come to me, and I had not much time.

She glanced at the centurion. He stared stoically ahead with the practiced look of someone who pretends not to see or hear but sees and hears everything. I assumed he must be absolutely loyal, or she wouldn't have brought him here. Perhaps she looked at him for reassurance. In any event, she finally told me her name.

"I am Flavia Titus Titianus."

She didn't need to say more; I knew her father intimately. Titus Flavius Titianus, the First Prefect of Egypt. He was a man of most peculiar—and demanding—tastes.

"You took a great risk coming here with only one guard," I told her. "In these times of turmoil, your life must often be in peril. I gather your errand is of some importance."

To her credit, Flavia wasn't one of those silly Roman women who prattle on about nothing. She didn't bother to respond but watched me with open curiosity as I settled on a facing divan, my left shoulder against the high armrest. I supposed she was intrigued to see Elektra of Canopus up close.

As custom dictates, I asked politely, "May I offer refreshment? My cook is quite a genius with pies. Savory or sweet."

She shook her head. I waited for her to speak. Having told me she was the daughter of the most powerful man in Egypt, she would surely now tell me why she had come.

Finally, she waved her hand at the guard, and then to her slaves. They crossed the mosaic floor and went out the open door of the library.

"May we speak in private?" she asked in the tone of the privileged class that automatically assumes compliance.

I nodded my head to Aeneas, who emptied the library of my slaves and closed the door after him. Outside, in the atrium garden, a fountain tinkled, and a nightingale sang. Insects swarmed against the linen drapes covering the open windows. In the corners of the room, small braziers burning a lemony mosquito-repelling incense gave off tiny popping sounds. Brass lanterns with star cutouts cast patterns on the walls and floor. Stars flickered on Flavia's gown.

She dressed in traditional Roman layers—*tunica*, then *stola,* and finally *palla*, the long shawl draped loosely around her shoulders with which ladies cover themselves outside the home—as Roman men wear the toga in public.

Such a cumbersome dress for the heat of Egypt. By the line of her breasts, I assumed she wore a leather bra.

Tiny beads of sweat glistened on her forehead, but they could easily have been from nerves as heat. She was decidedly ill at ease.

"Are you going to tell me why you are here?" I asked rather abruptly. "I do not desire to be discourteous, but I am expecting guests."

She took a deep breath, looked once around the room at the shelves of papyri and codices and then turned her eyes again to me.

I didn't like this reticent Barb. I wanted *my* Barb who set me in my place and scolded me when I was out of line.

"I am told that you know secrets."

I waited.

She started again.

"I am told that you know…ways…" She took a breath. "Ways to persuade…persons without them knowing."

"And whom do you desire to persuade?"

She looked down and then up again, obviously embarrassed, maybe even ashamed.

I laughed. I couldn't help myself.

"Excuse me for laughing, Flavia. I may call you that, may I not?"

"This is very difficult for me," she protested. "It is most…humiliating."

"Let me make it easier. You came here in search of a binding spell.

For a man or a woman?"

She looked startled. I couldn't tell if it was because I perceived her purpose or because I suggested she might seek to sexually dominate a woman.

"A man," she said hurriedly. "It concerns a man."

"Who?"

"Must you know his name?"

"Do you desire the spell to work?"

She took another sip of cordial from the blue glass. Two nightingales sang in the garden now. I was intensely aware of time passing. A party of the highest-ranking generals was due to arrive for a *convivium*. Aeneas had spent the entire day in the kitchen overseeing the preparation of the menu.

"Rufus Hektor Ptolemais," she blurted the name in a rush. Then apparently relieved that the confession had been uttered, she calmed herself and told me unnecessarily, "He is Greek Egyptian. But a Roman citizen, naturally."

I must have shown something of my shock because she asked me, "Do you know him?"

"I have heard the name." My voice was calm. I don't know how I managed it. Inside, my heart pounded so hard I thought surely she could hear. Hektor!

"His family is from Naucratis," she went on with details I didn't request. Once the dam was broken, her words gushed out. "They have been in Egypt for centuries."

Then instead of nervous, she looked disgusted in a way that reminded me so much of the good old Barb I knew and loved.

"You would never think it though."

"Think what?"

"That it has been five hundred years since they came from Korinth." She actually snorted then, just like Barb.

She even asked in a sarcastic tone, "I may call you Elektra, may I not? As you have taken the liberty to call me Flavia."

I liked the way this was progressing. The more we talked, the more Flavia was like Barb.

"I want Rufus Hektor," she stated petulantly in the way she might tell me that she wanted a new horse or a new necklace. "But he will not have me. *Me!* A Roman, *a true Roman,* not some foreigner with a purchased citizenship."

"Does he love someone else?"

"Love has nothing to do with it. He will not marry me because I am not Greek. Can you imagine? He says that his sons would not be eligible to join that precious club of his. So arrogant, these Greeks! All of them!"

Her eyes blazed by the time she finished lambasting Hektor and his pure lineage.

"There is a spell, Flavia. A special one." I did a credible job of keeping the glee from my voice, of sounding detached and professional. "But not tonight."

"Must I come again? It is…well, you can understand…awkward for someone in my position."

"I shall come to you. But I need something of Rufus Hektor. A lock of hair perhaps, a clipping of toenail? A bodily fluid is best. Can you manage?"

She smiled. "Oh yes, I can manage. Hektor does not object to sharing his fluids with me as long as it does not result in a son."

"Give me your ring," I told her.

Without any hesitation, without asking why, she handed me the cameo from her thumb. She was, indeed, desperate.

"Shall we make a toast, then?" I suggested, tilting my tiny glass goblet of rosemary cordial, herby and sweet, toward her. "To Rufus Hektor Ptolemais and his Roman wife!"

O Hektor! O Hektor! my heart sang at the joy of revenge for Leptis Magna. *You….are…going…to…pay!*

CHAPTER 30   GRAND WIZARDS

"Forbidden pleasures alone are loved immoderately; when lawful, they do not excite desire." – Marcus Fabius Quintilian

My dresser slave Ghazel chose an ankle-length, gossamer gown of scarlet sea silk painstakingly woven from the long filaments secreted by clams to attach themselves to the sea bed. Through the shimmering cloth showed my nipples and mound stained dark red. My lips were dark carmine, my face a redhead's natural stark white. By religiously shunning the sun, I avoided the use of the horrid and dangerous lead powder so in vogue among Roman ladies.

Gold earrings in the shape of Eros with tiny wings dangled from my ears. Thick gold bands circled my upper arms.

Brutus appeared with the ruby pendant just as Ghazel was drenching me in oil of gardenia. With his usual genius, he'd fashioned an intricate filigree setting of tiny wires of electrum in the shape of a septagram.

"The stone weighs six carats, Domina."

Ghazel hung the necklace around my neck. The huge ruby in the seven-pointed star fell precisely at my cleavage.

"Beautiful, Domina. The red of your hair lights the stone as the sun lights gold."

Like all Persians, she was a born poet.

Blue-skinned Gauls guarded my private entrance to the Temple. They weren't allowed their native dress or those hideous beaded braids. Their heads were shaved, and like the other male slaves, they wore knee-length red tunics. Except the Nubians. I preferred them in short white kilts that showed to advantage their magnificent chests, flat bellies and long, taut thighs.

In all, I owned six—or was it eight?—blue Gauls who stood guard in shifts. I never noticed their faces. In any event, staffing arrangements were under the purview of Aeneas, who only came to me with problems requiring more than ten lashes.

I entered the circular dining hall to find the *convivium* in full swing and my drunken guests rowdy. Nude teenagers with fit bodies and heads of barbered curls carried trays of fattened crane stewed in salty *garum.* The cook's signature dish, braised peacock in honey, vinegar, pepper and cumin sauce, had already been served.

"Elektra! We feared you would not grace us with your presence this evening."

"My apologies, Excellencies. Even a goddess requires time to cultivate her beauty."

The generals rewarded me with a round of toasts and cheers.

Platon the vocator, yet another Greek, had seated each man on his own private lectus in anticipation of the presentation of gift slaves to follow the banquet. Their couches were arranged out from mine in a semi-circle with the open arc facing the *orchestra* or 'dancing place.' A troupe of nude acrobats was performing to the accompaniment of pipes and flutes.

Oyster shells and bits of half-chewed smoked sausage littered the floor around the couches. With only a cursory glance to ensure every guest was attended by an adequate number of slaves, I picked my way through the *sputa*, smiling seductively, looking without seeing.

Draped in leopardskin and trimmed in silver, my lectus stood on a low dais at the foot of a triple-tall marble statue of me. For tonight, Ghazel had dressed my likeness in a matching scarlet gown of the same iridescent sea silk.

It was Aeneas who had identified the Athenian sculptor slave and arranged the commission.

"He is the best in the world, Domina. We shall be the envy of all Egypt."

The transport of the mammoth block of special Ephesus marble took weeks. The cost of the statue's red gold hair and nipples alone could feed my household for two months.

I nodded to Platon to serve the *piece de resistance*—a whole roast giraffe stuffed with antelope stuffed with wild boar, in turn dressed with fattened hares. Trumpets blared. Ten muscular men in red *chitons* entered with the massive bronze platter on their shoulders.

The generals burst into wild applause. "Brava, Elektra! Brava!"

Once Aeneas, through his network of spies, had sniffed out that our guests were Grand Wizards of the Mithraic Cult, he'd spared no expense.

"I have gone over the guest list with utmost care, Domina," he'd assured me. "They shall not be disappointed."

"I count on you, Aeneas. We can use allies such as these men."

It was common enough knowledge that no one advances in the army without joining the cult. It was likely that Mithraists commanded all Legions.

Their identity was supposed to be hush-hush, of course. Everything about the Mithraists was veiled in mystery—their secret handshakes, the underground temples, their blood-soaked bull sacrifices to the Zoroastrian Fire God Mithras.

"I hear it said, Domina, that Mithraists claim immortality. If one rises high enough."

"No one cheats death, Aeneas," I'd told him. "Not even a Grand Wizard."

But whatever cosmic forces these men believed in, I had my own magic. None was more potent.

I nodded to Aeneas. The music shifted to wailing flutes and throbbing drums. A cloud of blue smoke rose from the braziers and then cleared. Coppery ripe-breasted belly dancers, silver bells jingling at their wrists and ankles, shimmered in layers of silk. One by one, a sparkly-threaded veil fell away, revealing more, and then more, of their lush bodies.

The Grand Wizards cheered and make sucking sounds with their mouths. On the divan closest to mine, a man in his late prime with a shock of silver hair pulled up his gown and thrust his engorged penis in the air. I snapped my fingers, and a boy of about fifteen with a mop of blond curls rushed to take the Roman in his mouth.

With his usual efficiency, Aeneas had seen to every detail. Each of the eight Romans had five attendants—a feather boy to tickle his throat to induce vomiting, a pubescent nude girl to fan him, a child to shoo away insects with sprigs of myrtle, a Nubian *masseuse,* and a eunuch to help him urinate into silver bowls.

But those were amenities to be enjoyed at any banquet. Our spies had ferreted out the depravities unique to each guest; Aeneas had spent hours handpicking slaves to gratify those needs.

"Here is the list, Domina. Each guest and his taste."

More times than not, my clients liked to be bound and whipped and made to suffer pain in the way of the Tax Collector. For those tastes, I would have employed personally-trained slaves who knew just how far to go and when to stop. Tonight's entertainment had required specific purchases.

For Cassius Maximus Gallus—a twelve-year-old German virgin with wavy, spun gold hair. For Lucius Caecina Vestinus—a Persian youth with coffee skin and raven curls. A *mènage á trois* with an audience shouting suggestions for Caius Julius Capito.

Marcus Tiberius was the sole guest who desired only to watch. His preference was for two women, one blonde and one dark. Aeneas had noted that he liked it rough. The black-skinned Amazon would be equipped with an array of whips and nasty props.

A Syrian had given Aeneas the most trouble. His perversions involved animals—savage cats mainly, and certain breeds of dogs.

There were more names on the list, but I had left the particulars to Aeneas. After my cursory inspection, the boys, girls and young women had been sent for bathing and grooming.

Soon the Grand Wizards would retire to private rooms appointed with sparkling fountains, marble bathing pools, lion-head beds, gold chains, ankle irons, handcuffs and whips with silk or leather thongs.

I nodded for the lanterns to be doused and more colored powders thrown on the braziers. Perfumed smoke snaked through the still air. The musicians quieted their instruments, and the room fell silent with a hush of anticipation.

I waited. I let the breathless mood linger. I let them grow slightly restive before signaling Aeneas.

In single file, each preceded by a garlanded girl child carrying a lighted torch, the gift slaves paraded into the hall. Unlike the nude servers and scantily-clad attendants, these wore hooded red linen robes that hid their faces and perfect bodies.

One by one, they were led to the Romans reclining on couches. On cue, Egyptian musicians shook *sistrums*. The seductive jingle of hundreds of tiny silver bells grew increasingly louder and more frenzied. Drums joined in. With a flurry of drumbeats and a wailing of pipes, the oiled and perfumed slaves threw off their robes to stand naked before their masters for the night.

There were grunts of satisfaction. Hands reached out for flesh. Attendants moved to guide guests and pleasure slaves to their private rooms.

My job was done. I lay back and closed my eyes.

Not long now. Soon I would be in my atelier, preparing my special potion of venom and herbs that would bring Hektor's privileged life to a painful end.

CHAPTER 31 THE GENERAL

"Subdue your passion or it will subdue you." – Horace

D o we bore you?"

Startled, I sat straight up.

A gold eagle glittered on a massive bull chest armored in a leather cuirass studded with silver. The tongued leather-lappet skirt reached mid-thigh of legs sturdy as temple columns. Biceps bulged below pleated cap sleeves.

And the hands. I stared at them—big, square, and powerful—with thick fingers that could crush a windpipe as quickly as another man might squash a fly.

The General.

How could I not have seen him tonight? But I hadn't bothered to note the men lying on their couches around the circle; I rarely look closely at anyone. Clients. Slaves. They were a blur of eyes, noses and mouths set in unremarkable faces atop forgettable bodies.

Which one of the names on the list was the General? Thinking to identify him by depravity, I blurted out, "What is your taste?"

He laughed. And when he laughed, I saw those square teeth of his. "I have but one taste, Ishtar. You."

He plunked himself down on the other end of my divan, leaning back on the armrest and pillows, forcing me to move my legs so he wouldn't crush my feet. At least he didn't put his monster military sandals in my face. A slave hurried over with a high footstool.

"Your entertainment for this evening has been arranged, General. Go enjoy yourself."

"Do you imagine me to be so desperate as to buy my pleasure in a brothel? Marcus Junius Nepos owed me a favor, so I took his place."

He traced his finger up my calf, and I gripped his wrist to stop him. He chuckled, withdrew his hand and reached out to take a chalice of wine from a slave.

"How did you know to find me here?"

"You do not exactly hide yourself."

He took a deep swig of wine, tilting his head back, then wiped his lips with the back of his hand.

"In fact, my dear Ishtar, you are quite a star. A true evening star. All of Alexandria speaks of you. A living goddess, they say, capable of special powers."

He stared at me, expecting a response. I stared back.

"Is that true, Ishtar?"

"That I am a goddess?"

He threw back his head and laughed again. Another deep drink from the chalice. A slave was there immediately to top off his cup from a silver pitcher.

"Excellent wine," he commented.

"Thank you. I have my own vineyards."

"Of course. I would expect nothing less."

He studied me for a while from under hooded lids. I met his gaze.

"I made inquiries," he said finally in a too-casual tone. "It seems you have no history. Why is that?"

I'm sure he saw my eyes widen just a fraction. He always noticed every change in my expression, noted every shift in my tone. I was vaguely aware of music, raucous shouts, even the sound of retching, but all very far away. There was only the General and me in a vast vacuum.

He leaned forward to touch with his index finger the ruby hanging at the top of my cleavage before slowly tracing a circle on my skin around the pendant.

"If you are good to me, I shall arrange an introduction to Hadrian."

Good to him?

"Would you like that, Ishtar?"

"Why would you do that for me?"

He raised his eyebrows. "Do you not think it would be to your advantage?"

"Of course, it would be to my advantage. But what will it cost me?"

His eyes traveled the full length of my body, so provocatively and deliberately displayed to evoke desire. His gaze paused on my loins; he wet his lips with the tip of his tongue. In spite of my determination to resist his magnetism, my nipples rose to peaks in the red silk.

He shifted his weight, leaning forward, and before I could protest, slid his bear paws behind my back. He pulled me upright, into him, and put his lips to my throbbing nipple and my hand on his monster manhood. My breath caught in my throat.

"I see you still enjoy that," he whispered in my ear.

We both felt my heart race.

Before I could think to stop him, he scooped me up in his gorilla arms and rose in one sure movement to his feet.

"Where?" he snarled to a bewildered Aeneas.

Aeneas panicked, not knowing what to do. He stood paralyzed, his already protruding eyes enormous in his startled face.

I absolved him by nodding my head. The relief that washed over him was so complete, that I wondered for a moment if he, like the Tax Collector, would leave a puddle on the floor.

In giant strides, the General covered the distance to the interior courtyard. We stepped into the peristyle garden; Aeneas threw open the door to the best of our rooms.

Without ceremony, the General dropped me on the bed.

"Get out," he barked.

"But—" Aeneas started to protest. He never left me alone with a client but always made certain the Nubian twins were present.

The General picked him up by the back of his tunic and threw him out the door, slamming it after him.

I heard the bolt slide in the lock. And then with the speed of a charging bull, the General was on the bed, his fingers around my throat, his other hand under my gown and between my thighs.

"I have waited lifetimes for this," he snarled in my ear.

I struggled. I couldn't breathe. I gasped for air. Bright lights flashed in front of my eyes, and he was no longer the General but had morphed into Major Domo.

I beat about his face, yanking at his hair, scratching at his eyes. He didn't stop. All I saw was Major Domo, and I went wild.

In panic, I reached down along the edge of the bed. My hand found the hidden shelf I'd personally drawn into the design. With the help of my Greek architect slave, I'd designed the bed. I'd designed the room. I'd designed the Temple.

The hilt of the dagger was in my palm, and then the point was at the General's jugular. When he felt the cold steel at his neck, he stopped. His hand was still at my neck, but I could breathe.

"Get off," I commanded.

He blinked.

I applied more pressure. The point dug deeper. A drop of blood oozed.

He released my throat.

I pressed harder.

Abruptly, he leaned back with a look of profound surprise. And once he pulled away from the dagger point, I lost my power over him. If he wanted to wrest the knife away from me, I was no match for his strength.

But he didn't try to take the dagger. Instead he said quietly, "I thought you liked it rough."

"Not when forced. I do not like anything when forced."

Seconds passed. I heard the play of the Venus fountain with her gold-tipped breasts spouting water into a marble bowl. I could see the General was sincere in his confusion, but not about whether I would have used the knife. I'd ended his life once, in his Persian tent. Neither of us doubted that I'd do it again. If he pushed me too far.

Slowly, his eyes assuring me that he'd surrendered, he reached to take the knife from my hand. I let him have it, as freely as I would a chalice of wine we shared. Then he sat full back near my feet and tossed the knife aside. I heard the muffled thud of its weight hit the carpet.

"Forgive me," he said. "I miscalculated."

"Is that how you want me? Is that what I am to you?"

A shadow passed over his face. For a fleeting moment, I saw pain in his eyes, but it was quickly gone. Vulnerable only seconds, he leaned back on an elbow and gave me one of his little smirks that says there are no secrets between us. But I'd surprised him, taken him off-guard with the ferocity of my resistance.

"So how do we decide, Ishtar? What shall be our rules? Do you whip me—or do I whip you?"

"No one whips me—ever."

"Then we have common ground. I have no desire to strike you in any way."

He traced the septagram with his finger, barely grazing my skin. I felt my pulse quicken. He saw the stirring in my eyes and stood out of the bed. Watching me watch him, he unlaced his leather military cuirass with golden eagle and leather lappet skirt and tossed the uniform aside in the same casual way he had the dagger.

His stallion erection stood straight up in the linen of his tunic. His thick military sandals still laced up his shins.

"Come get it," his animal power dared me.

I rose to my knees on the bed, facing him. Carefully, as if unveiling a priceless artifact, I lifted the tunic. His monster manhood was inches away. I wet my lips and leaned forward to take his huge glistening head in my mouth.

He growled like a lion and dug his fingers into my elaborate hairdo with such force that the pins came undone. Fiery waves tumbled around my face and down my back.

I pinched the inside of his thighs, hard. He caught his breath and slowed, letting me set the pace. I licked and then nibbled gently while my fingertips massaged his balls covered in coarse black curls.

He growled louder. I wanted to make him roar. But more than that, I wanted to make him mine.

I could use a powerful man like the General.

Alternating tender caresses with more and more forceful, I kneaded and pulled. My lips, my tongue and my teeth matched the rhythm.

His hips began to slide backward and forward, trying to force me to take him deeper. Without mercy, I pinched his inner thighs hard again. My signal that I was in control.

I imagined that his erection grew larger.

Just when I swallowed him all the way to the back of my throat, a high-pitched, blood-curdling scream shattered the air. Even through the heavy wooden door, the wail was piercing.

I leaned back. The General and I both stared at the door.

Another scream, this one longer and more terrible. His erection melted.

The General grabbed his gladius and was at the door in two strides, sliding the bolt open.

"Stay here," he commanded. "Lock the door after me."

The screams went on and on until I heard shouts. Then it was silent.

There was a knock, and the General said, "It is I."

Blood stained his arm and the tunic with little pleated sleeves. I glanced at the sword still in his hand. There was blood on the blade.

"Cassius Maximus Gallus gets…carried away at times." He told me this while putting on his leather cuirass.

I didn't ask why the screams had stopped—if he had gagged the girl, released her or put her out of her misery.

I didn't have to. I knew.

"I need to get Cassius back to Alexandria. He is…shaken up."

I tried to recall more about the girl. I could vaguely remember that she didn't speak Latin or Greek. Aeneas had purchased her only two days ago. Or was it three? I'd only seen her for a few moments. Just to approve that she would do, that she was the right type.

But I remembered clearly her luxurious golden tresses and those big azure eyes wide with terror. Blond hair and blue eyes. That was what Cassius Maximus Gallus wanted. And the age.

Twelve to thirteen years old. And, of course, a virgin. The girl was yet another blur in the sea of unremarkable faces atop expendable bodies. Expendable lives.

I sat there mute while he struggled with the leather thongs of his cuirass.

"Could you help me with this?" he asked.

I found myself lacing the front to the back under his raised left arm while he gave me brisk orders.

"You must keep this quiet, Ishtar. Hadrian disapproves of the killing of slaves without just cause." His voice was matter-of-fact. A young girl wasn't butchered tonight, only a slave.

I knew by his detached tone that he'd seen worse. A Roman General sees much worse than the girl in the room.

"I have found him to be progressive," he went on about Hadrian. "He even extols tolerance of Christians, if they live within the law."

He belted his gladius on his right side and adjusted the balance.

"Caesar is superstitious, though. Which brings me back to the introduction I proposed."

He looked at me in the way of a fellow conspirator.

"Hadrian has dreams, it seems. Dreams that disturb his sleep." He paused, lifting an eyebrow. "You can interpret a few dreams, Ishtar, can you not?"

He leaned down and kissed me on the mouth, putting his hand on the back of my neck, gripping me firmly—very firmly, not letting go when he pulled his lips away.

"Now you are not going to call that *forcing,* are you?"

As an answer, I grabbed the back of his neck, kissing him hard, my tongue down his throat.

"I shall be back to finish up where we left off," he said gruffly, "but not tonight."

He opened the door and stepped out, closing it firmly behind him. I could hear footsteps in the portico, and voices, but they soon faded.

Aeneas was there almost immediately with the twin Nubians and Eunice, one of my personal slaves. The four of them looked shaken. I was shaken, too, but couldn't show it. I was Domina.

"Everything is being taken care of, Domina," Aeneas assured me.

"How much did we pay for her?"

"Six hundred denarii, Domina. No more than two horses."

He paused and then said, "Cassius Maximus Gallus left this purse. For the inconvenience."

"And this is in addition to our normal fees?"

"But certainly, Domina. Compensation for the *convivium* is quite apart."

Eunice, a tiny Thracian with miracle fingers, removed my sheer gown, helped me slip into a green linen caftan and then braided my hair into a long rope.

"It was a most profitable evening, Domina," Aeneas jabbered on nervously. "And most successful I would judge. Except for…the incident."

"I am not so concerned with the *incident* as I am with the breach in security. You failed to verify guests against names on the list."

He didn't look into my eyes but at the floor. I suspected that part of his avoidance was to hide his puzzlement at what he'd witnessed tonight. Not the girl, but the General.

And because I was humiliated that he'd seen the General overwhelm me, I spoke rashly.

"Thirty lashes. For the unexpected guest. You endangered me."

No sooner had I uttered the words than I regretted them. The punishment was too harsh. Aeneas was a frail man with fragile bony shoulders; thirty lashes could cripple him. Thirty lashes could kill him, and his death was out of the question. He managed my household and the Temple with unparalleled efficiency. If there were mistakes, he corrected them before they came to my attention. He never stole that I knew of. And he was loyal. More than loyal. Devoted.

I relied on him completely; he was my most valuable possession.

The twin Nubians stared straight ahead. Like Aeneas, Eunice looked at the floor. The play of the water in the Venus fountain was deafening in the silence. Three witnesses. If I weakened now, if only to reduce the number of lashes, my authority would be forever undermined. Who would fear me?

To exacerbate my dilemma, Aeneas was major domo; there was no slave higher in the hierarchy of my household. I employed no freedmen. Only I, Domina, could execute the distasteful flogging. And there would be no fooling anyone with half-measures and a light hand.

A part of me was livid with Aeneas that he'd put me in this untenable position.

"We still have much to do tonight," I said impatiently. "The lashing must wait."

"Yes, Domina. Of course. As Domina desires."

He kept his eyes on the floor, not wanting me to see his relief. He'd gained a reprieve, but by morning he will have died a hundred times in his mind. That would suffice as punishment enough for the moment.

"Now come," I commanded briskly. "We have work to do."

CHAPTER 32   CLEOPATRA'S SPELL

"Many a time from a bad beginning great friendships have sprung up."
– Sallust

My atelier housed a vast collection of ceramic urns, glass vials and carved chests of all sizes arranged neatly on wooden shelving.

Each container was meticulously labeled in Greek with the name of the specimen, herb or potion, along with an astrological notation as to the date it was collected, ground or distilled.

Sun 15 degrees Scorpio
Waning Crescent Moon in Taurus 3rd House
Venus square Mars

The storerooms were lit entirely by small oil lamps suspended on long chains from the ceiling. Like in the Cave of Bats, there were no windows to allow polluting sunlight. And like in the Hive, glowing mystic symbols and astrological glyphs covered the black walls and ceiling.

Live specimens were tended by a man and woman I'd stumbled upon in the slave market quite by chance. It might have been the honey-colored eyes that first drew me, but when after inquiries, I discovered that they were Berbers—Imazighen—from the Nafusa mountains outside Leptis Magna, I knew Lemta had sent them. Or at least, that's how I chose to see it.

From the beginning, the couple had demonstrated a remarkable affinity for nurturing the snakes, rats, spiders, beetles and white doves that are the base of Lemta's concoctions.

Menstrual blood, dog feces, placenta of a newborn rat and the eye of a dead crow placed in a door jamb when the moon was full, and a wife would desert her husband and child to fly in a fever to my client's bed. Or so he believed.

My tricks of the trade didn't always require animal parts. With his jeweler magic fingers, Brutus could carve a miniature beryl *intaglio* with a tiny winged Eros encircled by miniscule letters—a love amulet to be worn as a ring.

I didn't overly concern myself with the effectiveness of potions and midnight chanting. My clients believed, and that was enough.

Roman, Greek or Egyptian, they were all universally convinced that magical spells could render any man or woman a zombie without a will of their own. Merely summon up forces from the Underworld with "ABRACADABRA" or "ABLAMGOUNOTHO ABRASAX" to make anyone a sex slave.

I didn't bring the magic to Egypt; Egyptians had been masters of the black arts for untold centuries. But I delivered my spells with a dramatic flair that appealed to the Alexandrian ruling class. I was not some shriveled old woman in the market or eunuch creature from a temple.

And aside from the hypnotic incantations I memorized in the Hive, I pronounced my curses in eloquent Greek—not Egyptian gibberish.

The mystic mantras allowed me to take full advantage of fear and superstition. But more than that, the mere reciting of the sounds gave me power over my own fears, and that control gave me power over others.

For Flavia I'd promised a binding spell—*katadesmos*—designed to inflame Hektor with a love for her so consuming that he'd never leave her bed. All she must do is slip the potion into his wine, and he would be completely under her spell.

I smiled. Then again, my magic might be too powerful. Hektor might fall ill. Gravely ill. Deathly ill.

"Aeneas, prepare to sail to Alexandria at first light."

"Yes, Domina." The poor man quivered with relief. There would be no punishment this day.

Dawn on the Canopus Canal was a quiet affair. In lieu of the wild shouts and rowdy songs, the misty still air was filled with birdsong. These were the in-between hours. Those who partied all night now slept. Those who would party weren't expected until noon.

We glided silently through mercury waters with a soothing swoosh of our silver-tipped oars.

No one called out my name, but that was the plan. By leaving my conspicuous barge behind and concealing myself in a hooded cloak, I would arrive in Alexandria unnoticed. Under the cloak, I dressed as a Roman—yellow tunica, green stola the color of my eyes and a turquoise palla the shade of the Mediterranean in a white sandy cove. I wore Brutus' ruby septagram under my gown.

For bodyguards, Aeneas brought along three new slaves of average height and powerful builds—a red-headed Celt, a hawk-nosed Syrian and a coppery-skinned man with tiny bright eyes peering out from slits.

They were armed with short thrusting swords similar to the gladius of the Roman Legions. They also carried daggers, each different from the other. Long and slim with a heavy sheath for the Celt, curved like a crescent moon for the Syrian, and broad with serrated edges for the slant-eyed one.

As was customary for slaves, they stood with their eyes cast down when presented to me.

"Do they speak Latin?"

"Yes, Domina. Of a sort."

"Greek then?"

"Only the Syrian."

"At which market did you purchase them?"

"Not at a market, Domina. They were gladiators."

"Have you fought in Leptis Magna?" I asked them.

The Celt shifted his weight slightly.

"Speak up!" I snapped. "There is no right or wrong answer."

"I Leptis," he said in pigeon Latin.

"Did you meet a Nubian—a giant with tribal scars on his face? Three heads taller than you, maybe more? He might have worn a faience medallion with a seven-pointed star."

He thought a moment. "Past. One season."

"Did he live when you last saw him?"

He nodded his head yes. His language skills were too poor for me to insist on the "Yes, Domina" required of slaves.

So Goliath had survived the brutal Arena of Leptis Magna—as of a year ago, anyway. Tripolitana had a thirst for battles with wild beasts fed human flesh to whet their appetites for gladiator blood. He would have faced lions, leopards, bears and wolves starved and tortured to be made more vicious. He had to be good, very good.

I let myself believe that he might still live. Smart *lanistas* avoided certain death matches for their prize gladiators; they had too much invested in them.

"Make inquiries about the Nubian, Aeneas."

"Yes, Domina."

"And find out everything you can about the general from last night. Everything."

I didn't need to explain which of the generals I meant.

We docked at the Lake Mareotis wharf for pleasure yachts on the southern edge of Alexandria. Aeneas woke a sleeping porter, and we headed north into the city through the Gate of the Sun with me reclining on the cushions of a hired litter.

The streets of Alexandria were more crowded and raucous than when I was here as Athena and the city ruled by Greeks. Trash and stinking garbage littered the broad avenues. I had to cover my nose to dampen the stench of human filth. Ptolemy would never have stood for it. Certainly not in the Beta Quarter. We hugged the edge of Soma Avenue to avoid pounding horse hooves and clanking chariot wheels.

Everywhere was the clang and scrape of construction. My head hammered; the drawn curtains of my litter did little to filter the choking dust of stonework. Half the buildings still showed signs of the fire set fifteen years earlier by Jewish mobs. They'd come close to burning Alexandria to the ground; they'd succeeded in leveling Cyrene. Thousands of Greeks were massacred in both cities.

Alexandria hadn't been the same since the Great Revolt instigated by fanatical émigrés from Judea. The immense Jewish population had tested Roman power and been brutally suppressed, but they proved Rome could be damaged, if not defeated. And Greeks could bleed.

A pervasive pall of danger hung over the city. Criminals lurked in every shadow. Assassinations were carried out in broad daylight. No one went about the city unarmed.

Nighttime was worse. Under the Ptolemies, the streets of the Beta

Quarter were lighted with torches. Not so today. Romans and wealthy Greeks sequestered themselves in elaborate villas and ventured out after dark only under heavy guard.

The Syrian forced a path with his gladius through the mob of tourists at the entrance to the *Soma*, the mausoleum of Alexander the Great. Inside, his honey-mummified body reposed in a crystal sarcophagus.

There were shouts and curses. Someone tried to rip back the curtains of my litter, and we teetered to the side. I thought they might drag me to the street until Slant Eyes' serrated dagger flashed, and the crowd let us pass.

At last we arrived at the Gate of the Moon leading to the Great Harbor and what was known under the Ptolemies as the Royal Quarter.

Two Roman centurions demanded our pass.

Aeneas spoke quietly for a few moments, and then a small leather purse discreetly changed hands. We were waved through.

The Library of Alexandria was but a shadow of its previous self. But to Hadrian's credit, reconstruction had gone forward at an accelerated pace. Damaged buildings had been demolished, burned materials removed. Freshly hewn and polished marble sparkled in the morning sun.

Pharos, the Lighthouse, still dominated the entrance of the Great Harbor. A narrow neck of cobalt sea separated Pharos Island from the Royal Promontory on the east shore where Ptolemy's marble palaces sprawled. Romans lived there now—and the Greek bureaucrats who administered Egypt today as they had done since Alexander the Great.

Aeneas knew of a back entrance to the Prefect's Palace on the far side of the peninsula. We wound our way between a tall white wall and the short cliff that fell to the open sea.

He banged with a wooden staff on a green gate. We waited. When the gate finally opened, there were more quiet words before he handed over Flavia's cameo ring. The gate closed again, leaving us to wait outside like common beggars.

There was no shade; the morning sun was hot for this time of year. Time dragged on. I began to regret coming. Flavia could travel to me if she wanted a binding spell.

But as fate would have it, at the very moment I was to give the order to wait no more, the gate opened, and we were ushered in.

Lacy acacia and broad sycamore trees shaded the garden. Manicured paths bordered by disciplined rose beds connected elaborate mosaic fountains. Topiary in the shape of deer dotted the green grass. At least thirty statues of famous Romans stood about, mostly painted marble with a few bronzes gone green in the sea air.

Flavia was sitting for an encaustic portrait in an extravagant rose marble salon with a wide balcony overlooking the Imperial yacht harbor. The Lighthouse in all its majesty appeared so close that I could reach out and touch it.

She was dressed all in white, like a Muse. In her lap she held a small white dog with long, combed hair tied in blue ribbons. They came from China, these lapdogs that did no work; they were becoming quite the rage among Roman ladies. This one had buggy black eyes in a flat square face. It yapped when I came in.

"I am so glad for your visit, Elektra."

Flavia greeted me warmly enough. There was a sincere quality to her enthusiasm, and it occurred to me that she might welcome a friend to confide in. She motioned toward a wide divan close by her.

"Come. Do be close to me."

The artist mixed hot wax with pigment and then applied the paste with a metal spatula to a slender cedar plank. He worked rapidly, with precise, brisk strokes, smoothing and swirling before the wax could set. His stand of brushes for the fine detail of eyes, skin and jewels stood on an inlaid pedestal next to the easel.

Flavia's hair was piled high with a barrette of gold and pearls covering the center part. Four strands of pearls wrapped around her neck. In the center of the choker was a massive emerald. Giant pearl drop earrings dangled from her earlobes. More pearls mixed with strands of gold wrapped around her upper arms. The cameo ring was back on her thumb.

The bodice of her gown, cut for a cleavage that Flavia lacked, showed to advantage her glowing pearlescent skin. On the thin side for many tastes, she was yet a beautiful woman with the elegant bearing and elusive composure I find so appealing.

"These were once the rooms of Cleopatra," she said in a bright chirpy tone. "Can you imagine her here with the great Caesar? Do you not wonder if she used magic to enthrall him? Maybe a love spell of attraction?"

A slave removed my cloak, and I reclined on the sofa. A small silver cup of *passum*, a sweet raisin wine, was in my hand at the same time a third slave removed my sandals to cleanse my feet in rose-scented water.

"Cleopatra spent a great deal of time in Siwa," Flavia went on in her bubbly, carefree voice. "At the hot springs in the oasis. They say the Berbers there know magic that no one else knows."

Naturally, I thought of Lemta. There must be many women like her, hidden in secret spots, keeping alive the spells passed down from deep in Africa. Someone from Siwa might even have taught the woman who taught Lemta.

"No more," Flavia said in Greek to the painter. She settled to face me on the divan with her back on the opposite armrest. The little white dog stared at me suspiciously from her arms.

Our outstretched legs touched at the calf. Small gold rings encircled her second toes. Her toenails, not far from my hand, were stained with henna.

She was remarkably relaxed in our intimacy. I looked carefully into her eyes to see if I'd been mistaken last night. But I got no sense that she knew me from another life. She had no inkling she would one day be Barb.

"It is my father who insists I have my portrait painted now for my sarcophagus. He claims I am at the beginning of the decline of my beauty, and this is how I should be remembered for all time. Wretched of him, do you not find?"

I knew her father and his tastes. Any woman past sixteen was in decline.

"You *are* beautiful today," I told her. "You have a glow."

"Rufus Hektor has been here," she whispered.

I raised my eyebrow. Had I just missed him? What a treat it would have been to see his face. The woman he threw to the wolves in Leptis Magna—here—in his lover's quarters.

"He came to me at dawn," she confided.

Flavia was most definitely in love—or at least deeply infatuated. Her voice had that special lilt when she said 'he.' Her eyes sparkled; she was positively radiant.

Perhaps Hektor had invoked a binding spell—maybe even a drawing spell, a powerful *agôgai*—on *her*?

In my mind's eye, I saw a frenzied Flavia, burning with sexual abandon, performing the wild acts of a prostitute, perversions no proper Roman lady would dare.

"I have what you requested," she continued in a whisper.

She snapped her fingers for the slaves to leave us. From the folds of her dress, she produced a wide-mouthed tiny amber glass vial with a cork stopper.

"He never leaves his seed in me. *Coitus interruptus.* Always."

She looked terribly satisfied with herself. Maybe she was already making plans for the wedding. A pang of guilt stabbed me.

"You do realize, Flavia, that you shall have to do everything precisely the way I instruct or the spell cannot work."

She stared at me for a few moments. A new look came into her eyes that wasn't exactly suspicious, but definitely cautious.

"I like you. Elektra. I was not prepared to. I have heard much spoken of your temple and what goes on there. I thought you a wicked woman, but I was told there was no better sorceress."

She paused. "You are the best, are you not?"

I laughed. "And how should I answer? I am who I am, and I do what I do."

She considered me from the opposite end of the divan, her blue eyes staring into mine in a way so like Barb who missed nothing, who knew my own thoughts often before I was aware of them myself.

"Do you not believe in your own magic, Elektra?"

"I believe most in myself."

"That is not the most reassuring of answers."

"It is reassuring to me. And considering that the power of magic is dependent upon the practitioner, my belief in myself should be most reassuring to you."

She liked my answer. She could allow herself to believe once again that a spell to entrap Hektor was possible.

"What is Hektor's mother's name?" I asked.

"Eugenia. Why?"

"His matronymic must be used in the incantation. To identify him. It is essential for the spell to succeed."

I wrote 'Eugenia' in the blank space among Greek words on the papyrus and augmented two lines in the middle.

"Here are the words. Commit them to heart and repeat them exactly as written here. It will be most effective if you wait until the moon is full."

"So long?" As I hoped, she looked disappointed to wait.

"And what of your compensation, Elektra? You have not spoken of that."

"I shall think of something appropriate." I smiled and then said, "Now listen. This is what you must say. Exactly. Word for word."

I read the incantation in a modulated, low melodious drone emanating from deep in my throat. The drama of delivery is crucial to the effect.

ANOK THAZI N EPIBATHA CHEOUCH CHA ANO ANOK

O Lord Daemon, attract, inflame, destroy, consume him.

ANA A A NANA A A NANA

I bind you, Rufus Hektor Ptolemais, born of the womb of Eugenia, to the tail of the snake and the mouth of the crocodile, to the horns of the ram and the venom of the asp, to the whiskers of the cat and the penis of the lion, so that you can never have intercourse with another woman or man nor do anything for pleasure with other than me.

I bind you with your own seed spilled of your own body robbing me of your son to grow in my belly.

Neither gods nor men will procure a pure release for you. On the contrary, you shall love me, Flavia Titus Titianus alone, that you might forget your parents and all your family and all your friends and all other wants and pleasures and obligations for the entire length of your life. There shall be only me, Flavia, for whom you breathe.

ABLAMGOUNOTHO ABRASAX

Flavia sat completely still. If she breathed, it was so shallow I couldn't detect it. The dog glared at me with its buggy eyes.

It was when I came out of the toilet with its marble plank of multiple seats that I saw it.

Half-hidden in an obscure corner of her dressing room, I would have missed it entirely if I hadn't stepped over to admire her collection of silk gowns and rows of ornate sandals.

"Flavia," I called out to her.

"Yes?" she asked from the archway.

"I see something that I should like. As compensation."

I'm certain she thought I wanted one of her jeweled tiaras or the small chest filled with golden bangles.

"I should like *that*," I said, pointing to the Red Mirror.

CHAPTER 33 MOB

"You learn to know a pilot in a storm." — Seneca

B ut of course," Flavia gushed graciously. "Consider the mirror yours. A slave discovered it only yesterday in storage. I thought to take it to an antiquities dealer."

"I should be most pleased if you would have it delivered to my villa."

"Today. The mirror shall be there when you return," she promised, taking my hands in hers. "We are going to be best of friends, Elektra. I feel it. I shall invite you to my wedding."

I managed a smile. Flavia kissed me on both cheeks.

"Sisters! We shall be as sisters. And I promise not be jealous of your beauty. You may have all other men in the world, dearest Elektra, for I shall have Rufus Hektor."

Her eyes were so full of joy. Her happy laughter was the tinkling of bells ringing in my guilt. Oh why, oh why, did she have to be so ridiculously happy about this man, of all men? There are so many to be had.

For a brief moment, I weakened and considered not offering Flavia the tiny vial tucked in my gown. I'd leave her only the nonsense parcel of dried blood and herbs sprinkled with drops of Hektor's semen. She never need know about my special potion that would ensure he couldn't have sons with any woman, Greek or Roman. He would be sterile.

Sunlight sparkled on the sapphire waters of the Harbor. A great *trireme* with red sails passed by the Pharos on its way to open sea. Maybe west along the African Coast to Leptis Magna.

There under the same bright sun, Hektor had bid, won and then given me to Marcus Quintillus with his fiend wife. If not for my own boldness and a fair share of luck, I most likely would be dead now. I might have welcomed death.

Rufus Hektor Ptolemais deserved far worse than sterility, but for Flavia's sake, and hers only, I'd decided not to take his life. But pay a price he must.

"If you care not to wait for the full moon, Flavia, but wish to influence him sooner, I can offer this potion."

She stared for a moment at the blue vial in my hand before looking into my eyes.

"What is it?" she asked warily.

"The taste is akin to bitter almonds. Give him no more than two drops in a chalice of wine."

Her look was penetrating, so like Barb's. If she were near-sighted as well, I couldn't tell.

"It does not work right away," I cautioned, "but needs time. And several doses. Over a period of days."

"No incantation to memorize?" The hint of suspicion was back.

"ANA A A NANA A A NANA," I intoned. "The words are in the spell, if you recall."

She was silent for a moment, then took the vial from me.

"I *can* trust you, can I not, Elektra?"

"Say the chant three times, not out loud, while you are administering the drops."

She didn't look overly convinced; Flavia was savvier than I'd given her credit. But she would use the vial. She wanted Hektor that much.

"Elektra," she asked as the slave wrapped me in my cloak, "have you ever loved a man—as I love Hektor?"

Nemo's face was first in my mind. But that was more refuge than love. I had tired of him by the time we reached Cyrene and wasn't heartbroken to send him back to Lemta.

An orgasm is a beautiful thing, but I taught other men to please me. And I'd learned to please myself.

Love was between equals. Elektra had not yet met that man, so I shook my head to Flavia's question.

"Did you never marry?" she asked.

"How does a woman escape marriage? I was wed when quite young. To a man of my father's choosing, naturally."

"I have married twice. Both old as my father. Both political advantages. One died in battle and one of fever. That is why my father allows me to choose my husband now."

"So he approves of Rufus Hektor?"

"Father approves of his money. The family is far wealthier than ours. And I think Father is ready to be rid of me after coming home two times a widow."

On impulse I'm sure, she took the cameo ring off her thumb and put in on mine. She smiled and squeezed my hand. I felt as if she squeezed my heart.

"And your husband, Elektra? What happened to him?"

"He died as well."

I left before she could ask me how. I had lied to her enough for one day.

"Domina's guest last evening is close to Hadrian."

I raised an eyebrow at Aeneas referring to the General as *my* guest.

"They say the Emperor makes no military decision before consulting him."

"His name?"

"He is known as the Moor, Domina."

"Moor? Is he from Africa then?"

"Leptis Magna, Domina."

I'll admit that bit of news stunned me. How long before the General figured out that I was an escaped slave? He'd already begun investigating me. He might already know.

You have no history. Why is that?

I did my best to hide a reaction, fussing with my palla, pretending an interest in the curls around my face, reaching to adjust one or two. But Aeneas caught the slight halt of my breath.

It was how he stayed ahead of my displeasure, this keen attunement to my moods and nuanced changes in my expression. But I could also read him. His eyes were slate, guarded, still I caught the glint of interest.

"And the Nubian gladiator?" I asked in a brisk no-nonsense tone meant to divert him.

"I regret my inquiries have yielded no results as yet, Domina. But

I have put out word that there is a handsome reward for reliable information."

"Keep me informed."

"Of course, Domina," he said in a way that told me he wanted to say more.

"What is it?"

"It is only…that…" His voice trailed off.

"Speak. I do not have all day."

"Does Domina not find it curious that the Moor and the gladiator have a connection?"

I stared at him.

"Leptis Magna, Domina."

"Coincidence, Aeneas," I said with a shrug. "Nothing more."

"Certainly, Domina." He cast his eyes down then, as was proper for a slave, but he didn't fool me.

These clever Greeks have a way of putting things together. Puzzle-solvers all.

Finally I said, "I have not been to the slave market in many weeks. Perhaps there is something special to see."

He was pleased with yet another reprieve from his lashing.

The slave market by the docks was not far from the old Greek Agora where the principal trade was now religious dogma.

In place of the booths that once sold goods from all over the world, a medley of temples crowded the Square. Existing on alms, the shrines to scores of gods and goddesses competed to attract pilgrims and worshippers. Hawkers stood outside, shouting to passersby.

"Worship here! Baal awaits to grant your desires."

"You will see no more delightful women than the beauties who serve our Temple of Ishtar!"

Even the Roman gods had to compete. A small temple to Jupiter used a trick device invented at the Library that magically dispensed holy water when a pilgrim inserted a coin.

The satellite temple for Serapis, hybrid Egyptian-Greek god created for Alexandrians by the first Ptolemy, employed a hydraulic contraption that fooled the gullible into believing that the invisible hand of Serapis himself swung the gates open. Also for a coin.

Sects and cults of every belief preyed on the superstitious. Scruffy men in tattered robes shrieked out predictions of impending doom.

"Repent! The time is near. The Messiah comes."

Alexandria the seductress. The name was magic itself. From Britannia, Germania, Parthia, Sheba, Arabia, Persia, the Indus Valley, Mongolia and China, the pilgrims and missionaries came to study, pray, preach, persuade and recruit. Virtually every dogma in the world was represented in this once grand plaza.

Ignoring the calls of hawkers, pushing our way through the milling mass of hot bodies, we made for the slave market to see what oddity I might find to please my more discerning clientele.

"There, Aeneas! Do you see the hermaphrodite?"

Protected by a linen shade, a white-haired, chalky-skinned teenager with round breasts and shrunken penis stood chained to a stone post.

"An albino, Domina. A double prize."

"Indeed, Aeneas. This is a treasure I cannot miss."

A clever auctioneer had seen that the albino's shoulder-length hair was curled and adorned with a crown of poppies. The youth's body, an odd mix of soft curves and toned muscle, narrowed at a girl's slender waist and then sloped to the hard thighs of an athlete. For my taste, the face was more male than female and not at all handsome, but the high round breasts with bright pink nipples were a delight.

I could make a fortune with this creature.

The bidding was fast-paced; more than a dozen buyers drove the price higher and higher. I let it go on for a few minutes, then spoke quietly to Aeneas. He stepped in with a breathtaking offer that silenced the auctioneer.

The crowd turned in our direction. As it would serve only to raise the price if a pleasure goddess of Canopus were seen as interested in the albino, I stayed hidden behind the curtains of the litter.

"Twenty thousand denarii," the auctioneer stammered. "Do I hear twenty-five?"

The crowd mumbled and looked to the other bidders. But they were after a toy. For me it was business. Silence.

"Do I hear twenty-three?" asked the auctioneer.

Mumbling, but no counterbid.

"Do I hear twenty-one?"

Still no bid.

"Going once. Going twice. Sold then for twenty thousand denarii!"

"No tattooing," I cautioned Aeneas. "I intend to use this creature in a trade."

"The vineyards of Marcus Geta in Faiyum, Domina?"

"The vineyards *and* the villa. That pervert will give anything to suck on cock while fondling those breasts."

We'd made it past the Soma of Alexander on our way back to the yacht wharf on Lake Mareotis when traffic halted for a mob—bigger and angrier than anything we'd seen today—blocking the street ahead. We were two litters now, one carrying the albino hermaphrodite who, for obvious reasons, couldn't be in the sun.

Aeneas maneuvered us to the other side of the marble colonnade lining the avenue. We pressed against a massive edifice with no windows on the street. Double yellow doors, curved on top, were shut tight.

"Find out what is going on," I ordered.

The Celt and Slant Eyes stayed with me; the Syrian pushed his way through the crowd with Aeneas on his heels.

I waved away flies with a horsetail whisk. A chariot tried to pass but, like us, couldn't advance. The Roman cursed and shouted abuse while his driver struggled to rein in the horses. Snorting and pawing the stone pavement, their chestnut coats glistened with sweat.

Aeneas returned, tense and out of breath.

"A Jew, Domina. A *magus* who drinks the blood of newborns. The mob is on its way to the Prefect to demand he be crucified and burned."

"Will they not let us pass?"

"They are beyond reason, Domina. I suggest we turn back and take another route."

"There is no turning around, Aeneas. Look behind."

The traffic, blocked from here forward, backed up on Soma Avenue as far as we could see. Flesh pressed against flesh pressing against marble walls.

The litter rocked. It rocked harder. I grabbed the wooden poles holding up the canopy to steady myself. And then with the surge of a tsunami, the mob broke through, crushing our litters against the building at the street's edge.

Where were the Roman soldiers? Mounted *Singulares* were supposed to patrol the main avenues of the Beta Quarter to prevent these mobs from getting out of control.

Our porters, spineless curs that they were, deserted us, dropping their poles and letting me fall to the curb. I scrambled out of the litter to cling to the wall.

The hermaphrodite, weak and pale, tumbled from the litter onto the pavement.

"The Devil's child!" someone shrieked.

"Satan!"

Like a pack of hyenas, the mob fell on the piteous creature, beating at the fragile body with sticks, clawing at the white flesh. Its mouth opened wide in agony; horrible, high-pitched inhuman squeals pierced my ears.

I tore my eyes away from the horror of flailing white arms and legs streaked with blood. That's when I saw Eben in his heavy woolen robe with hood. No matter the heat, he always wore it. Held by both arms, he was half standing and half on his knees, right next to me. So close that if I reached out, my fingers could smooth the long tangled waves falling into his face.

He saw me at the same time I saw him.

"Help me," his desperate eyes pleaded.

Perhaps because the mob was frenzied with the mutilation of the hermaphrodite, the men who held Eben loosened their grip for a heartbeat. I grabbed his arm and pulled him into me.

At the same moment, Aeneas seized my hand. Then he was dragging me to a single lane alleyway a few feet ahead on the right.

With all my might, I held fast to Eben's wool sleeve. Heaving him almost off his feet, I stumbled after Aeneas into the alley with Slant Eyes just behind us. I didn't see the Celt and the Syrian. Were they ahead of us clearing the way or fighting to cover our escape?

There was no sun in the alley. A virtual tunnel between towering three-story marble monsters, the slim artery lay in perpetual shadow. We ran toward a narrow rectangle of blue sky at the far end, a long block away.

The stench of urine gagged me. Aeneas kept me on my feet and running forward as my sandals slipped and slid in piss and vomit.

When I glanced back at Eben, his eyes were glazed. But his feet moved; he stayed upright.

Behind Eben, I saw the Celt. Then I saw the Syrian behind him. The next time I looked back, the Syrian was behind me. Then he was passing Aeneas to lead the way.

The blue rectangle grew wider and wider until we burst into blinding sunlight onto a street narrower than Soma Avenue. Buildings on both sides abutted the pavement directly with no ceremonial colonnade. Immediately on our right was a construction site.

A cloud of dust choked the air. Hammers banged, and chisels clanged. The Syrian and Aeneas turned sharply into the heart of the chaos. I could hear the rabid cries of the mob whipped into a fury by being forced to run single-file through the alley.

A score of workmen in filthy loincloths and soiled rags over their noses and mouths kept pounding. Chunks of rock showered around us from overhead. Stones, large and small, littered the ground at our feet.

Aeneas grabbed my shoulders and shoved me into a shadowy space under a huge block of hewn marble. I never let go of Eben's sleeve.

Eben stumbled, fell to his knees and rolled in after me.

The ground gave way, crumbling all around. We slid a few feet downward and then a few feet more. I lost my grip on Eben.

"Ae-ne-as…" I called out as I tumbled head over heels down, down, down.

And then, everything went black.

CHAPTER 34   THE VISITOR

"Things are not always as they seem; the first appearance deceives many."
– Phaedrus

Domina! Domina!"
    I opened my eyes to the terrified face of Aeneas.
    "Domina, come back to us. Come back!"
His face was so pale—so very pale. Surely as white as the albino's. His whole body trembled.

When he saw me conscious, relief washed the panic from his face; he was suddenly ten years younger.

"I see, I breathe and I think, Aeneas. Let me now see if I move."

No broken bones.

I held out my hands, and Slant Eyes slowly pulled me to my feet. Not even a sprained ankle. Thank you, Universe!

"What do they call you?" I asked.

"Khan," he said, looking me directly in the eye. A capital offense in some households.

Eben stood to the side, staring blankly into another world. His shoulders looked too frail to support the weight of his ponderous robe. And while I wondered at how vulnerable he was, delicate as a gazelle, I noticed the fifth faience septagram hanging on a leather thong around his neck. But our roles were reversed; instead of Eben protecting me, I had saved him. At least, for now.

We were in a burial catacomb. Row after row of wooden sarcophagi filled deep niches in the walls. Moisture ate at the once bright-colored stucco ceiling now faded and peeling. By a caved-in doorway, a crumbling man-sized painting of the God Anubis watched the Celt and Syrian clearing stones.

The hammering had stopped, replaced by the mob's barking and baying. What sounded like hundreds of feet pounded the earth above. Chunks of the ceiling stucco fell on us.

We all began moving stones at the blocked doorway. Everyone, that is, but Eben, who truly was not with us.

Finally we cleared a hole, but no light shone through. We had the benefit of filtered sunlight from the shaft where I fell, but if there was an intact chamber on the other side, all was black.

Working together, we dug and tugged until the opening was wide enough for the Syrian to crawl through.

"Stay here," he said in Greek.

I thought nothing of following the command of a slave.

We waited an eternity while the earth trembled from the thunder of feet. Larger chunks of ceiling fell, landing with thuds all around us. Then came a shower of small stones. I feared the whole roof would cave in. Just when I could wait no longer and was ready to crawl in after him, the Syrian was back.

"Come."

The next chamber was pitch-black as only a cave can be. We formed a human chain; Aeneas held my hand, and I held Eben's. With the Syrian in the lead, we groped our way along the wall. I felt stucco crumble against my gown, then an open space where a sarcophagus must lie, then solid wall again.

We passed through a doorway and into another chamber. And then another. I lost count of how many.

Total darkness and total silence. I was acutely conscious of my too-rapid breathing. My heart hammered in my ears. I chanted *"ANA A A NANA A A NANA"* over and over.

My mind calmed. I willed my body to let go of tension. In the absolute darkness, I sensed the Syrian at the lead. I felt his energy distinct from the others. As was Khan's. As was the Celt's. We all vibrated at a different rate. And then we were vibrating together, as one. Eben's hand was moist. I heard the low murmur of his Kabbalah chant.

Miraculously, the next chamber was filled with gray shadows. And then at last, we entered a mellow halo of filtered sunlight glowing on limestone. A circular stone staircase carved out of living rock led up to the world.

Again the Syrian went first, followed by the Celt, both with swords drawn. Khan stayed glued to me, and I to Eben. Aeneas never let go of my hand.

We came out into a small courtyard surrounded by apartments. Laundry hung on balconies. Chickens clucked. Children played. The smells of cooking filled the air.

Within seconds, astonished faces stared down from three levels of ramshackle wooden balconies.

What a vision we must have been, covered in dust, climbing out of the castle of the dead. I heard shouted out the names of a multitude of gods, followed by incantations and singing. Those in the courtyard cleared a path for us, some kneeling, others making the sign of the cross. An old man sitting in the shade prostrated himself.

The Syrian slowly opened the gate to the street. He stepped out and quickly back in.

"Harbor."

I felt a wave of relief; we weren't far from the Royal Quarter and safety.

Across a wide street filled with two-wheeled carts pulled by slaves stood a mud brick warehouse. The docks lay just on the other side. A *trireme* mast waving a crested flag poked up over the palm thatch roof.

Following the Syrian, we hurried down the street and turned left into an alley. At the end were blue water, seagulls and the sound of waves licking at the stone quay. My nostrils filled with the salty scent of fish and rotting seaweed. The perfume of longshoremen.

We huddled in a group, the slaves waiting for my direction.

"What do you judge, Aeneas, to be our safest route home?"

"It might be best by sea, Domina."

"Then arrange for a boat."

While Aeneas went in search of a boat for hire, we hid like criminals in the deep shade behind a tall pile of amphorae. We could take no chances. I had stolen Eben from a mob convinced of his evil; I had robbed them of his death. Who knew what cult they belonged to? There were hundreds in Alexandria. Who knew what spies they had?

The Syrian watched every movement on the dock with the shiny black eyes of a hawk.

I felt the thunder of horse hooves vibrate through the stone quay and looked out through a space between the amphorae. Five horsemen approached. Roman cavalry. The Syrian and I exchanged looks; he frowned and shook his head. Caution. Wait.

It was rare to see cavalry inside the Gate of the Moon. The *ala* had quarters on the outskirts of the city near the old Hippodrome; the bulk of the *equites* quartered to the south in Faiyum where lush grasslands provided ample feed for their hundreds of horses.

I couldn't believe my luck when the riders halted just on the other side of the amphorae and the General's plumed helmet glittered in the sun. Not fifty feet away, he dismounted from a great black stallion sixteen hands high. *We were saved.*

I took off the ruby septagram necklace and gave it to Khan. "Take this to the Moor."

Khan walked toward the General, but before he took no more than a few steps, he was intercepted by one of the equites. There was a short exchange, and I regretted sending Khan. He spoke almost no Latin. The cavalryman took the necklace from him and turned to approach the General.

But the General put up his hand, and the soldier halted. Coming toward us from the direction of the trireme with crested flag was a small party of Romans in togas. A platoon of legionaries in black-brush helmets and leather cuirasses with lappet skirts marched behind.

The sun shone in my eyes; I could see only silhouettes with the General's back to me. He held out his right hand to a much smaller man, and they clasped arms. When he stepped to the side so the two could walk abreast, I saw the Roman's face.

Dominus! Marcus Quintillus! Here in Alexandria. And the General had come personally to greet him.

I must have cried out, although I wasn't aware that I did, because the Celt glanced at me and then followed my line of sight to the General.

"Get the necklace back! Get the necklace back!" I shouted silently to Khan.

But it was too late. The cavalryman was handing the necklace to the General who turned his face in our direction.

"We must leave *now*," I whispered urgently to the Syrian.

With the reflexes of a survivor of the Arena, he assessed the look on my face, the fear in my voice, the men on the dock and put them all together instantly. He signaled the Celt, and we were back in the alley heading away from the docks and then speeding down a side street.

Comatose Eben, the two ex-gladiators and me.

I had thought to seek refuge at Flavia's, but the Royal Quarters no longer meant safety.

With one command Dominus could have me crucified. He could do far worse to me before that. Crucifixion might be a blessing, in the end.

I had to get back to Canopus. There I could think; there I could come up with a plan. There I had my laboratory of potions that could silence Marcus Quintillus forever.

And there, I suddenly remembered—oh, how could I have forgotten!—I had the Red Mirror.

If Flavia were true to her word—and I believed with all my heart that she would be—the Mirror was waiting for me at home.

Home.

I could escape this nightmare scenario so easily. I had only the journey from here to Canopus. Then I could truly go home. Back to Las Vegas.

"To our boat," I commanded. "By every back street you know."

CHAPTER 35   EBONY AND IVORY

"An object in possession seldom retains the same charm that it had in pursuit."
– Pliny the Elder

The Syrian knew his way around the city, leading us through the old Jewish Quarter down quiet side streets and through empty alleyways. The sun was still well above the western horizon when we arrived without incident at the yacht wharf in the Lake Harbor.

If the winds favored us and our oarsmen rowed steady, we'd be home on my island not long after dark. Aeneas and Khan would have to find their own way. I left word with an Egyptian beggar who slept by the ramp.

"Look for two slaves," I told him in Greek. "One middle-aged, bony and bald, the other a copper-skinned square warrior with slanted eyes. Tell them this: *The Goddess will meet them at the Temple.*"

I handed him the yellow ribbon tied at my shoulder, saying, "Give this to the older one. There will be a reward when you deliver the message."

The beggar clutched my hand, held my eyes for a moment and then said, "ABLAMGOUNOTHO ABRASAX."

Stunned, I pulled my hand away. At the sound of the incantation, Eben stood up straight. He blinked once or twice in a startled way, then stared all around with the baffled look of someone awakened in an unfamiliar place.

When I took Eben's hand, he was ice cold in spite of his heavy robe, in spite of the sun baking down on the stone quay. At the base of his throat where a fragile patch of skin showed, the green septagram glowed. A purple vein throbbed in his temple. His lower lip quivered; tears glistened in his gazelle eyes.

"You are safe, Eben. You are with me."

"Thank you, Isis," he said humbly. "I knew you would come."

Not only did the Red Mirror await my return to the island but also a scroll hung with gold tassels and sealed in red wax with the Imperial Crest of the Emperor of Rome.

My presence was requested at a banquet the next evening on Hadrian's barge moored in Canopus.

The language was worded politely enough, but an invitation from the Emperor was, in fact, a summons. The General had made good on his promise for an introduction, although his timing couldn't have been worse.

Dominus. Here in Alexandria. Surely he had come to see Hadrian. Why else would the General greet him personally? I was certain Marcus Quintillus had also received such a scroll inviting him to the feast; his arrival could not be coincidence.

I lay my head on the armrest of the divan and closed my eyes. The Red Mirror floated in black space. I had only to step through.

"You cannot go back," I heard Eben say. "It is too soon."

"I am afraid, Eben," I whispered. "Very, very afraid."

"You are thinking to escape what is coming, Isis. But you must not." He paused before saying in a puzzled tone, "You have the power to influence events. Why do you not believe in yourself?"

In my mind, I replayed the dream with the gilded barge. Arms reaching out for me, but no one touching me, no matter how far the arms stretched and stretched.

"The Black Scroll," Eben said. "You came back for that."

"I came back for you, Eben."

"We are all One. Everything is One."

"If I am exposed, Eben, I shall die on the cross."

"The story is not yet written. It is you who holds the pen."

"And if you are wrong?"

"Have I ever been?"

I closed my eyes again. So exhausted, so utterly drained. Then I remembered what the General had said about Hadrian.

He has dreams. Dreams that disturb his sleep.
You can interpret a few dreams, Ishtar, can you not?
"I am going back, Eben. But only for a short trip. Only long enough to find out what I need to know."

My condo was dark. At first I looked around for Aisha, and then I remembered that I'd left her with Sonny before I went to Libya what seemed a thousand years ago.

There was a string of messages on my cell.

"I'm worried sick, Isis," Tony's third message pleaded. "Where are you? Have pity on me, will ya?"

I'd never lied or told half-truths to Tony; he was an anchor of honesty in my life. Of pure artlessness. And so to avoid his questions, I sent a text.

Me: *Everything fine. Out of range for couple days.*

He answered right back.

Tony: *You're not in Libya again?*

I didn't have to lie.

Me: *No. No more Libya.*

The General's message dropped the usual hint of knowing more. "Business complete. If you're listening to this, I assume you are back safely."

So he'd done the arms deal; I'd made my first fully deliberate, direct profit from death. I assured myself that he referred to being back from Paris, but I didn't really believe that's what he meant.

The message from Barb was typically astute. "As you aren't picking up your cell and not online, I assume you've done the stupidest thing in your life and gone back."

I knew exactly what Barb meant when she said 'back.'

Hector's voice was awash with relief. "Ingrid is out of the ICU. She's conscious. She knows me."

There was nothing from Rasheed.

It's up to you, Isis. It's all up to you. His last words before he walked away and left me at the gate in Charles de Gaulle.

His cell rang twice and went to voicemail.

"Rasheed–" I started and then stopped. I couldn't ask him to call me. I wouldn't be here. I couldn't tell him I'd given up the General. I hadn't. I couldn't tell him anything but the truth.

"Rasheed, I miss you. Don't you miss me?"

Had I no self-respect at all? I vowed never, ever, to tell Barb about that call.

I skipped over the message from an area code I didn't recognize and spent the next forty-five minutes on Google reading everything I could about Emperor Hadrian. That's when I saw the bust of Antinous of Bithynia. Hadrian's Greek lover. Tony.

There was no doubt. The likeness was astounding, right down to the rich mane of curls that I'd run my fingers through in three lifetimes.

With each click, more and more statues popped up. It seemed that every museum of antiquities boasted a likeness of Antinous raised to godhead by a heartbroken Hadrian. No one could say with certainty how he died. There were theories—accident, suicide, murder, and even ritual sacrifice. But regardless of motive, each supposition ended with his nineteen-year-old body floating in the Nile.

My cell buzzed. I picked it up without thinking, hoping it might be Rasheed.

"Hello," I said impatiently when I saw the 312 number on Caller ID.

"It's about time," said Gareth Greene in his Barry White voice.

"I've been out of town."

"Isn't that why people have cellphones?" But there wasn't anything in his playful voice that was accusative.

"I didn't have a signal." The truth. You can't beat it sometimes.

"Hey, did your being out of town have something to do with those bad guys? You ever find out who they were?"

"Not yet."

"But you feel safe now? I mean, you're back. Or are you back?"

"I'm in Vegas, yes. But just a short time. I came back to get... something."

"Time enough to see me?"

That took me enough off-guard that I didn't answer.

"Come on. You must have time for a drink? Don't you think you owe me that?"

I looked at the Red Mirror. I looked at myself *in* the Red Mirror. Not too bad. My hair looked pretty good.

I argued with myself that I didn't have time, and then countered, what was time? The old Isis in me had been waiting about 2,500 years for Goliath.

We may live more than once, but each life must be lived to the fullest.

What had the General called it? *A walk on the wild side.*
   "I've only got an hour."
   "I'll be there in ten minutes."

When I came out of the elevator, Gareth was standing at the security desk laughing with the guard Jack who held a piece of notebook paper in his hand with Gareth's autograph.

   In a way Goliath would never have dared, Gareth gave me a blatant once-over from my shiny copper hair right down to my black high-heeled boots. I was all in black—a Michael Kors slinky, long-sleeved, tight-fitting top over black leather pants. A thin snakeskin belt with brass buckle showed off my waist.

   On my wrist was a heavy Italian gold ID bracelet. Tiffany diamond studs glinted in my earlobes.

   "Nice. Very nice," Gareth said. His eyes said a lot more.

   The lobby was empty except for the valet, the concierge and two powerfully-built men in dark business suits, one sitting close by the front door, the other by the door to the parking garage. The General's men.

   I nodded to the one pulling out his cell. He looked at me, then at Gareth, and started speaking Corsu into the phone.

   Gareth drove one of those big shiny black Escalades that I always associate with drug dealers. The sound system played smooth jazz.

   Mixed with the new car scent was his cologne, more primal than spicy. I wore Sung—heavy, exotic, cloyingly sweet like jungle gardenia.

   "Where to?" he asked. "This is your town."

   "I told you an hour. We've got 50 minutes left."

   "My place?"

   We exchanged looks that said everything.

   "If it's close."

Gareth had a condo in the Cosmopolitan; like his car, his place was shiny black. The scent of new leather was here, too. So was the incomparable sound system that he switched on with a remote. Barry White.

   An array of mini-spots recessed in the glossy ceiling highlighted some impressive African art.

   A lounge chair was upholstered in zebra. A real zebra skin hung on the wall behind the glass dining room table surrounded by black leather and chrome chairs.

"Shall I take off my boots?" I asked when I saw the white carpet.

"At least."

I slid open the doors to the terrace and stepped out. The Bellagio fountains danced below; the Paris balloon was huge in the night sky. Glittering new high-rises dwarfed the iconic Eiffel Tower that used to dominate the Strip. North up Las Vegas Boulevard pulsed the lights of Caesar's, the Venetian and the Wynn.

Even someone like me who's seen just about every view in Vegas was moved to awe.

"Nice, huh?" Gareth asked from two inches away.

He held two flutes bubbling with champagne.

"How often do you stay here?"

"Whenever I'm in town. I could be here more often." His eyes asked me if I liked the idea.

"I'm gonna be straight," he went on. "I wanna fuck you. I think I've wanted to since you stood there in front of me in the Bellagio lobby wearing that sexy yellow sweater."

"I don't have much time," I reminded him as I unzipped his fly.

I reached into his jockey shorts and pulled him out. O Hathor! He was as beautiful as I'd daydreamed on the Nile. His black glistening head was big as my fist. He just kept growing and growing as I stroked him.

He set the two glasses on the railing and scooped me up with his giant hands spread under my butt. I wrapped my legs around his waist, my arms around his neck, and pulled myself into him. His huge cock pressed against my leather crotch. I gyrated my hips, grinding into him.

"Oh baby," he moaned.

Like a pro going for the dunk, he didn't take many strides to get to his king bed on a lighted platform.

His hands were inside my tight shirt and his fingers in my bra before my back hit the zebra bedspread.

I twisted and growled. His other hand was between my legs, his strong finger rotating on the leather. I squeezed his thick, iron penis in my fist, milking him, matching the rhythm of his fingers in my groin.

I came. Suddenly and unexpectedly. My hand stopped, my breath caught, my vagina contracted and contracted; heat flashed through my womb.

"Whoa," he said. "Man, you're easy."

"Don't worry. I'm not done."

I rolled him over and unbuckled his belt. His mammoth penis stood straight up, a basalt obelisk to the sky.

I took him all the way to the back of my throat. Just once. Then I pulled his trousers and shorts past his ankles and dropped them on the floor.

He reached for me, but I pushed his hands to the bed and held them there firmly until he got the message that I was calling the shots.

Then I unbuttoned his black silk shirt, alternating each button with a lick on his bulb, or a suck on his balls, or a swallow to the back of my throat. I never did the same thing twice. I never let him predict what was coming.

"Oh baby," he kept saying over and over. "Where did you learn to do *that*?"

When his shirt was off, I swayed between his ineffable long legs hanging off the foot of the bed, circling my hips to the throbbing beat of "Can't Get Enough of Your Love, Babe." With the delicacy of lifting a sea silk veil woven with sparkly threads, I slipped off each piece of my clothing.

First my leather pants, then my black top and then the black lace panties.

"Show me those tits," he begged.

I unhooked my bra and let my breasts fall free.

"Nice, baby. Nice."

And then, precisely as Isis had daydreamed of seducing Goliath on the Nile, I straddled him and placed him at my gate. He reached for my breasts, but I held his hands to his sides.

Slowly—so slowly—I lowered myself onto his giant pedestal. I couldn't sink all the way. He was too big. My throbbing lotus screamed each time I moved on his shaft.

Dangling my ripe breasts near to his lush lips, I teased him, never coming close enough for his tongue, offering him forbidden fruit that he must never taste.

Mesmerized, Gareth watched me act out my drama, eagerly playing his part, never imagining I was living a daydream twenty-three centuries old.

And when my aching bud fully flowered in its lust and the tsunami wave crashed in my surf, I threw back my head and howled, "O Goddess divine!"

"Far out," he shouted. "Far. Fucking. Out."

He grabbed me then and threw me onto my back and started pounding. He showed me no mercy, and I asked for none.

He shook all over in one final savage plunge and collapsed. We were both drenched in sweat. His male scent overpowered his cologne; I drank it in with deep gulps.

When he rolled onto his back beside me, we were glistening ebony and lustrous ivory on a zebra spread.

"Where have you been all my life?"

I laughed and got up from the bed.

"You don't wanna know. You wouldn't believe it anyway."

"Hey," he called out as I headed to the bathroom, "You're not a real redhead."

"I'm not a real anything," I said and blew him a kiss.

The valet didn't try to mask his surprise to see me at the glass doors sixty-seven minutes after I'd left. Even the Corsican gave me an odd look. Then the cellphone was at his ear, reporting to the General.

"When can I see you again?"

"I don't know, Gareth. I'm going out of town for a while."

"That sounds suspiciously like a brush-off."

"My life's pretty complicated. Why don't we just wait and see what happens."

"You mean like, 'Don't call us. We'll call you?'"

"Let's not spoil a great time, Gareth. I'll walk myself in."

I didn't have to go back. I could take my shower and go to sleep. Wake up tomorrow in my own bed. My life would go on. Whatever dangers were here, they seemed manageable after what I'd seen in Alexandria. Maybe Barb was right. Let the past alone.

But Eben was waiting for me. I'd promised him.

I brought up my bookmarked link to the Greek Magical Papyrus.

"Compiled in Egypt second century AD, the *Papyri Graecae Magicae* in Latin–*PGM*–is thought to be an opus of dozens of Egyptian scrolls collected by an ancient scholar and translated to Greek."

It was October 130 AD in Alexandria now, early second century. What Eben had been trying to tell me was that we were the scholars who created the *Papyri Graecae Magicae*—well, at least Eben was a scholar. And October 130 AD was when Antinous died. It was too much of a coincidence to be one. Everything was happening as it was meant to be.

I took a long look at the Internet image of the Prado marble bust of Antinous, and a possibility began to evolve, a possibility of altering his fate.

I'd gone back and saved Eben. I'd saved myself once.

Barb was wrong. I *could* change events. It was as Eben said—I held the pen.

And so in that way that we believe what we choose to believe, I chose to go back and write history. The Death of Antinous and the Black Scroll.

One minute I was lying on my bed, wrapped in a fluffy white bath towel, puzzling over words like 'ABRACADABRA' that I'd heard all my life and never considered their source, and the next I was in my marble bath in Canopus. Eben and Aeneas stood not far away.

"You were gone too long," Eben said anxiously. "You must prepare."

Aeneas stared at Eben and then even stared at me until I met his eyes, and he dropped his. But not before I saw his clever Greek mind puzzling, *Gone too long?*

"I am prepared, Eben. I am more than ready."

ABLAMGOUNOTHO ABRASAX. *Bring it on!*

CHAPTER 36   HADRIAN

"I came. I saw. I conquered." – Julius Caesar

G hazel went to great pains to ensure that my white skin was massaged with the finest oils, my hair rinsed with the sweetest scents and my cosmetics applied with the most meticulous care. She outlined my eyes with *kohl* in the Egyptian fashion and painted green mica on my eyelids up to my eyebrows. My lips were ripe with carmine. She piled my copper hair high in curls and elaborate twists held in place with gold sewing twine and garnets strung on golden wire.

Aeneas and she argued over which gown I should wear, Ghazel insisting on the emerald green silk to match my eyes, while Aeneas preferred the citrine woven with golden threads.

"I shall wear the citrine but carry an emerald palla."

On top of the citrine stola I wore a golden corset *mammillare* that pushed up my breasts and sculpted my narrow waist. A genius with fabric, Ghazel had developed a style unique to me that combined Egyptian daring with Roman elegance.

In honor of the occasion, Brutus had fashioned a stunning gold necklace with glittering crescent moons and seven-pointed stars set with emeralds and pearls. Sparkling stars and moons dangled from my earlobes. Golden serpents with emerald eyes twisted around my upper arms.

When the dressing was complete, I sat quietly sipping a chalice of infused herbs that calmed my nerves yet left my head clear.

ANA A A NANA A A NANA. Over and over, I called on the Universe to send me strength.

The setting sun signaled it was time to depart. With dread, I watched the sky flame on the horizon and the Nile turn red.

Aeneas would accompany me, of course—and for dramatic effect, the twin Nubians in their matching yellow-striped headdresses.

Eben handed me a miniature vial of red and green flecked glass, saying solemnly, "Two drops, and breathing stops, but slowly, over time. More, and it goes quickly."

I slipped the vial into a tiny pocket sewed discretely into my gown.

Ghazel with her flair for the theatrical had seen that my barge was decked in garlands of ivy and lotus blossoms. A flautist and a lyrist played seductively from the stern. Our long river oars dipped into blood red waters, pulling me to my fate in Canopus at the juncture of river and sea.

The torches on Hadrian's Imperial Barge blazed so bright we spotted his party from a mile away.

My heart raced. My palms were wet. I breathed deeply and slowly to ward off panic. I had the vial. With a dozen drops instead of two, I could put an end to Dominus at once. And if the worst happened and Eben was wrong about my powers, I had the vial for me.

Aeneas watched me carefully; all the glitter of my gown and jewels couldn't hide my distress from him. He had a puzzled look that vanished as soon as I turned my eyes to him. *Who is this woman?* he might have been thinking. Of course, he could never fathom the truth.

The pilot shouted out for the galley slaves to ship oars, and we pulled alongside the Imperial Barge.

Waiting aboard was the General.

He wore a gold muscle cuirass with white leather lappets and a gold helmet with a white brush. His monster sandals laced up the shin with golden twine.

Combed forward from the crown, thick, artfully-arranged black waves framed his rough face. But all the finery and plumage didn't tame him; he throbbed with raw animal savagery.

With a grace that always surprised me, he took my hand and led me onto the deck.

"Be careful, my beauty," he said after undressing me with his eyes, "You are certain to make enemies among the ladies tonight."

Then he leaned into my ear.

"I shall come after the feast to finish what we started."

"I cannot say that I shall be free. You forget I am a businesswoman."

With that, he laughed a good-natured laugh and pressed warm metal into my palm. The ruby septagram necklace.

"You left this behind on the docks yesterday," he murmured.

He waited for an explanation, but I gave him none.

"More secrets, Ishtar?"

Aeneas was immediately at my side to take the necklace.

"So General, just where is this Emperor you insist I meet?"

I was unprepared for the glory that was Antinous. His golden skin glowed. His eyes danced. Never had I seen a man—or woman—more radiant. So vibrant. So incredibly, fervently imbued with life force.

He stood close by Hadrian's lectus, dressed in a sky blue chiton in the classic Greek style, belted at the waist, with loose pleats falling to mid-thigh. Blue wool draped from under his right arm across his perfect chest to fasten on a muscular bronzed left shoulder. His mane of blond curls was expertly arranged to suggest no arrangement at all.

And because he was Hadrian's lover, I hadn't anticipated the force of his masculinity. Nor for his reaction when I entered the Imperial cabin.

His face was instantly attentive. His eyes lit, but not with recognition; he didn't remember me from another life. I met his eager look only briefly before quickly turning away. All the world knew Hadrian to be besotted with Antinous; he was with Caesar always.

The General brought me forward to where Hadrian reclined, and I dropped to one knee with bowed head.

"May I present to Caesar, Elektra of Canopus."

Hadrian proved not beyond arousal by a woman; his hungry eyes ate me up.

But he was tired. Haggard even. There was a sickly pallor to his skin that gave credence to whispers that he was in poor health. I sensed the rapid ebbing of male vigor past its prime. He had a sad dog look to his eyes. Old age was not to Hadrian's liking.

I'd envisioned him as the virile, confident man captured in bronze and marble with a full head of hair and a robust, wavy beard. This Caesar had scraggly tufts of hair combed over a bald spot. The manly beard was far from full and streaked with gray.

Yet he had some vigor left. His eyes shone with delight as he looked me quite thoroughly over.

"So you are the beauty of whom my old friend boasts," he boomed in Koine Greek.

"Caesar is more than kind. I am but a simple woman whom the Gods have blessed."

I answered him in Greek, relieved to avoid our native Latin. Although I'd largely succeeded in eliminating all traces of my Spanish accent, he might have detected a hint of the special lilt of Italica, our common birthplace. I wanted no questions as to my origin.

He waved his hand in the direction of the divan next to him.

"Come. Be here close to us. Let us feast upon your beauty. My old eyes, alas, see not well from afar."

I relaxed onto the silk cushions of the divan to his right and accepted a gold chalice of watered wine from a slave.

Conscious of every eye on me, I casually arranged my shoulders, hips and legs to present a seductive and inviting curve that narrowed at my waist and sloped along my thighs. My ripe breasts bulged the yellow silk; my oiled ivory shoulders and arms glowed in the lamplight.

Taking a sip from the chalice, I lowered my lashes in pretense of the demure and wet my deep red lips with wine.

Great sensuous waves rolled off me and washed over Hadrian. I beamed a laser of sensuality through him. His pupils dilated; his breath quickened. I cast a sidelong glance at the General, who watched me with a half-smile of amusement.

To the left of Hadrian, Antinous appeared mesmerized. He caught me looking at him and smiled altogether too warmly. I quickly turned my eyes back to Hadrian.

The silence went on, and the tension grew until finally relieved by the General.

"Caesar, I believe you shall find Lady Elektra's ability to see beyond the veil even more alluring than her charms."

"Yes, so you tell me, my Moor." Hadrian's voice had the telltale huskiness of a man drowning in sexual possibility. Still his eyes sharpened at the General's suggestion of my seeing what others could not.

"If Caesar would be so gracious as to give me something of his to hold," I breathed in a low vibrating tone. "Something personal, something that has been touched by his Imperial spirit."

Without hesitation, Hadrian took off his signet ring, the one whose insignia set in red wax carried the full force and might of Rome. A slave standing at his elbow passed the ring to me.

ANA A A NANA A A NANA, I murmured under my breath just loud enough for Hadrian to hear. My eyes were closed; I feigned the expression of one not quite of this world.

The lavish barge cabin with gilt-paneled bulkheads and deck covered in thick carpets was absolutely still. A coal popped in a brazier. From outside, I heard the sounds of guests arriving and slaves readying the banquet.

When I spoke, the timbre of my voice, tinged with wonder, was seductive as warm oil.

"I see a villa in the countryside. And rolling hills richly planted with olive trees. So gre-e-en." I drew out the word green as if in awe of the lushness.

"The sky is immense. It goes on forever." I paused a moment for dramatic effect before taking a sharp intake of air.

"Dogs! Dogs barking and barking. Hunting dogs. And horses. Such magnificent steeds."

I paused again before whispering, "A hunt."

Thanks to Google, I knew there were few things Hadrian loved more than a hunt. He'd spent his youth ranging the far hills of Italica in search of deer and wild boar.

"Caesar is young, but he outrides the older boys who struggle to keep up."

I felt Hadrian stir on his divan. I was tempted to open my eyes but kept them closed.

In a daring move calculated to stir old emotions, I addressed him in the familiar instead of third person, "Your mother worries; she has only you. Each time you ride out, her eyes are dark with worry."

I took another risk with the part about the mother, but what widow wouldn't worry when her only son rode recklessly after dangerous animals?

In minute detail, I described a special valley near Italica where I'd been allowed once to hunt with my brothers. So rare was the occasion they showed me kindness that each tree, stone, hill and scent of that afternoon was vivid in my mind.

Hadrian cried out, "Yes! Yes! I bagged my first boar there."

"Great Jupiter!" he shouted to the General, "the woman has the gift of Sight."

To ice the cake, I continued in my deep, resonating, trance-like tone, "I see another hunt. A hunt for lions. I see Caesar with Antinous. Chariots in the desert. The Egyptian desert."

Again I paused for dramatic effect before whispering in a hushed, urgent voice, "*Periculum!*" Danger!

Visibly shaken, Hadrian insisted, "I do not have this memory."

I opened my eyes and met his. With great coolness, I answered, "The hunt is yet to be, Caesar. It is written, but not the outcome."

"What is the danger?" he whispered.

I hesitated, pretending a reluctance to disclose my vision.

"Tell me!" he ordered. "I command you."

"The loss of Antinous," I said gravely.

Hadrian sucked in a long swallow of air. His right hand trembled; wine spilled from the chalice.

I glanced at Antinous, who seemed not at all disturbed. On the contrary, he gave me a small, knowing smile. I had the impression he didn't put much stock in my magic.

But Hadrian believed. I snapped my fingers for Aeneas to approach. The crack of the snap might have been thunder.

"It is not too late to alter events, Caesar."

I nodded to Aeneas who took the cue and passed the ruby septagram necklace to Hadrian's personal slave.

"Take this septagram, Caesar. Wear it on the hunt. It was crafted in my personal atelier under a waxing quarter moon in Aries with the sun in the 12th house. It shall protect and grant the strength to vanquish any peril."

Hadrian took the necklace and put it at once around his neck.

O Google! I worship at your altar for guiding me to the Pancrates poem eulogizing the lion hunt. The hunt where Hadrian saves Antinous only days before the fabled death in the Nile.

"Ask for anything within my power," Hadrian said solemnly.

"There is nothing I desire other than the satisfaction of assisting Caesar to live a long and fulfilling life."

"The response," he chuckled, "is that which I would expect from one who has the Sight to see what pleases me."

He made moves to stand. Antinous was already on his feet.

"And now, alas, I fear we must forego our intimacy. I am told the guests impatiently await my presence. Shall we make our appearance at the convivium, Elektra? There are many persons I wish you to meet."

I pushed aside my angst of who that might be. I had come this far. And I had now an Emperor as ally. Surely the Universe smiled on me.

But for extra protection, I murmured *ABLAMGOUNOTHO ABRASAX* and chanted *ANA A A NANA A A NANA* all the way to the torch-lit deck arranged with silk and fur-festooned divans.

CHAPTER 37   THE GRECKLING

"Tell me who is able to keep his bed chaste, or which goddess is able to live with one god alone?" – Sextus Propertius

Hadrian's wife, Vibia Sabina, lay in splendor on the couch to the left of his waiting lectus. She was known to be a cold and self-absorbed woman, a second cousin, who married Hadrian at her family's insistence.

No doubt they enticed her with his excellent prospects to follow their Uncle Trajan as Emperor. But brilliant as Hadrian was—scholar, musician, poet, architect, able military tactician and acute politician—Vibia Sabina had her own romantic liaisons and regarded him with disdain.

The two had evolved a barely civil marriage where both pursued their own pleasures. Vibia Sabina had given him no heir; she'd once boasted that she would never bear "that monster's" children. For reasons known only to them, Hadrian tolerated her. He seemed to have a weakness for strong women; they'd always dominated his life. Trajan's wife Plotina championed Hadrian's career right up to his election as Emperor and then guided his reign until her death.

According to Aeneas' sources, Hadrian was to sail on a grand tour up the Nile to Thebes accompanied by his mother-in-law, wife Sabina and her constant companion, an enigmatic woman named Julia Balbilla. I surmised that Balbilla was the woman reclining on the divan next to the Empress. Not particularly attractive, Balbilla had an arrogant yet intelligent face with a high forehead over cunning eyes. She was said to fancy herself a poet and was prone to the usual piques of temperament common to artists.

The pair of them gave me hostile glares of cold displeasure; my private audience with Hadrian had held up the banquet. I glanced quickly around for Marcus Quintillus but didn't see Dominus' pasty face or puffy white body in the circle reclining on gilded divans.

When I looked again at Vibia Sabina, she stared pugnaciously back. I bowed my head respectfully first to her and then to Balbilla, who held her chin with the arrogance of aristocracy. Her father, an exiled Greek king, lived a life of luxury in Rome at the expense of the state. Her mother was from a massively wealthy Greek Alexandrian family who arrived in Egypt with Ptolemy centuries ago. Imminently well-educated, Balbilla moved always in the highest of intellectual and social circles.

"Be cautious with Julia Balbilla," the General had warned. "The Empress and she are inseparable."

Whispering in each other's ears, the two scrutinized my every step. The General guided me to a divan occupied by a gangly Roman with knobby elbows who introduced himself as Gaius Valerius. He had a large pointy nose marked by prominent blue veins and wore a silly grape leaf laurel perched on his frizzy gray curls. Around his ostrich neck hung a garland of cloying sweet gardenia. I counted six rings on his fingers.

In what I thought to be rather an incautious demonstration of intimacy, Antinous joined Hadrian on his couch at the head of the circle. The General caught my eye just long enough for me to see the flicker of his disapproval. Whether it was of the open display or of the relationship itself, I couldn't tell. When I looked back at Antinous, he shot me a wide smile that made no attempt at discretion.

The Praetorian Guard, all in black from their capes to the lacings on their sandals, stood with unreadable expressions, eyes straight forward.

Overhead, hazy stars twinkled in an inky sky. The night mist on the river had risen and enveloped the barge in warm fog. Just enough air moved to keep insects from settling. Torches flamed, and braziers burned with the woody, lemony incense disliked by mosquitoes.

By the rowdy laughter and the snippets of crude jokes I overheard, Hadrian's guests had been drinking heavily. The usual bevy of gorgeous male slaves in Greek tunics stood around with silver urinals or pitchers for ladling wine.

"I have long desired to make your acquaintance, Madam," professed Gaius Valerius beside me. His hand slid to my thigh.

"I pray, Sir, that you excuse me, but this evening I am off-duty." This I said politely and firmly while gripping his hand and removing it from my leg.

He looked startled and then distinctly uneasy when the General took my other hand and raised my fingers to his lips. I felt him shift his weight away; he downed a deep swallow of wine.

Over the drunken babble and the trilling of flutes, I heard the splashing of oars and then the noisy lashing of ropes and ponderous creak of wood against wood.

A slave appeared and whispered in Hadrian's ear.

"At last," Hadrian boomed, "our honored guest from Leptis Magna has arrived."

Marcus Quintillus came into the light, and I buried my face in a chalice.

There was this terrible moment when I thought Hadrian would introduce us. But instead, the vocator led Dominus to a divan on Hadrian's right, and the party went on. While I watched Dominus, the General watched me. When I turned to meet his eyes, they were smoky and dark, too dark to read.

Sub-Saharan dancers swirled on the carpeted deck. Guests shouted, spilled wine and vomited. I couldn't look away from Dominus. He hadn't glanced in my direction once but appeared taken with the young man on his couch; they immediately fell into deep conversation.

The mood of the feast hovered well short of the usual abandon. I had the impression everyone was on his or her best behavior. There was no blatant fondling, either among guests or of the slaves. The servers were clothed. So far, none had been slapped nor any beatings ordered for casual spills of wine.

My stomach was in knots. I nibbled on white cheese, peacock tongues and peach sherbet frozen by glacier snows hauled in straw from mountains far to the north.

Each time I stole a glance at Antinous, he watched me intently. And each time he saw me look in his direction, he smiled back. I kept constant vigil on Dominus and did my best to keep my face in the flickering shadows of the torches.

Antinous' smiles didn't go unnoticed by Gaius Valerius.

"I see you know the Greek."

"We have only just met."

"Hadrian found him when traveling through Bithynia," he whispered. "He was young then, perhaps fourteen. The villagers organized a day of games in Caesar's honor. Apparently the slut is quite an athlete."

Slut. I was more than surprised that he dare be so open, but his audacity demonstrated how freely Romans gossiped about Hadrian and his consort.

A Spanish Caesar who wanted to be Greek. *The Greckling,* I'd heard him called when men felt safe. The Sodomite, too.

"You know the Greeks," Gaius Valerius went on. "They have a taste for nude boys. And so, it would seem," he sighed, "does Our Emperor."

I was on edge that Hadrian might feel compelled to boast about my visions, but he was more inclined to expound on his multitude of construction projects. He drank too much; his eyelids drooped, and his words slurred.

"We shall return the Parthenon to its former glory," he passionately promised the group in his Spanish-accented Latin. "Once more Athens shall be the center of all that is fine and beautiful in this world."

He verged on the tedious, even switching to Greek. I sensed a number of the guests who, in view of Rome's crush of Greece, would have challenged Hadrian's worship of all that was Hellenist.

And while an animated and inebriated Hadrian waxed on about the superiority of Athenians, Antinous the Greek fixed his attention on me.

Hadrian nodded off in the midst of reciting Homer. There was a little flurry of hand signals before two giants carried him away with the Praetorian Guard in the lead and behind.

A slave appeared by our divan and slipped a note in my palm. *Meet me. I have something I must tell you - A.*

Once Hadrian was gone, the mood of the party lightened. Dominus lay back on pillows. A slave massaged his neck. A slave's hand under his toga moved up and down. Sabina and Balbilla cackled behind chalices.

"I fear I have eaten something that does not agree with me, Sirs," I said, making my excuses. "Please forgive me, but I must take some fresh air."

I snapped my fingers, and Aeneas appeared. The General made no objection, but I felt his eyes follow me as I left by way of the shadows.

When I glanced back, I saw that Antinous had also gone. The Emperor's couch was empty.

CHAPTER 38 ANTINOUS

"Rare is the union of beauty and purity." – Horace

I have never had a woman," he told me in an exquisitely modulated voice, masculine yet sensitive. He might have been an orator or an actor. A poet perhaps.

His golden locks shimmered in a halo around his Adonis face. His lower lip was slightly fuller than the upper; they almost formed a pout. The cleft of Venus, Goddess of Love and Beauty, scored his chin. His blue eyes, without a trace of artifice, held me transfixed.

I had the sense he saw the world through the eyes of a man who'd lived twice his years. I certainly had no impression that I was inches away from a boy of nineteen.

In only a few days, this glorious Antinous would be no more. He had so little time left. I couldn't deny him. I put my palms on each side of his face and pulled him down to my lips. How sweet his mouth was on mine. Tender, tentative. My tongue found his.

Taking my hand in the way one would hold a priceless object, he led me below deck. Both of us on tiptoe, we moved stealthily along a narrow passageway with closed doors. His hand on the last door opened the latch, and we were inside. The cabin was simple and neat with none of the extravagance of a Roman stateroom. No wall murals showing satyrs frolicking with bare-breasted *maenads*.

One lone oil lamp burned on a wooden table laden with scrolls. A single bed with a simple coverlet stood in the corner. The Emperor did not come here.

Antinous locked the door and turned to face me. His breath was hot and moist on my forehead; my lips tasted the salt in the hollow of his throat. I took his right hand and placed it on my breast, watching him. He caught his breath; his pupils dilated.

Still holding his hand, I guided his fingers inside my gown to my swollen nipple and closed my eyes. My head fell back, and I breathed a sigh of real pleasure, with no acting on my part. Antinous waited for me to come back. Eyes fixed, totally in the moment, we swayed.

With the undulant molasses rhythm of the Hive, I inched my gown to my waist and slid his hand between my bare thighs just at the Gate to Pleasure. His eyes closed as his fingers dipped cautiously into my damp. He explored for the first time the dark, wet mystery of a woman.

We took our time; I wanted him to savor each moment, for each new touch to be divine. My lips were at his ear, blowing softly and then sucking gently.

Inch by inch, I slipped the yellow silk from my breasts. He drank in my white flesh and carmine nipples.

My hands on each side of his head, my fingers in his curls, I first wet his lips with my kiss, then guided him to my breast.

A born lover, he had the gift, tormenting me with his tongue, his finger deep in my canal. No wonder Hadrian adored him.

"And now," I whispered at the same time my hand caressed his pulsing erection, "I need you to come home."

He exploded. Hot semen sprayed my loins.

My lips went immediately to his; I kissed him tenderly, our tongues entwining. Not a minute passed before he hardened again.

I walked him backward to the bed, my hand slowly pumping him in a languid, easy rhythm that said we had time, plenty of time.

At the slight push of my hand on his chest, he lay back, and I mounted him, my legs straddling his thighs, my knees at his hips, my palm guiding him into me.

"Ah-h-h," he moaned when my warm wet swallowed him whole. I put my mouth on his, murmuring, "Sh-h-h."

His hands kneaded my breasts; I kissed his lips tenderly.

"Thank you," I breathed. "Thank you."

He exploded again. This time deep inside me.

I pulled away from him inches at a time, backing down his thighs until my lips were on his limp manhood.

But limp not for long.

It took only the touch of my tongue teasing his balls, and he was iron hard once again.

O Antinous, thrice-greatest! O glory of youth!

He grabbed my ass and flipped me over, ramming me again and again. I lay with my arms over my head, palms up while he pummeled me.

Antinous was in another world. He snorted and raged, driving into me with all his force. I locked my thighs around his waist and rode him.

We were both drenched in sweat. My intricate hairdo of sewing thread and pins came apart; thick red waves cascaded around my head to flow on the bed.

I couldn't remember the last time I'd been so thoroughly ravaged; I'd forgotten how delectable it is to do nothing but receive.

His hands were everywhere, exploring, memorizing, relishing a woman's softness—and wet.

When he came, he took me with him. Trembling, our bodies clung to each together. I found myself sobbing into his neck, with my hand over his mouth to quiet him.

Finally, he rolled over onto his back, holding me tight into his side with a grip that said he never wanted to let go.

With my fingertip, I traced his profile. The high, intelligent brow. The perfect nose, cupid lips, Venus chin.

I couldn't bear to think that such perfection would soon be gone. I kissed first his top lip, then the bottom, taking it gently between my teeth and tugging.

"I am sick of Hadrian's touch," he said quietly.

My fingertips stroked his muscled, sculptured hairless chest.

"I have to pluck my hairs—on my chest, on my face," he said bitterly. "I must not show I have a beard. Everyone knows it is time—past time, but Hadrian will not let me go."

There was nothing I could say. An *eromenos* must become an *erastes*, a penetrator, when the appearance of a beard announces he's reached manhood. The Greeks had strict rules about these alliances; rules that safeguarded a man's place as a man. But only when Caesar tired of him would Antinous be free. And I knew that there was no time for Hadrian to let him go. Antinous had only days to live.

"The soldiers despise me. I see it in their eyes. I am but a plaything to them. Less than a girl. More loathsome than a girl."

I didn't try to console him with silly words that both of us knew would be false; Antinous was too intelligent for platitudes.

He breathed in a long deep breath and then exhaled slowly.

"I am a man, Elektra. I can wield a sword or ride as well as any. Better than most. I want only to be what I was born to be."

He looked at me sharply, narrowing his eyes. "And you, Elektra. What were you born to be?"

"I remember nothing except to be used. By my father. Then my brothers. And then even my mother offered me to her idle friends. As I grew older, I learned to use others."

"Have you never known love?"

"The Gods withhold their greatest pleasure."

"Then I shall love you. And you shall love me."

How innocent he was of his fate, one far more tragic than any he imagined. I remained convinced that one act of daring might yet change events.

"Hadrian seems not in good health," I ventured cautiously.

Antinous, pure that he is, didn't take the cue. "I concede he looks ill, but I assure you he has the vigor of five men."

He paused and then admitted, "He is desperate though. He surrounds himself with charlatans who ply him with potions."

"It can be otherwise," I said softly, placing in his palm Eben's green and red vial.

I closed his fingers around it, saying "A few drops only. It is painless."

His eyes widened in shock. "I could never do that," he protested. "Hadrian has always been kind."

"How badly do you want to be a man?"

He studied me. The cabin was so still, I could hear the Nile rushing past the cedar boards. The quiet was broken by the muted cry over our heads of a gambler and then drunken laughter.

"Not badly enough to do what you suggest," he answered gravely. "My affection for Hadrian has changed, but I shall always love him for what he has given me. And he has given me much—including his devotion and trust. What honor would I have if I committed so base a crime?"

"There is being a man. And there is being a knight. Why set the bar impossibly high? Death is coming. I see it. I do not wish it to be yours."

"Do not play your magic games with me, Elektra," he teased, stroking my cheek with his fingers. "I do not believe in visions. And neither do you."

I rose from the bed and straightened my gown. Semen stained the front. The few ivory pins I found scattered about the covers and floor repaired some of the damage to my hair. The emerald green palla wrapped around my head and shoulders rendered me somewhat presentable.

"I must return, Antinous. We shall be missed."

"When may I see you again?"

I kissed him lightly on the lips. "Seeing should be easy enough, Antinous. But if it is more…"

He grabbed my face and thrust his tongue deep in my throat.

"You risk too much," I cautioned. "We could lose everything."

"I would give it all, Elektra—everything, anything—to be with you."

"Would you, Antinous? Would you give up your honor and use the vial?"

No sooner did I come on deck at the stern than Aeneas appeared. He had an anxious look that told me I'd been away too long.

I nodded for him to signal my barge. A light flashed, another answered; oars rose and fell with a steady rhythm. In the water, a slurp—then a swoosh followed by a sucking sound when the oars were pulled out.

The river was rippling black satin. Torches flamed onshore in Canopus. Beyond the town, a black velvet sea foamed white at the edge. Jewel-colored stars sparkled in a midnight sky; there was no moon. Mars was a cold, burning ember above the horizon. To the south, through the oyster river mist, I spotted my island in an glowing amber halo.

I didn't realize I was standing in a full circle of light until I heard that all too familiar menacing half-man, half-boy squeal.

"It is she! It is the witch!"

Not fifty feet away, on the port side of the barge, Marcus Quintillus pointed and shouted. His toga had slipped from his shoulder and dragged along the deck. A slave under each arm held him upright.

I stepped quickly back, out of the light and into the shadow. My heart pounded; vomit burned my throat. Too late, I clutched at the palla, dragging the wool to hide my face.

"Seize her!" he shrieked.

I thought surely the whole convivium would descend to the stern.

But no one came. Lyres strummed, and flutes continued to wail.

Aeneas stood stock-still at the starboard gangway. Beside him were the twin Nubians. In the dark of night, I could make out only the whites of their eyes and the glow of their snowy kilts. Thank the gods, they had the good sense not to look in my direction.

"Arrest her! I command it!" Voice cracking, Dominus lunged as if to come after me himself.

I stepped deeper into the shadow, silently chanting *ANA A A NANA A A NANA* over and over.

Then suddenly, coming out of nowhere, the General growled, "Calm yourself, man!"

He towered over Dominus, a mere shadow of virility in the best of comparisons. In the torchlight, the General's gold cuirass blazed.

"You have had too much to drink, Marcus Quintillus. Let your slaves take you back."

There were more words, mainly Dominus' incoherent mumbling with outbursts of "*fugitiva*" or "*striga.*" The General signaled with a brisk wave of his hand. Two centurions in red capes picked up Marcus Quintillus and propelled him across the port gangplank.

I watched from my hiding place, taking only the shallowest of breaths, afraid even to swallow.

It wasn't until Dominus was away and his barge's oars were moving in the river that the General turned toward me. I shook so violently that I couldn't have stood without the support of whatever solid object I leaned against.

"Get on your barge, Ishtar."

I was across the deck and on my boat without knowing that my feet touched the wood. My crew cast off at once.

Within minutes, we were rowing south, away from Hadrian's barge and Canopus, away from Marcus Quintillus, back to the safety of my island. At least that's what I told myself. Safe. But I didn't believe it.

I watched the General standing at the starboard gunwale until I could no longer see his golden cuirass and helmet.

My knight—my unlikely knight in shining armor.

CHAPTER 39   CRUCIFIXION

"In war there is no prize for runner-up." – Seneca

E arly, so early the kitchen slaves didn't yet stir, the beginning of a plan began to gestate, and I woke Aeneas. The instant fear in his eyes told me he thought the hour of his punishment had arrived.

"I am going to Alexandria. Get the boat. We take our own litter and porters. And the three gladiators."

"Three, Domina?"

"Yes, the men from the other day."

"But forgive me, Domina—" He stopped and then started again. "Khan…is not here, Domina."

"Where is he?"

"He…he never returned from the docks, Domina."

Aeneas tried his best to cover his concern, but it was obvious I should have known about Khan. He studiously avoided eye contact.

"Of course," I said as if my memory lapse was of no consequence. "I have much on my mind."

"Yes, Domina."

"And Aeneas…" I pretended to be absorbed in my hair.

His expression was carefully blank, but he had to be replaying the scene on the barge last night with Dominus shouting out *"Fugitiva!"* And now there was something about Khan that I was supposed to know but didn't. There was no better time to repay his loyalty and purchase more.

"You saved me in the city, Aeneas. Your quick thinking saved us all."

He looked cautious, wary of where I was going with my comments, perhaps fearful to find hope in their meaning.

"You may choose a slave to punish in your stead," I told him in an offhand manner. "You may deliver the blows, and you need not hang him up nor tie weights to his feet."

"Yes, Domina," he whispered. "Thank you, Domina."

In spite of the early hour, Eben was absorbed in his work, his face buried in tattered scrolls covered with hieroglyphs and the odd symbols I'd seen in the Hive. I suspected he'd worked through the night on translations.

"If you have any questions, Eben, the Berber couple knows their way around my atelier."

Startled, he looked up and asked, "Where are you going?"

"Alexandria."

He slumped in the ebony chair, staring blankly at me for a few seconds while processing this new and dangerous development. I thought he'd object, remind me of the near death we'd just escaped—*his* close call at the hands of the mob. But instead, he closed his eyes and, swaying back and forth, mumbled Kabbalah phrases under his breath. His thin body, overwhelmed by his ridiculous heavy robe, rocked and shook.

When he calmed and opened his eyes again, I asked, "Well? What did you see?"

"I see us working together on the Black Scroll."

"Excellent," I said with more relief than I'd like to admit.

And so I set off for Alexandria with renewed confidence. Who doesn't readily believe the prophecies that fit our purpose?

We made short time of it on the Canopus Canal and docked again at the Lake Harbor. The old Egyptian beggar still curled close to the ramp.

"ABLAMGOUNOTHO ABRASAX," I whispered in his ear and slipped a small bag of coins into his hand.

He answered, "ANOK THAZI N EPIBATHA." And then, saying something in Egyptian that I didn't understand, pressed a medallion in my palm. A green faience septagram. The sixth of seven.

I bent to the ground to look more closely at his face. A lifetime of care and trouble had etched deep lines; his eyes were inky pools of sorrow into which I dove in search of his soul. It reached out and grabbed my heart.

Qeb-ha! Centuries ago the old eunuch priest had led me to my father Hermes Trismegistus and the Emerald Tablet. In yet another lifetime, I had named him a Protector. He looked now to be the one needing protection.

"You are different," he murmured. "Your heart has hardened."

"This life has been hard, Qeb-ha. I have had little joy."

"You are better than you believe yourself to be, my child. Have you forgotten everything?"

"That which once saw me through my challenges is no use here. I can never be weak."

"Are kindness and compassion now weaknesses to you?"

"In this world, life is war. There is victory, or there is defeat."

"My poor, lost girl," he said, taking my hand. "There is still time for you. You may yet steer the vessel of your life on another course."

"Go to my island, Qeb-ha. Eben is there. We shall be together again."

He sighed and patted my hand in that kindly way of a fond uncle. "If you return here this day, I shall go with you."

"And if I do not return?"

"Then I shall pray for your soul."

I waited in the shade of a portico while Aeneas went in search of information as to where I might find Rufus Hektor Ptolemais. I gambled that he was in the city and not on his estates in Naukratis. The Hektor I knew would spend as little time as possible in the quiet countryside.

My germinating plan was a wild shot, but I saw no other recourse.

Aeneas returned out of breath; he must have run the entire way. His rain gray eyes had gone quicksilver with panic.

"Khan has been captured, Domina!"

"Captured?" Then remembering that I was supposed to know, I stopped short of querying why. Instead I asked, "Where is he?"

"The Hippodrome, Domina. He is to be crucified this morning."

"Crucified?" I whispered.

"It is as Domina directed," he answered with his eyes cast down.

O Venus! What evil have I caused when away fucking Gareth Greene?

"We must go there at once." But if I had known what I would see, I'd never have commanded it.

The first sign that crucifixions were taking place at the old Greek chariot racetrack was the wild cheering of the crowd.

Well before we reached the Hippodrome at the end of the wide east-west boulevard known as the Canopic Way, the ravings of the mob echoed off marble. As we drew near, the first pitiful cries for mercy and terrible screams of those being scourged and then nailed to wooden crossbars reached our ears.

Scores and scores of crosses were piled high. Most of the two-piece instruments of torture were *crux commissa*—ten foot long vertical beams with a horizontal brace to form a 'T.' Stretched along the oval racetrack to accommodate maximum viewing from the stands, dozens of crosses were already hung with the broken and bleeding crucified.

Lined up, stripped naked to loincloths, hands tied together in a long chain, a hundred more wretched creatures waited in abject terror to be whipped. Scattered among them were a few dozen women, their bare breasts exposed, all dignity gone.

With alarming efficiency, Roman legionaries went methodically about scourging bare flesh with glass-tipped leather flails, breaking legs with hammers, and nailing forearms and ankles to wood with iron spikes. There appeared to be no regulated manner by which someone might be fixed to a cross. The haphazard way in which they arranged limbs and hammered told me that the soldiers experimented to relieve their boredom. A few men hung upside down.

Dozens screamed from the agony of dislocated shoulders and metal piercing their bones. Close by, a soldier was driving an iron spike through the crossed ankles of a shrieking old man.

The stench of blood, feces and urine gagged me. I retched on the ground beside the litter.

Aeneas was there at once with a cloth and a jug of watered wine. I lay back on the cushions, squeezing my eyelids shut, whispering over and over, "ANA A A NANA A A NANA."

"Find Khan, Aeneas," I breathed out, exhausted. I put my forearm over my face and bit my lips to keep from weeping. I could close my eyes and shut out the horrifying sight of human slaughter, but I couldn't close my ears to the screams and piteous pleas for mercy. No! The pleas for *death*.

I wanted to stand out of my litter and scream at the world, "Are you mad? STOP at once!"

All the while the mob in the stands roared with each fall of the hammer and with each new cross raised. I waited numbly, eyes closed, clenching my jaw, until Aeneas came back.

"I found him, Domina! But the soldiers do not listen to me."

The porters carried my litter through the living hell of human agony and halted at a cross still lying on the ground. Khan was on his back, arms stretched out, wrists tied with coarse rope to the crossbeam of a *crux immissa*. The iconic cross of Jesus the Nazarene.

A spike had been driven through his right arm, just above the wrist. Dripping in sweat from effort, a broad-shouldered legionary bent over Khan's left arm with an iron spike in one hand and a wooden mallet in the other.

I pulled the litter curtains aside and dropped the palla to let the bright sun shine on my flaming hair.

"*Vale*, Legionary!" I called out in a husky tone.

Startled, he stood up straight and jerked his head in my direction.

When he saw my coppery hair, milky skin and warm smile, he boomed, "The Gods have blessed me this day to have this wretched work interrupted by Venus."

"It is I who is blessed to have found you," I oozed.

"What can a humble soldier do for so beautiful a lady?"

"You can release my man."

"Your man?" he asked blankly.

"Do you not see the tattoo on his neck? The septagram on the left side?"

He squatted down and brushed away blood and dirt.

"As you can see, the man bears my mark. As do these male slaves who accompany me."

First he looked at Aeneas, then at the Celt and finally at the Syrian. Their red-tinted stars showed clearly below the ear.

Still he was obdurate. "I regret I cannot, Lady. My orders say *fugitivo*. He is to be crucified."

"There has been a mistake," I contradicted. "He is *my* slave, he did *not* run away, and I do not desire him to be crucified. Kindly give him over into my charge."

I spoke with the utter confidence of one fully expecting her commands to be obeyed.

He stood a little awkwardly for a moment or two. I could see he was confused; perhaps he had no precedent to follow. More than likely, he didn't have the authority to stop an execution.

With a nod of my head, Aeneas discreetly passed the soldier a small drawstring purse. It disappeared into his leather cuirass.

"I really *must* return to Canopus, Sir. I expect guests."

Canopus. It said everything. I gave him my smile that promises the world.

"Perhaps you might like to visit my island, Legionary. The Temple of Elektra? Perhaps you might like to bring a friend?"

No common Roman soldier could dare dream of the pleasures my Canopus offered. Those delights were reserved for the wealthy and powerful—for officers of the highest rank. Grand Wizards of the Mithraic cult.

He grabbed a giant pair of pliers, put his foot with full weight on Khan's forearm, seized the nailed spike and pulled with all his force. It took four tries to free the nail from wood and bone.

As was customary, Khan had been scourged. The flesh of his back lay opened as by the blade of a knife. He'd already lost a lot of blood. To the Romans, it was a mercy to weaken a prisoner before he was crucified; death came faster.

But Khan's death was to have been slow. An escaped slave of which to make an example. They hadn't broken his legs.

To die on the cross was to suffocate slowly while the lungs were crushed from the body's downward pull. A man with broken legs was unable to support his weight. He died faster—normally within a day, maybe two.

Khan was silent. I feared they might have cut out his tongue. I feared he didn't live. But when I dared look into his face, his small, slant-eyes glinted back.

"Carry him to the Hippodrome docks," I ordered the Syrian and the Celt.

"Hire a boat, Aeneas, to get him back to the island."

An eternity passed while I waited on the sidelines of the killing field. The whippings, nailing, screams and cheers went on without pause in a macabre assembly line of torment and torture.

A sudden roar from the spectators greeted a new group with many women among them and even some children. Emaciated, huddled in trembling groups, they stumbled onto the field. On their foreheads and on their cheeks, flamed angry wounds from recent branding.

"Who are these wretched souls?" I asked one of the litter bearers. "Why are they branded three times on the face?"

"Christians, Domina. Worshippers of the Nazarene."

Unlike the slaves and criminals awaiting their fate, the Christians sang praises to their Lord and raised terrified, radiant faces toward the sky.

"What is their crime? Has Hadrian not said that Christians must be tolerated unless they break the law?"

"Who knows?" he answered with a shrug. "It is said, 'If the Gods do not send rain, lay it to the Christians.'"

And then, as I stoically watched the chain of human misery pass, I saw Rasheed. Perfect bronzed body still whole, naked save for the loincloth.

Alone of all the Christians, his expression was rock-hard, steeled to what he was about to endure. My head swirled, then the whole Hippodrome swirled, all of us in a vortex around him.

I yearned to stroke that proud face with chiseled jaw and cheekbone, to run my fingers across his bare broad shoulders and caress his naked muscular hips. I ached to massage his runner's thighs.

On his neck, from his shoulder to his left ear, coiled a flaming viper tattoo. On his forehead and cheeks festered the denarii-sized open sores of a brand not quite a cross and not quite an ankh.

"Centurion!" I called to the soldier in charge. "The man there. The one with the snake tattoo. Do you know his crime?"

"The Red Viper, Lady? Why, he is an assassin. Well known in the city. They say he slit the throats of at least one Roman and his wife. Most likely more."

"Who can stop his crucifixion?" I demanded.

"Stop it? No one, Lady. The Red Viper dies here in this field on the cross. But not quickly. We have orders he must beg for death and then live to suffer more."

Hadrian had promised to grant any favor. But I didn't have time to reach an emperor. There was only one other who had the power to help. The General.

He could stop anything. Or so I chose in that moment to believe. Because without that belief, I had nothing. Rasheed had nothing.

CHAPTER 40 THE MOOR

"It is kindness to immediately refuse what you intend to deny."
– Publius Syrus

Aeneas returned from the docks. Instead of ordering him again to find Hektor, I commanded, "Take me to the Moor." Sometimes the gods do indeed smile on us. After a few inquiries on Aeneas' part, we set off for the nearby makeshift parade ground where the General prepared for a military extravaganza in honor of Hadrian.

The earth had been packed hard in an area of about 1,000 by 500 feet. At the far end, carpenters hammered on a wooden tribunal with a green-and-gold striped awning. Next to the tribunal stood a turreted green tent. Yellow flags embroidered with boars and red banners with eagles waved from pike-poles. Scythian serpent standards, stitched from green, red and yellow cloth scales, snaked in the wind.

Several cohorts of mounted cavalry in full parade dress maneuvered around the rehearsal field. Hot sun glared off shiny mask-helmets adorned with white plumes. The equites wore close-fitting leather jerkins and tight trousers embroidered in scarlet and purple. Polished bronze greaves with a hinged knee cap protected their shins.

With ramrod backs and eyes straight forward, the horsemen balanced on leather-padded saddles. Bronze horns supported their seat in back and braced their thighs in front.

The horses were tall—fourteen or fifteen hands—with noble heads, wide barrels and well-muscled chests. Their thick manes, combed to the right, were braided in gold twine to match the tail.

Brightly-colored leather barding like an armored skirt shielded the horse's belly from spears. A chamfron made of hinged bronze panels embossed with images of gods protected the forehead and cheeks. A kind of ornate metallic mesh covered the eyes. Dangling from the harnesses, bronze suns and silver moons glittered in the noon light.

Horses thundered across the field stirring up clouds of dust. Big shiny medallions banged on the scarlet and green barding with each pounding stride.

A unit equipped with heavy lances practiced *testudo*, the tortoise. They rode first to the left, and then, halting in close formation, covered themselves and their horses with oblong shields. The line then divided in half, one group to charge, the other to receive the lance—every movement executed in disciplined formation.

A rider carried a red banner with gold fringe and gold-embroidered letters. FIRST MAURETANIAN COHORT OF THRACIANS.

"Eques!" I called out to a cavalryman standing guard.

He ran double-step to my litter.

"I must speak with the Moor."

"He is in council, Lady, and not to be disturbed."

"Inform him that Elektra of Canopus desires to see him on urgent business."

"That is not possible, Lady. He gave strict orders."

I leaned a bit forward, thrusting my cleavage into his face.

"Do you question that he desires to receive me?"

Wetting my lips, I gave him one of my come-hither looks that expunged all doubt that a man—any man—should refuse me.

He blinked hard and tried in vain not to stare at my breasts bursting from my gown. He glanced nervously toward the General's pavilion and back again. There was a half-witted look about him that told me he would take too long to coddle.

"Hear me, Eques," I hissed sharply. "I should not care to be you when the Moor discovers he was not advised that I was here."

His jaw contorted in a series of grotesque facial tics while he struggled to make up his mind.

"Go now!" I snapped. "Tell him that Elektra has come."

He took a deep breath through his mouth. And then having at last decided which wrath to risk, he straightened his shoulders, thumped his right fist on his chest and turned on his heels to march with purpose to the pavilion.

A few words were exchanged with a centurion guarding the entry to the tent. They both turned their heads in my direction. I met their looks boldly, making certain my hair flamed in the sun.

The centurion disappeared behind purple velvet drapes.

I waited. Trumpets sounded. Horse hooves pounded the packed earth. The air was clogged with dust.

Finally the centurion came out and barked indistinct orders to a handful of equites. They advanced march step to my litter, halted and then pivoted in unison to lead us to the tent.

"His Excellency awaits," the centurion announced as he pulled back the heavy drape for me to enter from harsh sunshine to shadow.

My eyes took a moment to adjust.

Green-and-gold striped couches stood on blood red Persian carpets amid a gleaming array of military regalia. The General's gold helmet with the mask of Mars stared at me from a mannequin wearing his gold muscle cuirass.

He reclined on one of the couches carved with lion paws as feet. By the look of the chalices and platters of half-eaten food, he'd been entertaining. We were alone; the others must have left through a side entrance.

He didn't give me a chance to speak before growling, "I sent word you should stay on your island!"

"Am I permitted to approach?"

He waved impatiently at the divan next to him.

Each step that I took was calculated to arouse. Never taking my smoldering eyes away from his, I glided across the carpets with hips swaying and breasts stabbing the air.

"I sailed before first light, Excellency," I offered in that throaty voice calibrated for promise. "I did not receive your message."

I sank onto the divan, careful to arrange the softness of my gown along the contour of my waist and loins. The green palla fell from my coppery hair, the stola slipped off a shoulder. My aura pulsed waves of desire to roll over him.

But instead of his pupils dilating and nostrils flaring as I anticipated, he snapped, "What is this charade, Ishtar? Do you expect me to believe you came here out of lust for me?"

"I expect you to want to finish what you started," I teased.

But he was having none of it.

"When I 'finish,' it shall be the beginning, Ishtar," he told me coldly. "And when it suits *me*. My guards advised you that I was occupied."

My first reaction was to glare at him, but in truth I was grateful to get to the point. I had no time to waste with seductions. At this moment, the soldiers could be scourging Rasheed with one of their odious flails hung with small pieces of glass designed to tear away flesh. They could be cutting away at his manhood. They might be poised to gouge out his eyes with a hot poker. I'd seen all of this today—and worse—in the killing field.

"What do you want?" he snarled. "What is so urgent?"

"I want you to stop a crucifixion."

His eyes, heavy-lidded like a crocodile until now, widened in surprise. "Whose?"

"A Christian."

He raised his eyebrows at my answer; it must have been the last he expected.

"What do you care what happens to those superstitious fanatics?"

"There is only one man who concerns me."

"A man?" He sounded puzzled; perhaps he didn't assign Christians gender. "Who is he?"

"They call him the Red Viper."

"The Viper?" he snorted with a laugh. "I think not, Ishtar. No one can prevent his death. He murdered a Roman."

I was fully prepared for his response and countered immediately, "Then make his death quick. You can do that. You have the power."

He leaned back against the armrest, contemplating me, mulling over my words. His eyes were so dark, I could read nothing in their expression.

After a moment, he asked, "And if I oblige you, what will you then do for me?"

"I shall do," I said without a trace of hesitation, "whatever you wish me to do."

"So you would be my slave?"

"No! I shall never be a slave—," I stopped before saying what was on my tongue.

"Again?" he supplied.

So now we arrived at Marcus Quintillus. He knew. Likely, he knew everything. About my escape. About Major Domo.

"I do not believe, Ishtar," he said in a too-quiet voice, "that you realize how precarious your situation is."

With all my strength, I pushed away the vision of myself, naked, bound and bloodied, hanging from a cross. Once, in Hispania, a slave had taken nine days to die. *O General! You are wrong. I do indeed realize.*

"Last night was…awkward," he accused me. "You disappeared with that sodomite of Hadrian's."

He was angry about Antinous. I'd never known him to be jealous; he was too sure of his own power. I chose not to reward him with a response but took a greedy swallow of watered wine. My mouth was like cotton. Sudden dread had swollen my tongue to twice its size.

He watched me in that dissecting way of his and then said, "I have known Marcus Quintillus all my life."

I suppose my disdain showed, because he added quickly, "Which is not to say I enjoy his company."

I said nothing, waiting for him to come to the point.

"He owes me a great many favors. Over the years I have righted a number of his…transgressions. Yet, he proves difficult in this matter. He refuses to negotiate. He is not always a rational man."

I held my breath in dread of what I knew he was going to tell me.

"He insists upon seeing you crucified."

Although the words came as no surprise, the shock of hearing them out loud caused my heart to skip a full beat. Tears welled in my eyes.

"Obviously," the General continued, "I endeavor to offer alternatives."

"Such as?"

"Such as his sale of you to me, of course. What else?"

I had come prepared for this. The germ of a plan. The one I hoped to cultivate this day. "What proof does he have that I was his slave?"

"Proof?" He considered me for a moment. "The word of a Roman against a—"

"Against a slave? But has he produced a bill of sale? Can he even prove that I am the woman he claims?"

"What are you suggesting?"

"When I was delivered to his villa, no title went with me."

"So you *were* in his villa. Did you murder his major domo?"

"Murder is a term I reserve for those who do not deserve death."

He chuckled and took a sip of wine, but his eyes never left mine. I gambled that he'd do anything for me to be his.

"Will you help me, General? Will you stop Red Viper's crucifixion?"

"You ask too much of me, Ishtar."

"In return, I shall do whatever you desire."

"Easy enough promised now."

"You shall have to trust me."

With that, he laughed out loud. "I trust you only to be yourself."

"So you will not help me?"

"I shall help *you* because I want you to live. But I shall not help your Christian."

There was a finality in his tone that told me not to waste more time here. I rose from the divan and wrapped the emerald palla around me in preparation to go.

"Am I free to leave?" I asked. My laser beam glare must have scalded his flesh.

"You are yet a free woman."

"Then remember this, General. If the Red Viper is crucified and I still live, then you face a most unpleasant end."

His smug expression melted just a little.

"One night when you least expect it. One hot night when your loins throb, when the taste of me is still on your lips, I shall thrill to watch you take a last painful breath."

I then rolled back my eyes, my green irises only emerald half-moons in bright white orbs. Raising my right hand with first and second fingers extended, I cursed him in my most black drama voice.

"ABLAMGOUNOTHO ABRASAX!"

Before he could speak or react, I was out the velvet tent flap. Aeneas waited with the litter.

"Take me to Hektor Ptolemais."

I'm sorry, Rasheed, I called out to the cosmos for him to hear. I have not forsaken you, but I can't save anyone until I save myself.

CHAPTER 41   HEKTOR

"I am convinced that life is 10 percent what happens to me and 90 percent how I react to it." – Scipio Africanus

G reek Egyptians carried on their centuries-old traditions in a manner quite apart from the Romans they still, after enduring defeat at their hands in all ways—military, economic and political—considered barbarians.

Rufus Hektor Ptolemais was exercising at one of the athletic fields on the old Library campus where Greeks had trained their bodies and minds for five hundred years.

His was a private field, open only to members of his club. Women were strictly prohibited. Proper Greek women, unlike Roman, kept to their homes.

Removing Flavia's cameo from my thumb, I directed Aeneas, "Give this ring to Hektor Ptolemais. Tell him that Flavia Titus Titianus desires to see him on a matter of utmost urgency."

Aeneas located a vacant shrine to Venus with a cobalt tile cupola and pink and white jasmine snaking up the columns. Hidden in a feathery glade of flowering myrtle, the white marble gazebo stood close to the calm surf of the Great Harbor. The Lighthouse rose above the lumbering *triremes* and *biremes* moored in sapphire waters.

I waited, powerless to clear my mind of the killing field and the vision of Rasheed the Red Viper being beaten and nailed.

Even with the whole of the Jewish Quarter separating the Hippodrome from the Library garden, his screams were in my head.

I'd arranged the emerald palla to hide my face and hair. When Hektor first arrived, he didn't realize I wasn't Flavia until he took my hand and raised my palm to his lips.

When he saw my green eyes, he took a step back, dropping my hand as quickly as he would let loose a poisonous asp.

"You!" he gasped.

"Me."

He stared at me in confusion. "The cameo ring?"

"Flavia gave it to me. Has she not told you that we are friends?"

His glossy chestnut mane was barbered in curls too long for a Roman. His warm eyes, flecked with iridescent specks of copper, had the expression of one seeing a ghost. But of course, that couldn't be the case, because the Hektor I've known through lifetimes doesn't believe in ghosts.

I moved to make room on the bench. "Come sit beside me."

He hesitated.

"Do not fear me. I mean you no harm."

I said the words in a most reassuring tone, but what I thought was, Has Flavia given you the drops that will end a thousand years of arrogant heritage?

He reacted to my suggestion that he feared me by sitting at once on the bench. How manly was he to be threatened by a woman? A woman he had once bought in a market?

His never-ending legs stretched out. I glanced at his long fingers, the ones that went straight to the Spot no other man knew. I resisted the urge to take his hand and guide him there—to lie back, spread my loins wide and dissolve.

"Why did you do it?" I asked.

He knew exactly of what I spoke, although his reaction was anything but what I expected. He looked away, staring at the Lighthouse, chewing on his lower lip.

Finally, squaring his shoulders, he turned to face me, blurting out as in confession, "It was a terrible miscalculation."

I don't know what I thought he would say. I'd gone over a hundred explanations in my mind, struggling to understand. When given the chance to save me, he'd walked away. Hektor, who always saved me.

He'd gone through the Red Mirror once—passing into a reality he didn't believe in.

"I needed a way to gain entry to Marcus Quintillus," he said simply. "He refused my requests."

"You gave me to Marcus Quintillus in hopes of an *introduction?*"

His explanation was so banal. I had thought of so many reasons but never that. He deserved to be made sterile. He deserved worse. He deserved to be castrated, and I would gladly have done the deed myself, right then, if I'd carried a knife.

"I saw you across the marketplace," he went on, not answering my question.

I had the impression he was more there than here with me.

"It was the red hair that first drew me. But when I got closer, I *recognized* you. But from where?"

He gave me a puzzled, uncertain look. "Why do I feel I have known you all my life? "

I could see he anguished; I almost pitied him, but not quite. He didn't wait for me to answer but endeavored to explain an enigma he couldn't resolve.

"Yet drawn as I was to you, I felt a deep resentment. An inexplicable thirst for revenge. But revenge for what? It made no sense at the time. It makes no sense now."

As hungry as he was for an explanation, Hektor the skeptic would never believe that he wanted revenge for my betrayal two thousand years from now.

He paused, running his fingers through his waves. His eyes had the most bewildered look. "You called out my name that day. How did you know? Have we ever met? Surely I would have remembered."

We sat very close to each other; he yearned to touch me, but I wanted to hear more. I wanted to hear everything. And he wanted very badly to tell me; I believe he carried his guilt as I carried my anger.

"You were so beautiful. Your hair was like fire. Your skin white as milk." Even now, his eyes burned with excitement at the memory. Oh, how earnest he could be.

"I planned from the beginning to get you back. You must believe me. You were not a gift. You were…a loan."

A loan. If I'd had that knife, he would have been dead.

"When I saw you at the baths, you were not dressed as a slave." He rattled on in the eager narrative of someone at long last unburdening his soul. "I convinced myself that you were treated well."

His eyes begged me to forgive him; a fine layer of moisture gave them shine. "I was a coward. I thought only of my own ambition."

"And the ring?"

"I brought the ring from Egypt, thinking to use it as a bribe. It is very old. Very valuable. Instead, I was compelled to give it to you. As if the ring belonged to you. And as a message that I was coming."

"But you did not come."

"I could not," he protested. "Everything went wrong. I was summoned that night to meet with a Roman they call The Moor."

"The Moor?" I repeated in disbelief.

How small the universe. How closely entwined our lives. Goliath, Hektor, Jason and the General. All of us in Leptis Magna at the same time. The General might have come to his old friend's villa that night. He might have rescued me. Instead, he prevented Hektor.

I felt a softening in the wall of rage around my heart; the knife edge of pain dulled enough to allow me to reach out and stroke Hektor's cheek. He was so lost in his story, he didn't respond to my touch.

"Early the next morning, not long after the sun had risen, I came to the villa of Marcus Quintillus. No one could understand how you escaped. All the gates were locked from the inside."

His voice took on a ferocious intensity. "I have never stopped wondering what happened to you. I have never stopped regretting that day. What can I do to right my wrong?"

I leaned forward and brushed his lips with mine. My hand went under his tunic; my fingertips slid up the inside of his taut thigh and under the loincloth. Then I kissed him with a great tenderness designed to relax.

"Do you still have the bill of sale?" I breathed into his mouth.

I took his sacks in my palm and rolled them gently together. He grew harder.

"Bill of sale?" he gurgled. "I…I do not know."

I placed my palm over his nostrils that he might smell his own scent on my hand.

"Yes!" he blurted. "Why not? My accountant keeps everything."

"Marcus Quintillus is in Alexandria." My breasts brushed against his chest.

"What?!" he cried out.

"He recognized me," I whispered, circling his ear with my wet tongue. My hot palm stroked his iron post.

I put his hand inside my bodice. He moaned. His lids closed; his mouth went slack.

"He demands my crucifixion."

His entire body jerked; his eyes flew open. My tongue still circled his ear.

"But without proof of ownership," I crooned, "he has nothing."

Suddenly, my old Hektor was here. He sat straight up—keen, resolute, fervent to come to my rescue.

"I shall go to a magistrate at once! I shall claim you as my property."

"There is still the matter of the major domo," I cautioned.

"One slave slays another," he said with a dismissive shrug. "I shall pay compensation. You belong to me. Only I may determine your punishment."

"And that shall be?" I whispered, guiding his fingers up my gown to my wet.

There, lying on my back on the hard bench, I cooed like a dove while his long fingers explored me, caressed me, dipping into my canal. He went to the Spot. The G-Spot that only his fingers found.

The world faded for a few blissful moments. Even the horrific screams of Rasheed were gone from my head.

I felt only warmth spreading through my pelvis, up my womb and down my buttocks. My thighs wide open, legs dangling on each side of the bench, I rode the wave of ecstasy to sublime.

"You are so beautiful," he crooned. "I could never tire of touching you."

He bent to kiss the base of my throat.

"To think you could have been mine all this time."

I loosened the ties of his loincloth and gently took his fingers from my canal, placing them in his mouth so he might taste me.

With expert, practiced moves, I maneuvered his long legs, placed him at my gate and ushered him into me.

I matched each thrust with a rising of my pelvis to welcome him. He went deep. He would have crawled inside me if he could. Then he pulled all the way out. His steel erection with glistening head stood up between my open thighs.

Coitus interruptus always, Flavia had told me.

But not with me. With me he would know full, addicting consummation.

I gripped his butt with one hand and guided him back to my gate with the other. Locking my legs around his waist, I pushed upward into him.

He moaned, resisted only a heartbeat and then surrendered, sliding deep once more. My palms stroked his butt muscles, tight from daily workouts in the athletic fields of the Library. His thighs were rock hard, the muscles long and taut.

Using all the little tricks I know so well—the pull and tugs on his balls, the teasing of my finger in his anus—I led him inexorably to where I needed him to go. In a great shaking and trembling and gulping of air, he exploded inside my hot cocoon.

I waited what I thought was a decent passage of moments before whispering, "I must go."

"Are you not my slave?"

"You have not yet produced the bill of sale."

When I'd straightened my gown and my hair, I put my hand on his cheek.

"I would not mention this meeting to Flavia, Hektor. It is best she knows nothing of us."

I kissed him, my tongue deep in his throat.

"Can I count on you to take care of Marcus Quintillus?"

"What is your name?" he called after me. "How shall I find you?"

"I am Elektra. Ask anyone on the Canal the way to my island."

CHAPTER 42   MONKSHOOD

"Luck is what happens when preparation meets opportunity." – Seneca

F ind me an apothecary, Aeneas."
I chastised myself that I'd been in such a rush this morning that I'd left my satchel behind. Never travel without a vial. Every minute counted, and I was losing hours.

What might the soldiers be doing to Rasheed this very moment? I refused to let my imagination fill in details I knew my heart couldn't bear. Instead I fumed at the General, scheming of ways to make him suffer, and rather than let images of a tortured Rasheed flood my mind, I envisioned the General writhing in agony from a few toxic drops concocted in my lab.

With Aeneas in the lead, the porters headed west along the harbor, traversing the same docks where I saw the General greet Marcus Quintillus. At the depths of a shadowy alley that twisted and turned in the curves of a cobra, Aeneas called for the litter to halt in front of an open doorway covered with tattered cloth, and I climbed out. Above the door lintel were pastel traces of a large eye-of-Horus painted centuries past.

The stall, without a single burning lamp, was shadowy as twilight. There were no windows. When I came through the curtain, a parrot with bright feathers squawked from a perch. There was an air of indolent chaos about the shop. Bunches of herbs hung helter-skelter on lengths of twine stretched from wall to wall. A filthy pallet lay on the floor next to a wooden counter slightly taller than my waist.

In the corner I could just make out the silhouette of a bony hunched figure grinding away at a mortar and pestle.

The woman looked up and hurried over. Behind her white hair frizzing in all directions were wooden shelves stacked in no apparent order—dull metal urns, cloudy glass flasks and ratty baskets of dried snakes, birds, spiders and lizards.

In spite of the disorder and the dim light, I spotted right away what I needed.

"Monkshood."

Her squinty black eyes held mine for a moment, assessing me—trying to decide if I knew the result of the plant's ingestion. I must have passed her test, as she didn't warn me of any dangers.

"Lady want powdered leaves?" she asked in broken Greek. "Or Lady want oil?"

"The oil," I answered in relief that she had just what I needed. I didn't have time to distill leaves.

I called for Aeneas, who appeared with his sack of coins. Coppers exchanged hands, and the crone handed me a red vial slightly smaller than my little finger. Blue veins popped up from her paper-thin skin. Orange-red henna stained her long, curved claws.

Her touch lingered longer than necessary, but I didn't pull my hand away. I sensed she was reading me through her fingertips. I half expected her to show me the seventh septagram. Everywhere I went, I waited for it appear. The closing of the circle. The last Protector.

I nodded to Aeneas to pull out another coin, and when she dropped my hand to take it, I removed the cork stopper and sniffed. Aconite. High concentration.

I gave her a nod of approval, asking, "May I rely on your discretion?"

"Certainly, Lady," she assured me with a smile that showed a few black teeth set in black gums. Opium.

"Give me some of the poppy oil as well."

Another vial appeared, this one green and containing about twice the volume of the red vial.

"ABLAMGOUNOTHO ABRASAX!" she called after me.

When I turned back, she was already at work with the mortar and pestle. The parrot squawked goodbye.

With a great deal of concentration and meditative calming, I steeled myself for our return to the Hippodrome. By the time we arrived—having traversed the clogged center of Alexandria and wound our way through the back alleys of the Jewish Quarter, inhabited in fact by anyone not Roman or Greek—at least two hundred more pitiful souls anguished on crosses. Their moans and cries chilled me, but I did my best to ignore their agony. I couldn't save everyone.

Crosses ringed the ovoid track; soldiers had nailed fish to those hung with Christians. Drunks shouted abuse from the tiered marble stands.

"Where is your Messiah now, Christian? He couldn't save himself. How can he save you?"

"You'll burn tonight! We need light for the chariot races!"

"Drinker of blood! Cannibal!"

Food vendors hawked small cakes of sweetmeats, round loaves of bread, roasted nuts and sticky black dates. Wine merchants poured watered sour wine or thick frothy beer into crude clay cups.

"Aeneas!" I shouted in a panic. "Find the Christian they call the Red Viper."

I waited in the litter and manifested a scene in my mind, willing it to unfold precisely as I desired and with the desired outcome. I refused to allow doubt to cloud my vision.

Once found, I would bribe a guard to allow me a closer look at the Red Viper. Not a particularly unusual request for a Roman lady. Once I got close, I would find a way to give him the poison.

I had selected Monkshood because the active ingredient aconite causes arrhythmic heartbeat leading to asphyxiation. Death takes longer than I would have preferred, but the end is remarkably akin to the suffocation of crucifixion. No alarms would be set off.

I refused to think of the precise details—of what I would say or how I would administer the oil.

When faced with the legionary, I would know what to do. He would be, after all, a man like any man.

If the gods smiled on me, I could also give Rasheed the opium.

"He is not here, Domina."

"Of course, he is here. Perhaps he is not yet on the cross."

"The soldiers say, Domina, that the Red Viper was taken away by cavalry from the parade ground."

And so, the General turned out, as well, to be only a man like any man.

Did Rasheed yet live, or had he passed from this life into the void? How many lifetimes before we would meet again at the Stirling Club and have our night at the Wynn?

"Take me back to the Moor."

But when we arrived at the parade grounds, the *ala* no longer exercised. A few slaves busied themselves cleaning the field of horse manure and smoothing the dusty sand with rush brooms. The equites had retired to their billets to gamble and drink.

The General was gone. No one knew where. Or in any event, no one admitted to knowing. My threats reaped no results.

There was nothing to do but return to my island.

"Let us go to the nearest dock. There we can hire a boat to ferry us to the Yacht Harbor. I want away from here. I want out of the city."

But Aeneas stood his ground, shifting his balance ever so slightly before looking me in the eye.

"I have news, Domina."

"What news?"

"Of the Nubian, Domina."

"It must be news that shall displease me. Why else have you waited to tell me?"

"Forgive me, Domina, but I have only just learned."

"Well, out with it, man. What have you heard? Does he live?"

"He lives, Domina. And he is to fight in the Elesius Amphitheatre this afternoon."

"Here? In Alexandria?" It seemed the whole world converged on me.

A black fly bit my forearm. The nasty monsters swarmed all around. But if there were hundreds of flies on the parade ground, it was nothing compared to what we would find at the Arena.

Oh, how I detested that wretched hellhole. The heat, the crowds, the repugnant stench. There wasn't a sweet oil potent enough to mask the vile odors of mass death.

Always making my excuses, I steadfastly avoided the Games, refusing to sit on a bench for hours to watch the slaughter of too many men and animals at once to take note of any single death. Only rarely was there a contest worth viewing.

"What is his specialty?"

"Wild beasts, Domina. The trident and the net. It is said he is also master of the gladius."

"Who owns him?"

"An Armenian, Domina. A freed gladiator with a school outside Timgad near Lambessa. Far to the west of Leptis Magna."

"Armenian, you say? Loosen your purse strings, Aeneas. Count on a hard bargain."

"Bargain, Domina?"

"I shall have this gladiator, Aeneas. I shall have him today."

"Is Domina thinking of going to the Arena *now*?" His question was as close as a slave could come to objecting.

"Are we prepared for this evening's convivium?"

"Yes, Domina. All is arranged."

"You have secured the slaves for the Parthians?"

"Yes, Domina. Six blondes, all lactating."

"And the drug?"

"Yes, Domina. I gave each the potion last night and again this morning. One dose more this afternoon, and their milk shall be sufficiently infused."

"Then send for our boat to pick us up on the Canal docks nearest the Arena."

"Yes, Domina."

"And Aeneas, ensure the old Egyptian sails with us."

Still he stood there.

"What else, man? More news you have not shared? Speak! We have not enough time as it is."

"I cannot advise Domina to continue without an armed escort. It is most unsafe in the Amphitheatre Quarter."

"What then do you propose?"

"Perhaps the young gentleman might be of assistance to Domina?"

I followed his line of sight to a cohort of crack Praetorian troops in menacing black leather, black helmets with black brushes and black capes. In their midst sat Antinous astride a golden stallion.

"Well done, Aeneas. Please ask His Excellence to join me."

Antinous was at my side before I could finish dabbing on oil of gardenia.

"Elektra!" he cried out with far too much joy. "Fortune blesses me to find you here!"

I cast a cautious glance toward the Guards, who, as always, pretended to see nothing but saw everything.

The sun turned Antinous' curls to spun gold. A short blue tunic fell mid-thigh. His clear, direct eyes, somewhere between the azure of his tunic and the sapphire of the sea, hid nothing.

I saw he was all mine to do my bidding. Unfortunately, I feared the Guards saw his eagerness, as well.

"Salve, Most Excellent!" In hopes of dispelling any suspicion of our intimacy, I flashed the too-bright smile of a courtesan teasing a youth. "What a delight for my eyes weary of the city's harsh ugliness."

"You play with me, Elektra," he said solemnly over my hand. "Do I merit your scorn?"

"Careful," I whispered, then said loudly, "I find myself in need of escort, kind Sir. I must go to the Amphitheatre, and such is the sorry state of Alexandria that my good slave insists that I may not go alone."

"Guard!" he called out. "We accompany the Lady to the Arena!"

With a noisy stamping of feet and banging of swords on shields, the Guards executed a complicated maneuver at the clipped command of the centurion. We waited as the front troop filed past in march step. My porters fell in after them. The rear guard closed up behind.

"You cannot know how it gladdens my heart to see you, Elektra."

Antinous leaned in close, hanging down from the saddle, gripping the golden stallion with the powerful thighs of a young athlete in his prime.

"I have thought of nothing but you." His lips were inches from mine. Only the most expert of riders could have stayed so level with my mouth. "When can I see you?"

"You see me now, Sir."

"Do not toy with my heart, Elektra. When? Where?"

"I cannot promise now when it may be."

"Then I shall come to you whether you are ready or not."

With that, he coiled back into the saddle in one smooth, effortless motion, dug in his heels, and the golden stallion with its golden knight leapt forward, flinging small pebbles into the dusty air.

CHAPTER 43   THE ARENA

"The world turns aside to let any man pass who knows where he is going."
– Epictetus

The Games were in the second phase of the day when we arrived at the new *Amphitheātrum* on the Elesius Plain between Alexandria and the resort town of Canopus.

Fresh paint was vivid on the marble gods and emperors ringing the three tiers. Around the top, multi-colored pennants snapped in the sea breeze.

The roar of the crowd, louder even than the mob at the Hippodrome, shook the ground. Millions of flies swarmed around high mounds of wild beasts slain in the morning's mock hunts.

Thick, dark smoke rose from dozens upon dozens of cook fires. At least two hundred lions were being gutted and prepared for roasting. Blood-spattered slaves skinned leopards and bears. Boar and hippo lay in piles. A dozen giraffes were already turning on giant spits.

Tonight, the crowd at the Hippodrome would feast on roast game while cheering chariot races lighted by human torches.

Leaving the litter behind and surrounded by Praetorian Guards, I followed Antinous through a gate in the southern façade that opened to a gloomy arched passageway on level with the Arena field.

The walls were of concrete and stucco-covered brick. Hadrian himself had designed the monster structure, using the latest in construction techniques. Just last night he'd boasted of it.

It was well known that Alexandrians weren't easily impressed. In Egypt, one builds monuments in eternal stone. We had all listened politely, of course. No one wanted to end up like Apollodorus. His exile and death had shocked the empire.

One would have thought that his genius protected him. After all, he had engineered the Pantheon, the largest unreinforced concrete dome in all history. Trajan had given the equivalent of a triumph in his honor.

But in a foolish clash of egos, Apollodorus had apparently said one time too many that emperors should stick to ruling empires and leave building to architects.

In any event, it turned out that Hadrian was not one to brook criticism of his art.

Or, I suspected, to tolerate the sharing of his lovers.

"Wait here," Antinous said with the authority of a man on a mission. "I shall find this Armenian and the Nubian."

"Thank you, kind Sir," I said coolly, careful to give the appearance of distance.

He left us with four Praetorian Guards.

"Move along," they growled at drunkards stumbling to the toilets.

A combat had just finished. By the boos, jeers and throwing of food, the battle of *essedarii* chariots against pairs of pedestrian *andabata* blinded by helmets with no eyes had ended too quickly for the crowd's taste.

Aeneas and I took refuge in a stone archway with an iron grate. I kept my hair covered and my face in shadow to avoid being recognized. Any of my clients could be here and insist I join them.

On the other side of the bars, slaves cleared the Arena floor of entrails, mangled flesh and brains. The entire length of the field was one long pool of blood; slaves hurried to spread bucketful after bucketful of fresh sand before the next match.

In the very center was the *crux quadrata* outline of the subterranean elevators that raise war machines and wild animals to the surface. Beasts that Goliath might battle today.

The day was hot, the sky without a cloud. Massive linen canopies stretched by an intricate system of ropes and pulleys formed a giant central oculus, shading the stands and leaving the field in blinding sunshine.

From my vantage point, the upper two stands looked to be filled to capacity; I estimated a crowd of at least twenty-five thousand. Only a handful of spectators sat on the First Tier seats behind the wrought iron rail meant to keep drunks from falling from the stands into the battles. Scores of slaves fluffed cushions and washed down stone aisles with perfumed water.

Now was the hour of private refreshment, but at the start of the main match, the privileged would return to their ringside seats atop the marble podium with walls too high for animals to escape.

A waving banner at the Prefect Box announced that Titus Flavius Titianus was in attendance. The Box was vacant. Like the other First Tier spectators, Flavia's father and his party would be sipping wine and snacking on cured meats in one of the cool interior reception chambers.

No doubt they settled their wagers from the morning games and placed new bets for the afternoon. I had spent too many hours in rooms like that, laughing falsely at inane and vulgar jokes, feigning interest in their tedious replays of this thrust or that slash.

Was Flavia here? Had she sat in the Prefect Box, watching men die at the very moment I had seduced her Hektor in the little shrine by the sea?

To the east yawned the Triumphal Gate, where gladiators entered. To the west was the *Porta Libitinaria*, the Gate of Death, named for the Goddess of Funerals. Through this point of final exit, slaves carried the corpses of the vanquished.

Trumpets sounded. Giant blue-skinned Gauls with polished helmets topped by elaborate bronze fish burst onto the arena floor. Trumpets blared again. Stocky Thracians, armed with rectangular *parmulae* shields and curved *sicae* swords, ran onto the field. The Thracians' helmets had white feather side plumes and silvery visors pierced with tiny eyeholes.

The bloodbath began with the jarring clank of sword on sword. The first Gaul went down not three feet from me in a crimson fountain of blood. The crowd roared. A curved sword ripped up into his gut, spilling pink intestines. I tried to melt into the cool stuccoed wall, squeezing my eyes tight, but I couldn't shut out his screams.

There were those who deserved dying; I had no pity for them. I'd ended life more than once and never regretted it. But that was death with purpose, not this mindless sport.

In the bowels below, starved lions tormented by slaves with flaming torches roared. In the stands above, the thirsty screamed for more blood.

According to the flyers, Goliath was billed in the final combat of the day. The Grand Finale. Ten pairs of star gladiators in a fight to the death.

"This contest, Aeneas, is an intolerable waste of talent and investment. Has Hadrian not forbidden the killing of a slave without just cause?"

"There is an exemption for gladiators, Domina. To fight and die in the Games are their purpose."

At one time a talent like Goliath stood a fair chance of survival. He could even live to retire. But Hadrian had changed that. No new territory, he proclaimed. Fortify borders. Rebuild within.

In ending Rome's expansion, the unending stream of men captured in battle dried up. No more prisoners of war marched by the hundreds of thousands to perish in every backwater Arena of the Empire. Yet, there must be death. The Games required it.

What remained were wild animals, rebels, criminals and a few condemned slaves and Christians. And trained gladiators.

This day in Alexandria, nineteen noble, precious, gifted warriors would be slaughtered to satisfy the mob's blood thirst.

Not Goliath, though. I wouldn't allow it. He'd saved me in the past—and in the future. Now I would save him.

The crowd thundered when the last Gaul fell, his head severed from his blue body.

Where was Antinous? If he didn't return in the next moments, I'd go off myself in search of the Armenian.

When I glanced at Aeneas, his gray eyes had darkened to slate; deep furrows creased his brow. Whether he was concerned for my state of mind or for what a star gladiator might cost, I couldn't say. Perhaps both.

I thought of reassuring him that we would find new strategies for milking our clients when Antinous appeared.

"I have found him!" he declared rather triumphantly for what, in truth, was a simple task.

We followed Antinous down the long arched corridor, Aeneas trailing me with more Guards behind him. Filtered sunlight fell in long dusty shafts across exquisite murals depicting death and killing. The Praetorian Guards' hard-soles clomped on the stone. Drunks scattered before us, pressing against the walls.

At the point where the oval curve sharpened to the left, Antinous turned into an arched doorway, and we went down stone steps to enter an unadorned, windowless brick chamber. The ripe, adrenaline- and testosterone-infused air was hot and close.

Every vicious weapon devised by man hung on the walls or leaned against wooden racks—broad swords, sharp pikes, heavy rods, wooden lances, trident forks, iron hammers, ropes of chains and ponderous flaxen nets. A handful of slaves in coarse brown tunics sorted the various regalia—spiked and plumed helmets, gruesome silver masks, ornate studded leather vests and polished bronze cuirasses.

Ten gladiators in loincloths, muscles bulging, oiled skin glistening, prepared to battle ten more warriors arming themselves in another brick chamber somewhere along the corridor. Only one of them would survive. The nineteen others would be dragged, broken and slashed, virile life force extinguished, through the Gate of Death.

I saw Goliath at once, a giant among giants. Pink scar tissue scored his ebony arms; blue-black slashes crisscrossed his belly. A long gash had not quite healed on his left cheek. The septagram faience medallion on the leather thong glinted in the torch light. He glanced at me briefly and went back to lacing his sandals.

The *lanista* in his *pileus*, the woolen cap given to gladiators awarded freedom, stood up straight and looked me over from head to toe with crafty, avaricious eyes. He possessed a powerful compact body built of unforgiving muscle covered by nut brown flesh raked with battle scars.

"How much to purchase the Nubian?" I demanded without greeting or introduction.

"I regret to disappoint the Lady, but he is not for sale."

"Everything is for sale," I corrected him.

"Not this man. He is my best."

"Your best will do you no good if he dies."

"He will not die. The omens are favorable."

"Omens?" I scoffed. "What do *you* know of omens?"

He didn't have an answer but licked his thick lips once with the tip of an orangey tongue. I could see his mind asking, *Who is this bold woman?*

"And if he should be the last man standing?" I challenged. "Do you dare gamble that the Prefect is in a mood to please the mob? That he could choose to grant today's champion his freedom? What then? You might gain the purse yet still lose your man."

The room had stilled; all eyes fixed on me. I kept absolute focus on the Armenian who looked warily at Antinous and back again at me. Beads of sweat glistened on his upper lip.

"Save your investment!" I snapped. "Name a price for the slave."

"No, my Lady!" he protested but then added hurriedly, "Please forgive me, I care not to show disrespect."

"I shall match the purse and give you fifteen thousand *denarii* more. No risk. All gain."

He took a sharp intake of air at the staggering offer, and I was certain I had him. His mind rushed in all directions; he wanted to look away, but I held his eyes.

Aeneas, too, caught his breath when he heard the sum. I could read his thoughts as if they were my own. *Twenty thousand lost just yesterday for the hermaphrodite—and now?* Who knew how large today's purse might be?

But the Armenian wasn't as shrewd a businessman as I gave him credit. Instead of taking my offer, he tried reasoning with me.

"After today's combat, my Lady. The Nubian is favored by long odds to win. Bets have been placed. There could be a riot in the stands. You know these Alexandrians."

Unmoved, I gave him a hard look that said I was losing patience.

He paused and then tried, "The Prefect shall be displeased."

When he saw he didn't get the desired reaction, his tone turned to pleading. "Surely the Lady understands. I cannot anger the Prefect!"

I was set to better my offer when Antinous interceded.

"Whose displeasure do you wish to incur this day—the Prefect's or the Emperor's?"

"The Emperor, Sir?" Startled, the Armenian looked from Antinous to me and then back to Antinous. "What is Hadrian's interest in this affair?"

"Do you not recognize Elektra of Canopus? Have you not heard how highly Caesar regards her? The Emperor desires nothing more than to see the Lady pleased, yet you persist in effecting her deep disappointment."

At that moment, the heralding of trumpets called spectators back to their seats for the final match of the day. The Grand Finale fight to the death.

"Arm yourselves," he bellowed. "What are you louts waiting for?"

I glared at him. He hadn't taken the Emperor threat seriously but rather made no attempt to mask his derision of what he saw as a youth attempting to impress an older woman.

That's when Antinous called out, "Guard!"

Three Praetorians in black leather with the Imperial Crest emblazoned on their chests stepped through the portal at the top of the steps.

The Armenian stammered, "Are you…the…the—"

He stopped short of saying 'Sodomite,' but we knew the word was on his tongue. Instead, he finished his question with, "Greek?"

I don't know if Antinous held a formal position. Surely he wasn't known officially as 'the companion.' But if he had a title, he didn't offer it.

"Do you agree to the sale, man?" Antinous pressed. "Or do you risk Caesar's wrath?"

Antinous' eyes were the most shocking blue, quite electric. An electric aura vibrated around him. The whole chamber was electric.

Metal clanged as men tackled their weapons and shields, tied the last thongs of their greaves and secured spiked helmets. The trumpets sounded again. Goliath took a heavy net in one hand and a trident in the other. His mask was the face of Neptune cast in pure silver.

The Armenian was now in full sweat with the desperate look in his eyes of a cornered animal casting about for escape. The orange pointed tongue appeared again to wet his lips, surely bone dry from tension. I imagined the inside of his mouth like cotton.

Over our heads pounded the feet of a thousand spectators hurrying to their seats. Soon, very soon, the Amphitheātrum would fall silent. Then the first solemn notes accompanying the *pompa triumphalis* would fill the air.

In that mystic hush, the gladiators would parade through the Triumphal Gate to stand before the Prefect with their ritual pledge, "We who are about to die, salute you!"

But the gladiators, armed and ready, were still in the dressing room.

I dragged the palla from my fiery hair and stuck my face into the Armenian's. We were exactly the same height. He took a step backward. I advanced on him.

"Listen to me, you *little* man. You sell me that Nubian, or I shall place a curse on you that will raise boils on your skin and make your pee run crimson with blood. You shall wish you were dead rather than endure the agony of a piss."

Then I straightened my spine, rolled my eyes back with lids fluttering wildly and intoned with all the melodrama of the Hive, "ABLAMGOUNOTHO ABRASAX!"

No sooner had I delivered my curse, than the stomp in unison of twenty-five thousand pairs of feet shook the room. Swords and shields rocking on hooks rattled against the walls.

The Armenian's eyes were beyond wild.

I let escape a long *hi-s-s-s-s-s,* rattling from deep in my throat, just as Lemta had taught me. At last, he surrendered.

"Find the Thracian!" he screamed. "Get him armed. Move!"

And then they were gone, leaving Goliath behind, silver Neptune mask covering his face, silver greaves up his shins, heavy net slung over his Hercules shoulders, silver-tipped trident clutched in his massive fist. In the holes in the mask, I saw his eyes wide with disbelief. He recognized me, but I couldn't tell if from the slave market or from our other lives.

"Yes, it is I," I said simply. "You are safe."

I wanted to take his giant hand and kiss his palm. I wanted to tell him that I would soon set him free, that he would no longer be a slave. But I resisted saying more—much less touch him—in front of the Praetorian Guards.

"Congratulations," Antinous was saying. "You have your slave, although I have not yet understood his importance."

"I thank you most sincerely, Sir. I am in your debt."

"I like that," he murmured, taking my hand and kissing *my* palm.

For a young man with no experience with women, he caught on fast. Too fast. And with too much daring. Over his shoulder, the hard eyes of the Praetorian Guard pretended not to see every gesture of his affection.

"You tread a dangerous path," I murmured.

But I could see he was blinded—blinded by something more perilous than infatuation. I saw adoration.

Adoration drives men to foolish acts.

In that moment, a scene unveiled in my mind. A scene I'd not anticipated. A scene I would have done anything never to see.

If I couldn't alter events, Antinous would die in a few days. But instead of saving him as had been my intention, I saw that I would be the instrument of his death.

CHAPTER 44   THE PROTECTORS

"In difficult and desperate cases, the boldest counsels are the safest."
– Titus Livius

Qeb-ha waited as promised with my boat at the arranged quay on the Canopus Canal. His whole face lighted when he saw Goliath who still wore the expression of a man unsure of what is happening. He certainly didn't recognize the old Egyptian, at least not yet.

I said my goodbyes to Antinous in the most formal manner possible.

"Thank you once more, Sir, for your gracious assistance. Please be so kind as to thank the Emperor for the loan of his Guard."

"I shall come to your island, Elektra." His blue eyes teased; he appeared impervious to risk. "We shall picnic on the grass as we do in Bithynia during the Dionysus Festival. I shall make sweet love to you on a bed of flowers."

My glance at the Guard didn't tell me if they heard his words.

Night fell quickly on the Canal. Our crew lighted red glass lanterns strung on ropes around the deck. The silver tips of the oars flashed against the dark water when raised, disappeared below the surface and then flashed again as the rowers urged us forward. The sky, filled only a short time ago with hundreds of feeding birds, darkened from mauve to deep purple and finally to black velvet speckled with stars.

Like the hypnotic trill of a snake charmer's flute, the music of pipes and lyres of the Canal drew us away from the city's squalor and pain.

Wondrous scents from countless incense burners diffused themselves along the banks. And through the wispy, scented haze of rising mists glowed the fairy lights of a thousand gazebos. No screams of agony here, only the carefree melody of laughter.

I hoped to never see Alexandria again. At least, not in this lifetime.

"Domina, we are almost home."

I woke with a start. Torches blazed along every path. Two barges approached the quay. At least three already moored there. Across the still waters of the Nile, I heard the faint strain of the flautists lined up for the greeting ceremony.

"Sail around back, Aeneas. I shall join our guests after I bathe."

Docking on the far side of the island at a secluded private quay, I sent Aeneas on ahead to the Temple. Then, with Goliath and Qeb-ha, I made for the hidden path to my villa. The front gate was in sight when Ghazel stepped from the shadows.

She had the face of death; her black eyes stared out from a white mask of terror.

Goliath tensed and moved beside me.

"Soldiers are here for you, Domina," she said in a hushed voice.

I stepped into the trees, away from the light. With the reflexes of a gladiator, Goliath at the same instant pulled Qeb-ha to follow me.

"Praetorian Guard?" I whispered, my first thought being of Hadrian.

Foolish boy! Didn't Antinous realize the peril he put me in?

"No, Domina," she shook her head violently. "They carry a Procurator's seal."

So Marcus Quintillus then. He'd wasted no time. Even if Hektor managed to find a magistrate he could bribe to rule in his favor, it would be too late once I was in Dominus' hands. I should have arranged his death rather than think to outmaneuver him.

The night was deadly still. Mosquitoes buzzed around my ears. Frogs croaked from the river banks. The distant shouts of revelry drifted through the mist.

We could return to the boat. Just weigh anchor and sail away. Make for the sea. But even as I thought it, I knew there was no escaping Rome in a little boat.

My world melted. Colorless, without form, the cosmos returned to the primal matrix. It was over.

"Domina," Ghazel whispered, "We must pray."

"Pray? Pray to whom?"

"To our Lord, Domina. We must have faith. Only He can save us."

For the first time I noticed she wore around her neck a small wooden ankh, the Egyptian icon for eternal life. But it wasn't quite right. The top was a circle rather than an oval. A hybrid of both ankh and cross. Like the brands I saw today on foreheads and cheeks.

Oh Ghazel, Ghazel. Prayer hadn't saved the Christians in the killing field today. I needed to get to the Red Mirror.

"How many soldiers, and where are they?"

"Six, Domina. They are in the vestibule."

"Have they searched the house?"

"Yes, Domina. They have searched everywhere."

"Go to the atelier door. Signal if it is safe."

Following her white tunic through the dark, we stayed a few hundred paces behind. She opened the green door cautiously and entered. A moment or two passed—not long—and the door opened a crack. When she waved, we hurried across the herb garden and slipped in.

Eben in his heavy robe held a brass oil lamp in his hand. I had thought he would be as terrified as Ghazel, but his face was remarkably calm.

He registered no surprise to see that I wasn't alone.

"I have been meditating," he said quietly. "It was revealed to me that we would be four Protectors."

"Alert Aeneas," I told Ghazel. "No one is to say I have returned."

She disappeared back into the night.

"You think of the Red Mirror, Isis," Eben said gravely, "but you must not. All will be lost if you leave."

"And all is not lost now?"

"The outcome has not yet been written."

I didn't know my hand was shaking until Qeb-ha took mine in his. He was so thin; I felt only bone. A current flowed from him. First my hand warmed, then my arm. My screaming nerves quieted.

"You are the Chosen One," he soothed. "The Gods have set us on this path. They shall not forsake us, my child. Everything is as it must be."

We all stood close together, jammed between shelves in the narrow passage between the door leading to my atelier and the one to the garden. Goliath, his back against the outside door, could scarcely stand; his head poked up between the racks of drying herbs.

I think Qeb-ha must have prepared him during the sail here, because he didn't look at all surprised by the septagram symbols all around him, or my being called the Chosen One. Or Eben calling me Isis. In fact, I saw a genuine spark of recognition when he heard that name.

"Come," Eben urged. "You created this moment. Only you can lead us from it."

Eben had been working on his translations. A dozen scrolls covered the top of a marble desk. Maps filled the space on the wall above; the largest, a map of the world, had been drawn by Claudius Ptolemy of the Library. The desk and carved ebony chair stood on the rich red wool Persian carpet that cost me three highly-trained pleasure slaves.

To the right of the desk, a tall window of opaque colored glass reflected burning lamps. On an inlaid cedar stand nearby stood one of Ptolemy's complex kinetic models of the Sun, five planets and the Moon, all revolving around the Earth.

The three doors were closed. One led to a storeroom and a second to the laboratory where we distilled essence from herbs, flowers and reptile parts.

In less than ten paces, I could fling open the third door and step into the corridor with its ceiling covered in delicate paintings of every species of bird. At the end of that passage, a gilded door opened to my bedchamber where the Red Mirror waited.

In the blink of an eye, I could leave all this behind.

Qeb-ha took my hand again. The current flowed. I knew without looking that Eben sank to the small prayer rug in the corner and rocked to and fro. His breath came quicker; he muttered Kabbalah phrases, calling on his Higher Powers, looking to the Light.

Goliath's controlled breath was heavy and deep. Like the trained fighter he was, he stayed alert, tense, primed to act.

Qeb-ha's breath was so quiet that even though he stood next to me, I more felt than heard him.

I had my hand on the latch, about to open, when the door shook on its hinges.

Bang! Bang! Bang!

I don't know how I kept from bursting into tears. Poor Qeb-ha's hand was crushed in my grip.

"Open up!" bellowed the General. "I know you are in there."

Eben was on his feet. Goliath, still armed with his trident, moved between the door and me.

"If you do not open, Ishtar, I shall break the door down."

Touching Goliath's arm to tell him to stand aside, I unlocked the latch.

When I pulled the door toward me, the General filled the open frame; the force of his fury pushed me backward. His blazing black eyes took in the room at one glance.

"Have you come to arrest me?" I asked.

He answered by grabbing the back of my neck and pulling me into his face.

"Thank Mars," he growled, crushing my mouth with his.

I placed soft palms on his rough cheeks, and looking deep into his eyes, said, "Marcus Quintillus must die."

"Do not concern yourself with him," he answered flatly.

"Is it over then?"

"Not yet. But for now, you are under my protection."

Before releasing the back of my neck, he kissed me hard again.

"Do not leave the island. Wait for my return."

He had turned to go down the painted corridor when I called out to him.

"The Red Viper, General." I did my best to control my voice, but a tiny tremor of hope vibrated when I asked, "Does he live?"

He stared at me for a moment before saying, "You did not ask for his life. You asked that his death be swift."

"So he is dead?" I couldn't stop the tears from welling.

"He lived for life after death. Now he has it."

When he saw my shoulders collapse, he came back to me and stroked my cheek with a tenderness of which I always forget him capable.

"He would have despised you as a harlot, Ishtar," he whispered. "You would have been less than dirt to him. Be content you never met him."

Of course, I believed that I could have persuaded the Red Viper to love me, but it was too late for such vain dreams.

The General kissed me once more, this time his lips barely brushing mine. "Play with your magic potions, Ishtar. Conjure up the future. And when you do, you shall find me there, waiting."

CHAPTER 45   THE BATH

"Life's like a play: it's not the length, but the excellence of the acting that matters." – Seneca

Eben was anxious to share his work. Drawing from as many as twenty scrolls—some recorded in hieroglyphs and some in the squiggly scratching of Demotic, a script version of the ancient pictographs—he translated Egyptian text into precise Greek letters to form an encyclopedia of magical spells.

His compilation, written on crisp new papyri, was carefully rolled onto ebony rods, similar to Eben's Torah, the sacred book of the Hebrews.

"Here it shall be stored," he said with pride. Reaching under the desk, he pulled out an ebony tube inscribed with golden eyes-of-horus, ankhs and unicorns.

The Black Scroll of my dream in the Hive.

"With Qeb-ha's help," Eben explained, "I am transcribing to Greek with the use of these seven additional letters." He pointed with an inky finger to unfamiliar symbols that looked vaguely Greek. "They have been devised for Egyptian sounds not in the alphabet."

Perched on a low stool, Qeb-ha poured over a scroll so fragile that I feared the papyrus might crumble in his hands.

He blurted out loud in Coptic; I caught a few words. *Thebes. Temple.*

Although my Egyptian was poor—I rarely heard it spoken in Alexandria—I found it not like learning a foreign language, but rather more as remembering something I'd once known but forgotten. And there was much about Egyptian in the sounds and cadence very close to the Tamazight of Nafusa. Coptic and Berber—ancient languages from one primal source. Like Lemta's magic.

"Why a scroll, Eben?" I asked. "Why not a codex?"

"This is a holy book," he sniffed, "and must be treated as such."

"The Christians record their holy books in codices. It seems more practical."

"I wish not to speak ill of the new faith, but the followers are an uneducated lot, and their myriad of sects have no tradition."

"I see the codex as a step forward, Eben. Easy to transport and easily stacked. The binder both protects the pages and shows clearly the title. Much better than a tag that's always getting lost. And you turn directly to the page you search, rather than unrolling a scroll."

"Our holy Torah is written on a scroll," he insisted. "The Magic itself was first written on scrolls. It is only fitting that the translation also be in the ancient way. The proper way."

I left him to his work; I had more pressing issues than to debate a scroll versus the codex. Matters of life and death. My own.

The General was true to his word. Equites from his cavalry—minus their horses—surrounded my villa. I felt safe, at least for now. Safe enough to grieve the Red Viper, to grieve Rasheed.

The bathing pool in my tepidarium was heated to just above body temperature. Eunice dripped oil of gardenia from the silver spout of a cobalt and white glass flask.

I settled on a yellow linen divan to let the masseuse slaves work their wonders. Nubian women massaged my feet and calves, hands and forearms with warmed almond oil. Eunice loosened the weaving in my hair and brushed the long mass one hundred strokes with a soft bristle brush backed with silver. After the brushing, she piled my hair on top of my head and fastened it with ivory pins.

Once in the scented waters with my head leaning back on a wooden headrest, floating in delicious warmth, I allowed myself to drift.

Nightmare visions of a battered Red Viper forced me to sit straight up. Even with my eyes wide open, the images wouldn't go away. The sounds of his screams wouldn't fade.

"Bring me the yellow flask."

This was a potion I brewed for my own use; I added only a few drops to my wine.

"Leave me."

Like one counts sheep to fall asleep, I counted the golden stars on the blue corbelled ceiling above my marble bath.

"Forty-nine. Fifty. Fifty-one."

My lids closed. The Red Viper was a tiny figure far, far away. I kept counting imaginary stars.

"Fifty-two. Fifty-three. Fifty-four."

My cells melted; I was one with the water.

I can't say how much time passed. The pool never cools but is kept at a constant warmth, just as the tepidarium, by water pipes running under the marble floor. Somewhere, out of sight and hearing, slaves were stoking fires in an underground furnace.

I felt a presence and opened my eyes to a naked bronzed god perched on the edge of the pool. Antinous.

When he saw my eyes were open, he slipped into the water and glided toward me.

"I told you I would come."

I wanted to ask how he got in, but my tongue was too thick to form words.

"You are the most desirable of all women," he murmured.

His fingers touched the base of my throat. I leaned my head back and felt his warm lips there.

Then his fingertips grazed my breasts rising up from the water, and I felt his lips again.

Down across my belly, over my shaved mound, his fingers traveled, followed always by his mouth.

He stroked between my thighs, down one loin and back up the other.

"Tell me everything that gives you pleasure, Elektra," he whispered. "Teach me."

He didn't need instruction. His finger found my swollen bud and rotated. My nipples rose to aching peaks. His tongue licked, moved, and licked again.

My brain, the small part of it that wasn't numbed, shouted, "Stop! Don't do this."

I heard, but I didn't listen.

To lie in the warmest of scented waters, for a god to caress me, for me to be pleased and not please, was a temptation the drug rendered irresistible.

Antinous nibbled my neck. When hearing my moan of pleasure, he bit just a little harder, sucking the skin, teasing with his tongue.

All the while his finger rotated on my aching bud.

When the orgasm rolled through my womb, I cried out, lifting my pelvis to his touch.

"Again, Elektra," he breathed in my ear. "Let me take you there again."

Then his finger deep inside me found the Spot. The magic spot that only Hektor knew.

He felt me melt, and although never having touched another woman, instinctively knew why. His finger stayed exactly where it was supposed to, massaging with exactly the intensity he was supposed to.

"You are a goddess," he crooned. "I shall worship you forever."

Heat radiated from the Spot; a hot flush spread through my hips and belly.

"O-o-o-o-o," I breathed out as the wave crested. His lips brushed mine with a kiss sweet as poetry.

He stood to his feet, his erection piercing the air. Scooping me up in his wrestler arms, he carried me from the pool to the yellow linen divan with gilded lion legs.

The room swirled; my head still reeled from the drug. For a brief moment, I thought I might be sick.

"Wait," I managed to whisper. And he answered by sitting on the divan beside me and pulling the pins from my hair to bury his face in my scented waves.

"Can you give me a vial with your smell?" he teased.

Only the slimmest circle of blue rimmed his huge pupils. His wet hair hung in ringlets about his face and neck.

I climbed onto his lap and straddled his thighs. Wrapping my legs around his waist, I guided him into my wet, pulling myself into his groin.

He went wild. Grabbing my buttocks with both hands, he sat on the edge of the divan, thighs spread wide and rocked me.

His erection deep inside, he stood to his feet and carried me, my legs locked around his waist, across the mosaic floor to a ledge holding an urn. Using the ledge to support my hips, he pummeled me and pummeled me against the wall. The urn crashed; I heard it break into a hundred pieces, but he didn't slow.

My mouth was on his, my tongue down his throat, when he climaxed with the bolt of a stallion. His body jerked once, then twice; he rested his forehead on mine.

"Oh Gods," he said, "there is nothing else like it."

He was careful to step around the shards of ceramic to carry me back to the divan.

"Give me a minute," he breathed.

A minute was all it took.

"How many positions are there?" he asked, rock-hard again. "I want to try them all."

On the third position, my head began to clear. This was wrong. Very wrong. I had to get him out of here. What if the General came back?

To hurry the climax, I reached between his legs to caress his balls.

He exploded, as I knew he would, and I allowed him to lie beside me for a few moments.

His curls had dried to gold. His flawless golden skin glistened with sweat. Never had I known a man more perfect. So lacking in guile, so pure. Innocent. Innocent of his fate.

The Greeks would claim that his beauty made the gods jealous, and that is why they took him so young. The Romans say that he whom the gods love dies young, with health, full senses and sound judgment.

But by coming here, I had my doubts that Antinous was of sound judgment.

"You must leave, Antinous. You risk both of us by being here."

"I have come on Hadrian's command, sweet Elektra. We set sail tomorrow for the South, and you are invited!" He positively glowed at the prospect of my joining the cruise.

When he saw me frown, he said quickly, "You may take your own barge."

"Do not go, Antinous. You must find an excuse."

"Why should I not go? We can be together. I can see you every day."

Out of desperation to keep him from the Nile voyage leading to his death, I whispered, "If I stay behind, will you stay with me?"

Alarmed, he warned, "You cannot refuse. Do not think of it. Hadrian does not care to hear 'no.' Trust me on that."

The interruption I'd feared turned out not to be the General.

I had only just pulled on a caftan of fine Egyptian linen when the door opened. Antinous sat on the divan, tying his sandals up his shin.

He was dressed, thank the gods, although it would take an idiot not to see what had gone on in that chamber. Broken urn and silk pillows strewn on the tiles. The scent of sex hanging in the air.

Towering over Ghazel in the doorway stood Hektor. His chestnut waves and carefully barbered curls were disheveled. His toga hung askew. I knew at a glance that he had come in haste from Alexandria.

"Hektor Ptolemais," I oozed graciously, "what a delightful surprise. May I present Antinous of Bithynia on an errand from the Emperor."

Gentleman that he was, Antinous stood to his feet and bowed his head.

Hektor nodded brusquely back. His angry eyes took in the telltale signs of wild abandon so like the upside-down Manhattan hotel room in another life. I saw he struggled to understand why this scene was so familiar. He had asked me then, *Did it have to be the Greek?*

Antinous leaned over my hand in a formal farewell.

"I bid you goodnight, my Lady. We sail at dawn."

Then he was out the door, and Hektor and I were alone. Except for Ghazel.

"Leave us," he told her.

She looked at me, and I nodded.

"You might have sent a message that you were coming, Hektor. This has been a most eventful day."

He slammed the door.

"You fuck him the same day you fuck me?"

"It *is* what I do, Hektor."

It wasn't until then that I noticed the scroll in his clenched fist. When he saw my eyes fall on it, his face grew darker.

"Your bill of sale," he snapped.

"May I offer you some refreshment?" I asked politely.

"Are you offering me a taste of you?"

"Is that what you want?"

"I shall not stick my penis where that Greek has been. He is Hadrian's Sodomite. But you know that. You *do* play with fire, Elektra."

"There is nothing about any of this that is playful, I assure you. Can I trust you to say nothing?"

He snorted, shaking his head. "You humiliate me and yet ask of me more. An escaped slave. A *whore* slave!"

He plopped himself on a cushioned tripod, long legs bent at the knee, and leaned forward to demand, "What is this about sailing tomorrow?"

"Please, Hektor. Let us go into the next room. Allow me to serve you some wine. You have endured a long journey. And I am grateful for your efforts, truly I am."

"Grateful?" he snorted again. "You must think me a fool."

"I think you a very perceptive man who, when he hears the facts, will act with intelligence and foresight."

Once I had him settled in my library, reclining on a wide divan covered in a robust wool woven with golden suns and silver moons, I told him of Hadrian's invitation.

"You sail tomorrow on a cruise with the Emperor?"

By his tone I could tell he was much impressed.

"Hadrian favors my visions."

Before he could offer his opinion on visions and those who put stock in them, I raised my hand to stop him.

"You are well aware, Hektor, that people are passionate about their beliefs. And because of those beliefs, they can be influenced."

I phrased my words carefully, not saying anything overtly critical of Hadrian while hinting at the opportunity his superstitious nature offered.

Hector took a sip of wine and let me continue without interruption. I definitely had his attention.

"I do not need to point out how invaluable to both of us my connection to Caesar might prove."

My use of 'both of us' elicited the desired reaction. We could be a team, both sharing an emperor's favor.

Hector sat more erect; I was proposing something far greater than an introduction to Marcus Quintillus. What might Hektor be willing to do to gain access to Hadrian?

"I am certain you have many interests I could promote."

I watched him take another sip of his wine. I'd added only two drops from the yellow flask. Not enough to numb as I had numbed myself, but enough to make him more pliable. If he proved obstinate, I'd have to use more. A healthy dose could put him to sleep for a day. More might put him to sleep forever.

"Hadrian would never invite a slave, Hektor, even a freed one, into his inner circle. We can let Leptis Magna be our secret—and both gain. Or you can persist in your claim, and have me. But am I worth it?"

"What about Marcus Quintillus?"

"He is being taken care of."

"Taken care of?" he sneered. "That sounds sinister. And to think that I anguished over your fate."

He looked around the room, at the shelves of fine codices and scrolls, at the gilt doors and the superb mosaic tile floor of Athena, the Greek Goddess of Wisdom, surrounded by the Nine Muses.

"You have done well for yourself," he admitted begrudgingly.

Sensing I wouldn't need more of the drops, I refilled his chalice with undoctored wine and placed the ewer on the ivory-inlaid table between us. The yellow flask stood on a tray across the room.

"More than well," he continued. "I believe you might live better than I. How did you do it? And do *not* tell me magic."

"What does one ever do to succeed? Know the right people. Take advantage of opportunity. Maximize talents. Work hard."

There was a new respect in his eyes when he began to realize that all the riches around him were mine—and that I had earned them myself. Well, almost. Admittedly, I'd had quite a bit of help from Aeneas.

"So if not my slave, then what will you be to me?"

"I shall be your ally, as you are mine."

"And that is all I may expect?"

"We can have that, too. But I shall never be yours exclusively."

He considered me over the rim of his cup, openly hungry in spite of his earlier scorn of the Sodomite.

"Not tonight," I told him. "I join Hadrian's entourage tomorrow and have much to prepare."

A burning ember popped. The strip of fine linen over the open doors to the peristyle garden kept out most of the insects. Heavy incense discouraged the rest.

Frogs croaked in a garden pool. Cicadas sang in the trees. A nightingale warbled. The fall of water from three fountains played a continuing refrain.

Quite unexpectedly, he pulled out an intricately jeweled, hinged silver box and put it on the table between us.

"I might as well give it to you. It is a twin to the other. Somehow, the rings belong on your hand."

Inside was the second Hathor Ring. The very ring Rasheed gave me in Las Vegas when we both thought we had a chance. The other ring was in the wall of Dominus' bath in Leptis Magna, waiting for me to find it two thousand years from now.

"You were correct, Hektor. The rings do belong on my hand. Thank you for returning them to me."

"Returning?"

"Just a little of the magic that you don't believe in. I do not expect you to understand."

I refilled his chalice and took a seat across from him.

"I am curious, Hektor. How is it that you have not been to my island before? I judged myself well-known in Canopus."

He made that dismissive snort of his. "I avoid Romans when I can, Elektra. They are an uncivilized, brutish bunch."

Poor Flavia. I was certain that all the spells and potions of the Black Scroll would never give her Hektor.

He was preparing to leave when I asked, "The bill of sale, Hektor? Here is where it, as well, belongs."

CHAPTER 46 NILE CRUISE

"In these matters the only certainty is that nothing is certain." – Pliny the Elder

Dawn came to the Nile in a golden mist at one with the river. I hadn't slept at all, but spent the night overseeing the packing of potions and herbs, scrolls and lead curse tablets, jewelry and gowns. And the Red Mirror.

Ghazel and Eunice would provide for my personal needs, along with a cook, hairdresser, cosmetics slave and masseuse. Although I put more trust in the Syrian and Celt to protect me, I chose the Nubians, trained to serve me. What danger would I face in Hadrian's pleasure fleet?

Besides, I had Goliath. When I told him that he was a free man, he shook his head. How rarely he spoke. I wondered that I ever recognized his voice in the Bellagio lobby.

In my absence, Aeneas would run the Temple. I trusted no one else.

"And who do you propose to act as hostess in my stead? Think carefully on it. If she handles the role well, I might yet free myself from these tiresome convivia."

"May I suggest Phaedra, Domina?"

Yet another Greek. Thoroughly loyal to *him*. If Aeneas had his way, all my slaves would be Greeks. Godfather to his own mafia.

"The path is clear for your work, Eben. I shall be away for some time."

Black ink smudged his fingers; his hair was more unkempt than ever. Immersed in his work, only my hand on his arm tore his attention from the scrolls.

"I shall see you on the other side," he said absentmindedly and then went back to his translation.

"Do good, my child," muttered Qeb-ha in Coptic. Patting my hand in the way he has of a kind and loving uncle, he repeated what he'd first told me centuries before, "You are the Chosen One. The Gods have set you on this path."

"And where does the path lead, Qeb-ha?"

"Why, to your destiny."

Of course, where else?

There were some last-minute tussles with the General's men, who insisted I was not to leave the island. But when shown the scroll with Caesar's seal, they let me pass. I boarded my barge as the first of the Hadrian's retinue sailed past.

I wasn't sure exactly what I expected when invited on an Imperial Nile cruise, but it wasn't the flotilla of ships led by the Hadrian's mammoth barge with double banks of oars. Battalions of Roman soldiers marched down the East Bank trampling under their thick-soled sandals the fruits of a thousand slaves' labor.

Today was the 24th day of Octobris. Antinous had six days to live. Or for me to save him.

My galley slaves pulled the long, silver-tipped river oars to push us upstream, against the current, toward the south. A brisk wind from the sea rose with the sun, and our red sail snapped and then billowed. At the top of the cedar mast, my red and gold banner with silver septagram announced to the world my arrival.

After a breakfast of dates, honeyed herb tea, white goat's cheese and fresh baked bread, I relaxed in the soft fur of my divan on the poop deck. A gold-spangled canopy shielded me from the morning sun. The twin Nubians in their yellow-striped headdresses stood poised to wave palmiform fans if the breeze died.

Lulled by the swoosh of the river against the gilded hull and the steady rhythm of the oars—in the water, through the water and out again—I dozed.

Shortly before noon, a skiff pulled alongside with a welcome greeting from Hadrian. A banquet tonight, the scroll announced. I was both relieved that Antinous hadn't delivered it personally and disappointed not to see him.

Ghazel served watered wine cooled in the Nile. I settled under my awning to watch the shore glide by. Lush with green wheat, the verdant Delta stretched without end to a blue horizon.

Here the Canopus branch of the Nile had narrowed; river traffic jammed the water lanes. Our mighty armada plowed on, scattering oncoming boats to wash on papyrus-clogged shores.

Farmers bending to their crops straightened to stare in awe at the floating golden palace that was Hadrian's barge. Running as fast as their thin legs could carry them, brown boys in loose white tunics waved and shouted.

One obscure village melted into another. The glare of the sun on gilded wood blinded me. All around the hull, the silver Nile shimmered and swirled.

We passed the walled city of Naukratis. It was there that Greek traders first lived in Egypt, invited by a long ago Pharaoh. When Egypt belonged to Egyptians and not Persians, Greeks or Romans.

I thought I might recognize Hektor's villa along the shore. Not this Hektor, but the Hektor who'd forsaken his wife for me. Barb was barren Eugenia then and had pleaded to raise Hektor's and my child as her own. He broke her heart, and yet foolish Flavia wanted him again.

While the household slaves napped under a striped awning on the deck below, Goliath stood watch from the helm.

"Domina, a boat approaches."

After a great deal of back-and-forth shouting, a skiff with a green triangular sail and powered by four oarsmen lashed onto our starboard side.

"Elektra! I only just heard that you were here!"

So again in that odd way of thinking of someone causes them appear, Flavia stepped onto the main deck. Her hair had been piled in another of those impossible arrangements requiring hours of weaving and more than one hairpiece. She wore a turquoise palla streaked with sparkly silver threads over a rose stola with the sleeves and hem of a grass green tunica peeking out. In her arms she carried the ever-present white Chinese dog done up with pink and green ribbons.

She hadn't come alone. Julia Balbilla, constant companion to

Hadrian's wife, Vibia Sabina, was at her side. Balbilla had chosen a sapphire stola with a sunny yellow palla and matching tunica. But there was nothing sunny about sullen Balbilla. Her lackluster brown hair was arranged in too-tight curls rising ridiculously high off an already high forehead. The bright sun showed her no mercy. Her nose was too big and her lips too thin, yet I couldn't deny that she had a most commanding presence. I might even call her striking—in a masculine way.

Intelligent, too. And calculating. I saw her take in everything at once.

"We have come to have our fortunes told," Flavia announced gaily.

The Nubian twins hurried to carry up two divans. Ghazel and Eunice arrived with trays of wine and fruit and a silver bowl of water for the dog.

"You must forgive my humble hospitality," I told them. "I have but one cook, who must perform miracles in a tiny galley."

With the bearing of a queen, Julia Balbilla surveyed the poop deck; her watery eyes, washed of almost all color, noted every detail. She coolly assessed every carpet and urn and calculated the cost of each gilded railing. There was a wrinkle to her nose, not quite of disdain, but rather that she'd found nothing wanting and was therefore disappointed. I suppose she didn't expect a pleasure goddess to demonstrate good taste.

At last, she turned to me.

"Flavia cannot stop raving about the power of your Sight, Elektra. And of course, Hadrian is enthralled."

Julia Balbilla was one of those women who so adroitly says one thing while thinking something entirely different. She wasn't here to have her fortune told.

"And how shall we see the future, my ladies?" I asked obligingly. "Have you had your stars read?"

"Astrology is too complicated," Balbilla protested. "All those planets and houses and angles. Too much mathematics for a woman's mind, do you not agree?"

We both knew that there was nothing too complicated for her labyrinthine mind.

"Then I would suggest bones," I offered in an amicable tone.

"Bones?" repeated Flavia. "What do you think, Julia?"

"It seems very…Nubian," she answered. "Raw. Intriguing."

At my nod, Eunice appeared with an ornately embroidered black velvet drawstring bag.

"What are those strange symbols?" Balbilla demanded.

"A magician never reveals her magic. It would no longer be magical." She frowned and settled unhappily back on the divan. Flavia looked from her to me, not liking what she saw. The pug-faced dog had the same suspicious look in her buggy eyes as the morning in Cleopatra's chamber.

"Come," Flavia urged in an attempt to regain the gaiety of their adventure. "Let us see the bones."

I tumbled the contents of the bag into a large silver bowl set on the low cedar table between us. A dozen bleached vertebrae, each marked with black lines, clattered like ivory tiles.

"Am I allowed to know what *these* symbols mean?" Flavia asked hopefully.

"This is the cobra," I said, picking up a bone marked by a curling S with two dots over it. "And this one, with a triangle and rays, is the lion."

"And this?" Balbilla pointed to a bone with a long thick line that ended in a V.

"The crocodile. And the last is the vulture." A wide-angle V sat on a short line.

"Four animals. Three bones each."

"A bit simple," Balbilla sniffed.

"The truth always is," I replied, holding the bowl out to her. "Would you care to go first, Julia Balbilla?"

I wasn't at all prepared for her reaction. She stared in horror at the silver bowl in my hand.

"Do I have to touch the bones?"

I would never have expected her to be frightened; she seemed too clever for common superstition. But there was no judging people's fear by outward appearances. By any other standard, highly suggestible Hadrian had a fine mind.

"No. But you must touch the bowl."

She hesitated. Then, as if the act required great courage, she squared her shoulders, took the bowl in her palms for one brave moment and set it back on the table at once.

Oh, how I would delight to have this woman in a dark room, throw some colored powders on the fire and intone a few hair-raising chants.

Although the invocation of magical names wasn't something I'd normally do when throwing bones, I couldn't resist a long onomatopoeic chant. With a dramatic raising of the bowl, I took a deep, cleansing breath and rolled back my eyes until only half the iris showed.

"CHAOR, CHTHOR, CHARABA, CHOLBAS, CHTHRYTHTYR," I chanted. "CHORBATH, CHTHAMNO, CHITHODYCHRA, CHYCHCHYCH."

Then I looked directly at Balbilla and asked in the deep, vibrating voice of Lemta, "What do you wish to know?"

I must have terrified the question right out of her head. She sat there, her small eyes big, thin lips closed in a tight line. Flavia shifted her weight on the divan. The dog growled. We all stared at Balbilla—Flavia with concern, me with a blank mask, the dog with slightly bared teeth.

"I have changed my mind," Balbilla announced in that arrogant tone of hers. "One should not tempt the Gods."

Flavia blinked, glanced at me uncertainly and offered brightly, "Well, I have a question! Let *me* touch the bowl."

We went through the routine, and she asked the question I expected.

"Shall I marry soon?"

I didn't need to ask whom, and Balbilla showed no interest. She appeared restless now, anxious to leave.

I threw the bones onto a leopard skin. Again they clattered like ivory tiles and fell into random groupings. I took a few moments, pretending to study their positions and the combinations they formed.

"I see a positive outcome but only after some difficulties."

"Thank you," Flavia breathed out in relief.

"I am only the messenger," I said humbly.

"We should return. It is late," declared Balbilla. "Vibia Sabina will be wondering what happened to us."

"It is a pity she could not come with you today," I remarked politely.

Her head jerked slightly. I could see her thinking, *Do you imagine that the Empress of Rome would visit a whore?*

No, but the Empress can send you.

"May I use the toilet?" Flavia asked, leaving Balbilla and me alone.

"Antinous is a charming young man," she said idly.

"He is indeed," I replied. *So Antinous is the reason you've come?*

"You cannot imagine how fond Hadrian is of him."

"I think I can."

Her icy eyes registered mild annoyance; she tilted her head to one side, almost defiantly thrusting her sharp chin toward me.

"He has arrived at an awkward age." She waited for my response.

"Antinous or Hadrian?"

She surprised me again by chuckling; cold as she was, Balbilla had a sense of humor. I believe I even detected a smidgen of respect.

"We are not certain who of the two is more enthralled with your magical powers." Her use of 'we' was clearly meant to underscore her intimacy with the Empress.

I'd like to have said that both were too impressionable. Antinous young and foolhardy. Hadrian an old fool.

"Shall we, Julia Balbilla?" Flavia was back. "Thank you, my dearest Elektra. You have made me most content."

I considered and rejected asking if the General sailed with us. Julia Balbilla was a woman I judged should know as little as possible about me.

"Until this evening," Balbilla said formally. Then just before she boarded the skiff, she turned and asked pointedly, "Do you ever divine the future for yourself?"

They hadn't been gone half an hour when yet another skiff pulled up to the starboard side. This boat had a lemon yellow triangular sail and carried six Praetorian Guards. Antinous stood in the bow poised to jump onboard.

Could he be more obvious? Every gossip in the flotilla watched the little skiffs with colored sails to see which barges they visited. In no time at all, the entire fleet would know of his visit.

"Are you comfortable?" he asked. "Do you need anything?"

"I need for you not to visit me."

"We shall be here on the poop deck in full view of the world," he said grandly. "I promise to behave myself."

I sighed and waved for a chalice.

"What did the high and mighty Julia Balbilla have to say?" he asked as soon as he took the divan. "Did you discuss her poetry? I suggest that you do, if you wish to gain her friendship. She considers herself a new Sappho."

"They came to have their fortunes told."

Antinous found that worth a hearty laugh. "I hope you gave her a good show."

He stretched out his legs and flexed his calves, tightening golden thigh muscles exposed by the short tunic skirt. My eyes lingered a little too long—long enough that he noticed.

"Do you have any of that wonderful Delta wine you served me last night." His eyes twinkled when he said 'last night.'

He gave me a long sideways look and stuck the tip of his tongue out the corner of his mouth. Had he no idea what danger he was in? The danger he put *me* in?

"Balbilla did say something about you arriving at an awkward age."

The smile disappeared. Sobered, he said in a flat voice, "Hadrian will not set me free. How awkward is that?"

"He is the Emperor," I reminded him quietly.

"And his Guard resents me."

"To what extent?"

"They would not harm me, if that is what you imply."

"Are you certain?" I held his eyes to reinforce just how serious I was.

He put his hands behind his head, his fingers where my fingers enjoyed teasing his thick golden curls. His eyes, a most remarkable enamel blue, bluer than the sky behind him, were somber.

"Do you truly believe my life is at risk?"

"Yes, Antinous. I do. In fact, I want you to leave the cruise."

"Hadrian will never allow it."

"Perhaps I might influence him." I had only the germ of an idea, but Hadrian just might be superstitious enough to fall for it.

I filled Antinous' chalice with more of the Delta wine, asking idly, "Does the Moor sail with us?"

"He has not yet arrived. Something about a task in Alexandria."

Antinous didn't elaborate, and I didn't press. He'd lost his earlier bravado; the furrow between his eyebrows, deep for someone so young, was back.

"With you, I am happy again," he said gravely. "I feel alive."

He stared intently and then said with ferocity, "I make you happy. I can feel it. Do not deny it."

"Yes, you make me happy—very happy. I admit that."

He didn't need to be bound with silk yarn or flogged with leather whips; he didn't crave for me to urinate on his face. We didn't play games; we didn't act out roles. Sex with him was pure joy. I wanted to tell him the joy he brought me but didn't for fear of encouraging him.

"But we cannot be together. You know this to be true."

"Do not say that! Life can be different. Circumstances can alter. You must leave me hope for the future."

I hated listening to him speak of hope. Unless circumstances altered very quickly, he had no future.

"Of late, I sense…a change." Antinous didn't look directly at me but out over the shimmering Nile. "A change in Hadrian."

"What kind of change?"

"He looks at me with sadness," he answered, turning his gaze back to me.

If it had been anyone but Antinous, I would have asked, *Does Hadrian still make love to you?*

I didn't have the heart to further humiliate him.

"Let us run away, Elektra. You and I. Let us weigh anchor and sail. Tonight!"

I felt a stab of guilt. If I truly wanted to save him, would that not be what I should do?

"Where would we go?" I reasoned. "There is no place we can escape Hadrian's reach."

I thought he might come back with suggestions like Sheba or far away Parthia, but instead he stared mulishly at nothing. The muscles in his jaw worked; he nibbled a bit on his lower lip.

"Is there no way out then?" he asked.

Should I tell him that his final exit was only days away? That he should enjoy every moment, for he would soon gain the release from Hadrian he so desperately sought. Was I wrong not to tell him? Would I want to know the hour and means of my own death?

"Tell Hadrian I had a dream. A dream about him."

Just after the sun slipped below the western horizon and the flotilla anchored for the night, another skiff, this one with purple sails, glided through mauve waters toward my barge.

A summons from Hadrian. I was to return with the Praetorian Guard.

CHAPTER 47   BLACK COBRAS

"Afflicted by love's madness, all are blind." – Sextus Propertius

The mood on the Imperial Barge wasn't as light-hearted as I'd expect for a pleasure cruise. There was a heaviness in the air that, like a thick cloak of sobriety, dampened all gaiety.

Hadrian was in audience, an audience that didn't include Antinous, who stood in a gold-trimmed white toga on the second deck, just below the poop deck holding Hadrian's pavilion. His face brightened slightly when he saw me, but the furrow was there; he looked worried. My unease increased.

At the base of each set of steps stood two Praetorian Guards. Backs erect, fully armed with gladius at the belt and shield on the arm, they stared, as always, stonily ahead.

I felt everyone looking at me, which wasn't at all unusual, yet tonight I suffered an odd paranoia that they stared because they knew my fate.

Under ordinary circumstances, I would have relished their eyes drinking in the crimson silk gown, lingering on cleavage deep enough to invite without giving everything away. In the Egyptian style, a golden sash encircled my ribcage. From there, the shimmering scarlet cloth followed the lush curves of my body right down to my slender ankles and gold sandals tied with gold twine finished with golden tassels. My toenails, carefully pumiced, were henna-stained brick red.

The Greek major domo who oversaw Hadrian's household greeted me politely, led me up a flight of steps and indicated I should take a seat on a low-backed carved ebony chair with leopardskin cushion.

No sooner had I sat than a tall comely slave with chestnut curls offered me watered wine in a gold chalice etched with Hadrian's Imperial Crest. On my right middle finger glowed the Hathor Ring Hektor had given me on my island. I closed my eyes for a moment, focusing on the lapis lazuli, summoning its power.

ANA A A NANA A A NANA.

A rose sky darkened to violet. The last glimmer of day cast a thin glowing line along the western horizon.

I passed the time watching an army of slaves light torches around the perimeter of the main deck. Thin plumes of smoke rose from brass braziers. The pungent scent of frying garlic drifted from the kitchen barge. Ashore, fires roared under roasting meat.

Fifteen red and gold striped couches on the forward deck clustered around a massive circular inlaid table. Hadrian's empty lectus stood on a slightly raised dais in front of a screen carved with his crest.

A mosquito buzzed at my ear; I adjusted the palla of fine burgundy wool to cover my head and shoulders. The October night was still warm; later there would come a damp chill as the mist rose from the river.

I did my best to still my pounding heart by chanting over and over. In time, I calmed.

Under the weight of fiery curls and elaborate twists, my head buzzed. I closed my eyes, focusing on my crown chakra. The hum heightened; vibrations sang higher. A white beam streamed down through the top of my head. Golden rain fell around me. The beam broadened to press all over my body; every cell throbbed. I was overcome by a sudden pulse of heat and opened my eyes to curb the nausea.

Footfalls on the nearby steps brought me back.

Five Egyptian priests in traditional long white kilts, heads shaven, leopardskins draped on their shrunken brown shoulders, filed down. One after one, they turned to look at me. Their eyes, outlined in kohl, burned with an inner fire I imagined only from hell. "Evil!" screamed their auras.

Black cobra tattoos snaked around their arms; upside down wooden ankhs hung on their bare chests.

These were priests from the cult of Seth, God of Chaos, God of the Desert. Everything dark, all things sinister, come from Seth. Slayer of Osiris. Widow-maker of Isis. Malevolent uncle of Horus.

I watched the back of their shaven skulls, each tattooed with a head of a cobra with hood flared, sink lower and lower down the steps until they reached the main deck.

What could Hadrian want from the worshippers of Seth?

"Caesar awaits," whispered the Greek major domo.

I floated up the steps to the poop deck; my feet didn't touch the wood. The white beam streaming into my crown chakra held me erect.

A Praetorian Guard pulled aside the blood crimson velvet drape hemmed with gold braid for me to enter Hadrian's pavilion.

No one announced me. Hadrian reclined on a deep purple divan, his elbow slung over the armrest head of a mighty lion with gilt mane.

"What a vision you are, Elektra of Canopus," he said in a tired voice. "That glorious red gown with your fiery hair. I think the mere sight of you is better medicine that all the vile potions my physicians concoct."

He looked utterly exhausted—and older than he had just the other night.

"Εδω," he said, switching to Greek, waving me in the direction of a gold-and-green striped lectus. "Here, close by me."

"Most Excellent Caesar honors me by his summons."

His eyes watched me appreciatively as I navigated a low table to glide to the divan just across from him.

"I wished a small, private talk," he told me.

Small? Like a word to the wise?

I'd already noticed there was no one else in the tent. Not even a Praetorian Guard. No one had searched me. I might have pierced him with a poison needle.

His illness would have been short. He would have demonstrated all the symptoms of cardiac arrest—or perhaps stroke.

But I hadn't come prepared to solve Antinous' problem by killing Hadrian. At least, not this night.

"I am told that you create a new encyclopedia. A collection of all the magic of Egypt."

I hope I didn't show how his words stunned me. If he had spies in my household, he certainly knew about Antinous.

"Yes, Most Excellent Caesar, I have able assistants, schooled in languages, to execute the translations into Greek."

"And how shall this knowledge be known?"

"We call it the Black Scroll, Caesar."

"Why black?"

I shrugged. "The name was revealed to me in a dream, Caesar."

I saw no reason to go into details about the black arts and the power of absolute dominance the magic promised. Hadrian had power enough. Power over my life certainly. And that of Antinous.

"Ah-h-h," he said. "A dream."

In the way he said it, I understood that dreams were not a place where Hadrian was comfortable.

What demons stalked his sleep? And how could I use them?

"I have heard, my beautiful Elektra, that the Black Scroll, as you call it, contains powerful spells. Perhaps I am in need of such magic."

Would he ask me for a spell to control Antinous?

"Magic is often revealed in dreams, Caesar," I baited, hoping to elicit the nature of his nightmares.

But instead of confiding the source of his torment, he gave a heavy sigh, leaned back and closed his eyes. For a moment, I thought he might have dozed off.

"Did you recognize the priests?" he asked, still with his lids shut.

"I did, Caesar."

"Do you believe they can deliver what they promise?"

"What have they promised, Caesar?" I asked quite calmly, but inside I choked.

He opened his eyes and stared into mine.

"They promised what the Grand Wizards promised but have not delivered."

They claim the secret to immortality, Domina—if one rises high enough.

I didn't bother to insult him by feigning ignorance of the Grand Wizards. Hadrian was no fool, at least not when it came to judging people.

After a moment, he continued in his weary, resigned voice. "My work is not finished, but my strength wanes. I fade every day. The doctors can do nothing but do not admit it. I need more time. Not forever. I flatter myself not so much."

"Have the priests made a proposal, Caesar?"

Would he be so shameless as to tell me that they offered the sacrifice of Antinous to steal his youth and vitality?

Hadrian aged another year in that moment. Such anguish etched his face. A tortured soul. His whole body shrank before my eyes.

"Do you believe, Lady Elektra, that life force can be transferred from one man to another?"

"I do not," I said forcibly. "No person has seen evidence of such a rejuvenation."

"There is not evidence of everything that happens. Much is beyond proof. You, of all people, should know that."

"No one is given back their youth by the death of another, Caesar. These priests are not gods."

Rather than respond to my argument, he asked, "What is death?"

"I can best say it is the transition from one state to another, Caesar. What that 'other' is—the nature of it—I cannot know."

If I told him about past and future lives, would it encourage him to die with grace? Or would it encourage him to take Antinous' life?

"There are many opinions, are there not?"

"As many as there are gods, Caesar."

He sighed again, a sigh of exhaustion.

"I find it very confusing. I am not sure what to believe. I have counsel from so many."

He stared regretfully into his chalice. He didn't drink. He appeared stunned. I decided that he was heavily drugged.

"I wish for time to stand still. Not to age. Not for—" He stopped and then started again. "Not for anyone around me to age. Do you have a magic spell for that?"

"I have yet to see time stand still for anyone, Caesar."

"Is he frightened?"

Hadrian's question to me was as unexpected as his query about death. He didn't need to name Antinous.

"Should he be, Caesar?"

Hadrian didn't answer but clapped his hands to summon his major domo.

"Send in Antinous. And bring some of those cheese tarts I smelled from the ovens."

Antinous came into the tent and went directly to Hadrian's left side to stand a bit stiffly at the armrest. Hadrian reached out and took him by the hand.

Antinous looked away so I wouldn't see the pain of humiliation in his eyes.

Then Hadrian tugged on him, pulling him closer and forward, more to his side. He raised their entwined hands to his lips and kissed the back of Antinous' hand.

Antinous stared stonily at a point past me, avoiding my eyes. The muscles in his jaw had tightened into acorn-sized knots.

"I hear you two enjoy each other's company," Hadrian said quietly in a tone that, although not exactly menacing, caused a bristly, tingling feeling to crawl up my neck.

Antinous glanced at me and then down.

I kept my voice perfectly level, saying, "Antinous is like a sun that shines enthusiasm on us all."

"Then it is his spirit that you admire?"

"But certainly, Caesar. He is most admirable." I was at the same time terrified of letting anything show and dismayed that we spoke of Antinous as if he weren't here. As one would a slave.

"He is so young and impressionable," Hadrian mused out loud, then shocked me by saying, "But, I am reminded daily, not young enough."

Hadrian had a faraway look on his face for an instant before continuing, "His good heart is easy prey. He is subject to whims."

"He is subject to the same ambitions as any young man, Caesar."

Antinous controlled himself well, but it was impossible not to sense his boiling resentment of being discussed so openly. Surely Hadrian could feel the tension in him. How long before Antinous exploded?

The tray of cheese treats sat undisturbed between us. None of us had touched our wine. The rhythm and depth of our breathing was each different. Hadrian labored a bit. Antinous's breath came a little too fast. I concentrated on the beam of energy still teasing my crown chakra and forced myself to take discreet breaths, in through my nose and out through my mouth.

"I had a vision, Caesar," I dared say.

Hadrian roused from his lethargy. His back straightened; he gripped Antinous' hand tighter.

"Tell me," he whispered.

I truly believe he looked for a way out. A way that would not cost him Antinous.

"We sailed through a thick mist, Caesar, but not so thick as to prevent seeing the veil of tears ahead. In the quiet, the absolute utter stillness, the Gods urged us to leave the river of sorrow."

"Which Gods?"

"All the Gods save one. All speaking with one voice."

"Who did not speak?"

"Seth. For the veil of tears is of his making. And the black world on the other side, the world I could not see but knew was there, is also of his making. Seth's realm of chaos and death. His abyss of grief."

Hadrian heaved a long sigh. "So our destiny is sorrow."

He looked defeated—and so incredibly sad.

"We make our own destiny, Caesar. My vision was not of what must be, but of what shall come to pass if no action is taken. It is within Caesar's power to send Antinous away. To save him from the future."

As if in answer to my suggestion, he released Antinous, who lost no time moving to another divan. He didn't recline but sat on the edge, knees slightly apart, leaning forward, his forearms on his thighs.

He hadn't yet learned the guile of hiding his feelings; hope beamed from his eyes.

"I cannot live without him," Hadrian said simply, pathetically.

How repugnant it must be for his Guard to watch the great Hadrian, builder of walls and cities—progressive of mind—play the role of an old fool in love.

Hadrian's confession made me fear the Praetorian Guard more than ever.

"But can Caesar live *with* him?" I asked.

We had come to the point in our conversation where nothing needed to be said. He knew the implication of my words. It was one thing to be infatuated with a young boy. All were willing to give the Emperor his little Greek fantasy, his *eromenos*. But Antinous was no longer a child; the whole affair had become quite intolerable. Hadrian not only made a fool of himself, he brought dishonor on all.

He had a dazed look. And why wouldn't he be, a man caught in such a dilemma? A man conflicted. A man contemplating the death of one he so loved that he couldn't bear to send him away?

Antinous was visibly crushed; dark despair replaced hope. The three of us were alone in the pavilion, but I sensed spying eyes. The Emperor of Rome was never free of those watching over him; their lives and power were intrinsically entwined with his continued well-being.

Unless the Guard sought a replacement.

It had happened before—the assassination of an Emperor by the Praetorian Guard. But I didn't sense they'd made that decision. Hadrian was no madman like Caligula. He had only one serious flaw. An obstacle easily removed. The Nile could be a treacherous playground for a young man who drank too much.

The silence bore on so long, I began to consider speaking again. Had Hadrian fallen into a trance? Or to sleep? His breathing made a slight wheezing sound.

Then from behind closed lids, he spoke wearily, "Your benefactor will join us soon. I hope in time for tomorrow's hunt."

Benefactor?

Hadrian opened his eyes and gave me a significant look.

"I have heard tales," he said in a quiet voice. He let those words hang for a moment in the air before continuing in a brighter tone. "But the Moor vouchsafes for you."

He smiled a little. I do think he was, in his way, fond of me.

"You are indeed a woman blessed with good fortune. And I believe you to be quite clever. Clever enough, I hope."

I felt myself mesmerized by the movement of his lips forming words. He waited, and I understood he expected me to speak.

"I am indeed fortunate to benefit from Caesar's presence and trust."

He chuckled a little. "And did I not say clever?"

He expected no answer, and I gave none.

"Tomorrow we arrive at Giza," he announced. His suddenly clipped tone indicated that our audience was over. "There we shall hunt lion in the shadow of the Pyramids. If your vision proves correct, my prescient Elektra, we shall face danger but return victorious. Is that not what you predicted for the hunt?"

The hunt where Hadrian would save the life of Antinous. Three days from that hunt, Antinous would die.

"It is the first step in the road to a destiny that is not yet written, Caesar. There is still time."

"Perhaps. And then perhaps the Sphinx shall answer our questions."

All my hopes for persuasion faded with his words. Hadrian didn't accept my prophecy or my caution. He intended to sail into the veil of tears.

In the end, we believe that which we choose to believe.

CHAPTER 48   O HEKA!

"So potent was religion in persuading to evil deeds." – Lucretius

Hail Caesar!" saluted the Praetorian Guard.

"Hail Caesar," came the refrain from the guests reclining on divans.

No one rose to greet Hadrian's entrance. No trumpets or fanfare. This was a casual affair, a meal among friends on a pleasure trip. The company appeared to be exclusively Roman. I saw no evidence of a purchased citizenship in this inner circle.

Wife Vibia Sabina and her companion Julia Balbilla again shared a lounge. Tonight, Antinous took the empty sofa to Hadrian's right. He wore a sullen frown without a trace of the sunny enthusiasm I'd just praised so highly.

Flavia waved from a divan a few places to the left of Sabina and Balbilla. In her lap slept the little white dog, and to her side reclined a handsome young Roman in the *laticlavus* toga of a Senator.

Forget Hektor! my mind shouted to her. *He is not who you think he is.*

The vocator led me to a lounge directly across the wide, food-laden table from Antinous. I studiously avoided eye contact with him and focused on my dinner partner for the evening.

"Good evening, Most Excellent," I greeted him in a Latin artfully devoid of Spanish accent.

He smiled agreeably, inclined his head, and made a place for me on the couch.

"I am Quintus Tineius Rufus, Lady," he announced with some pride. Rufus was a military man, nearly bald and of middle-age. He wore a short white tunic topped by a leather cuirass embossed with the golden emblem of the Palestine Xth Legion. Unlike Romans who'd adopted the Eastern custom of adorning themselves with gold and jewels, he wore a solitary signet ring on his right index finger. A ring that said he commanded the Legion.

We exchanged a few idle remarks, commenting on the fair weather and the low waters of the Nile now suffering a second year of disappointing flood.

"It is a pleasure to be away," he confided, "from those agitated Jews. They are never content. And now that Caesar in his great wisdom has outlawed circumcision, the threat of insurrection grows each day. My men anticipate ambush on every outing in that Gods-forsaken hell."

"Circumcision is at the heart of their faith, Most Excellent. To be denied that is to be denied covenant with their One God."

"It is a barbaric custom that defiles the natural beauty of the manly form. Are you sympathetic to them?" he demanded.

"I am sympathetic to all those who wish to honor their gods—if that worship harms no others, of course."

"Humph," he snorted. "Followers of the Nazarene as well? I find Christianity a superstition taken to extravagant lengths."

The words of Pliny the Younger. But he didn't give the historian credit.

"A fast-growing superstition, Most Excellent."

"Yes," he grumbled. "The contagion continues to spread. What *is* the attraction? Do you know any of these people? Most seem to be slaves."

"Eternal life?" I suggested. "The belief that all men are equal?"

"Pure nonsense and wishful thinking. They deny the great Chain of Being where we all have our place."

He took a swig of wine and wiped his lips with the back of his hand.

"The meek inheriting the earth?" he sneered. "It is a radical and dangerous thought that must be checked and set straight."

"And you, Most Excellent, to what school of thought do you adhere?"

"I am a Stoic," he sniffed, "as are all good Romans."

Tineius Rufus didn't add that he was a Mithraist, although I was certain he was high-ranking—maybe even a Grand Wizard—to be in command of a Legion once led by Julius Caesar. No doubt he worshipped with a secret brotherhood in underground caves just as the

Christians he despised. The two sects even shared a fascination with drinking blood. One symbolic, the other quite real.

"A Stoic, Sir? A noble path for the strong." I gave him an admiring smile. "You must welcome Caesar reviving the old Sumptory Laws. I have heard that excessive luxury in Rome is subject to fine."

"Luxury is the cause of crime and lust—and more deadly than armies," he declared pompously.

Now he plagiarized Juvenal. He obviously didn't expect a woman like me—the very antithesis of his Stoic ideal of virtue—to recognize the words of a renowned poet.

"It was the extravagance of the East that corrupted Rome," he declared in the too loud voice of a man who'd had too much to drink.

Extravagance in drink was apparently not considered by him to be a corrupting influence. Entirely self-absorbed, he was oblivious to the quieting of conversation around us.

"What need have we of silks and perfumes?" he plowed on. "Or men who adorn themselves like women?"

"Careful, Tineius Rufus," challenged a long man of regal bearing from the adjacent sofa. "You sound like one of those Christians who deems worldly pleasures as—how do they call it?—*sinful*. Would you also have us retreat to the desert to meditate upon a life hereafter?"

"To the desert," shouted a woman with hair hennaed flaming orange. "Not to pray but to fornicate!"

The banquet laughed and cheered, "Hear! Hear!"

"Do not speak to me of those heretics," Rufus snorted. "I look not to the Christians for other than calamity. Jews and Christians—all the same. Troublemakers. I say do away with the atheists. To the lions—all of them."

"Why fret over a religion of slaves, superstitious Egyptians and weepy women?" He spoke quietly, this burly Roman with a shock of white hair, but everyone listened. "No Roman—or Greek—takes it seriously."

"I should not be so certain," objected a young man to my right. "Let us take the case of Justus of Alexandria, once a student at the Library. He argues their teachings within the framework of *Logos*."

"Watch out, Rome! A Christian with wit has come!"

"I have read Justus myself," the youth came back. "I tell you he makes something of this superstition that an educated man may examine."

"You can dress up their words in the robes of Socrates if you will,"

Rufus retorted, "but you cannot deny that they worship a common man. A *Jew*."

"A Jew who rose from the dead. Not a common thing."

"Who else saw him but a handful of his devotees?"

I'd rarely seen a dinner party more animated. Everyone seemed to have formed an opinion of Christians. Clearly, they were fascinated by this cult that had come from nowhere and grown so fast, but I didn't sense that they understood the force of history at work.

"They say this Jesus came to Egypt to learn the magic arts. When he returned to Palestine, he declared himself a god."

"Any fool can call himself a god, my good Sir. Mark my words. The cult is doomed—already split into dozens of sects in Alexandria alone. They battle over whether their Messiah was a man with the nature of a god or whether he was a god *and* a man."

"Yes! They have indeed been infected by Greek rhetoric! Never a straight solution but always divergent points of view."

"I say it is a good thing if these Jews follow a new faith. The old one has brought us nothing but headache."

"It is not the Jews, Gaius Scipio, who follow the teachings of the Nazarene but everyone else."

I kept my thoughts to myself. I had, after all, an unfair advantage. There was no point in warning them about the sea change ahead. They would never believe that this renegade cult would one day take over the Empire.

Then Julia Balbilla said, "Pilate should never have crucified the man."

Such was her authority that she could still a robust debate. It was as much in her tone as her bearing. A woman who knew all about everything.

"But one Jew, Julia Balbilla," someone dared protest. "How many Jews have been crucified? Thousands. Tens of thousands."

"Perhaps only one Jew," she argued in her sublimely arrogant manner. "But the wrong one. He broke no Roman law. We should never have gotten involved. It was the beginning of an age of trouble. And we have not seen the end of it."

So Balbilla proved the most prescient of the lot. A perceptive lady deserving of her reputation.

Hadrian didn't offer an opinion or deliver his usual sermon on tolerating law-abiding Christians. He drank too much and spoke not at all. In truth, he wasn't really with us.

I hadn't once looked directly at Antinous but felt his eyes constantly on me.

The conversation moved on to the hunt the next day. I made my excuses to Quintus Tineius Rufus and left under the pretext of a headache.

I'd reached the stern of the barge where Goliath waited when Antinous caught up with me.

"Are you mad?" I whispered fiercely when he took me by the shoulders.

"Do you condemn me to this life?" he begged. "Have you no pity?"

"I can do nothing more at this moment, Antinous. I shall not give up, I promise you. But *this*? This is foolhardy. Surely you see the danger."

"Come away with me, Elektra. Now!"

"You know my answer."

"Then you do not love me as I love you."

That much was obvious, but I couldn't find it in my heart to shatter his. My silence was enough.

"Is it because you think me too young?"

He sighed then and leaned against the gunwale, throwing back his head, his eyes drinking in the sea of stars overhead. Mars, fiery orange in the black sky, glowed near the horizon.

"Is it not ironic, my sweet Elektra? Too young for you. Too old for Hadrian. I am but a plaything tossed about by the Gods."

"We cannot escape, Antinous. There is *nowhere* beyond Hadrian's reach."

"If I were free, would you have me?"

In my heart, I honestly didn't know. He *was* very young. But before I was forced to answer, perhaps with a lie, two Praetorian Guards stepped out of the shadows.

I wouldn't have been surprised if the Guards had each taken an arm and arrested me. Instead, they maneuvered me, without touching, to the gangplank leading down to a floating quay with half a dozen skiffs tied on. Goliath followed and helped me into a boat manned by four rowers.

The oars pushed through the slick waters, rose into the misty air and dived down again. The sound of the creaking oarlocks was deafening.

I felt both hot and cold. I tried to hold back tears, but my eyes would have none of it. Dread overwhelmed me. And for a time, under the canopy of eternal stars that witness the short lives of men, I surrendered my quest to save Antinous. There was nothing I could do. Not in this life, anyway.

When I dared to look back, the two Guards stood there still, watching us row away. Antinous was gone. The moon, waning in third quarter, had just risen, forming a conjunction with Mars. I took it as an omen. But whether it was good or bad, I couldn't decide.

Against all logic, I lighted seven lamps set on seven bricks and began to mix powders and gather ingredients—dried placenta, my own coagulated menstrual blood, and dog excrement.

A potent cocktail. But not potent enough. I needed a living being. The formula called for a cat, but there was none on board. The best I could do was one of the caged doves the cook kept on hand for stew.

Holding the plump gray bird in a brass bowl filled with Nile water, I drowned it. But not quite. It struggled in my hands; I held its wings tightly against its body until the dove was still, yet breathed.

Then I cut open its living abdomen with a tiny silver blade and pulled out its entrails, noting the color and shape of the liver. Auspicious.

Finally, I slit the writhing dove's throat over a small golden bowl rimmed with septagrams, harvesting the remaining blood.

Lifting the bowl toward the east, I intoned the ancient spell taught to me by Lemta.

"I call upon you, Mother of all men—O Heka! Goddess of magical power, OROBASTRIA NEBOUTOSOUALETH, O Entrapper! Mistress of corpses, LETH AMOUMAMOUTERMYOR."

I mixed seven drops of dove blood with seven drops of my own pressed from a pricked finger. Then I combined the blood with seven drops of the Nile.

I drew a series of sacred signs and magic words on a clean sheet of papyrus with cinnabar ink blended with the blood. Words of power. Words that conjure up demons. Words that bring the dark side to the light. ABLAMATHANALBA ABRASAX. ABRACADABRA.

"I conjure you, the *daimon* that has been aroused in this place, and you, the *daimon* of the dove that has been endowed with spirit; come to me on this very night and at this very moment, and perform for me the death of Hadrian."

After rolling the papyrus carefully, I tied it with a long coppery strand of my hair. Then I tore the pigeon into seven pieces with my bare hands—two wings, two feet, the head, the body and the tail—and cast them all onto hot coals. A metallic powder turned the smoke blood red. The stench of the burning feathers mixed with frankincense and myrrh.

Black splotches of dove blood dampened the front of my red silk gown; gore dripped from my fingers.

Then to make absolutely certain that the Underworld got my message loud and clear, I etched an ancient Phoenician malediction on a lead curse tablet.

I saw no other way to save the life of Antinous than to end Hadrian's.

The sun rose, we cast off anchor, and I fell into a deep sleep—the sleep of dreams.

A gray mist hovered above steely waters swirling in mercury arabesques. The form of a man coalesced, first in the dull sheen of pewter, then with a golden glow.

I couldn't tell if it were Christ or Antinous rising from the dead.

The dazzling aura burned so bright I was blinded. When my vision cleared, the light had gone. The beautiful and pure Antinous floated face down in the mackerel water, his life spirit drained from his Adonis body.

I woke with a sob, clutching in my fist the small leather pouch of placenta, blood and papyrus fragments summoning Hadrian's death.

The sun was high when Ghazel woke me to a splendid October day with the clearest of skies and most tender of breezes. The air was dry and warm, but not hot.

"Domina, a boat approaches."

It couldn't be Antinous, of that I was certain. Confined to quarters, perhaps. Certainly not free ever again to visit Elektra of Canopus.

I braced myself, fully expecting an arrest warrant. By the look of her terrified eyes, so did Ghazel.

She quickly arranged my hair into a wreath of twisted braids, sponged my naked body with fragrant water and helped me into a white caftan with silver embroidered crescent moons around the hem and bodice.

As the skiff with orange sails neared, I could make out no telltale black capes and black helmets.

When the General stepped onboard, I nearly wept with relief and went down at once from the poop deck to welcome him.

"Are you a fool, woman?" he snarled as a greeting.

"I attempt to avoid it."

"You do a poor job. I killed a Roman so that you might live."

By that I took him to mean Marcus Quintillus.

"Is he dead then?"

He answered by opening the door to my cabin, plopping himself on a divan and shouting at Ghazel to bring wine.

I motioned for the Nubian masseuse to remove his sandals. She washed his feet in scented water and dried them with soft linen before rubbing his soles with warm almond oil.

The tension in his shoulders relaxed. The dark scowl lightened somewhat; he glared at me with slightly less intensity.

His eyes traveled around the cabin until they fell on the Red Mirror. He looked surprised, and then curious.

"You brought the mirror with you?"

I saw him thinking. *Why that piece above all others?*

"Leave us," I said, taking the flask of oil from the Nubian. "Close the door."

I started with his right little toe, rubbing with oil, then the next toe and the next, pulling gently on each until I heard the gentle pop of a joint. I massaged gently his calloused and torn big toe and repeated every touch on the left.

His anger drained. I felt it flow through me and out my crown into the still air of my cabin made sweet by fresh gardenia and jasmine.

Using my thumbs, I pressed hard into his calf muscles. My fingers found a tiny knot and massaged until it disappeared.

My thumbs on his inner thigh brought the erection rising from a mound to a pillar between the leather tongues of his lappet.

I put my mouth on him and took him deep in my throat, tunic cloth and all. When he grabbed my braids in his fist to push my head further, I bit down. With a cry of pain, he released me.

Faster than he could realize what was happening, I grabbed the silk rope stored under the divan and lashed his wrist to a little post in the armrest.

Startled, he watched me with open lips. I lashed the other wrist to a second post.

While he stared and panted, I tied his ankles spread-eagle to the foot of the sofa.

His erection grew taller, thicker.

I held his eyes while I moved his tunic aside, straddled him and poised above his throbbing manhood.

He breathed short quick breaths through slack lips. His irises were so black I could scarcely see his pupils dilate.

Slowly, so slowly, I lifted my caftan, exposing first my white thighs, then my shaved and carmined mound and soft rounded belly. Finally I pulled the robe over my head to bare my ripe breasts. He couldn't tear his eyes away from them.

Slowly, so slowly, I lowered myself onto his pedestal. We locked eyes again. He held his breath as I took him deeper and deeper, until I was filled. And then I pushed more, and then more, using all my weight to bear down.

O comet ride! O flight to the stars!

I cried out in a frenzied release born of ecstasy and pain. The General's great mass shuddered under me with the force of an earth tremor.

The door to my cabin flew open, and a panicked Goliath filled the frame. First stunned, then confused, he stood in the doorway with gladius in his hand, staring with wide eyes at the General tied to the lounge and a naked me impaled on him. I would have thought a gladiator had seen most everything.

I shook my head, and he stepped back and closed the door. But I knew he didn't go far.

I settled into a chair just next to the General's spread-eagle legs, crossed my own bare legs and poured myself a chalice of wine. I made no move to loosen his ties.

He struggled against the ropes, twisting from side to side, trying to free himself, bellowing like the bull that he was.

I popped a big juicy purple grape in my mouth, chewed and then spit out the seeds onto the deep green Persian carpet.

"Untie me!" he demanded.

"Not until you tell me how Marcus Quintillus died. Did you make him suffer? Tell me he suffered."

"He was Roman!" he snarled back.

"He was a pig and deserving of slaughter."

From under my divan, from the same shelf that had held the ropes, I pulled out a steel dagger, double-edged, razor-sharp—a shiny blade as long as my hand. I didn't recall ever seeing uncertainty in the General's eyes, but I saw it now.

"Do you want to know what *I* would have done if given the chance?" I asked.

My chair was close enough that I easily lifted the hem of his short tunic with the tip of the blade. I tossed the rest of the cloth back, fully exposing his belly.

"I would have tied him down, just like this. Then I would have carved away at his balls, taking only tiny pieces until there was nothing left but a gaping hole."

As I spoke, the tip of the blade nicked at his testicles. The look on his face was priceless. I think he finally understood what I was capable of.

"His penis I would have taken off in one piece and stuffed down his throat. In the end, before he gagged yet could still breathe, I would have disemboweled him."

With each step of my tale, I traced the knife. First his balls, then around his penis, then down the thick black line of hair on his belly from his navel to the black bush.

He looked quite terrified, more than I imagined possible.

I laughed out loud and leaned over to slice the silk bonds tying his ankles.

"What will you do if I loosen your hands?"

"I shall strangle you."

"Will you stop in time?"

"I have not decided."

"Then why should I untie you?"

"You have enough troubles without the Moor dying of starvation in your cabin."

I had to laugh. And while still smiling, I sliced the last cords with the dagger.

His gorilla hands were at once around my throat, dragging me to the lounge. Our eyes fixed. His were wild as one of the beasts tormented for the Arena.

I put my fingers in his short, curled hair and pulled his face toward me, pressing my lips to his, opening my mouth to swallow his tongue.

He pressed harder; my vision blurred. I could no longer kiss him. A flash of light exploded into a kaleidoscope of high-intensity color, stronger than neon, brighter than the sun.

Then a curtain fell and darkened the light at the moment I climaxed.

This was death, I told myself. No more painful than this. Why does everyone fear it so?

But I didn't die. My vision came back, and when it cleared, the General was kissing my neck where his hands had been, his erection in me again, but not for long. He exploded when he saw my open eyes looking with wonder into his.

He raised up on his elbows, his face so near, our noses nearly touched. I saw each tiny capillary in the whites of his eyes.

"Is this finally to be our lifetime?" he asked.

"You tell me. You are the one who knows everything."

CHAPTER 49   PROPOSAL

"You can accomplish by kindness what you cannot by force." – Publius Syrus

Word of the hunt and the near death of Antinous by lions spread rapidly from the shore to every barge. I learned of it from Hadrian's messenger, who delivered a scroll addressed expressly to me.

Elektra of Visions, it started. *Hadrian, Caesar and Emperor of Rome, saved Antinous this day from the jaws of a beast.*

With the scroll was the ruby septagram necklace I'd given Hadrian as an amulet to imbue him with strength for the hunt.

I'd let myself imagine the hunt going differently. Hadrian, in his attempt to save Antinous, fails and is himself killed by the lion. But the hunt unfolded just as the poet Pancrates related. They both lived, for now.

The hunting banquet that night at the feet of the Sphinx quickly morphed into a drunken brawl of celebration. How Hadrian actually saved Antinous was a tale that grew more exaggerated with each telling. By the time sweets were served, the story had Hadrian dragging the beast from Antinous and choking the life from it with his arthritic bare hands.

Antinous was alternatively too gay or too morose. He glanced constantly over at me; I watched him with guarded eyes. The Praetorian Guard stood conspicuously close by Antinous—and not far from me.

He drank excessive amounts of wine and ended with his head in the vomit bowl before being carried off by slaves to bed.

The General behaved himself. Neither of us mentioned the scene in my cabin, although he occasionally toyed with the fringe of the emerald scarf covering the bruises on my neck. Once he put his index finger on the lapis lazuli stone of the Hathor Ring.

"The ring always seems to find its way to your hand," he commented. "Who in this life gave it to you?"

"Hektor Ptolemais."

"And yet he is not here," he said with a smug smile. "What a pity his efforts fall short of the prize. But I suppose the man has become accustomed to losing."

"I am more concerned with another loss."

"Why do I sense, my dear Ishtar, that you are about to tell me more of this loss and how I may help you avoid it?"

"Antinous will die in less than three days," I whispered.

"I know that."

I blinked and stopped myself from asking how he knew. Hadn't I told him only this afternoon that he knew everything?

"Do you intend to let it happen?"

"Why should I stop it?"

"For me," I said petulantly. "You should stop it for me."

He laughed so loud that the couple on the next divan stopped arguing and looked over.

"You come often to drink at this well, Ishtar, always expecting the water to be fresh and plentiful. First the Christian, now the Greek. How many others on your list?"

"It would mean everything to me," I wheedled, stopping short at fluttering my eyelashes.

"I should save the Sodomite so you can fuck him? What is *my* interest?"

"Do you imagine Echo swept off her feet by Narcissus?" I snapped. "I want to save him because he has not yet begun to live! He is nineteen years old and brilliant. Surely you can see his promise."

"You want him to live for his *mind*?"

"The world needs more beautiful souls, not fewer."

"Do you dream of having him, if he lives? You must know that is not possible."

"It is not for *me* that I ask. It is for the love he has given me, for the joy we have shared over lifetimes." I looked at him with scorn. "Have you never felt loyalty and true affection?"

"You dare ask me that?" he said quietly.

He took me quite off guard; I'd never expected him to bare his soul.

"And after Antinous, what then, Ishtar?"

"I have not seen the future. I have not wanted to."

"I see you alone," he said solemnly. "Without the intimacy you so crave."

I stared at him. How close he was to my fears.

"Without love," he added unnecessarily.

"There is no one to offer me that."

"And what of me?"

"You? Love? Is that what you call your paws at my throat? You use me, as all men use me. All men except Antinous."

I signaled Goliath, who appeared with my cloak.

"Come to my cabin again, General," I hissed. "I shall whip you with my velvet flail, and we can pretend that the anticipation of pain and the thrill of mastery are endearment."

I had risen and was making to leave when he reached out to stop me.

"If you wish to be loved, Ishtar—love."

In his hand he held the seventh septagram. The final Protector.

The General didn't come that night, as I was certain he would. I tossed restlessly, expecting to hear the skiff lash to our stern, waiting for his weighty footstep creaking on the deck.

When sleep refused to come, I swallowed a mild potion, climbed the steps to my deck lounge and lay down under the stars. The moon sank below the river, and all was quiet. My lids grew heavy. The last I saw of the heavens was Mars burning bright as an ember overhead.

We were under sail when I woke to a dazzling sun sparkling on diamond waters. The slaves had set up my awning, and I lay in the shade.

Ghazel was there at once with a steaming mug of a honeyed infusion of herbs.

"A gift came while you slept, Domina."

She clapped her hands, and Goliath appeared with a black kitten, but no ordinary one. It was a baby black panther, already larger than a full-grown house cat, with sharp claws and fierce pointed teeth. Around the kitten's neck was a silver chain hung with a septagram pendant set with a ruby.

The General.

"What shall we feed her, Domina?" asked Ghazel.

"Not Christians." I quipped, and then immediately regretted it.

She flushed and lowered her eyes. We hadn't spoken of her faith since the night on the island when the soldiers came. She always wore the morphed ankh around her neck, and I allowed it, choosing to afford her some comfort in her miserable life.

The seven branches of the Nile had merged into one mighty river a half-day sail north of the Pyramids. Hundreds of brown Egyptians, nude save for loincloths, toiled in green fields of winter grain along both banks.

As Egyptians had through millennia, fishermen balanced on narrow papyrus boats to cast their nets onto the glassy water. Hippopotami, 'river cows,' lumbered in the tall reeds; crocodiles dozed in the mud. A million birds—some migrating to escape the Northern winter across the sea, some at home on the Nile—feasted on clouds of insects.

To the east, craggy purple mountains rose from the vast fertile plain. Beyond was the land of Seth. The land of chaos. The Desert.

Heading south, the fleet sailed on, silver-tipped oars pulling against the current, northerly winds filling the colored sails, speeding us inexorably closer and closer to the veil of tears.

Tonight we would dine again on the shore's rise, reclining on ornate, carved couches under the stars. Massive bonfires of roasting giraffe and hippopotamus blazed on the ridge.

I dressed for the evening banquet with meticulous attention to detail. The slaves waxed, pumiced and scraped. They coated my flesh in a silty mud that, when dried and washed away, left my skin soft as a child's. Finally, they massaged gardenia-scented almond oil into my arms, my legs, my breasts, neck, hands, feet, and buttocks. My skin glowed like moonstone.

I chose the formal attire of a noble Roman lady. First a leather bra and panties, then a lemony linen tunica with sleeves to mid-forearm. Next came a cap-sleeved, emerald green stola, again of linen. My outer wrap, a rich purple palla, was woven of wool soft as cashmere.

In the end, little of my carefully oiled skin showed—my ankles above golden sandals, my wrists adorned with *cloisonné* armbands, only a hint of flesh at my bodice.

The Hathor Ring went on my finger and the septagram ruby pendant around my neck with the bruises left by the General concealed by white lead powder.

Ghazel and Eunice spent an hour on my hair, using thin heating coils to form five-inch high curls. A gold filigree bun holder with three golden chains secured a chignon high up on the back of my head.

Rigid and formal, the latest fashion in hair screamed, "Don't touch! I am virtuous. I am Stoic. I am Roman."

My reflection in the Red Mirror confirmed that all trace of harlot was gone.

Again I was paired with the General. Flavia was again with the handsome Senator who openly doted on her. Radiant in white silk, she positively beamed. But her father was right; she had that kind of fragile blond beauty that doesn't age well. I returned her smile, silently shouting out, *Waste no more time on Hektor!*

Julia Balbilla arrived late. She surprised me by pausing by our couch. Her sharp eyes missed nothing, not the General, not my Roman dress.

"I did not realize you were so well-acquainted with the Moor," she remarked with the smile of a viper.

She really was audacious to speak of the General as if he wasn't there. No doubt she considered a general from provincial Libya, even one favored by the Emperor, to be chaff to her royal wheat.

"But then," she continued ruthlessly, "I suppose you are well-acquainted with a number of men."

I made a mental note to cast a spell on her—make her already putrid skin erupt in nasty boils. Better yet, I'd put a curse on both of them, she and Sabina. I knew the perfect one, devised for a jealous husband seeking to turn his wife against her lesbian lover.

With the cold look of a predator, the General fixed his hard stare on Balbilla until she nodded curtly and moved a little too quickly to her lounge.

"Thank you for the cat," I said while we watched Balbilla's iron-spined back move away from us.

"Which one?"

I laughed lightly, and he showed his square teeth in a smile that lighted his face.

"Have you named her? The kitten, I mean." His tone had a slight tease.

"I was hoping you might have a suggestion." My tone held more invitation than I'd planned.

The corners of his mouth turned up; I saw a warm glint in his eye that I hadn't seen for centuries.

"Perhaps if I spend more time with the beast," he suggested, "an idea will come."

In that moment, an altogether too healthy Hadrian arrived. We applauded and called out greetings. As was befitting the Emperor of Rome on a formal occasion, trumpets blared and drums pounded.

Antinous beside him was already drunk; his face was marred by a slack expression and half-closed eyes. He looked around the circle of lounges until he found me; my heart broke to see his despair.

"He loves you. I give you that," the General whispered in my ear. "But there is no hope for that love. Would it not be the greatest mercy to let death relieve him of his misery?"

"Not the priests, General! Not those Sethists."

I knew their work only too well. Incantations summoning demons. Partial drowning. Disembowelment while still living. In my mind's eye, I saw Antinous the Dove ripped open by a cadre of demon priests.

"Might I not bring him one last night of joy?" I begged. "Can you not allow me a last time to see his smile?"

Sparks from the fire rose. A log cracked. The laughter around us had the muted and wobbly sound of a world in slow motion. The General and I were alone in that vacuum again. He was silent for the longest time, never taking his eyes from mine.

Finally he asked in the quietest of voices, "Do you love him that much?"

"The Guard would never suspect *you*," I whispered.

"You risk everything for him," he said in awe.

He stared at me for a moment, and then turned his eyes to the fire. Fearing that my next words might push him to refuse, I stopped myself from saying more.

When he turned his face toward me, we were inches apart. The longer I looked into his hooded dark eyes, the deeper he let me go. And in letting me go deep, he let me see his need for me. A need that frightened him. A need that, when I saw it and realized its depth, frightened me also.

"And if I do this for you, what will you do for me?" He spoke quietly and soberly.

"I shall try to love you," I answered immediately and with absolute sincerity.

He laughed out loud then and said amicably, "I guess that is the best I can expect."

After a swig of wine, he turned to me again; in the firelight his eyes danced with pleasure.

"I can always count on you to be frank with me. That is something to build on."

Then in a completely unexpected move, he took my chin in his thick fingers and said, "I think you should marry me, Elektra of Canopus."

"Marry?" Oh, the General could, indeed, surprise me. It was impossible for me to mask my astonishment.

"Why?" I asked. "You can have me as I am."

"I want to make an honest woman of you." He paused. "A citizen again." He let the portent of those words sink in before going on. "No one would dare reproach my wife."

"I...I never considered it."

"Have you not?" he chuckled. "Then why dress tonight in this unbecoming costume of a Roman matron if not to demonstrate the possibility?"

In the middle of the night, while everyone slept, a small boat without lights, smaller even than a skiff, rowed by only one man, pulled alongside my barge. In the bow was Antinous. At the oars was the General.

Antinous reeked of wine and vomit when he stumbled on board. The General said nothing except, "Two hours." Then he rowed away toward the rushes of the river shore.

I bathed Antinous as a mother tenderly bathes her child. He wept in my arms while I kissed his curls.

When he had calmed, I led him to the divan and lay him down gently. Under my silk caftan, I was naked and oiled with jasmine scent.

I kissed his perfect mouth—gently, unhurriedly—with a touch so light my lips were the flutter of butterfly wings. He opened his eyes. Blue as the spring sky over Thebes.

"I love you, Elektra. I do not wish to live without you."

He was so very young; he wouldn't have the chance to learn that life goes on even with a broken heart.

"Sh-h-h," I whispered. "Be nowhere else but here. Be here with me in this moment."

I lay beside him, molding my flesh into his on the velvet couch prepared with soft furs. The sweetest of incense burned in the glowing braziers.

I would not cleanse myself tonight; I would not wash away his seed. And if the Goddess Hathor blessed me and my cycle followed its natural course, I might bear the child of Antinous.

"I love you, Antinous," I whispered when he entered me. "I shall love you for all time."

There was nothing I did not do for him; there was nothing he did not do for me. We were one soul in two bodies, then one soul in one.

"Is this our goodbye?" he asked. "Shall we never watch the sun rise together? Shall I never wake in your arms and kiss the sleep from your eyes? Shall we never make love in the grass among spring flowers?"

"Imagine the sun is rising now. Can you not smell the flowers? Kiss my eyes."

I was strong until the last moment. But when he opened the door to step out of my world, I weakened.

"Leave, Antinous. Leave now," I begged him. "Take the boat and row. Get away!"

"What is a life without reputation or honor?" he asked in the purest and calmest of voices. "What is life without love?"

He took my face in the palms of his hands. When I looked into his eyes, I saw quiet resignation and no pain.

"If I step from here into the darkest abyss, I take the light of your love with me, Elektra. You are a goddess. You have blessed me. I carry your love to eternity."

I watched from the upper deck as they rowed away. Antinous sat in the bow, facing me. He never took his eyes away.

The General had looked only once at me. He kept his face forward, his eyes perhaps on Antinous watching me.

Finally the speck of their boat disappeared in the pre-dawn mist.

CHAPTER 50   MISTY END

"I am dying, Egypt, dying." – Marc Antony

That day, in the early afternoon, we reached the spot on the Nile where Antinous would die.

With black dread, I watched the barges of our mighty armada drop anchor on the East Bank across from Hermopolis. Here, six hundred years before, Goliath and I had moored our ferry and climbed the rise to the hunting lodge.

The day of the hunt. The day everything changed.

I couldn't bear to attend the nightly banquet, but the General arrived in a skiff and forced me to dress.

"You cannot refuse Hadrian. He is in the foulest of humors." He snapped his fingers to call Ghazel.

"You will put on your gown," he commanded, "fix your hair and come with me."

And so I acquiesced. I had no choice. If Elektra was to have a life, I had to finish the scene. And I still held out hope that somehow, I could rewrite the play.

For that, I would recast my role. I chose a coal-black Egyptian wig, shoulder-length with golden tassels, and an Egyptian gown of the finest white linen. Barely covering my breasts, wide straps attached to a wide band encircling my ribcage. From there, long gossamer sheer pleats molded to my waist and clung to my thighs.

Ghazel drew dramatic black kohl lines around my eyes and out to the temples. Sparkling green mica glittered on my lids to the eyebrows.

Transfixed, the General watched each step of my transformation from Roman to Egyptian.

"Ishtar," he whispered.

I saw in his eyes that he was back in his Persian tent lifetimes ago when I stood before him as a young Egyptian priestess.

I didn't remember leaving my cabin but was vaguely aware of forcing my feet forward, not feeling the ship's deck beneath me, moving through a cold, silent world without form. Gooseflesh rose on my numb skin.

"You are cold," the General said, wrapping his scarlet wool cape around me. With a firm grip on my upper arm, he propelled me into the skiff and sat me on a cushion.

All the while, I stared stoically ahead, not allowing tears to spoil my makeup. I must be powerful this night of all nights.

Oars dipped into dark water. The current of the river hummed. Overhead, the canopy of stars blazed. Is that where the souls dwell awaiting their next birth?

At the muddy riverbank steeped in tall reeds, Hadrian's army had performed one of its engineering marvels. Within the space of a day, the legion had constructed a long floating pier of logs hauled from across the Nile.

We lashed on among dozens of other brightly painted skiffs and made our way to climb the rise. Banquet bonfires burned on the exact site where the hunting lodge had once stood. A grove of ancient sycamores still cast silhouettes against the sky.

Ghosts called out to me, "Isenkhebe, Isenkhebe, Queen of the Hunt!"

The sun glinted once more on the brass rails of chariots and the tips of spears. Long-legged Berber dogs, panting to hunt, roamed in packs. Tugging at chariots, proud stallions snorted and stamped, eager to fly across the desert.

O Egypt! I was reborn here.

The scene faded; torches replaced sunshine. The laughter of Romans silenced the baying of dogs.

Hadrian was drunk. He looked a hundred years old. But the demon kept on living. Even after my curse, Hadrian refused to die. The vile Cult of Seth offered him a way out.

How easy it would have been to touch his hand and prick him with a poison needle.

Antinous was more in a stupor than awake. I was certain he'd been drugged. His eyes were sightless without a trace of blue fire.

At their own table, set apart from the Romans, huddled the Sethists with their cobra tattoos. They glared at me with their windows-on-hell eyes.

I gripped the General's arm, and he turned, frowning when he saw my expression. Then his eyes followed my line of sight to the Sethist table, and his face darkened. I felt his muscles tense, but he took my arm firmly and led me away to our divan.

"Not the priests, General," I pleaded.

"Eat," he said. "We are being watched."

The menu was birds. Birds and more birds. Ostrich stuffed with goose, stuffed with duck, stuffed with pheasant, stuffed with quail dressed with cracked wheat, onions, garlic, rosemary, dates and almonds. And black pepper. Always pepper. In everything. The desserts. The poached fruit.

I gagged on every morsel, washing down each bite with wine. Every mouthful was a piece of the dove I had torn into seven parts. My head began to spin. I called for the vomit bowl, but nothing came up except bile.

The evening wore on. Antinous didn't look for me. He seemed already more dead than alive. His dauntless sun no longer shined enthusiasm and never would again.

Bedouin musicians sang their ancient haunting melodies and beat their narrow drums. Mars rose to join a million stars in a velvet sky. Orion, Ursa Major, Berenice's Comb—I found each constellation. And each brought back a memory of a different Antinous, but always the noble knight.

"Can you not do something?" I begged the General. "Please, I implore you."

"This night has been written. There are many who wish Antinous gone."

I sobbed into his shoulder; he held me as one would a child.

When I looked up at him, he said, "I would bless the day you shed such tears for me."

"There are many kinds of love," I whispered.

"Not for me," he answered.

Swaddling my shivering body in his scarlet cloak, he lifted me from the lounge, saying to the guests around us, "My wife is unwell."

I looked back. Antinous no longer was at Hadrian's side.

The mist on the river tonight was heavier than I'd ever seen. Descending to the water, we moved through dense fog. No more stars. The fires on the rise were no brighter than the faint glow of distant galaxies. Without the torches that blazed along the floating pier, we might have fallen off the edge into the deep black mud.

Slaves waited in skiffs beside amber-haloed lanterns. Somewhere, beyond the impenetrable mist, on the West Bank, stood once-mighty Hermopolis now fallen into decline.

We rowed through nothingness toward nothingness. In the distance, from the ridge, shouts and laughter rang out sharply; the high notes of flutes carried easily through the mist. The beat of drums pulsed in the night air.

Our lantern didn't serve other than to warn boats of our presence. The world was woolly gray and wet. A flash of silver. Oars rose from the water and slipped in again.

"Turn back!" I cried out without any thought. It was nothing I saw; it was nothing I heard.

The oars stopped, and with their halt, the creak of the oarlocks was silenced. Not a breath of air moved the mist. Far, far away, a flute trilled the song of a lone nightingale.

"Go back," I repeated.

If the slaves looked to the General for confirmation, he didn't countermand my order. The port oars pulled through the water instead of driving. The prow swung to starboard, the stern to port, and the boat turned. Tiny pinpoints of orange lights surrounded by hazy halos directed us toward the pier.

At an indefinable distance from the shore, maybe a few yards, maybe many, we collided with another boat. A boat that sailed without lights.

First our prow scraped, and then came the crunch of oars entangling with other oars. Wood snapped in a deafening crack. Our boat tipped, water poured in over the side, and then the skiff righted again.

I could scarcely see the General next to me, much less the other boat. But I sensed it much larger than ours. Whoever was on board made not a sound.

"Who goes there?" demanded the General.

Silence.

"Identify yourself."

Silence.

"Ship the oars," he commanded, and our slaves hauled the entangled oars up as best they could.

The broad blade of the General's gladius flashed, but not to strike. Using the sword's hilt, he grappled the gunwale of the other boat and heaved us alongside. I made out Goliath lashing our stern to theirs.

The river spirits breathed the slightest of breezes, and the mist cleared in a circle around us. The current was carrying both boats down the river, away from the pier.

Twelve priests with shaven heads and glaring kohl-lined black eyes huddled around Antinous slumped at amidships of a long canoe. I knew it was him although I couldn't see his face. They'd put the horrid jackal mask of the God Anubis over his golden curls.

In a low tone, starting as a murmur, the priests began to chant.

"Ar eq-kua er seta au eh-heh hah
Tet hru ent kshesev neseni t'a pa ma-ehti."

"Hand him over," growled the General.

The hilt of his gladius was in his hand now, the blade thrust toward the priests. Lantern light turned the steel to red fire. Another blade flashed as Goliath stepped from our boat into theirs.

The Sethist canoe, narrow and shallow, tipped and rocked wildly; the Nile rushed over the sides. I think their boat might have capsized if not anchored by us. All the while, the priests chanted the ancient Egyptian curse, their high-pitched sinister voices screeching louder and louder.

"Ar eq-kua er seta au eh-heh hah
Tet hru ent kshesev neseni t'a pa ma-ehti."

Spreading wide his long legs to maintain balance, Goliath lifted the lifeless Antinous and passed his slack body to the General.

Our boat teetered for a moment before stabilizing. By the time Goliath stepped back into our skiff, the chant of the priests had risen to a roar. A roar of fury. The roar of a thwarted Seth.

I pulled the wig from my head and shook out my hair to cascade in a flaming frenzy around my milk white face. I must have been a dreadful sight, heavy kohl eyeliner streaking where tears had run. Still,

I willed my eyes to blaze green fire.

With the General's red cape around my shoulders, I stood up, white gown shimmering in the mist, stretched out my arms in the cloak to sprout crimson wings and rolled my eyes back in my head.

"Nekhbet!" a priest hissed. "Mother of Mothers!"

At the base of my neck, the septagram pulsed, the ruby blazed; the electrum grew so hot I thought it would brand me.

"I conjure You, O Lord Osiris! I summon You by Your Holy names OUCHIOCH! OUSENARATH! OSORNOUPHE!"

The priests' wild, heated, enraged chanting dimmed to a murmur. I shouted out, "OUSERSETHEMENTH!"

A beam flooded my crown chakra, poured down my spine and lifted me skyward above the planks. Higher and higher I floated.

The Sethists fell silent. I heard not one more odious syllable of their malicious Egyptian chants. From the distance of a star, I watched their canoe disappear into the mists.

"ERATOPHI ERACHAX ESEO IOTH ARBIOTHI AMEN," I shouted after them, and the Goddess Isis released me back to this world.

The General had taken the grisly mask from Antinous and laid him across the seats. Goliath tenderly arranged his legs and arms.

"He still breathes, Domina."

Antinous' perfect body was whole. We had stopped the priests before they reached the sacrificial altar. There, under the foul eyes of Seth and Anubis, in a tawdry river hut, surrounded by obscene incense burners in the shapes of demons, they would have wielded their ritual knives to harvest his organs while he lived.

"Antinous," I whispered.

He opened his eyes and turned toward my voice.

"Have I passed?" he asked.

"Not yet," I answered gently. "Soon."

"And I am with you. The Gods are kind to grant me my wish."

Sweet Antinous. Even now, so close to the end, he saw kindness in the universe.

"I drank of the vial, Elektra. The one you gave me for Hadrian. You were right. There is no pain."

I didn't bother to ask how long ago, for I knew of no antidote. Once ingested, death was inevitable.

"Will you hold me, Elektra? Hold me in your arms?"

Pulling his body into mine, I cradled him more as a mother than a lover.

I kissed his parted lips. His breath was weak. As I watched, the potion drained him of another ounce of life.

"I go to eternity," he whispered, "with the vision of your fiery hair and green eyes to remember forever."

His eyes closed. He was so still, I thought he had passed. But he opened them one last time and breathed, "You blessed me with the greatest gift, Elektra. I became a man with you."

And then he was gone.

I kissed his closed eyelids and his open lips. I stroked his golden curls.

"I shall see you again, Antinous. We shall love each other again." As I whispered, I hung my ruby septagram around his neck. He would take a part of me with him to the void.

What happened afterwards is not that clear. I think the General and Goliath tipped Antinous into the river. I know they removed the septagram. I believe I protested, but my whole body was one sorrow, my mind nothing but grief.

"We must," I remember the General insisting. "You cannot be associated with his death."

The fog lifted more. Dawn was not far away. The river was molten mercury with a slick oily sheen. The current carried him gently, face down, curls golden against the leaden water. I watched until I saw the golden light I'd seen in my dream. He belonged to the gods now. He had risen.

Later that morning, the General woke me with a kiss.

"He has been found. By the Praetorian Guard."

"What did Hadrian say?"

"He said, 'The light of my life has been extinguished.' And then he wept like a woman."

I wept again without shame. I am a woman. I am allowed tears.

And through my tears, I saw the Red Mirror hanging on my cabin bulkhead and knew it was time, finally, to go home.

PART THREE
LONDINIUM

CHAPTER 51   REALITY CHECK

"Every man, however wise, needs the advice of some sagacious friend in the affairs of life." – Titus Maccius Plautus

Sunshine in narrow beams streamed through the slats of the plantation shutters. I sat up. The dark green velveteen bedspread was wet under my butt. I'd peed in my sleep. How long had I been lying here?

I made for the bathroom, emptied my bladder, drank a tall glass of water and stared at the reflection in the vanity mirror. Me, not Elektra, stared back. I was really home.

Tony's cell rang three times before he answered.

"Isis! I've been worried sick. Why haven't you returned my calls?"

I couldn't help myself. The sound of his voice, just like Antinous, cracked a dam; great sobs wracked my body. Having held myself together for so long, I lost control.

"Isis!" Tony was shouting into the phone. "What's wrong? Speak to me!"

"I'm just so glad to hear your voice. To know you're alive."

"Of course, I'm alive."

"Oh Tony, I've seen such monstrous things!"

"I can be there tonight."

"No! Don't come here! I—I want to come to you." I hesitated a moment before whispering, "I want to be…somewhere safe."

"Jesus, Isis, what's going on?"

"I want you to hold me, Tony."

I must have stunned him because the airways between us remained silent for a moment.

Then he said quietly, "I'll be at Newark to pick you up."

I pulled myself together and booked the red eye out of McCarran. The date on the e-ticket told me three days had passed. Three days! No wonder I was starving.

I scarfed down four yogurts and nibbled on a chunk of Parmesan cheese while the water boiled for Assam tea.

There were no messages from Rasheed. I fought back new tears.

No calls from the General, either. Were his men still in the lobby? Waiting three days without my coming down?

Barb had called only an hour ago and sent a text. "If I don't hear from you soon, I'm coming over to wake you up."

Hektor called yesterday. I sincerely—truly and sincerely—hoped he had good news about Ingrid.

And then there was Gareth Greene. He could wait.

Tony, my knight, proved the most frantic and insistent. He'd called four times and sent five text messages.

Worried sick about you. CALL!

The General answered on the first ring. "You're back."

His voice was exactly the same. He might have said, 'And then Hadrian wept like a woman.'

"I wasn't really gone," I answered, more to see what he'd say than anything.

He was quiet for a moment, perhaps surprised that I was so forthright.

"There's gone and *gone*," he said finally.

"Thank you," I told him, truly meaning it.

I waited a minute, and when he didn't answer, I said, "You turned out to be quite a star."

"Did I now?" he chuckled. "That seems out of character. Did you finally tame me?"

"Maybe we tamed each other."

"Now there's an enticing thought." Then he asked, "When do I have the pleasure of seeing you?"

"Not right away. I'm leaving town for a few days."

"Let me guess. You're going to see Tony."

I shouldn't have been caught off guard, yet I was.

"You're more predictable than you think," he went on. "But Tony's not enough for you."

"People change," I said defensively. "I've changed."

"I haven't."

I was about to ring off, when he said, "I can make you happy. You know that now, Elektra."

Elektra. A bristly tingle crept up my spine. He had, at last, admitted openly to knowing all.

Barb was a tad icy when I called and didn't warm when I told her about Flavia and Hektor.

"Flavia and I schemed for you to get him," I said, thinking to bring us close again.

"Did you give him up for me?" she asked in an acid tone.

I changed the subject. "I'm going to Princeton. To see Tony."

"Will you stay?"

"No. I mean…I don't know."

"You could do a lot worse."

"I couldn't do better." And I meant it. I really did.

"I haven't talked to you for so long," Elaine said when she heard my voice. "Still got your four men?"

In my mind's eye, I could see her surrounded by dried herbs and fresh vegetables in her Pennsylvania country kitchen.

"The pool is shrinking fast," I answered with a laugh. "A couple of them refuse to be juggled."

"So, are you getting ready to make your choice?"

Elaine has this uncanny ability to go right to the heart of anything. She strips away the fluff and leaves the core exposed to examination. She's always been like that, even back in college when we shared a dorm room and she listened to my woes and dried my tears.

I don't remember Elaine ever vacillating about her life. She knew what she wanted and went after it with calm certitude. She found her man in college. Steve and she were raising their two kids, a handsome boy and a sunny girl, in a gracious gray brick colonial with a big attic and cozy paneled basement set on a wooded acre in Amish country.

Azaleas and hydrangeas border a kidney-shaped swimming pool with striped deck chairs. House with green lawn, picket fence, husband and kids. The American dream.

What was wrong with me? Why couldn't I want the ideal?

"I'm going to see Tony in Princeton."

"Is the plan to test him out?"

"At least he hasn't dumped me yet," I said with a laugh a little more nervous than I'd like.

"What about Hector?"

"He's been taken."

She was quiet for a second before asking, "Are you going to make me guess who's left?"

"Would you believe the General?"

"I believe you'd be well taken care of. Protected."

"Funny you say that. That's what he claims."

"You haven't mentioned Rasheed."

I couldn't help myself; the tears just came.

Elaine let out a sigh. "You always did have a thing for the heartbreakers."

I sniffled a bit and let myself wish that Elaine could hand me a cup of tea and make everything better, like in the old days.

"Call him," she said. "Maybe he'll make you miserable. But at least you'll know."

"He terrifies me. I lose myself in him. I don't know where I end and he begins."

"You're stronger than that. Are you sure that's not an excuse?"

"Excuse for what?"

"Rasheed's the only one, isn't he, who doesn't lie at your feet?"

Isabel answered Hector's cell. "What do you want?"

Her tone was more than icy. It was glacial.

"I'm returning Hector's call, Isabel."

"Leave him alone, Isis. Haven't you done enough?"

"*He* called *me*. I think he deserves a call back, don't you?"

Apparently I didn't deserve an answer. I thought maybe she'd hung up, but after a few seconds, Hector was there.

"Don't pay attention to my mother, Isis. She blames you for the accident. I can't understand why."

"It's okay, Hector. It's a woman thing. How is Ingrid?"

"She's going to be fine. Absolutely fine." His voice was pure joy. "I was hoping you could come by the hospital."

"I'm flying to the East Coast tonight."

"She asked to see you."

"Ingrid? Me?" I hope my voice didn't sound too scared—or guilty.

I packed a carry-on with a pair of jeans, a black sheath, rust cashmere cardigan, running shoes and black pumps. At the last minute I threw in a slinky coral negligee I'd bought on impulse. The pink with my red hair was pretty electrifying.

The General's septagram necklace with black Tahitian pearls went in my purse, the Tiffany diamond studs in my earlobes. I wrestled a bit before deciding to wear the Hathor Ring Rasheed had given me that night in my old condo. I put the second ring, the one I'd retrieved from the villa by the sea in Leptis Magna, in a sapphire blue velvet pouch.

When I came out of the elevator into the lobby, I fully expected the General's men to be there. Maybe even Orsini. But not Moe. Poor Moe. He'd bled out in the Cave of Bats.

But there weren't any Corsicans in dark business suits and Ray-Ban sunglasses. The orange-haired old lady with the gray cat in a stroller argued with the concierge. Two tall, tan guys in white tennis shorts and polo shirts checked their mail.

"Yes, Ishtar," the General answered his cell.

"Your men are gone." My voice had a slight tremor that I'd rather wasn't there.

"Do you miss them?"

"Please don't play games. Does this mean I'm not in danger anymore?"

"You, my dearest Ishtar," he chuckled, "attract danger like lavender attracts bees."

"Are you punishing me because I'm going to Tony?"

"Do you want punishing?"

"I want you to talk straight. Have you called off your men because there's no threat, or have you called them off to make some kind of point?"

"You haven't asked the right question."

I took a deep breath. "Okay. *Have* you called off your men?"

"Do you want me to?"

"Why are you doing this?" I demanded. "I thought we had—"

"What? An arrangement where I do everything to protect you while you do anything you please?"

"You've never been jealous before."

"Who says I'm jealous?"

"Every time I begin to think you're human, you show me you're a monster."

"I'm very human, Ishtar. Never doubt that."

Then he hung up on me. The connection went dead. I'd have gone back upstairs to get my Glock, if I hadn't been catching a flight.

Halfway to the hospital I gave the driver new directions.

We pulled up in front of one of those imposing fortress banks with marble floors and high ceilings.

"I need to make a quick stop. Can you wait?"

The safe deposit boxes were in the basement behind a massive steel door with a forbidding wheel lock. An armed guard stood just outside as the attendant turned her key and waited for me to turn mine.

A few moments later I was behind a closed and locked door alone with the Emerald Tablet.

Rows of precise Greek letters eternalized its message.

And the following to be the truth
That which is below is like that which is above,
and that which is above is like that which is below,
to the accomplishment of the miracle of one thing.
And as all things come from the One,
through the meditation of the One,
so all things were born from one thing by adaptation.

Placing my palm on the cool glassy surface, I chanted the mantra Hermes Trismegistus had given me 2,200 years before.

Alpha to Omega, We are All One.

Seven words that explain everything. From A to Z, we all come from the One. We are all One.

With each repetition of the phrase, the Emerald Tablet grew warmer and brighter until the faience glowed green and the blue of the fluorescent light shone aquamarine. My palm burned, but I felt no pain. I repeated the mantra.

Alpha to Omega, We are all One.

The chant was soothing, the energy light. Not dark like the incantations of the Black Scroll. The power of the Emerald Tablet, harnessed for good, was a healing force. White Magic versus Black. Good versus Evil. Trust versus Control.

I wasn't being entirely honest with myself. I wanted control. Control was at the very heart of my desire.

Convincing myself that influencing another person's behavior with benign intent was not the same as stripping them of their will, I made my request.

CHAPTER 52 INGRID

"The sum of all sums is eternity." – Lucretius

Isabel was waiting when I got to the hospital. Her black eyes with spiky lashes flashed when she saw me exit the elevator.

As always, her shiny dark hair, streaked with silver, was pulled tightly off her face into a chignon. Very few women her age could dream to carry it off. On Isabel, the severe hairdo only served to accent her aristocratic features and, thanks to the genius of South American cosmetology, her ageless complexion.

Her favored emerald studs glittered from her earlobes. Artfully applied makeup highlighted cheekbones and outlined lush youthful lips. More cosmetology magic. A testament to the buttress of money against the onslaught of time. Still, I'd be thrilled to look as good as she did at her age. Half as good.

I had to give her extra credit for keeping her slim figure and holding herself erect. Disciplined. That's Isabel.

Even today, she held her anger in check. But I knew her too well to be fooled. Under her icy surface, resentment over the pain I'd caused Hector smoldered. I was the enemy, and it saddened me. I couldn't help my heart. It wants what it wants.

Ever the savior, Hector rescued me from her wrath. I still found him so handsome that my heart skipped a beat when he came out of the hospital room. His shiny chestnut waves were slightly disheveled in the way I imagined they mussed when he removed his polo helmet.

And rather like in my Canopus bath when he'd rushed from Alexandria with the bill of sale.

I'd never seen him play polo. I'd never been home with him to Buenos Aires. I'd never even slept with him. Not in this life, anyway. That would have meant commitment. And I couldn't promise fidelity. At least, I'd been that honest.

His ever-present polo shirt was today the perfect shade of lemon yellow to contrast his mahogany tan. He still had that Apollo shine. He wore his usual blue jeans that bulged a bit indecently in the crotch. Never-ending muscular legs, with tight thighs that control polo ponies, ended in alligator cowboy boots.

In spite of my resolve to let him go without a fight, the Spot began to burn. I could have that. Lucky Ingrid.

And then I saw her.

Right leg hoisted up in one of those slings held by a confusing array of pulleys and cords, she leaned against white pillows.

Hector had told me the danger from the accident came from internal injuries. I suspected that her divine body, covered now with hospital sheets, was violated by a swath of ugly stitches that would heal into flaming scars.

But it was her face that made me want to sob. I don't think I would have recognized her.

Exquisite, flawless, Swedish blond beauty Ingrid had been smashed, twisted and torn. Her aquiline nose was set in some kind of metal brace held by strips of tape.

I couldn't see how even the genius of South American cosmetic surgery would ever repair that face. A long gash, terrible and grim, screamed from her right temple down to her jaw. A grotesque turban of bandages replaced her golden hair and padded her right eye.

She was looking at me now through the black slit that was her left. "Isis," she said gratefully. "Thank you for coming."

I so hope that I didn't show my horror; I really tried to hold my face a mask.

I glanced at Hector. His eyes were on Ingrid. Love and adoration. I don't think he saw a single cut or bruise. He raised Ingrid's good hand to his lips and kissed her fingers with a tenderness that wrenched my soul.

I could have had his devotion, but I threw it away.

Would anyone look at me in that way if *my* face was a horror of broken flesh and bone? Maybe Tony.

"Take a chair, Isis. Here. Close to me." Ingrid's voice was surprisingly strong.

She spoke clearly in the self-possessed tone of a woman who had come to terms with her fate. I detected no note of resentment, no anger. No *poor me* as I'm certain I would moan.

Hector had done well to rid himself of my narcissism.

Once I was seated in the oak chair with blue woolen cushion and severe straight arms, he left us to be alone.

"Are you in a lot of pain?" I asked rather stupidly. How could she not be?

"I am drugged to the teeth, I believe you would say."

"I'm so sorry, Ingrid."

And as soon as the words came out, I began to cry. I couldn't help myself. Ingrid's mangled face brought back nightmare memories of broken bodies on crosses begging for death.

I was a wreck, falling apart, fluctuating between erratic bursts of adrenaline and shock waves of pity. Pity for others, yes. But self-pity, too. I disgusted myself. Ingrid's purity made me feel unclean.

Only five minutes ago, I'd coveted Hector. No wonder Isabel despised me. *She knew.*

"Sh-h-h, Isis," Ingrid consoled me—*she* lying in the hospital bed.

I stopped my tears and pulled myself together. I was stronger than this. Elaine told me so. I was *not* a bad person. I'd just lost my way. *Un camino malo*, Isabel had called it.

"I know you blame yourself for the accident," Ingrid was saying.

I looked up with a start.

"Isabel blames you. But I want you to know that I don't. And Hector doesn't."

Oh Ingrid, you don't know how wicked I am.

"This was all meant to be," she continued in her calm, soothing tone. "I am meant to be with Hector, at least now."

I think I really stopped breathing. My heart pounded in my chest.

"You see, Isis, Hector belongs also to another circle, a circle with me. And at this point in time, your circle and mine are intersecting."

She paused and then asked, "You understand what I'm saying, don't you?"

I nodded, not at all sure of what she meant. Could she really be saying what I thought?

"Isabel refuses to accept it. She sees only the circle you know. But the universe is much more complicated than her vision. I'm afraid she has a rather simplistic view."

I could hear Ingrid tiring. Her voice grew deeper and more pebbly. I was thinking that I should tell her to rest when she reached out her good hand to me.

"You must rid yourself of all guilt. You have been gifted with powers that would be heady for anyone. If you listen to your inner being, you will know the right path. You will use your powers to heal and not harm."

"Does Hector know?" I whispered.

"Hector is slowly awakening. We are to travel a long, difficult but beautiful journey together. This moment has been many lifetimes in the making."

I think she might have smiled if her damaged face had allowed.

"Thank you, Isis, for the joy you have given Hector. He truly loves you. You are a goddess to him."

"You are the goddess," I told her. "Surely you come from a higher plane."

But she had closed her eyes and dropped into sleep.

"Will you have a cup of coffee with me?"

Isabel struggled for a moment before agreeing with reluctance. Had we come so far that she didn't wish even to be alone with me? I wanted to shake her and say, "Straighten up, woman. You were my mother once!"

The hospital basement canteen was one of those dreary places that decorators try in vain to make cheerful. Painted in lurid orange and green, the long, windowless walls were made more garish by cold fluorescent lighting.

Neither of us was tempted by the soggy sandwiches in clear wrap, and after filling white Styrofoam cups with watery coffee, we found a table away from the clanking of trays.

Isabel sat across from me on a plastic chair; her body language was one of extreme discomfort. I suspected her unease stemmed both from being in my presence and from the tawdry surroundings. The Bellagio was her normal milieu, French champagne in crystal flutes her usual props.

"I have a gift for you," I told her when we'd settled.

An eyebrow arched. I enjoyed her surprise; it was a bit of a challenge to catch Isabel off guard.

Without saying more, I dug in my purse until I found the blue velvet bag and slid it across the orange Formica tabletop toward her. Her eyes fixed on the Hathor Ring on my finger. The one Rasheed had given me.

"I wish I could have done this in a more appropriate setting," I apologized. I truly meant it.

She looked from the ring on my finger to the velvet bag. She stared without making a move to pick it up. I had the sudden thought that she might, out of spite, refuse to look inside.

But I was too paranoid. Her antipathy toward me didn't extend so far as to stymie her curiosity.

Her long fingers with perfectly manicured, scarlet-lacquered nails reached out to lift the sachet. With all the respect the gift was due, she slowly and carefully loosened the gold cord drawstrings.

Each movement seemed to take forever; both of us watched her aristocratic hands acting out a ceremonial ritual. This is how Sit-hathor would have handled a *Menit* necklace sacred to the Goddess.

The velvet pouch finally opened to reveal the ring. I'd never, in all our lifetimes, seen Isabel drop her mask to such a degree. She made no attempt to conceal her shock—or her pleasure. She looked up at me and blinked in disbelief.

"It belongs on your hand," I said simply.

Cautiously, she slid the ring with the gleaming lapis lazuli set between golden horns onto the middle finger of her right hand. A perfect fit.

Then to my utter amazement, she took a sudden sharp breath that ended in a shudder racking her whole body. On impulse, without a single thought, I reached out with my hand, the one with my ring, and took her right hand.

Side by side, our two Hathor Rings gleamed. Supreme Priestess and High Priestess. Mother and daughter.

She finally looked up. Instead of cold and brittle, her black eyes, wet with tears, glowed. Her careful eyeliner had run a tad; the faint shadows under her eyes hinted at her age.

"I have missed you, Isis."

In her voice I heard both regret and relief. She finally let go of a burden carried too long—the burden of discontent that she couldn't mold me in her own image.

"I have always been here, Mother."

I don't know why I said it; I certainly didn't know I was going to until the word came out. Mother.

"Can you forgive me?" she asked.

"You were right. Hector deserves better than me."

She didn't answer that I, too, was deserving. I would have liked that; I was badly in need of her approval.

Neither of us spoke for a few minutes. The dreadful coffee cooled without us taking a sip.

"Do you love someone, Isis?"

"I thought I loved several men. No! I *know* that I loved—love—all of them. But in different ways."

"There must be one. There always is."

"What about Hermes?" I asked. "Did you love him?"

Her face lit up when I said his name. Her cheeks flushed. Suddenly, I saw her as young Sit-hathor with a youthful Hermes Trismegistus—a forbidden couple with a forbidden love.

Was that the last time her eyes had shone with this special light?

"I loved him more than you can imagine," she whispered.

She looked past me. Her eyes focused somewhere else. Embarrassed to intrude, I looked away from her face.

Then she came back and laughed a little.

"It is quite an experience to be loved by a magician." Her eyes twinkled; suddenly, she was more beautiful than ever I'd seen her.

I thought of the love of the women in the Hive and knew exactly what she meant.

"Don't you have a plane to catch?" she asked unexpectedly.

I looked at my watch. I had forty minutes to departure.

"Damn! I'll never make the flight."

"Go," she urged. "Try."

But I didn't make the flight. By the time I got through security, the gate had closed. To avoid the crowds, I went out a side exit, around the corner to the taxi queue, and took a place at the end of the line.

"Sorry, Tony. I can't get a direct flight until tomorrow morning. There's a big convention ending today."

"Are you going to be all right?"

"I'm fine, really. It was a silly meltdown, that's all. I feel sort of stupid."

"Call me later. Let me know you're okay."

As soon as I rang off, my cell buzzed.

I took a deep breath and said, "Hello, Gareth."

He took a split-second to answer, probably surprised to hear my voice and not a recording.

"Thanks for taking my call." His Barry White voice was a bit flat, with a tiny tinge of sarcasm.

"I feel guilty."

"You should."

If I'd treated him so badly, why was he calling? I was waved to a cab and crawled onto the back seat.

"I didn't want to leave it the way we did," he was saying. "The way *you* left it."

What a nerve. How many times had the great Gareth Greene banged a groupie and never given her a second thought?

"I've got a pretty complicated life already, Gareth."

"So you've got a guy. Why didn't you say so?"

"I don't want to be rude, but is it really any of your business?"

"You've got a pretty sharp tongue, you know that?"

I exhaled while counting to ten.

"There's something between us," he said in the interval of my silence. "I can't put my finger on it. It's not like anything I've ever experienced."

I listened. I knew what there was between us. Several lifetimes.

"Don't you feel it?" he asked. "The connection?"

Then he dropped a bomb. "Do you believe in reincarnation?"

"What do you want, Gareth?"

"I want to talk about this."

"Talk?" I snorted.

"Hey! Seems like I was the one who got used."

I weakened. "Are you in town?"

"I'm at your place. Parked out front."

He said it at the exact moment my cab turned into the circular drive. He was out of his big shiny Escalade and opening my door before I could pay the driver.

As I stepped out, he opened his hand. A green faience medallion with seven-pointed star glinted in his giant palm.

"Now will you talk?"

CHAPTER 53   GOLIATH REDUX

"Love can be put off, never abandoned." – Sextus Propertius

W here did you get it?" I asked as soon as I opened the door to my penthouse.

"*What* is it?" Gareth countered.

I looked directly into his eyes, trying to see how much he knew, but more than that, to decide how much he could handle knowing.

"It's old," I said.

"I know *that*. I paid enough for it."

"You *bought* it? Where?"

"London. An antique shop. A little place, not fancy."

I moved to the bar, poured Highland Park into a pair of short, Waterford crystal tumblers and waved Gareth to the sofa. The mirror wall reflected his black magnificence towering over my flaming red hair and then the two of us sinking onto teal leather.

"How much are you ready to hear?" I asked.

"Try me."

Before continuing, I let the smokiness of the scotch settle on my tongue.

"You're right that we've known each other before," I said matter-of-factly. "In fact, I've known you in three other lifetimes. There could be more."

I looked hard at him, expecting an expression at least of disbelief, if not shock. I saw none. He stared back at me, slowly nodding his head, even smiling a little, looking very satisfied. I had the clear impression that I confirmed what he'd already suspected.

"So, what was the deal? Were we lovers?"

"We were...close. Like family—but not related."

I struggled a little to describe the relationship. It didn't seem like a good idea to tell him that once he'd been my slave. Who knew how he might react if I touched that raw nerve? Slavery was a hot-button issue with the power to dredge up ugly collective memories.

"Never lovers," I added firmly. It was true, at least for the past lives I knew about.

"I find that hard to believe. You ate me alive."

I took another sip of the amber scotch.

"You see, in one of our lifetimes, I was...well, you might say...a little obsessed with you."

He liked that. His eyes flashed with possibility.

"But I moved past it," I added quickly, so as not to encourage him. "I realized it was wrong, that I would have been taking advantage of you."

"No problems the other night, huh? You didn't have any qualms then."

"Do I have to apologize for having sex with you? Do you do that, Gareth? With your women?"

He grinned. "Okay, point taken. Give me the story."

Gareth was total concentration as I ran him quickly through the saga of my father Hermes Trismegistus, creator of the Emerald Tablet, and his choice of me as its guardian. The Chosen One.

It was an incredible relief to share with someone besides Barb. Even she didn't know the full story; I'd told her nothing of the Tablet's power.

"I believe the septagram you bought in London is one of seven commissioned by me in Amunia. In Egypt. Third century BC. You see, I once formed the Order of the Tablet with seven Protectors and gave each a green faience medallion identical to the one you have."

I paused to let it sink in before saying, "You were one of those seven."

Gareth finally took his first taste of the whiskey. Only it wasn't a taste. He downed the whole shot. I went to the bar, grabbed the bottle and poured him another generous splash.

"So these Protectors—this Order you call it—our job was to protect...
what? An *Emerald Tablet*? And protect it *from* what?"

"The forces of evil."

I couldn't help but smile. It sounded so ridiculous, sipping 18-year-old single malt in my penthouse off the Strip. "We started out protecting the Tablet, but ended up...well...protecting me, I think."

"That's some family history." Then he asked, "Are there others out there? Have you met other Protectors?"

"Some. Not all. And not everyone who has a medallion today is one of the original seven. I think maybe roles morph over time. Perhaps during lifetimes I don't know about yet."

"Maybe something big's going to happen," he said. "Maybe we're gearing up for it."

"Maybe your imagination is even wilder than mine."

"Think about it. We meet. I save you. Then I'm in London and see this septagram. I have to have it, and I don't know why. And when I hold it in my hand, I think of you. And the more I think of you, the more I'm convinced we've known each other before. That we have this ages-old, cosmic connection."

By this time, I'd refilled our glasses more than twice. My head was too light; the three yogurts had been hours ago.

"How do you know all this?" Gareth was asking. Then a light came into his eyes and he said, "You've been back, haven't you? Back in time. *How?*"

Gareth was so tall that his head was cut off in our reflection in the Red Mirror. His black silk shirt, open four buttons at the top, showed a gold chain on lustrous muscle. I saw Goliath's gladiator chest in a warrior's cuirass.

The giant bulge in his black cashmere pants throbbed at me. Behind us, also reflected in the mirror, was my wide bed.

I tore my eyes away. This was *not* what I intended.

"It's hard for me to believe that we haven't been fucking our brains out through the centuries," he growled in my ear.

"I'm flying tomorrow to see someone."

"That's tomorrow," he crooned, massaging my tight shoulders in his mammoth hands.

Hot, wet lips sucked on my neck. Against my will, my nipples hardened.

To give in or not to give in.

While I was deciding, Gareth took charge. Palm pressing on my womb, his long basketball player's fingers were between my legs, rotating on my clitoris.

"Relax, baby, " he whispered in his Barry White voice.

And so I did.

A series of dog-bark sounds woke me from sound sleep; Gareth snored. He stretched out on his back the full length of the bed and then some. In the low glow of the indirect lighting, his nude body shone black as polished obsidian against the snowy white Egyptian cotton sheets. How he managed to have a hard-on was worthy of the Mithraic Mysteries.

The God Min with erect penis.

That's when I heard the sliding door to the terrace scratch along the track. I instinctively looked at the altar-niche where the Red Mirror should hang. Gone.

"The Mirror!" I yelled.

Gareth was immediately awake. He leapt from the bed and crossed the silvery carpet with the speed of a forward going for the dunk.

I was close behind.

We went through the open sliding door and onto the balcony in time to see the edge of the Red Mirror disappear over the railing.

Gareth lunged, caught the corner of the frame with his right hand, doubling from the waist to hang down. I grabbed his left biceps and hung on with all my strength, bracing myself against the wrought iron railing.

Twenty-eight stories down shimmered the swimming pool. One story below, balanced like a performer from Cirque du Soleil, a wiry figure in a black leotard perched on the railing of the terrace under us. He hung onto the other end of the Red Mirror.

Gareth pulled; the muscles rippled across his powerful shoulders. The acrobat-robber used his weight hanging on the Mirror to counter Gareth's strength. I thought that surely with the size and force of his hand, Gareth would wrench the mirror away.

But instead, in one long heartbeat, the Mirror slipped, slipped more, and then began a slow motion tumble to the tiled deck far below.

It took forever for the mirror to fall. I watched each twist and turn as in my dream in the Hive. And just like my dream, the Red Mirror shattered into a thousand shiny shards of splintered glass.

Our eyes had been fixed on the mirror while the proverbial cat burglar nimbly scrambled from terrace to terrace down the face of the high-rise. As we watched helplessly, the black shape hit the ground from the second floor and fled into the shadows.

There was nothing to do but sweep up the pieces. The glass was shattered. The wooden frame, painted and repainted over millennia, had split at the corners into four pieces.

"Does this mean no more trips to the past?" Gareth asked.

I looked at him. Like an unexpected death, the finality hadn't fully penetrated my shock.

"Too bad," he was saying. "I was thinking we'd take a trip."

"Gareth," I started cautiously, wanting to tread carefully, to cause no pain. He was a straight up guy, and I owed him a lot—he was, after all, a *Protector*. But going through the Red Mirror together was more of a commitment than I could offer.

"Don't say it," he said gravely, his black eyes burning. "Don't make up your mind. Give me a chance."

"I warned you. I'm going away this morning."

"Don't you want to see the other septagram?"

Obviously, I didn't give Gareth enough credit; he knew how to move the ball down the court when he needed to.

Five septagrams. The General. Orsini. Lars had two. And now Gareth had one and held out the possibility of a sixth.

I didn't need to question if I was meant to locate them all. That was a given. Why else were they coming into my life? Gareth was right. We were gearing up for something.

"Where?" I asked.

His answer was a crooked smile; he'd won, and he knew it

"This is extortion," I accused him. "You're holding me for ransom."

"I don't like to lose."

"And what if I don't care where it is?"

"Oh you care, all right. I see it in your eyes. Nothing could keep you away."

CHAPTER 54 TONY

"If you have a garden and a library, you have everything you need." – Cicero

I'm sorry, Tony. I'm not going to make it, after all."

Silence.

"Tony? Are you there?"

I heard a deep sigh.

"You really push the limits of patience, Isis." The unfamiliar tone in his voice was not reassuring.

"Something's come up," I said lamely. "It's business."

"Right," he said in a flat voice.

Then there was silence. I started to say something but stopped. It seemed pathetic and doubly lame to say sorry again.

"You know, Isis, if it were just me, maybe I'd put up with it. But I have to think of Jen." His voice was very matter-of-fact when he started but then slipped into frustration. "She baked a cake, for Christ's sake! She even picked up her room."

My stomach turned over. Jen, only thirteen, kidnapped once because of me—the woman who slept in her dead mother's bed—had baked a cake to celebrate my arrival.

"What if I stop by on my way home?" I offered.

"I don't know," were his words, but his tone said he did.

Now even Tony was deserting me.

"Am I still welcome if I come today?" I asked quietly.

"We're here. You know the address."

No offer to pick me up at the airport.

Gareth accepted my departure without much of an argument. Had he been bluffing, like a feint on the court?

"I envy the guy," he admitted with a shrug.

"It's complicated. I warned you."

"I'm not giving up."

Now I shrugged—and continued brushing my hair. "Surely you don't need the sex that bad."

"Man, you can be cold, girl."

"Look, I'm not in love with you. And you aren't in love with me. Let's just leave it as it is."

His long muscled legs, hard as sculpted basalt, stretched out on the trashed bed. He leaned back against the mirror headboard with his hands behind his head, elbows pointed out. My heart skipped a beat. Not because of him, but because Rasheed sits like that.

Rasheed. I hated every time I thought of him.

"Why don't you meet me in London after your stolen weekend?" Gareth suggested casually.

I stopped brushing and turned.

"Is the septagram in London?"

Then before he could answer, I asked in a bit of a panic, "Is it for sale?"

In my mind I was already telling him to go there now. To buy it now. Today.

"No."

I waited for more, but it didn't come. "Would you stop playing this game? It's tiresome. Just tell me where it is."

"Meet me, and I'll show you."

"I think I liked you better as Goliath."

"Hey, what can I say? I've evolved. Isn't that the point?"

I was on my way to the airport to catch the plane to Newark, this time with a bag of warmer clothes, suitable for London, when the General called.

"Where are you?" His voice was gruff, demanding.

"You never ask that."

"You didn't take the flight last night."

"So you *are* having me followed."

"If I were, would I be asking where you are?"

"Maybe. To keep me off balance."

Silence.

"Shall we talk business?" he said finally.

"What kind?"

"The kind where you earn a lot of money. Isn't that the kind you like?"

"I might be more choosy than you think."

"Meet me in London, and make up your mind."

For a moment, I seriously considered that he'd bugged my place.

When I didn't answer right away, he added, "After Princeton. Or have you changed your mind about Tony?"

"I'll be in touch," I said as the taxi pulled up at Departures.

"I'll be waiting," he chuckled.

Late afternoon traffic was beginning to build up, but I made the drive from Newark to Princeton in just over an hour.

All along the shaded streets lined with comfortable two-story houses, most with porches or wrapped verandas, kids biked and skateboarded on wide sidewalks or dribbled balls in driveways.

When I rang the bell, Jen threw open the sturdy, fire engine red front door.

"I thought you weren't coming!" she beamed. "Dad's been *so* weird."

The front hall bookcases were in their usual disarray. A rainbow-colored rug lay slightly askew. Jackets, sweaters, caps and umbrellas hung from hooks above running shoes and galoshes.

Jen grabbed my bag and started lugging it up the wooden stairs.

"This is heavy. Does it mean you're going to stay awhile?"

"Is your Dad home?"

If she said yes, I'd know I was in real trouble. Tony hadn't exactly rushed to greet me.

"He's at the lab. I'll call him."

Sure enough, in the middle of the kitchen table stood a chocolate cake, a little lopsided but iced thickly with real frosting. Rich, dark and glossy.

Jen had scribbled "Welcome" in thin squiggly letters with one of those squeeze tubes of colored icing you get in the grocery store.

"It's a gorgeous cake."

"Thanks. I made it myself," she said with a proud grin. "From scratch."

A surge of warmth rushed through me. That eager face. Those hazel eyes. My Jason. Athena's Jason. Now Jen.

I felt at the same time both grateful and guilty to be standing in Tony's country kitchen with painted white cabinets and black-and-white checkered linoleum. A big window over the sink looked out onto an impossibly green backyard ringed with rhododendron bushes and a white picket fence. A robin splashed in the blue birdbath.

"Do you want to see my room? I've done some new things."

Curled up together on a quilt spread out on the worn oak floor, sipping mugs of Earl Grey laced with milk and honey, we pored over old photos from summers on the Jersey Shore.

"There's Mom and me. Before she got sick."

A beautiful young woman robbed by cancer in the prime of life. Her pictures were all over the house. She always had a smile. How much fun she must have been. Fun until she caused the greatest pain of all.

It was so unfair. All the mean-spirited bitches who live out full lives. I drew some consolation that they'd meet again—Tony, Jen and her mom—in another life. Like Hector and Ingrid, the three belonged to yet another circle of souls.

Would Jen understand if I tried to explain? But I dismissed the idea as soon as it came. Tony the cosmologist, rational scientist *extraordinaire*, certainly wouldn't approve of my corrupting his daughter with tales of past lives.

And at the moment I thought of Tony approving or disapproving, I looked up to see him leaning against the door frame—every bit as breathtakingly beautiful as Antinous.

We ate cake as the main course, with hamburgers on the grill for dessert. Tony and I shared a bottle of a good Barolo I'd picked up at a wine store on the way into town.

Jen kept us laughing with stories from school. She had an amazing talent for mimicry. I could see each quirky kid muddling his way through eighth grade.

When the kitchen grew dark, Jen insisted on lighting candles.

"More romantic," she teased.

It was almost ten o'clock before Tony ordered, "Bed!"

Jen gave Tony a kiss on the cheek and then me a big hug.

"It's okay if you make noise," she whispered. "I know about these things."

And then Tony and I were alone.

He'd been warm all night; I detected none of the chill in our phone conversation.

"Thank you for coming, Isis." His tone said he meant it, really meant it.

"I'm glad I came. It was the right thing to do." I paused just a second. "No. I said that wrong. It feels so good to be here."

He leaned across the kitchen table littered with ketchup-smeared plates and kissed me lightly. When he pulled away, our lips clung together for an instant.

"You're very beautiful with red hair. But then, you'd always be beautiful. You're a beautiful person."

I wanted to shout, No, I'm not! I'm a selfish, horrible person who makes money from war.

Our minds must have been on the same track because Tony went on to say, "I hope you're not still involved with Libya. That isn't the business you were talking about, is it?"

Other than that comment, it was the first he'd spoken of our phone call with his silent ultimatum. For Tony it was never about power; it was about what was reasonable and fair. Noble. Noble through the ages.

"I have to decide."

"Not tonight," he said. "Tonight I have other plans."

A last log cast a red-gold aura that lit the tips of his blond curls with fire. The lines etched into Tony's forehead, around his eyes and at the corners of his mouth marked life's passage in a way stolen from Antinous. Otherwise, they were the same pure soul with the same enthusiasm and joy.

I felt lighter, more hopeful when in his arms. The world was brighter. Less complicated. I was a better person. I believed I could be better still.

"What if I told you that we've known each other before?"

"I'd say I'm a lucky man."

"I'm being serious, Tony."

When he looked into my eyes and saw my gravitas, he pulled back, then rolled over to sit up straight beside me with his back against the sofa. I sat up too, and he wrapped a giant crocheted afghan around our shoulders. Our bare legs, parallel on the oval braided rug, stretched toward the open hearth with glowing embers.

Even his toes were perfect, each one straight and just a tiny bit shorter than the one before, forming a precise diagonal from the big toe to the little.

"Remember, Tony, when we went to the Metropolitan Museum? How the statues were more than stone relics to you? How you felt like you knew some as people?"

He handed me a wine glass with the last of the Barolo.

"I remember everything about that day, Isis. It was the first time I recall being happy since Susan died."

"We were married once," I blurted out. The words just came. I'd thought to take him along in stages, but I heard myself say what I'd wanted to tell him for so long, but never dared.

He blinked.

"In another lifetime."

Our faces were close enough that the blue of his eyes was the thinnest of circles around huge black pupils.

"I know it sounds crazy. I would have thought it crazy, too—not that long ago."

The furrow between his eyebrows deepened, the one he gets when struggling to reconcile disparate thoughts.

He didn't ask how, or what, or why. He didn't say anything. I wanted to crawl inside his head. His eyes had that detached quality of a mind separate from a body.

I rose to my bare feet and padded across the floor to find my purse and take out a folded paper.

While he stared at the printout of a bust of Antinous at the Prado Museum in Madrid, I curled back down beside him on the floor.

"It's you. You can see that. I'm surprised no one has pointed it out to you before."

I was certain he was going to say that it was a coincidence. That the striking resemblance was due to an anomaly of genes programmed to produce eyes, ears and noses. That given the number of human beings on the planet throughout time, doubles were statistically predicted to happen. *Doppelgängers*. The Germans had a word for it.

But he didn't respond like I thought he would.

"I've had the strangest feeling since I met you. The first time in Vegas when you told me your name. Isis. And then in New York. It's never been like we were strangers who'd met randomly. Not for me."

"Then you don't think I'm some kind of nut?"

"You are definitely some kind of nut." His eyes twinkled; his face glowed. "A very delightful one."

Leaning into me, taking my chin in his fingers, he kissed me on the lips, his tongue probing just a little. Just enough that we both stirred.

"It explains so much, Tony," I argued earnestly. "Why you're instantly attracted to someone—or repulsed. Why people are drawn to a strange land—or a time in history. Why it's easier for some to play the piano. Or for you to do math."

He smiled and blew gently in my ear.

"It's all happened before," I insisted. "We're building on the past."

"Does that mean we have a future?" he asked, his fingers holding my chin again.

"It means we have now," I answered.

He smiled and quoted Epicurus, "We have this moment only. There is only here and now."

When he saw my surprised look, he laughed out loud. He had the exact, mischievous, heart-stopping look in his eye as young Antinous.

"I've been studying up on the Greeks," he grinned. "I may be more in tune with the universe than you think."

And then Antinous Thrice Greatest kissed my lips, my breasts, my belly.

His manhood first pierced the air, then me, driving deep into my wet, his palm muffling my cries.

O Aphrodite! O Gods divine!

CHAPTER 55   LONDON

"A mouse does not rely on just one hole." – Titus Maccius Plautius

O ur 747 dropped through a fuzzy blanket from leaden skies to a glossy tarmac. Judging from the size of the puddles, the recent rain must have fallen in torrents. For the moment, the skies rested.

Heathrow is always a zoo, but this morning I made it through customs and, within an hour of landing, was waiting 'on line' for a taxi. A long row of wet black umbrellas dotted with glistening beads stretched to the front of me and behind.

I can't say I was all that surprised when Orsini appeared.

"He's waiting for you in the limo."

Orsini with my bag in his hand motioned toward a black Rolls Royce limousine parked in the outside lane—illegally. Small peril, no doubt, for Corsicans.

"Are you sure you didn't implant a chip under my skin?" I said as soon as I was in the car. I didn't bother to ask how he knew what flight I was on.

"I'm meeting someone," I warned him.

"I know," he answered.

The limo moved through obverse traffic in that confusing way I find jarring until I adjust to the steering wheel on the right, the hair-raising left-turns and the intimidating challenge of roundabouts.

"I'm flying to Scotland for a tasting—a single malt reserve."

I took his amicable tone to signal an invitation.

"It's reputed to be quite special," he added in a way intended to be tempting.

"I told you I'm meeting someone."

"Ah yes, the basketball star. One could never accuse you of going for a certain type."

He had the good sense not to bring up Tony.

Rain began to fall again in earnest; the windshield wipers beat right and left, right and left in their mesmerizing thumping rhythm. My lids closed.

When the Rolls stopped, we were in front of The Lanesborough Hotel where I was to meet Gareth.

"You see, Ishtar? No tricks."

He waited until I'd stepped out of the car before he told me the reason he'd met me at the airport.

"Have you heard about the bank heist in Las Vegas?"

I stared at him. He didn't try to hide his amusement at my shock.

"The biggest in history is the headline. Apparently it happened during the night. Hundreds of deposit boxes emptied. CNN reports that it's impossible to put a number on the loss."

Orsini closed the car door. I saw myself reflected in the tinted glass—open-mouthed with orangey hair frizzing in the rain.

Registration was a blur. After returning my passport, the desk clerk said something about everything being taken care of.

I must have followed the bellhop to my room but can't remember. All I could think of was the Emerald Tablet. In the hands of the General. It wouldn't take him long to discover he needed more than the Tablet itself. And when he figured that out, he'd be back for me.

Emerald Tablet gone. Red Mirror smashed. I had nothing left.

Nothing except the Hathor Ring. I touched it just to make sure it was still on my finger. That the General hadn't taken it while I dozed in the car.

A fruit basket with chocolates stood on a round, curved-leg Queen Anne table. Beside the basket was an ice bucket with a bottle of *Cristal*. Two flutes, rimmed with gold, sparkled beside it.

The note said, *Call as soon as you do your girl thing. Gareth.*

My 'girl thing' was a hot shower to calm my nerves and a blow dry to calm my hair. My brain worked on a loose plan.

I'd take my purse and passport when I left. Nothing else. Certainly not my cell with GPS. I'd find a back door, preferably through a dark basement.

The house phone rang, and I jumped. My pulse went through the roof. I couldn't decide if I should answer.

Calm down. It's probably a courtesy call from the front desk. It wouldn't be the General, not yet anyway. He didn't yet guess my next moves, or I wouldn't be here. I'd still be in his limo going who knows where.

In spite of having convinced myself the call was routine, I answered cautiously, "Hello?"

"You're not answering your phone." Relief washed over me to hear Gareth's voice.

"I must have forgotten to take it off airplane mode."

"How's your room? Do you like the view?"

I hadn't looked out the window. Hyde Park. Upper-class London. Heads of State and all that. Rain fell in steady, metallic sheets. I couldn't tell what time of day it was. The sky was one unarticulated shade of gray.

"It's nice."

"Nice? You're tough to impress," he said with a good-natured laugh. "Come see my suite."

I could see the gleam in his eye over the phone.

"You could move up here, you know," he suggested playfully.

"I think two rooms were a good idea."

"Yeah, I got that message."

"When can I see the septagram?"

"You don't let up for a minute, do you?"

"The septagram, Gareth. That's why I'm here."

The Petrie Museum wasn't much to see. A dirty, two-story brick building on a walking street identified as University College London. Glossy black-painted double doors had small glass panes. White Helvetica font on a school bus yellow and black sign read "UCL Petrie Museum."

The entry was just wide enough to go straight through to the back or to the right up narrow linoleum-covered steps with a simple wood pole railing. On the white wall along the stairs was painted "PETRIE" in huge black letters with smaller "Museum of Egyptian Archaeology" below.

When we stepped inside, we walked back in time to the nineteenth century. From what I could see from the tiny foyer, the museum was a rabbit warren of small, connecting rooms filled with wooden cases about seven feet high and five feet wide. Priceless, millennia-old artifacts were crammed on glass shelves behind wood-framed glass doors that lock with little brass keys.

The first room displayed four-and five thousand-year-old ceramics packed like sardines one and two deep. There wasn't an inch between them. Little yellowed labels identified the black-and-red glazed clay as 'Badarian' or 'Amratian' and other pots with primitive reddish-brown etchings as 'Naqada II marl.' Any one of the ceramics would be a centerpiece in a lesser museum.

Gareth went into the room on the right. I followed, my footsteps creaking on the scuffed hardwood floors. We passed more wood and glass cabinets filled with wondrous treasures. Simple descriptions of the ancient Egyptian pieces had been typed with an old-fashioned typewriter in Courier script on index cards.

```
Yellow curly hair and scalp from a body which
had long black wig. Dyn. XVIII-XIX. ca 1550 bce
```

A yellowed index card explained that a Pharaoh's twelve-year-old concubine had worn the beaded gown with pointed metal breast cups. Another label identified the model wooden boats with tiny crews, sails and miniature braided rope as Middle Kingdom. An entire case held only copper knives and razors like those Isis used to shave her head and mound.

In the third room, we stopped in front of an unlit cabinet. The fluorescent tube in the ceiling above was off; there were no windows. The whole corner lay in shadow.

Gareth went away and came back with a flashlight.

"The display lights are broken," he said with a grin. "They gave me a *torch*. No shit. That's what they call it."

The beam bounced back into our eyes, and Gareth moved right up to the glass. Right away, he found the septagram.

The green disk, lustrous like polished glass, was etched with a seven-pointed star. There was no doubt this was number six of the seven.

"How did you know to look here?"

"The guy at the shop where I bought mine. 'Old enough to be in a museum,' he told me. That's why it cost so much. I didn't believe him until he gave me the ID number so I could check it out."

The black Courier script typeface on the card told me next to nothing, but the time period fit when I lived as Athena.

```
?Provenance          UC. 16882
Faience.
Faiyum. Ptolemaic Period. ca 200 bce.
```

"Excuse me."

The woman looked up, startled. Short and slender, she sat on a hard straight-backed chair at a mammoth dark wood desk. In front of her was a laptop and a stack of five by three inch white index cards. The top card had the same typewriter text in courier font.

"I was wondering if you could tell me something about a piece in the collection?"

Her watery brown eyes without any lashes blinked through thick lenses set in wire frames. Dishwater blond hair was pulled back into a scraggly ponytail. She wore the kind of clothes that you don't notice and can't remember afterwards except as vaguely wool.

Either she wasn't accustomed to people asking for more information, or she was surprised to hear an American accent. I don't think the museum got many tourists. The Petrie, founded on the collection of William Flinders Petrie, an Oxford man known affectionately as the Father of Egyptology, was a museum made for academia.

"I have the catalogue number," I offered, smiling politely.

"I'm sorry for the wait," she apologized after a lengthy search. "We're in the process of digitizing. I'm afraid we haven't come very far."

She held a card in her hand like the ones stacked on the desk.

"There really isn't much more. But I can give you the email of Professor Harriston. Professor *emeritus*," she stressed, perhaps to press home that he was retired and not to be disturbed without due cause. "He's written a paper on the object, but unfortunately we don't have a copy."

She wrote the name and email address in a careful hand on a small square sheet of paper from a notepad. She started to hand it to me, then stopped and wrote the title of the paper on the back.

"The significance of the septagram in pre-Roman Alexandria mystic cults."

"I hate to be difficult," I wheedled, "but I'm only in London for a day. This is *terribly* important."

Her eyes grew a little rounder; she looked a bit fearful of what was coming next. I imagined she thought I'd ask for his home address.

"I wonder if you could give me his phone number? I'm a little anxious that he might not check his email."

She hesitated; I sensed I'd struck a chord. No doubt the retired professor hadn't quite come into the digital age.

Smiling reassuringly, I chanted *ABRACADABRA ABRASAX* in my head.

"I suppose it'd be all right," she said cheerfully. "He's in the book, anyway."

"Can I use your phone?" I asked Gareth. "I left mine at the hotel."

Gareth's reduced entourage had waited in the street. Only three people accompanying us was his idea of going it alone. He hadn't objected, though, to leaving through the hotel kitchen.

"Leave it to me, babe. I'm used to escaping by the back door."

The professor's phone rang and rang with the odd trill of an English landline. I started counting at the third ring, wanting to make sure I gave him plenty of time to answer. Four. Five. Six. Seven.

In my mind's eye, I saw a hunched codger in a gray knit sweater with leather patches on the sleeves scraping along in tattered plaid house shoes. The phone was at the end of a long dark hallway lined with bookcases.

"Professor Harriston's residence," a woman stated crisply.

I decided a housekeeper.

I told her my name and that I was on a very brief visit from America. She could obviously tell I was American, but I wanted to emphasize the urgency.

"I am doing some research on a piece at the Petrie Museum. Professor Harriston has written a paper on it, and I have a few questions that only he can resolve."

The woman started to say something about an appointment, and I interrupted.

"A very few questions. I would only need an hour of his time. Less."

She snorted into the phone.

The ugly American. I'm sure that's what she thought.

"Will you hold, please?" she said curtly.

I waited. A few feet away, Gareth and his entourage stood in a tight group, talking in animated voices punctuated by peals of laughter.

"Can you be here at half four?"

"Yes. Absolutely."

She gave me the address with directions from the Petrie. The professor must have walked to work; it wasn't far.

Now to get rid of Gareth.

A break in the mackerel sky brought out the sun. The doors opened in an adjacent building; a stream of students poured out. It took them about five seconds to recognize Gareth Greene. Basketball has its fans even in Britain.

They swarmed around him; his entourage struggled to hold them back. I turned and walked quickly away, dropping his cell in a trash bin.

Professor Harriston lived in one of those narrow brick London row houses with glossy front doors painted black or red and hung with heavy brass knockers, each unique. The professor's was a lion's head with the number '7' in polished brass above.

A weighty black wrought iron fence ran along the street from one neighbor to the next, all of about thirty feet. On the other side of the gate was a short flight of stone steps up to the phone box red door.

Sunny yellow pansies bloomed in white window boxes below a bay window facing the street. The housekeeper. Definitely a woman's touch. At the window, heavy drapes, a rust brown velvet, had been pulled tight.

I lifted the brass knocker and banged. Out of the corner of my eye, I saw a crack in the drapes widen.

The door opened without warning, and I was greeted by the robust voice on the phone.

"You are early," she admonished me with an icy blue glare. A hair net covered gray hair set in pin curls.

She was taller than I imagined but otherwise as round. Her brownish dress with a green leafy pattern came to below the knee. Sturdy calves in thick nylons ended in a pair of sensible brown shoes tied in neat bows.

"I'm terribly sorry. Shall I come back?"

But her point being made, she opened the door for me to pass, and I stepped through.

Straight ahead was the predictable steep flight of narrow wooden stairs leading to the master bedroom. There would be another flight to the third floor. The only bathroom would be at the top of the first flight, unless Harriston had modernized by converting the closet under the stairs to a WC.

Directly down the Lilliputian hallway was the kitchen. The enticing aroma of baking drifted in the air.

She must have noticed my nose twitch in an appreciative way, because she snorted slightly as she opened the white paneled door to my right.

"The professor said you'd be wanting tea."

"Come in. Come in, my child," Hermes Trismegistus commanded from deep shadow.

Heavy curtains like the ones at the bay window covered the French doors onto the back garden. Small lamps with old ivory-colored shades gave off the yellow glow of oil lanterns. The long walls of the narrow room were entirely covered in bookshelves stuffed with hardbound volumes of all sizes. Deeper cases held what looked to be atlases and loose maps.

When my vision adjusted to the gloom, I made out papyrus scrolls stacked in the same chaotic way as in Hermes' study at the Library of Neith.

He stood with his thick mane of gleaming silver hair beside a massive desk strewn with papers and books.

In place of a sapphire blue gown spangled with silver stars, Hermes wore a tattered gray sweater with leather patches on the elbows and brown corduroy slacks. There was no slump to his shoulders; he had the erect posture of a man half his age.

I glanced down. Scottish tartan slippers.

"I've been waiting quite some time," he said kindly.

He motioned for me to approach, and when I was near enough, he took my hands in his giant palms.

"You are more beautiful each time I meet you, Isis."

I kissed him on both lined cheeks.

"I approve of you as a redhead," he commented and then added with a sigh. "It was an awful time, was it not? The Romans were a cruel lot."

I didn't bother to ask how he knew about Elektra. Hermes Trismegistus, creator of the Emerald Tablet and the Red Mirror, knew all.

"I've been holding this for you." He handed me a small wooden box inlaid with silver ankhs.

Inside was the seventh faience septagram. A thin gold chain went through the drilled hole at the edge of the circle.

I immediately hung the amulet around my neck.

"Can you get the Tablet back?" he asked.

Could he read my mind? Is that how he did it?

"I'm fairly certain who has it."

"Then you know what you must do."

Hermes' eyes were the same pale blue, a shade so transparent that even the steely skies of London would be too glaring.

"Do you believe I can succeed?"

"I have always believed in you, Isis."

I'd once said I wouldn't die for the Tablet. That I'd give up the mantra rather than suffer pain. But now that it was in the hands of the General, I feared for the world.

"Do I have to die?"

"Not if you prove clever enough."

I was inclined to think the cleverest thing for me to do was disappear.

A light knock on the door preceded its opening.

"Ah, here is Mabel with our tea."

Mabel carried a square silver tray, properly polished. On the tray balanced flowered china teacups and saucers, a teapot in a yellow cozy, a bowl of sugar cubes and a matching pitcher of steaming milk.

Freshly baked scones were stacked on a tiered silver server, along with triangular sandwiches of white bread with the crusts cut off.

"There's raspberry jam and clotted cream for the scones. And I thought you might like to try some of my lemon curd." Mabel didn't manage a smile, but her tone was warmer.

I believe she meant the lemon curd as a peace offering. The door closed, leaving us alone again.

"He frightens me, Hermes. He knows things. He's always a step ahead."

"But you have the advantage, Isis."

"How is that?"

"It should be obvious, my dear. He wants two things, Isis, and he wants them equally."

I set my cup back on the saucer harder than I intended; the china clattered in a silent room. A clock ticked. A horn honked on the street.

"I think you overestimate the General's attraction to me."

"I think you underestimate your power over him. Especially now.

Now that you have knowledge of the spells."

Hermes opened a deep drawer in his desk and pulled out a paper scroll bound with golden twine.

"This is not the original, of course," he said, handing it over to me. "The papyrus would be too fragile to handle."

Even though the scroll was a copy, I unrolled it with reverence.

It was a bit of a surprise to me that I was able to read it so easily. Formulae in Greek and then gibberish incantations.

I read out loud, "BOR PHOR PHORBA PHOR PHORBA BES CHARIN BAUBA."

"Excellent! You have identified the correct incantation." Hermes beamed his approval, patting my hand with the kind, fatherly affection he'd shown me in the Temple of Amun.

"You see, I have a special collection, a kind of apocrypha of black magic outside the known canon."

"Do you have the original?" I wanted to see if I might recognize Eben's distinctive handwriting.

"I have the complete works, Isis. The Black Scroll. The very papyri Eben and Qeb-ha transcribed. The document you—Elektra—made possible. Eben was correct. You had to go back. Everything depended on it."

I stared at him, incredulous. Not because he knew what Eben had said to me, but because I think I finally understood.

"You planned all this lifetimes ago? You knew the General would one day get the Tablet?"

In lieu of an answer, Hermes took a long drink of Earl Grey, his eyes smiling over the edge of the cup.

"*You* are his fatal flaw. That is why, Isis, *you* are the Chosen One."

CHAPTER 56   PROVIDENCE

"Perhaps believing in good design is like believing in God, it makes you an optimist." – Sallust

A glob of dog feces, a dash of menstrual blood, the hearts of two cats sacrificed under a full moon, breasts slashed open with a malachite blade while hearts still beat.

The recipe read like one of hundreds.

"Do you have an apothecary?" I asked, my brain searching for easier ways to secure these ingredients in central London than the obvious.

Hermes Trismegistus leaned back in his chair and popped the last of a buttered scone into his mouth.

"I am a tad disappointed, Isis. I should have thought you would have discovered by now that these props are unnecessary. Devised for the ignorant masses."

"You mean…"

"Precisely. Magic, my dear, is all in the mind. Principally, in the mind of the magician, who by cunning, device and a great deal of drama, controls the minds of others."

"But how will I be able to control the General?"

"Cunning, device…and drama."

"Then why the spell?"

"Because of the *words*, Isis. Never underestimate the power of words. Commit the spell to memory—BOR PHOR PHORBA PHOR PHORBA BES CHARIN BAUBA. You must summon the forces to help you."

"Summon from where? Surely you don't mean from the Underworld?"

"Is it important from where you draw your power?" he asked mildly.

I touched the Hathor Ring on my finger. A cold lump of lapis lazuli set in a few carats of gold. How many times had I called on this inert chunk of inorganic matter for courage?

"You're going to need this," he mumbled while rummaging in the center drawer of his desk. "Ah! Here it is."

Inside the large brown envelope was a thick wad of British pound notes and seven cellphones.

"Disposable," Hermes said with a smug little smile of satisfaction. "And the password on that paper is for a portal."

I blinked and frowned. "Portal?"

"A secure bulletin board, if you will. I've assigned you as joint-administrator. I believe it more prudent than phone communication, do you not agree? I shall check for messages twice daily."

It would appear the Professor emeritus was more in the digital age than the Petrie staff gave him credit for.

"Will you be traced here?" he asked without seeming particularly concerned.

"I did all I could not to be."

He nodded, his pale eyes shining with affection, his love flowing to bathe my soul in confidence and hope. The last thing I wanted was to fly from his cocoon.

"I should leave," I said in a voice more determined than I felt. "The longer I'm here, the greater the danger."

We rose simultaneously. There was a brief awkward moment when I was seized with the fear that I might not see him again. Had we learned all we needed? Had *I* learned?

"Oh, Hermes!" I sobbed, throwing my arms around his neck. I hadn't realized how deeply lonely I was. "Now that I've found you in this life, I don't want to let you go!"

"There, there, my child," he crooned, patting me fondly on the shoulder. "Let us focus on the task at hand."

In a flash of inspiration, I blurted, "Change the mantra. Without the mantra, the Tablet is useless."

"If only it were that easy," he said with patient eyes.

I gathered my bag and Burberry trench coat, making ready to go when Hermes stopped me.

"How is that handsome Antinous, by the way? Such a clever boy."

I felt a stab of guilt.

"It *is* difficult, I could imagine," he mused while helping me on with my coat. "Permanence frightens you."

"Am I so terribly hopeless?"

"About the Red Mirror," he said matter-of-factly and out of nowhere. "It never was about the glass. That's not where the magic is."

"Do you mean—"

"I mean it's all up to you, Isis. Everything is up to you."

At the last moment, before I was to go out the heavy front door, I dug in my purse for the phone numbers I'd copied from my cell before erasing data and destroying the SIM card.

I scribbled Isabel's number on a scrap of paper.

"Sit-hathor," I said quietly, handing the paper to him.

He looked at me, startled. A little shaken, too. For once, I was a step ahead of Hermes Trismegistus.

"She would love to hear from you. I have it directly from the source."

And then, I was out on the street in the thickening dusk, alone and in search of the Emerald Tablet.

Rain had fallen again while I'd been inside. The street was shiny, the sky gun-metal gray.

I stood poised at the bottom of the steps for a moment, not knowing whether to turn left on the sidewalk—or right. In the end, I let the shout of a child be my beacon and headed in that direction, hopscotching through a checkerboard of puddles.

Just as I raised my arm to flag a cab, the man caught my eye. Standing on line at a bus stop, bundled in a sublimely British trench coat, he had a pallid face white as marble distinguished by a carefully trimmed goatee streaked with gray. He wore a black fedora with a neat brim and discreet red feather in the band. Shortish graying hair peeked out around his ears. Longer hairs curled at the back of his neck.

A bit slope-shouldered, he leaned toward me, arms akimbo, bulging pot-belly tugging at his center of gravity. A crook-handled black umbrella, its wooden ferrule planted firmly on the pavement, supported his weight.

When he waved his free hand for me to approach, I looked around, thinking that surely he meant someone else. His smoky, urgent eyes locked with mine, and over the space of the fifty or so feet between us, I recognized Qeb-ha.

Out of all the streets in London, he stood here. Qeb-ha looked as astonished as I felt.

We climbed onto the double-decker red bus and found two seats together at the rear.

Before he could say a word, I grabbed his hand and kissed the blue-veined back. His immaculate nails were neatly trimmed with cuticles pushed back. A professional manicure to go with the artfully groomed goatee.

"The Gods have sent you!" I gushed.

"So now you believe in the Gods?" he teased.

"I must believe something put you exactly where I needed you to be. It can't be coincidence."

"*On the road, one finds a companion,*" he quoted from our past.

"*And in battle, one finds a brother,*" I completed the ancient Egyptian proverb.

"Are we to do battle?" he asked with wide eyes.

"Yes, Qeb-ha. We are to save the world."

"Again?" He sighed, but he still had a smile.

"Have you got Internet at your place?"

"I shall do my best not to be offended," he answered as he pulled a smart phone out of his trench coat pocket. "Do you need to search now?"

So while the bus rumbled its way through tangled traffic and drab passengers with a rainbow of skin colors hung on straps, I googled the General's favorite distilleries, looking for any upcoming tasting of special reserves.

I called Lars from one of the disposable phones.

"Can you come to London? Right away?"

He was quiet, no doubt thinking of our little adventure in Libya. I didn't hear him say, "Rah! Rah! Let's go again!"

"Can I know why?" he asked at last.

"I can't explain on the phone. By the way, it's no use calling my number. I'm not picking up messages."

"How do I contact you?"

"A secure message board. A portal."

I gave him a login and password.

"Don't check it from your own computer," I cautioned.

I paused and then said in a brisk voice, "And don't tell anyone where you're going—or even that you *are* going, if you can avoid it."

"I'm not sure why I'm doing this, Isis."

I gave him one final instruction.

"Wear the septagram cufflinks, Lars."

It was silly, really. The medallions meant nothing on their own, but in my mind, they'd come to represent the balance of power. Our four septagrams against the General's two. One neutral in the museum. He was outnumbered.

Now he had to be outsmarted.

"BOR PHOR PHORBA PHOR PHORBA BES CHARIN BAUBA," I chanted, summoning the powers that be—wherever, whatever or whoever they are.

CHAPTER 57 Q

"Make the best use of what is in your power, and take the rest as it happens."
– Epictetus

If I had imagined Qeb-ha's London flat, it would never have been what met my eyes when he opened the door.

Snowy white carpet ended at ceiling-to-floor windows with the fairyland lights of Thames bridges twinkling through evening fog. An aquamarine jellyfish Chihuly glass fixture hung above a glass table surrounded by white leather and chrome chairs.

Qeb-ha took off his shoes inside the door and placed them precisely parallel on a gray mat to the right. I put mine beside his.

"Welcome to my humble abode," he said with unabashed pride.

A fluffy white cat twirled around my ankles, lifting her lush tail in seductive anticipation.

"Sasha! Behave yourself," Qeb-ha admonished. "Such a slut," he giggled as he took our coats and hung them in a mirrored closet.

Suddenly I missed Aisha terribly. I could imagine her green eyes narrowing when I went to pick her up. It'd be a while before she forgave me this long absence.

White leather sofas and lounge chairs trimmed in chrome grouped around a birch coffee table with long-stemmed white moth orchids in a white porcelain pot. Around the room burned discreet recessed lights that he adjusted with a remote.

Qeb-ha had a respectable collection of fine, primary-color abstract paintings, but most of his art was chrome-framed, black-and-white George Platt Lynes or Robert Mapplethorpe photographs of nude men—all Antinous-level gorgeous. Each photo was a sensitive study of muscle and line, rather like the Greek marbles displayed in museums.

We sipped a glass or two of port and nibbled on Stilton and crackers. Sasha crawled into my lap and purred. Qeb-ha slipped on a Vivaldi CD.

"What do I call you?" I asked.

"What about 'Q'?" He looked pleased at his cleverness.

Very James Bond, I could see him thinking. In spite of my warning of battle, I wasn't certain he'd grasped the portent of our meeting.

"You do understand the danger. You won't tell anyone you met me?"

"Tsk tsk, my dear Isis. Where is your faith?"

He handed me a key on a silver chain attached to a miniature Eiffel Tower. Sasha purred in his arms.

"Do tell me if there's anything you need," he offered graciously at the door of the guest room.

White carpet, white walls, fluffy white towels in a white-tiled bath, a queen bed covered in hot pink satin.

"I need an Internet cafe, but not in the neighborhood."

"Take the 9 Line and hop off when you see one. They're everywhere. And if you don't want to be seen leaving the building, use the service entrance just past my bedroom. It leads directly to the stairs."

He paused. "By the way, I'm gay."

"Then I take it I don't need to lock my door?" I said with a grin.

Rain was coming down in sheets; only a handful of miserable-looking strangers waited for the bus. No one from my past that I could see.

About ten minutes into the ride, I jumped off, crossed the road, hopscotching more puddles, and ducked into a small cafe with a neon sign in the window. "Internet."

The room was dimly lit; a dozen computer screens cast an eerie glow on concentrated faces. Overhead, a lurid fluorescent tube flickered. On the whole, the cafe was a joyless and gloomy spot frequented by a motley group in damp jackets. The smell of stale tobacco mingled with wet wool.

I couldn't help but wonder if some of those hunched over the screens were accessing secure portals with nonsense posts coded to communicate plans to bomb the Underground.

One terminal was free. To my right sat a young man with an untidy beard and a red-and-white checkered Palestinian *keffiyeh* head scarf twisted around his neck. He stared intensely at an Arabic website and didn't look up when I sat down.

When I entered the ID and password, the first message in the thread appeared.

Welcome A-Team.

Hermes didn't lack a sense of humor.

I stared a little at the screen, uncertain where to begin. Finally, I typed, **Pls sign in with an Avatar.**

Although the odds of the General hacking this portal were next to nil, if he worked with the CIA, who knew what connections he had? NSA? Anything was possible. I didn't want to take a chance with names.

I waited. Would Lars post tonight? I decided to check in the morning and was about to sign off when a message popped up.

This is Big Bird about to fly.

I typed, **Black Magic is playing at Hyde Park Corner.**

It wasn't very clever, but Lars seemed to get it.

Roger that.

I took the bus back to Q's, stopping at an Indian drug store to pick up some brown hair rinse. Rita Hayworth hair wasn't the way to go about London unnoticed.

From Hyde Park I had a clear view of The Lanesborough. On the top floor where I reckoned Gareth's suite to be, lights burned in the windows.

I kept checking my watch. It had been six hours. Enough time surely for Lars to fly from Copenhagen to London and catch a cab to Hyde Park. I'd wait thirty minutes, then find another Internet cafe and check the message board.

It was a few minutes later that I saw him step out of a black London cab. He stood there for a moment, orienting himself before he turned and headed in my direction, his black leather jacket shiny in the streetlight, his flaxen hair silver.

No other cars stopped. From what I could tell, he hadn't been followed, but I stayed back in the shadows until he was opposite me.

"Lars!" I hissed.

He pivoted in surprise.

"*Gud*, Isis! Is this really necessary?"

"I'm hiding from Cesari."

"Cesari? Weren't we just in Libya saving the guy?"

"Everything's changed."

"Yeah, I'd say so."

I'd thought of sending Lars into the hotel but realized that wouldn't work. If the General had men there, they might recognize him. I insisted we walk to the opposite side of the park to grab a taxi back to Q's.

He was deep asleep; loud snores rumbled through his door. I rinsed my hair with the brown color and then decided I couldn't wait any longer. Dawn would be breaking in a couple of hours.

"Q," I whispered, shaking his shoulder lightly. "Q, I need you to wake up."

He appeared a minute later in a white terry cloth robe, barefoot, tufts of gray hair poking out at odd angles. When Q saw tall, Nordic Lars, neat platinum hair framing a golden tan face, eyes blue as Persian enamel, he immediately put his hand up to pat the wild strands into place.

"How's your acting?" I asked.

He blinked two or three times and dragged his eyes away from Lars.

"I was quite a talent in my day," he said rather proudly. "Nothing professional, mind you. But at university, I played—"

"Can you deliver something to the Lanesborough? You've got to think of a pretense for being there this early. The room is probably being watched."

"Just…leave it…to…me," he slurred, swaying on his feet.

He straightened his shoulders and smiled winningly at Lars. "One of my best roles was a stage version of Arthur. I brought down the house."

Then he squinted a little in my direction.

"Did you change your hair?"

Lars and I dozed in white leather recliners in the living room. I woke with a start; the sky was pearly. The lights on the bridges were out.

I was making tea in the white and glass kitchen when I heard the key turn in the lock and then Q's cheerful "Good morning!"

"A virtuoso performance if I do say so myself," he crowed as we gathered on hard Arne Jacobsen chairs around a blinding white architect-designed kitchen table.

"Did you make sure you weren't followed?"

"You wound me," he sniffed.

"Q, if someone wanted to buy a weapon in London, where would he go?"

I thought he'd be taken aback at my question, but instead he set his mug on the table and raised an eyebrow.

"May I assume you have liquid?"

"Didn't you have enough of guns in Libya?" asked Lars.

I counted out a stack of pound notes. Q sealed them carefully in a white envelope that disappeared inside his trench coat.

We left together, Q with a light step on his second mission of the day, and Lars and I away from the flat to call Gareth.

Using one of the disposable cellphones, I dialed the number of the phone that Q had delivered to Gareth's suite.

Gareth answered immediately.

"I should be pissed at you for running off with my cell. It's a fuckin' pain in the ass to replace!"

"I'm sorry, Gareth, but I can't risk being traced."

"Woman, you're dangerous to be around."

"You've known that since the beginning," I said sharply.

"There you go being cold again."

When I didn't say anything, he asked, "So what do you want from me, Isis?"

"Muscle. Back-up."

"What are you offering?"

"A trip through the Red Mirror maybe." I didn't promise with me.

I heard him take a sharp breath.

"I thought it was smashed."

"Very little is what it seems, Gareth."

Lars and I stopped at an Internet cafe on the corner.

"Let me check for messages."

I didn't mention whom they might be from. Lars was on a need-to-know basis.

When I logged on, there was one message in the thread. I stared at the words.

Ishtar. You have nothing to fear from me.

I looked quickly around the cafe, fully expecting Orsini to be watching me from a dark corner. A kind of wind roared in my ears. My head pounded. My mouth was as dry as it had ever been in the desert

"I need to tell you something," Lars was saying from a distant galaxy. In a daze, I turned toward him.

"I told Rasheed."

"Told him what?" I asked stupidly.

"That I was coming to London to see you, what else?"

"Did you call him on your cell?"

"He called me. Out of the blue. I wasn't expecting it."

"Did you tell him about London…on…your…cell…phone?" I carefully enunciated each word.

I saw by the look on his face that he had.

"Shit." I leaned back in the chair and closed my eyes.

A kaleidoscope of thoughts flashed simultaneously in my mind. The General knew. Rasheed was in danger. I'd had only a couple hours of sleep; I must look a mess. *Would Rasheed like my hair?*

"I thought you'd want him to come, Isis. I thought that if you asked for *my* help, you could use his, too. *Gud!* Rasheed was with us in Libya. Has that changed too, like with Cesari?"

"Nothing is the same as it was."

I watched out the window at people walking briskly by. Cars whizzed past.

"Isis," Lars said a bit sharply to bring me back. "You have to tell me what's going on."

I turned toward him again and held his eyes.

"Cesari has stolen something from me. Something I have to get back. He'll do anything to keep it. And I mean, anything."

I paused for a second, giving time for my words to sink in.

"*Anything*, Lars. You know what happened in that cave."

CHAPTER 58   REUNION

"Remember when life's path is steep to keep your mind even." – Horace

W hen Lars' cellphone buzzed, we both jumped. We were wound that tight. No sleep didn't help. Or the chaotic, unrelenting press of humanity that is London. Or the constant mind-numbing rain. Or the ominous presence everywhere of the General.

"*Det er Lars.*" he answered in that no-nonsense Scandinavian way.

He was quiet for a moment, and then his eyes met mine.

"*Rasheed,*" he mouthed.

I had an urge to cry—no, weep!—so powerful, it took everything I had to keep from bawling out loud. I was strung-out, like a junkie, taxed to my limit, holding onto my resolve with bloodied fingernails.

Lars tried to pass the phone to me. I looked at it in horror and stifled the urge to knock the cell out of his hand. A venomous asp couldn't have elicited a more desperate reaction.

"*For helvede*, Isis. *Talk* to the man!"

Taking in a breath that filled my lungs down to the diaphragm, I bit my lower lip and opened my palm.

The phone burned my hand. I closed my eyes and lifted it to my ear

"Hello, Rasheed." My voice was calm, steady—composed.

"I've been trying to reach you on your cell."

"I'm not using it anymore." My voice faltered a little.

Silence.

Then he asked, "Why did you call Lars instead of me?"

I heard irritation in his voice but also something else. Hurt. Rasheed sounded as if his feelings were hurt.

"I can't talk about this on the phone."

"Well, you can tell me in person. I'm here."

Like an idiot, I looked up at the cafe door onto the street. No Rasheed, of course.

"I'm fairly certain this call is being intercepted," I warned. "By someone you once told me to get rid of."

Silence again. I could sense Rasheed thinking of a way to tell me where to meet him.

"Remember our dinner the first night we met, Isis?"

Remember? How could I ever forget? The Eiffel Tower in Las Vegas. Barb and Lars had been there. The night of the Wynn.

"In an hour," he said and rang off.

He couldn't mean Vegas. Or Paris. I googled 'Eiffel Tower London' and to my surprise, up popped several links to the ArcelorMittal Orbit.

I scanned quickly.

> The ArcelorMittal Orbit is a new observation tower in the heart of the Olympic Park in East London…London's Eiffel Tower…Closed to the public while the park is redeveloped.

Lars and I grabbed a big black London taxi and swung by the far side of Hyde Park to pick up Gareth.

"Who's Blondie?" he asked as he uncurled his giant frame on the back seat, dwarfing Viking Lars.

I took the jump seat facing them.

"Lars has two septagrams," I said significantly.

Gareth looked at him with new appreciation. He probably thought Lars was getting twice as much sex, no doubt from me.

My septagram was warm against my skin, hotter, I was sure by far, than my body temperature.

Then Gareth told me, "You're all business with that dark hair."

"Did you leave by the back?"

"The backest of backs, babe. No worries."

"We've got someone else to pick up," I told him. "Someone you might recognize. Someone from another life."

Lars gave me a quizzical look but didn't comment. I think he'd given up trying to follow what was going on.

Gareth flashed a mouthful of white teeth. "Right on! It's the magic bus. Time for a w-i-l-d ride. Anybody got any weed?"

The skies opened; slate sheets of driving rain pounded the pavement. *Thump, thump, thump* went the windshield wipers.

You hide things from me, Rasheed had accused that bleak afternoon in Copenhagen when he'd left me standing in the rain. Rain. Not good for Rasheed and me. We needed sunshine to nurture our dark love.

When our cab approached, he got out of an idling taxi. That Rasheed stood alone, in the rain, leaving Gamel and Marcos in the car, made my heart pound.

The downpour had slowed to a drizzle. He hunched a little in that odd way people do to protect themselves from raindrops. His raven waves glistened. A hat would have helped. An umbrella would have been better.

Who knew from where Rasheed had flown? No doubt a shiny city under harsh azure skies and an uncompromising sun.

I opened the door before our taxi came to a full stop.

"Wait here."

Twelve, maybe fifteen feet separated us. I was reminded again of Copenhagen. Dark skies. Light rain. Taxis. Rasheed and I staring at each other across cold, wet space.

Rasheed had worn a suit that day. I'd been dressed to kill in black stiletto heels and pearls. All dolled up to impress him.

Today I was a mess. Blue jeans and V-neck sweater I'd slept in. Drab hair unlike my natural color—unlike any color I'd ever had in any of my lifetimes—frizzed all over the place.

I stood there, knowing that a rapt Lars and Gareth watched the scene, maybe even holding their breath like I was.

I knew that Marcos and Gamel were watching, too. There wasn't much between Rasheed and me that they hadn't witnessed.

And then, there was no distance at all between us. Rasheed's arms were around me; his perfect mouth chiseled by a master sculptor devoured me. His tongue down my throat, his manhood a stone post at my belly, I melted into him. Where I ended and he began was impossible for me to know.

"Ride with us," I breathed in his ear. "We're going after Cesari."

I didn't need to say it, though, because the General was precisely why he'd come. *Get rid of him, Isis. It's up to you. It's all up to you.*

When Rasheed opened the door and I crawled into the back of the cab, I locked glances with Gareth.

Please don't spoil this for me, I begged with my eyes.

Gareth looked from me to Rasheed. I knew by the wonder on his face that he recognized the man he'd once worshipped. We'd both loved Black Falcon then and wept together at his death.

Of course, Rasheed knew Goliath. Rasheed always recognized the players in our drama of reincarnating souls; the past was a wellspring of anger and jealousy. Thank Hathor, I saw no signs of jealousy now. He suspected nothing between Gareth and me.

They nodded to each other in that special way men acknowledge comrades-in-arms, and Gareth slid over so Rasheed could take his place facing me.

Gareth turned out to be a man who took defeat as gracefully in love as on the court. He grinned and said, "So *you're* the lucky guy."

All the way to Q's, Rasheed leaned forward in the seat, knees spread, gripping my hands in his. Once, he raised my fingers to his lips and kissed them.

His eyes studied my face in the way Black Falcon had memorized the angle of my jaw, the curve of my lip, every freckle across my nose, sensing he'd not see me again.

I wanted to shout at him, *You don't have to do that. You can keep looking at me every day!*

We bumped along, four men, one of them a giant, none of them small, and me on the jump seat in the back with Gamel in the passenger seat next to the driver. Not even for the drive through London would Marcos and Gamel leave Rasheed's side.

Six of us. Only one more, Q, to complete the New Order. Seven Protectors on a magic ride to find the General and the Emerald Tablet.

CHAPTER 59 CONTACT

"No one is so brave that he is not disturbed by something unexpected."
– Julius Caesar

Flanked by my posse of black leather-jacketed warriors, I waited for the elevator up to Q's flat. Unable to settle on one plan, my mind raced through a dozen scenarios.

Visions of Libya and the *pop pop pop* of execution kept playing over and over like a scene from a film noir movie stuck on repeat. I couldn't get a clear picture of how this was to enfold. I couldn't see us, guns blazing, storming wherever the General was holed up.

Rasheed squeezed my hand, bringing me back to earth. I turned toward him, and he mouthed, *I love you.* His eyes said, *We're in this together.*

I should have been ecstatic. Over the moon. Rasheed was here, holding my hand, *supporting* me. He just told me he loved me, words I thought he'd never say. He *believed* in me. But instead of feeling joy, a black foreboding weight dragged at my heart.

My nerves tingled. Spiders crawled on my midriff. All my senses—smell, hearing, sight, touch—were acutely alert. My mouth had a metallic taste.

The miniature lift arrived, and I got in with Rasheed, Lars and Gareth. With a look, Rasheed told Marcos and Gamel to wait for the lift to return.

I watched the numbers blink one after another. Then the stainless steel doors slid open. We strode the hundred paces to Q's door, the wet soles of our shoes squeaking a little on the tile.

My key on the Eiffel Tower chain turned the lock, and I stepped first through the door.

Q's shoes were lined up neatly on the mat. His still-wet umbrella hung next to his Aquascutum trench coat on the chrome clothes tree. Vivaldi played through the hidden Bose speakers; the CD was near the end of the track.

Gareth whistled when he caught the unending white vista that morphed into oyster sky.

"Nice digs."

"Q! Are you decent?" I called out. "I've brought guests."

No answer. No Sasha swirling at my ankles with uplifted, yearning tail.

I turned to Rasheed and said without conviction, "He must be in the shower."

Rasheed nodded. Following my glance, he went down the hallway to the bedrooms. Lars made for the kitchen.

Dread had burgeoned into a black monster that squeezed my lungs and refused to let me breathe. I stepped through into the living room.

Q lay in that rag doll position of a man who has died instantly, with no time for his muscles to contract in a final spasm. A single red dot was between his eyes, not so different from the *tilaka* of devout Hindus.

Sasha mewed at his neck, her white fur tipped with blood.

Dark crimson pooled around his fragile head with thinning gray hair. His smoky eyes were open, glassy and empty, yet there was imprinted a look of surprise on his face that I'll never erase from my mind.

I felt my psyche file the image away with other monstrous things my eyes had witnessed. The General bleeding out from a slashed throat. Black Falcon's flailing legs when I choked his life away with a scarf. Pink intestines spilling on the *triclinium* floor. The agony of the crucified in the Hippodrome.

"Jesus," I heard Gareth whisper.

I sobbed and went to my knees beside Q's funny little body with pot-belly and short stubby legs.

It wasn't until I started to stroke his cheek that I saw the green faience disk on his chest where the assassin had placed it.

The General.

"You bastard!" I screamed. "Why kill Q? WHY?"

Marcus and Gamel rushed into the living room at the same time as Lars.

"Where's Rasheed?" I asked in a voice an octave too high.

Lars said in a quiet, tight voice, "He's not in the bedrooms; I was just there."

"The service entrance," I shouted to Gamel. "At the end of the hallway."

A 9mm Beretta appeared in Gamel's hand. Marcus pulled a snub-nosed, compact submachine gun from inside his jacket. They were gone in an instant. I heard them run down the short hall and then sling open a door.

Gareth, the best forward in the world, of whom I would have expected the fastest reflexes, stood planted like a basalt statue, staring at Q.

I think until now, he'd taken it all as a game.

"You want out?" I asked.

"The thought crossed my mind."

"I don't blame you. I want out, too."

But there was no out for me—I was the Chosen One.

Like Eben in one of his Kabbalah trances, I found myself rocking on the white carpet, my arms wrapped around my shins, murmuring, *ANA A A NANA A A NANA.*

Lars and Gareth must have watched me in bewilderment. The longer I chanted, the further they floated from me. Only it wasn't them floating, but me.

I no longer felt the floor. The light beam streamed into the top of my head, pouring white rays into my skull, performing a kind of cosmic laser surgery first on my crown chakra, then on my right frontal lobe.

My spine straightened. I stopped rocking. Without being aware of any willful action on my part, I settled with my hands calmly in my lap, at my solar plexus—the power chakra. The back of my right hand rested on the palm of my left.

Through my Third Eye, between my eyebrows, just where Q had been shot, I traveled through a swirling spiral—out, out, out into the Light. And there I saw what must be done.

"I have to go shopping."

Incredulous, they stared at me.

"And we shouldn't call the police. At least, not right away. They'll ask too many questions."

Lars the pragmatic Scandinavian took charge of that one. "We're going to wipe the place down for fingerprints, then we're getting out of here."

Marcus and Gamel glared at me with such hatred that I wouldn't have been surprised if they'd trained their guns on me in that moment and fired.

"I'm sorry. I'll get him back. I promise."

Somehow I had the presence of mind to make sure Sasha had food and water. I remembered vaguely that Q had a cleaning lady and felt a stab of guilt that she would find him like that.

We left Q's and checked into a hotel. Lars used his real name. There was no point any longer in subterfuge.

"There are CCTV cameras on every street corner in London, Isis. If Cesari has the high-level security connections you claim, he's been watching every move. It's not that hard when you know who you're looking for."

Face recognition software, digital surveillance, hacked portals. There was nothing or nowhere secure in the world if you have the right friends.

My first stop at Harrods was the lingerie department. A black lace push-up bra with matching lace panties. A black lace bustier. Black silk stockings with seams. Black and red garters.

Next I bought black cashmere slacks, tailored to fit perfectly at the waist and hips and fall in a straight line to Saint Laurent black patent, spike-heeled boots. Then a tight-fitting, black cashmere turtleneck and a narrow crocodile belt with an understated brass buckle.

For the *pièce de résistance*, I chose a knee-length, Greek-inspired, white silk gown that crossed enticingly at braless breasts and melted into a narrow waist to flow around my hips and thighs. Giuseppe Zanotti silver sandals with delicate chains draping the ankle straps had heels high enough to be sexy but low enough to be mobile.

My last purchases were a crocodile overnight case and a bottle of Caroline Herrera 212 perfume with notes of gardenia, camellia, white lily, jasmine and musk. Heavy on the musk.

The stack of pound notes I counted out was nearly as high as the one I gave to Q to purchase black market pistols and Uzis.

If he'd bought any weapons, they weren't in the flat. Poor Q. Had I ever brought Qeb-ha anything but worry and pain?

Untrue, I reminded myself. Elektra brought him out of the gutter.

I liked to think that he'd lived out his days in comfort, helping Eben transcribe the Black Scroll.

The cabbie didn't blink an eye when I directed him to an adult store with fur-lined handcuffs and velvet ropes in the window.

Back in the hotel room, I washed my hair with a stripping shampoo that took out most of the dulling dark rinse. It fell to my shoulders in a warm chestnut cascade. Just the right amount of red. All the orange was gone.

The General answered after three rings.

"Yes, Ishtar."

"I don't want to do this anymore," I said quietly.

"You have nothing to fear from me. I've always wanted you whole."

"Will you leave my friends alive?"

"Do you mean Rasheed?"

"Everyone," I answered. "That's the deal."

"I'll pick you up at your hotel."

It wasn't necessary for me to tell him which one.

After we rang off, I sat for a few minutes on the edge of the bed, chanting the incantation Hermes had given me, calling on the powers—from wherever they come—to work their magic.

CHAPTER 60   CROCODILE

"Power has no limits." – Tiberius

By some bizarre stroke of synchronicity, at the moment I exited the hotel, the sun broke through a slate sky and spotlighted the General's shiny black Rolls.

Orsini stood by the passenger door. As soon as he saw me, his hand reached for the handle.

I tried to see his eyes behind the dark lenses, to read if he felt guilt, to discern if he felt anything for me, for his comrade-in-arms. His face was set in an expression of no expression—unreadable, unreachable. We might never have been together in Malta, might never have together saved the General in the Cave of Bats.

The General waited with a self-satisfied curl to his lips; his mass seemed to fill the whole of the limo. The dark navy blazer tailored on Saville Row did little to conceal those bull shoulders and chest.

Stretching out his thick-fingered paw, he patted the black leather seat beside him; I caught a glimpse of a gold crocodile cufflink with the glittering ruby eye.

"Surely you are not afraid *now*, Ishtar? Not after we've been through so much."

The septagram at his throat was a startling green against the nest of coal black hairs in the V of his white shirt. So, it was Orsini's septagram I'd found. *He* had killed Q. But not without the General's order.

Orsini shut the door. I heard the lock click. I waited to hear the trunk open for my case, but a second or two later, he was climbing onto the front seat.

An impregnable black glass window slid up with a quiet electric whir; Orsini and the driver disappeared.

"Why Qeb-ha?" I hissed. "He was harmless. You know how much I loved him. Couldn't you have spared him for *my* sake?"

"I regret that, Ishtar," he told me in a sincere voice filled with genuine regret. "I truly do. My man was…overzealous."

"Are you not in control of your men? I *know* you are in control of Orsini."

The General answered by handing me a green Harrods sack, saying, "I need you to change your clothes."

His tone was so polite and his manner so mild that under any other circumstance, I might have characterized him as pleasant.

Inside were twins of the slacks and sweater I was wearing. He held up another sack, smaller. I knew without looking that it contained duplicates of my bra and panties.

I think I succeeded in denying him pleasure by not showing surprise. At first I was inclined to change as rapidly as possible. But as I silently chanted the spell Hermes had given me, my movements slowed.

Back slightly arched, in one long fluid, studied motion, I eased the turtleneck over my head and tossed it to the carpeted floor. My hair crackled with static electricity.

The General watched, as I knew he would, transfixed. His breath came a little quicker at the sight of my ripe breasts pushed up in the French lace bra.

I slid my fingertips under the left strap. Slowly, with a smooth caress, I slipped the black lace down my upper arm. Then, without any hint of hurry, my fingers eased the right strap from my shoulder.

It wasn't much really. Two bare shoulders with straps hanging down He couldn't see more flesh than before. But it was enough for the General's bull chest to heave.

Always in slow motion, with smoldering Elektra intensity, I unsnapped the bra, but held the two ends together.

How I would have loved to laugh out loud at the electric jolt when he heard the unfastening. And at the longing in his eyes.

Spaniel eyes. Well, not quite. But he was close. I never dreamed I'd see him beg.

In the silence of the limo, the air throbbed.

I wet my lips and released the ends, shrugging my shoulders ever so slightly. The bra slipped down, and my breasts fell free.

His breath caught. His lips parted. I thought he might reach out with those bear-sized mitts of his and crush me. I thought he might put those thick lips to suck in that way he had that rendered me helpless.

I'll admit to a perverse excitement. My nipples ached for his mouth; I felt suddenly wet.

Never in this life had he come so close to having me as now. Oh, he hungered for the pleasure we both knew only I could give. I could see it. I could feel it.

Pure animal. Glorious carnal lust. Contained. *Controlled*. Under my spell, or rather that of Hermes.

"BOR PHOR PHORBA PHOR PHORBA BES CHARIN BAUBA," I intoned over and over in the low vibrating voice of Lemta.

When I eased out of my slacks, his eyes drank in my loins. When I slipped down my panties, I thought he might weep.

All pubic hair gone—*à la arabe* as they call it in North Africa. Like Ishtar in his tent, like Athena in the desert, like Elektra on her barge. I'd stopped short, though, of rouging the smooth, seductive, nude mound of womanhood.

I had no plan. I flowed into Hermes' chant and fell under the spell of its rhythm. In a trance, I rode the moment and let it carry me to the next.

Under us, the road bumped and thumped. There on the back seat, behind those tinted windows, I sent wave after sensuous wave to crash over the General.

His breath came fast; his chest heaved. Why he didn't pull out his god-sized penis and cram it down my throat or plunge it up me, I don't know. In a Herculean effort of self-control, his monster hands curled into fists.

I can't explain what happened in the back of that limousine. But everything changed. I felt it. He felt it. The loss of power. His.

Some might think that he and I were being swept to a foregone conclusion defined by fate. But I didn't believe it. I intended to write the final act to our drama; I held the pen.

When I'd pulled on the new sweater and slipped into the new boots, the General lowered the electric window and tossed everything—my purse, boots, slacks, bra—all except my passport and the faience septagram at my throat—out of the car to scatter by the motorway.

It was magnanimous of him, I suppose, to leave me my passport. And Hermes' septagram on a gold chain around my neck. The General did have a heart—in a way. Or, at least, he had a weakness for me.

I imagined the odds and ends of my things settling here and there on the motorway. The tiny emitters Lars had placed in my bra, right boot heel and in the waistband of my slacks, would no longer show as speeding dots on his laptop map, but stationary blips.

The General fell quiet; a heaviness settled on him. I didn't look at him but stared out the tinted windows, focusing on the hum of the tires on pavement as we sped south out of London.

The driveway was gravel. Small stones crunched under the tires and pinged against the undercarriage of the limo. I pressed the button for the window, and it rolled down with a smooth electric whir.

A clump of other limousines—two more black Rolls, a silver Bentley and a white stretch Hummer—parked on this side of the drive. Across the circle drive a shiny red Maserati gleamed next to a yellow Lamborghini. A thug in a black leather jacket was unloading crates of Roederer Cristal from a black Range Rover.

Orsini had gotten out of the front but didn't open our car door.

"You know what I need, Ishtar."

The General's voice had an odd, hollow sound to it. He didn't need to say that he'd discovered the Tablet was useless without my help. That I held the key. I sensed he was desperate for me to cooperate. Terrified, even, of the outcome if I didn't.

"And if I don't give you what you want?"

"It won't be pleasant for your friends." He paused, and then added unnecessarily, "Especially Rasheed."

"And what if I prove to be like you?"

"Then you have an Achilles heel. Just as I." In spite of everything, he could still smile at the irony of his own weakness. "We are so very alike—more than you know—or rather than you wish to admit."

"Where do we go from here?"

"That depends on you, Ishtar. You command quite a bit of power if you haven't noticed."

"Who belongs to all these cars?"

"Interested parties."

"Are you in control?"

He smiled and squeezed my hand, the first time he'd touched me during the long ride. His eyes glittered. I do believe that in his own twisted way, he was thoroughly enjoying himself.

"Shall we go in and see?"

The Great Hall was tiled in a classic black and white marble *rialto* pattern. At the very center of the hall, a majestic Venetian chandelier dripping with crystals hung down from the second-floor ceiling.

Under the chandelier, a round rosewood table held a jungle spray of a dozen purple orchids. Under the table was a malachite and onyx floor mosaic of a crocodile. To our right, a sweeping staircase carpeted in deep burgundy curved up to where a bedroom most certainly waited.

"This way," the General said, smiling with all the intimacy we've shared through the ages.

The suite had a four-poster king bed with a blood-crimson velvet spread. I saw right away that the rosewood posts were too far apart to bind his wrists with the velvet handcuffs I bought in the shop. And then I wondered, Had he duplicated those, too?

A fire crackled in the curly-carved fireplace with a hearth tall enough for me to stand. The massive gilt-framed mirror over the mantel reflected the General looming behind me, and behind him, the crimson bed.

How fragile I looked beside his bull mass.

French doors opened onto a balcony with a curved balustrade not unlike my hotel room on Malta. But instead of a medieval city, we looked out on a green lawn edged with ancient oaks. At least a dozen Corsicans armed with Uzi-like pistols or automatic carbines roamed the grounds.

Seagulls circled and squawked; we were very close to the coast. The lawn ended so abruptly, I knew there had to be a cliff that dropped to the gray Channel. If I were still enough, I might hear waves crashing on a rocky beach.

"I want to see him," I said without turning around.

"All in good time."

There was a discreet knock on the door, and our suitcases arrived— the General's, my luggage from the Lanesborough, two Harrods sacks and a crocodile overnight case. Not the one I had bought, I was certain, but yet another duplicate.

"You thought of everything."

"Would you expect less of me?"

"I've learned always to expect the unexpected."

I took a seat on a chaise lounge covered in the same crimson velvet as the bed, leaned back and looked around.

"I assume you have the Tablet. Is it in this room?"

"I have always admired your directness." There was genuine affection in his smile. "That, and your ability to morph before my eyes."

"What do you want from me, General?"

"The secret to the Tablet, of course. But as you surely have surmised, I also want you."

"Am I to be a possession as well?"

"Not at all, Ishtar. The offer I made in Tahoe still stands. I want to share my life with you."

"I don't think you know how to share."

"I didn't do too badly in Egypt, did I? "

"That was then. This is now."

He snorted a little at that and turned to fill a small stemmed glass with port wine.

"I took the Tablet to protect it," he confessed quite casually,

"*I* am the Chosen One. The Emerald Tablet belongs with me."

"You cannot keep it safe. I can. *We* can. Together."

I think he believed it. A team, that's how he saw us. A team to rule the world.

"Is that who the cars belong to? Your New World Order?"

"Shall we dress for dinner and find out?"

"I'll never forgive Q's death," I told him as I went into the dressing room. "Never."

When I came out with my arms and shoulders bare in the halter top and white silk clinging to my breasts, the General in a white dinner jacket stopped weaving his bowtie and stared.

The dress elicited precisely the desired response. His eyes softened to smoky charcoal. Waves of yearning rolled across the room to break on my shore.

He went directly to a black velvet case on the dressing table and took out the Tahitian pearl necklace with the ruby septagram. I didn't bother to ask how he got it from the hotel room safe or even how he knew to look for it there.

He smiled and raised his eyebrows to ask permission, and I obliged by lifting my hair from my shoulders.

His touch, I regret to say, was electric. His fingertips seared the back of my neck as he unclasped the thin gold chain with the faience septagram. I held out my hand, and he dropped the necklace in my palm.

His fingertips were hot when he fastened the black pearls. I felt his moist lips on my top vertebra, then the second and the third. Thick fingers trailed down my spine, past where a bra strap should have been, to stop at my waist and then trace around the band.

His eyes had a satisfied look when I turned to face him.

"Don't think you've won," I warned him.

"I've learned, Ishtar, not to take anything for granted with you."

CHAPTER 61   PROOF OF LIFE

"Time discovers truth." – Seneca

Much as I appreciate your beauty, Ishtar, and your efforts to display it this evening, I don't want you to catch a chill." The General took a soft shawl of white angora wool interwoven with the most delicate of silver threads from a green Harrods box and draped it quite lovingly around my shoulders in the same way he'd wrapped me in his Roman General's cape.

He took my chin in his thick fingers, holding my eyes for a long moment, inviting me to see what I'd seen that night on the Nile. The depth of his need. In his own perverse way, he did love me.

"We make quite a team, Ishtar. You inspire me to greater heights than ever I imagined."

"I want to see him now," I said evenly. "I want proof of life."

He hesitated scarcely a moment before acquiescing, "Of course. I understand."

I thought he might lead me down into an ancient dungeon of seeping stone walls overgrown with foul-smelling mold. Or at least up to a tower with one tiny window through which the cold night wind blew.

But instead, he took my arm and led me along the wide carpeted hallway to double doors not far from our bedchamber. Orsini stood guard. At the General's nod, he turned the knob and stepped aside to let us pass. Following us in, he closed the door behind him.

Plush ivory wool carpet covered the floor. Two Chinese vase lamps cast golden halos. Sometime in the last hour, without my noticing, night had fallen.

Rasheed sat back into a brown leather Chesterfield couch, a black cloth sack over his head, his legs in black jeans bound with white plastic zip ties and his hands behind his back, no doubt also bound. His knees were spread open in that way he has of sitting that makes it almost impossible for me to look away from his bulge.

His head was turned toward the door when we came in.

Behind Rasheed, I saw closed French doors that must give onto the same grassy lawn. The movement of a man's form near the dark doors caught my eye. I saw the gun first. A Glock. Then my heart seized for a full second when his face came into the light.

Major Domo! Or rather his current incarnation, the monster who tried to drag me into the van at the Bellagio.

I twirled to face the General; how shock must have bleached my face. "*You!*" I hissed.

Rasheed sat up straight when he heard my voice. He didn't call out but twisted at his bindings. I had a flash that he was gagged as well under that horrid, sightless hood.

"It was you, all along!" I spat at the General. "The kidnapping attempt? Was that your way of driving me to you?"

"He wouldn't have harmed you."

"This man is an *animal*," I snarled. "How *dare* you sic him on me!" I squelched an urge to grab a poker from the fireplace and beat them both about the face.

The General took a few steps and held out his palm for Major Domo to hand him the pistol. In a fleeting millisecond of panic, I thought the General would shoot Rasheed.

But in one swift movement without any warning, he lifted the Glock, put the end of the silencer between Major Domo's eyes and with a hollow pop, squeezed the trigger. Exactly as Q had died.

Stunned, I stared at what had been Major Domo, collapsed on his back where he had stood, legs bent under him in an impossible contortion. He had the same surprised expression frozen on his face that I'd seen in Leptis Magna.

Brains splotched the green silk brocade wallpaper behind where his head had been only seconds before.

"He killed your friend Q," the General said calmly. "Are you satisfied now?"

Blindfolded and bound, an enraged Rasheed struggled to stand up from the Chesterfield.

Rushing to him, I went to my knees and jerked off the hood and then the gag. I took his head in my hands and pulled his face into mine, saying, "I'm okay, Rasheed. *He* hasn't harmed me."

It was in the way I said *He,* that I think crushed him. The General let the Glock drop to the floor where it landed with a soft thud on the thick carpet. To my eyes, he looked suddenly tired, even old.

He'd killed Major Domo to please me, and still I chose Rasheed. No matter what he did, nothing changed.

"Do you know how impossible a situation you've created?" I demanded.

His face went black; his fists clenched and unclenched. I had a brief vision of those paws around my throat, choking the life from me—not for pleasure but in earnest.

"There is no exit from this, General. If you harm Rasheed in any way—any way, at all—you might as well kill me now. For I *will* kill you."

He glared back, a tower of fury that I spoke the truth.

He couldn't kill Rasheed and have me. He couldn't release Rasheed; he could fly him to the furthest corner of the planet, but Rasheed would come back. For this indignity, the same humiliation as the General suffered at the hands of the Libyans, Rasheed would hunt him down.

Then he morphed. Quickly as his anger had risen, it subsided. He calmed. His breath came evenly again. Far from ready to concede, he gripped my upper arm and hauled me to my feet.

"We have guests, Ishtar."

He led me to the door, leaving Major Domo spread-eagled on the ivory carpet with his halo of dark blood and Rasheed bound on the Chesterfield sofa.

"Have someone clean up this mess," he told Orsini.

Because the General hadn't seen anything but my lips so close to Rasheed's that we might have kissed, he didn't notice that I slipped the faience septagram on gold chain into Rasheed's jacket pocket. Drilled into the back was the last of Lars' micro emitters.

The General propelled me down the curved staircase toward the plaintive strains of Mozart. Orsini followed close behind.

The dining room was a vast dark wood-paneled hall lighted by ivory candles in wall sconces and a dazzling five-tiered chandelier over a banquet table. Rows of crystal goblets sparkled in a sea of gleaming silver set on snowy damask. Each plate, knife, fork and spoon lined up with a precision achieved only by the ruler.

On the opposite side of the room yawned a monumental fireplace where a half dozen men could fit in the hearth. A fire blazed. Over the mantle hung an eighteenth century oil painting of someone's ancestor decked out in burgundy velvet and a powdered wig.

From behind an immense Chinese screen, a string quartet played the tedious Mozart Quartet in G major. Every note set my teeth on edge.

We weren't long in the dining hall when the chatter among the men and women standing about the room stopped. Most had their backs to the door when we came in. One by one, they turned to face us.

Ibis Man and the Russian, supposedly both killed by the General at Tahoe, raised a gold-edged champagne flute. I read the triumph in their eyes, *Did you really think you had won?*

How could I have been such a fool? The General had played me from the beginning.

"I'm sorry, Ishtar. It would not have worked out if you knew." His voice didn't hold that much regret.

"What else don't I know? What other lies have you told?"

A millisecond passed before I saw it in his eyes. How could I have been so stupid?

"The Red Mirror! The Cirque du Soleil stunt. It was you all along. It's always been you."

"I needed the mirror, Ishtar," he said with a shrug. "You wouldn't have given it to me."

"What if *he* had gone rogue like that bastard did with Q? He might have killed me."

"You weren't supposed to be home. Orsini screwed up. He saw you go into the terminal and didn't see you come out. I assumed you were on your way to Tony."

"Is there anything you've ever said that I can believe?"

"I think you know the answer to that. I've always wanted you. I always will."

Our arrival was the cue for the party to be seated. Dinner-jacketed men paired off with painted women in daring gowns and gaudy jewels. Across the table smirked Marcus Quintillus—or whoever he was in this life.

I held his eyes until he sneered and turned to the blond hanging on his arm.

To my right sat a well-muscled Frenchman who was quite handsome in a sinister way. He tried polite conversation, which I rebuffed. Further down the table was a tall scarecrow with a flinty face. I decided they belonged to another circle of souls, a circle I had no desire to intersect.

"The music's morose," I complained to the General. "Please ask them to play something else."

As in a lavish convivium, the courses came one after another. *Paté de foie gras* served with tiny toast triangles. Lobster *bisque* thick with cream. Venison filet in blackberry sauce.

I picked at my food, pretending to eat. My mind was on Rasheed upstairs. We couldn't blast our way out of here. The place was a fortress. The General's death wouldn't be enough to stop these men. And I didn't want him to die. Not again. I'd had enough of death. I'd had enough of guns.

"You're overconfident," I warned. "Look around. There's not a man here you can trust."

His response was a glare burning with the cold fire of resentment.

"I hope for both our sakes, they don't know you have the Tablet. If they do, then we are soon dead."

I gave him no peace, but in a soft voice, step-by-step, reasoning each argument with cold logic, I quietly demolished his dreams.

"You know in your heart," I murmured, "that this will never work. You've come to a dead end, General. There is no way out."

Glasses emptied and were refilled. Peals of laughter rang out; women giggled. Hands disappeared under the table.

I didn't need to guess where fingers went. Drooping eyelids, lax lips and heavy breathing told me all. The only difference in the groping between tonight and ancient Rome was that the servers escaped abuse.

The General put his heavy burning hand high up on my thigh, close to the Gate to Pleasure. He thrilled me even then, knowing the heights to which he could take me. But I wouldn't give him anything—no until I got everything I wanted.

"Surely you don't expect me to fuck you here?" There was no hin of anything in my voice but disdain. "Even in Canopus you showed me more respect."

Startled, he turned to face me. What had he expected? I'd warned him. *Not when forced. I do not like anything when forced.*

How different this feast was from those on the Nile. What the General saw in my eyes tonight gave him no hope.

"You said yourself I'd changed."

He aged years in that moment. I saw something of Hadrian's haggard look when all doors closed to a future with Antinous.

I touched his rough cheek with my fingertips. I leaned into him, my eyes holding his, and kissed him lightly on the lips.

"Will you spoil now, all that we've had together?" I whispered. "You made me happy once. I think I made you happy."

The sounds of raucous laughter melted away. We were alone in our vacuum.

Between us played holograms of our passion. The scene in his tent when Isis rode his comet to the stars. The twilight and rising moon on the desert when Athena crossed the line between ecstasy and pain.

The scenes that played the longest were ones of which I had no memory. Tender nights and savage afternoons in Canopus when we lived as Roman and wife. Those memories were his, and he shared them with me.

"BOR PHOR PHORBA PHOR PHORBA BES CHARIN BAUBA," I chanted softly in his ear, not to elicit fear or control his will, but to ease the separation that we both knew was coming. He was near surrender. So close.

"Give me the Tablet," I crooned, wet tongue in his ear, gentle hand caressing his bull manhood. "Give me Rasheed."

Kissing him full on the mouth, I drew his soul into mine and sucked away the last of his resolve.

"Let us keep our memories, General."

Then I delivered the *coup de grace.*

"Let us keep hope for a future."

CHAPTER 62   CHOICE

"Everything that has a beginning comes to an end." – Marcus Fabius Quintilian

I would have made love to him in a last goodbye. I would have worshipped his swarthy, furry body with my lips, my tongue and my teeth.

I would have engaged in every depraved, animal mating his wretched soul desired. I loved him that much still, sick as it is.

The General reclined against a pile of pillows on the blood crimson spread. White silk draping my body, I kissed his broad chest and fondled his stallion jewels to ready us for one last comet ride.

Orsini burst through the door, eyes sharp, the FNP-9 pistol from Libya in his hand.

"He's gone!"

Thank the gods, the General had time to get to his feet, button his shirt and jam his erect penis back in his pants before Rasheed found us

In a blind rage, Rasheed rushed him; his hands went to the bull throat, his thumbs on the windpipe, pressing with all his fury, propelling them both from the bed to the fireplace.

In any other circumstances, the General's sheer mass would have repelled Rasheed, but the adrenaline surging through Rasheed's veins drove him to a madness that no force could contain.

I grabbed hold of Orsini's arm to stop him from shooting Rasheed He knocked me back. I lunged again. Then Marcos and Gamel appeared from nowhere, and Gamel put his 9mm Beretta to Orsini's military crew cut.

"On your knees," growled Gamel.

Orsini dropped to the floor and tossed the pistol aside. It landed a few feet away from me.

The General tore at Rasheed's ears; his fingers gouged Rasheed's eyes. Still Rasheed drove his thumbs into the General's windpipe. They crashed to the floor. With every second they struggled and flailed on the red Persian carpet, the General's face grew darker. His eyes bulged; his lips opened and closed in the struggle for breath.

Had I, too, looked like a gasping fish when the General's hands at my throat started my slide to unconsciousness ending in ecstasy? Would death come to him as an orgasm?

"Stop Rasheed," I yelled at Marcos and Gamel, who had no intention of doing anything of the kind.

Marcos' scathing look said he'd love nothing more than to put a bullet in me after he'd put one in the General.

I was on my way to try to stop Rasheed myself when Lars and Gareth burst into the room.

"Pull Rasheed off!" I shouted at them.

Neither of them moved. I could see Lars thinking, *Isn't this what we came for?* Gareth's face told me that he was ready to help Rasheed finish the job.

"Gareth! I need Cesari alive. He has the Emerald Tablet."

Orsini's FNP-9 was a matte black blob on the carpet. I had started for the pistol, not sure what I would do once I had it, when Garth and Lars bolted across the room to pull Rasheed off. It took both of them using all their sizeable combined strength to drag away the savage beast Rasheed had become.

Gagging, almost retching, his chest heaving to take huge gulps of air, the General was a fraction of a second on his back before he erupted with a roar. With a speed unimaginable in a man his size, and before I could shout out a warning, he rolled twice, grabbed Orsini's pistol and fired.

The crack split my head. I stared in horror as black blood bellied in Rasheed's shirt.

"No-o-o-o-o!" I screamed, hurling myself at the General, knocking the pistol from his hand.

He was half-prone on the parquet floor, eyes wild as an enraged bull. Immediately I covered his body with mine, protecting him from Marcos who had the compact submachine gun trained on us. One pull of the trigger and that lethal weapon—scarcely larger than a pistol—could fire nine hundred rounds per minute.

"STOP!" I commanded. "No more!"

In that moment, I'm not sure if I meant to save the General's life because I didn't want him to die—never, in all our lives, had I wanted him to die—or because he was the only one who knew where the Emerald Tablet was.

Rasheed rasped, "Don't shoot. Don't hurt her."

Marcos stood for an eternity before he finally lowered the snub barrel to point at the floor instead of me.

Pounding footsteps in the hallway warned of more men, certainly some of the Corsicans who roamed the grounds armed for war.

"Stand down! Everyone stand down!" I heard myself shouting.

Turning to the General under me, I whispered, "It ends here, Cesari. It's over."

I'll never forget the look in his eyes. A look so like Hadrian's. All hope lost.

Seeing his loneliness might have broken my heart once, but he'd crossed the line I'd warned he must never cross.

"Tell them, General. Tell them it's over."

He knew by the icy finality in my voice that it was.

As incredible as one might believe it, there was a doctor in the house The scarecrow from dinner with the angular face.

He immediately went to Rasheed and examined the wound I'd stuffed with the white cashmere shawl the General had given me.

"The bullet went straight through, here on the side," he announced to the room.

"Good work," he said to me.

At first I thought he referred to my stopping the slaughter but then realized he meant that the shawl had staunched the bleeding.

"You'll live," he told Rasheed.

I collapsed on the floor, rocking back and forth in one of Eben's trances. My white silk dress was wet with Rasheed's dark blood.

By the time the ambulance left with Rasheed transferred to a gurney, I walked briskly around the bedchamber, gathering my things.

Transfixed, the General watched from a chair. His eyes were quite dead.

I slipped out of the stained dress, leaving it in a pile by the side of the bed. I was naked under the gown. No stockings. No bra. No panties. I didn't consider going into the other room to avoid arousing the General's lust; for me, he no longer existed. Not after shooting Rasheed.

I dressed as if alone, pulling on a bra, underpants, and jeans. Buttoning up the rust cashmere cardigan with no-nonsense tugs and pulls.

When I was ready, I crouched before him, bending at the knees, my haunches resting on my heels. I felt nothing for him, except maybe pity. He was broken. A man like him should never be broken.

"Where is it, General? Where is the Tablet?"

He looked into my eyes briefly and then stared stonily past me; I turned my head to follow his gaze. There, standing on its end, ready to roll on its sturdy inline wheels, was the new crocodile overnight case I'd never opened.

CHAPTER 63   BURIAL AT SEA

"From the end spring new beginnings." – Pliny the Elder

Cotton clouds floated on the blue horizon. In the distance, the white triangle sails of Marcus and Gamel's yawl billowed. Not that far, really, but far enough.

We'd dropped anchor just offshore of a tiny, kidney-shaped emerald isle with an empty white crescent beach edged with feathery palms. A thousand shades of Caribbean turquoise stretched from our boat to the sandy shore.

If I imagined another coastline, one with white rocks and green cypress, I might have been back in North Africa the day Black Falcon gave me up for silver.

But there was no giving me up today.

Barb had answered at the first ring when I called.

"Can you fly to St. Martin's?"

"St. Martin's? I thought you were in London."

"I am. But I'm getting married, Barb." I paused to give her chance to absorb what had to be startling news. At least, I don't think she'd expected to hear it. I was still a little in shock myself.

"And I want you to be there," I continued. "You know, be my bridesmaid. But without the silly dress."

She didn't say a word. Not because she didn't want to come to the wedding, but because she couldn't guess and was afraid to ask.